THE
WOMEN
OF
TROY

PAT BARKER

HAMISH HAMILTON
an imprint of
PENGUIN BOOKS

HAMISH HAMILTON

UK | USA | Canada | Ireland | Australia
India | New Zealand | South Africa

Hamish Hamilton is part of the Penguin Random House group of companies
whose addresses can be found at global.penguinrandomhouse.com.

First published 2021
001

Copyright © Pat Barker, 2021

The moral right of the author has been asserted

Set in 12.5/17 pt Fournier MT Std
Typeset by Jouve (UK), Milton Keynes
Printed and bound in Great Britain by Clays Ltd, Elcograf S.p.A.

The authorized representative in the EEA is Penguin Random House Ireland,
Morrison Chambers, 32 Nassau Street, Dublin D02 YH68

A CIP catalogue record for this book is available from the British Library

HARDBACK ISBN: 978–0–241–42723–1
TRADE PAPERBACK ISBN: 978–0–241–42724–8

THE WOMEN OF TROY

Pat Barker was born in Yorkshire and began her literary career in her forties, when she took a short writing course taught by Angela Carter. Encouraged by Carter to continue writing, she sent her fiction out. She has now published sixteen novels, including her masterful Regeneration trilogy, been made a CBE for services to literature, and won the UK's highest literary honour, the Booker Prize.

The Silence of the Girls began the story of Briseis, the forgotten woman at the heart of one of the most famous war epics ever told. It was short-listed for the Women's Prize for Fiction, the Costa Novel Award and the Gordon Burn Prize, and won an Independent Bookshop Award 2019. *The Women of Troy* continues that story.

Pat Barker lives in Durham.

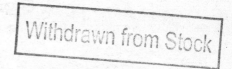

For Jack, Maggie and Mr Hobbes;
and in loving memory of Ben.

Inside the horse's gut: heat, darkness, sweat, fear. They're crammed in, packed as tight as olives in a jar. He hates this contact with other bodies. Always has. Even clean, sweet-smelling human flesh makes him want to puke – and these men stink. It might be better if they kept still, but they don't. Each man shifts from side to side, trying to ease his shoulders into a little more space, all intertwined and wriggling like worms in a horse's shite.

Redworm.

The word sends him spiralling down; down, down, into the past, all the way back to his grandfather's house. As a boy – which is what *some* seem to think he still is – he used to go down to the stables every morning, running along the path between the tall hedges, breath curdling the air, every bare twig glinting in the reddish light. Turning the bend, he would see poor old Rufus standing by the gate of the first paddock – leaning on it, more like. He'd learnt to ride on Rufus; nearly everybody did, because Rufus was a quite exceptionally steady horse. The joke was, if you started to fall off, he'd stretch out a hoof and shove you back on. All his memories of learning to ride were happy, so he gave Rufus a good scratch, all the places he couldn't reach himself, then breathed into his nostrils, their breaths mingling to produce a snuffly, warm sound. The sound of safety.

God, he'd loved that horse — more than his mother, more even than his nurse, who, anyway, had been taken away from him as soon as he was seven. Rufus. Even the name had formed a bond: Rufus; Pyrrhus. Both names mean 'red' — and there they were, the two of them, spectacularly red-haired, though admittedly in Rufus' case the colour was more chestnut than auburn. When he was a young horse, his coat used to gleam like the first conkers in autumn, but of course he was older now. And ill. As long ago as last winter, a groom had said, '*He*'s looking a bit ribby.' And every month since then, he'd lost weight; pelvic bones jutting out, sharp points to his shoulders — he was starting to look skeletal. Not even the lush grass of summer had put fat on his bones. One day, seeing a groom shovelling up a pile of loose droppings, Pyrrhus had asked, 'Why's it like that?'

'Redworm,' the man said. 'Poor old sod's riddled with 'em.'

Redworm.

And that one word delivers him back to hell.

At first, they're allowed rush lamps, though with the stern warning that these would have to be extinguished the minute the horse began to move. Frail, flickering lights, but yet without them the pelt of darkness and fear would have suffocated him. Oh, yes, fear. He'd deny it if he could, but it's here, unmistakably, in the dryness of his mouth and the loosening of his bowels. He tries to pray, but no god hears, and so he shuts his eyes and thinks: *Father.* The word feels awkward, like a new sword before your fingers grow accustomed to the hilt. Had he ever seen his father? If he had, he'd have been a baby at the time, too young to remember the most important meeting of his life. He tries *Achilles* instead — and it's actually easier, more comfortable, to use the name that any man in the army can.

He gazes along the row of men opposite, seeing each face lit from below, tiny flames dancing in their eyes. These men fought beside his father. There's Odysseus: dark, lean, ferret-like, the architect of this whole enterprise. He designed the horse, supervised its construction, captured and tortured a Trojan prince to get details of the city's defences – and finally concocted the story that's supposed to get them through the gates. If this fails, every leading fighter in the Greek army will die in a single night. How do you carry a responsibility like that? And yet Odysseus doesn't seem at all concerned. Without meaning to, Pyrrhus catches his eye and Odysseus smiles. Oh, yes, he smiles, he seems friendly, but what's he really thinking? Is he wishing Achilles were here, instead of that useless little runt, his son? Well, if he is, he's right, Achilles should be here. *He* wouldn't have been afraid.

Looking further along the row, he sees Alcimus and Automedon sitting side by side: once Achilles' chief aides, now his. Only it's not quite like that. *They're* in control, have been from the moment he arrived – propping up an inexperienced commander, glossing over his mistakes, always trying to make him look good in the eyes of the men. Well, today, tonight rather, all that's going to change. After tonight, he'll look into the eyes of men who fought beside Achilles and see nothing but respect, respect for what he achieved at Troy. Oh, of course he won't brag about it, probably won't even mention it. No, because he won't have to, everybody will know; they always do. He sees these men looking at him sometimes, doubting him. Well, not after tonight . . . Tonight, he'll –

Oh my god, he needs a shit. He sits up straighter, trying to ignore the griping in his gut. When they'd climbed into the horse, there'd been a lot of joking about where to put the latrine buckets. 'The arse

3

end,' Odysseus said. 'Where else?' This produced a burst of laughter at the expense of those who were sitting at the back. Nobody has used the buckets yet and he desperately doesn't want to be the first. They'll all be holding their noses and making wafting movements in the air. It's just not fair, it's not *fair*. He should be thinking about important things, the war ending tonight in a blaze of glory – for *him*. He's trained for this for years – ever since he was old enough to lift a sword. Before that even, five, six years old, he'd been fighting with sharpened sticks, he was never not fighting, pummelling his nurse whenever she tried to calm him down. And now it's all happening, it's actually happening at last, and all he can think is: *Suppose I shit myself?*

The griping seems to be easing off a bit. Perhaps it'll be all right.

It's gone very quiet outside. For days, there's been the noise of ships being loaded, men singing, drums beating, bullroarers roaring, priests chanting – all of it as loud as possible because the Trojans were meant to hear. They've got to believe the Greeks are really going. Nothing must be left inside the huts, because the first thing they'll do is send reconnaissance parties down to the beach to check that the camp has actually been abandoned. It's not enough to move men and weapons. Women, horses, furniture, cattle – everything has to go.

Inside the horse, now, there's a growing murmur of uneasiness. They don't like this silence; it feels as if they've been abandoned. Twisting round on the bench, Pyrrhus squints through a gap between two planks, but can't see a bloody thing. 'What the fuck's going on?' somebody asks. 'Don't worry,' Odysseus says, 'they'll be back.' And indeed only a few minutes later, they hear footsteps coming towards them up the beach, followed by a shout: 'You all right in there?' A rumble of response. Then, what seems like hours later, though it's probably only minutes, the horse jerks forward. Immediately, Odysseus holds up his hand and, one by one, the lights go out.

Pyrrhus closes his eyes and imagines the struggling sweaty backs of men as they bend to the task of hauling this monster across the rutted ground to Troy. They have rollers to help, but even so it takes a long time – the land's pitted and scarred from ten long years of war. They know they're getting close when the priests start chanting a hymn of praise to Athena, guardian of cities. Guardian of cities? Is that a joke? Let's bloody hope she's not guarding *this* city. At last, the lurching stops and the men inside the horse's belly turn to stare at each other, their faces no more than pale blurs in the dim light. Is this it? Are they here? Another hymn to Athena, and then, after three final shouts in honour of the goddess, the men who've dragged the horse to the gates of Troy depart.

Their voices, still chanting hymns and prayers, fade into silence. Somebody whispers: 'What happens now?' And Odysseus says: 'We wait.'

A goatskin filled with diluted wine passes from hand to hand though they daren't do more than moisten their lips. The buckets are already more than two thirds full and, as Odysseus says, a wooden horse that started pissing might arouse suspicion. It's hot in here; the place reeks of resin from freshly cut pine logs – and something very odd has started to happen, because he tastes the resin and smells the heat. The inside of his nostrils feels scorched. And he's not the only one who's suffering. Machaon's streaming with sweat – he's carrying a lot more weight than the younger men, who're as lean as the feral dogs that even now must be sniffing around the doors of the empty huts, wondering where the people have gone. Pyrrhus tries to imagine the camp deserted: the hall he'd entered for the first time ten days after his father's death, sitting down in Achilles' chair, resting his hands on the carved heads of mountain lions, curling his fingertips into their snarling mouths as Achilles must have done, night after night – and feeling all the time like an imposter, a little boy who'd been allowed to stay up late. If he'd looked down, his legs would have been dangling a foot away from the floor.

By tomorrow morning, he may be dead, but there's no point thinking like that: a man's fated day will come when it will come and there's nothing you can do to push that moment further back. He looks from side to side, seeing his own tension reflected on every face. Even Odysseus has started chewing his thumbnail. The Trojans must know by now that the ships have sailed, that the Greek camp is indeed deserted, but perhaps they don't believe it? Priam's ruled Troy for fifty years; he's too old a fox to fall for a trick like this. The horse is a trap, a brilliant trap – *yes, but who's inside it?*

Odysseus lifts his head and listens and a second later they all hear it: a murmur of Trojan voices, curious, nervous. What is it? Why is it? Have the Greeks really given up and gone home, leaving behind this remarkable gift? 'Remarkably useless,' somebody says. 'How can you say it's useless when you don't know what it's for?' 'We mightn't know what it's for, but we do know one thing: don't trust the fucking Greeks.' A roar of agreement. 'Anyway, how do we know it's empty? How do we know there isn't somebody inside?' Voices edging up from suspicion into panic. 'Set fire to it.' 'Yeah, go on, burn the bugger. You'll sharp find out if anybody's inside.' The idea catches on; soon they're all chanting: 'Burn it! Burn it! Burn it!' Pyrrhus looks round and sees fear on every face; no, more than fear – terror. These are brave men, the pick of the Greek army, but the man who tells you he's not afraid of fire is either a liar or a fool.

BURN IT! BURN IT! BURN IT!

A wooden box crammed full of men – it'll go up like a funeral pyre larded with pig fat. And what will the Trojans do when they hear screams? Run and fetch buckets of water? Like bloody hell they will; they'll stand around and laugh. The army will return to find only charred timbers and the bodies of burned men, their raised fists clenched in the pugilistic attitudes of those who die by fire. And above them, on the walls, the Trojans waiting. He's not a coward, he really isn't, he got into this bloody horse prepared to die, but he's buggered if he's going to die like a pig roasting on a spit. Better to get out now and *fight* –

He's halfway to his feet when a spear point appears between the heads of the two men sitting opposite. He sees their faces blank with shock. Instantly, everybody starts shuffling deeper into the belly, as far away from the sides as they can get. Outside, a woman's screaming at the top of her voice: 'It's a trap, can't you see it's a trap?' And then another voice, a man's, old, but not weak, carrying a lot of authority. It can only be Priam. 'Cassandra,' he says. 'Go back home now, go home.'

Inside the horse, men turn to stare accusingly at Odysseus whose plan this is, but he just shrugs and throws up his hands.

Another burst of shouting. The guards have found somebody skulking outside the gates, and now he's being dragged in front of Priam and forced to his knees. And then, at last, at long last, Sinon starts to speak, his voice wobbly at first, but strengthening as he launches into his tale. Pyrrhus glances across at Odysseus and sees his lips moving in time with Sinon's words. He's been coaching him for the past three weeks, the two of them pacing up and down the arena for hours at a stretch, rehearsing the story, trying to anticipate every question the Trojans could possibly ask.

Every detail is as convincing as it can be made; how the Greeks believe the gods have abandoned them – and particularly Athena, whom they have grievously offended. The horse is a votive offering and must be taken immediately to her temple. But it's not the details that matter. Everything really depends on Odysseus' reading of Priam's character. As a small boy, not seven years old, Priam had been captured in a war and held to ransom. Friendless and alone, forced to live his life in a foreign land, he'd turned to the gods for comfort, and in particular to Zeus Xenios, the god who commands kindness to strangers. Under Priam's rule, Troy has always been willing to take in people whose own countrymen have turned against them. Odysseus' story is calculated to appeal to Priam, every detail designed to exploit his faith and turn it into weakness. And if the plan doesn't work, it certainly won't be Sinon's fault, because he's giving it everything he's got, his voice rising to the skies in a great wail of misery. 'Please,' he keeps saying. 'Please, please, take pity on me, I daren't go home, I'll be killed if I go home.'

'Let him go,' Priam says. And then, presumably speaking directly to Sinon, 'Welcome to Troy.'

Not long after, there's a clattering of ropes lassoing the horse's neck and it begins to move. Only a few yards on, it shudders to a halt, sticks fast for several agonizing minutes, then lurches forward again. Pyrrhus peers through a gap between the planks – the night air unexpectedly cool on his eyelids – but sees only a stone wall. Though that's enough to tell him they're passing through the Scaean gates into Troy. They look at each other, wide-eyed. Silent. Outside, the Trojans, men, women and children, are singing hymns of praise to Athena, guardian of cities, as they dragged the horse inside the gates. There's a lot of excited chatter among the little boys who are 'helping' their fathers haul the ropes.

Meanwhile something peculiar's happening to Pyrrhus. Perhaps it's just thirst, or the heat, which is worse now than it's ever been, but he seems to be seeing the horse from the outside. He sees its head level with the roofs of palaces and temples as it's pulled slowly through the streets. A strange feeling: to be locked fast in darkness and yet be able to see the wide streets and open squares, the crowds of excited Trojans milling around the horse's feet. The ground's black with them. They're like ants that have found the chrysalis of an insect, big enough to feed their young for weeks, and they're dragging it back to their hill in triumph, unaware that when the hard, shiny pupa splits open it'll release death on them all.

At last, the lurching and swaying stops. By now, everybody inside the horse is feeling sick. More prayers, more hymns; the Trojans crowd into the temple of Athena to give the goddess thanks for victory. And then the feasting starts, singing, dancing, drinking, more drinking. The Greek fighters listen and wait. Pyrrhus tries to find room to stretch his legs; he has cramp in his right calf, from dehydration and sitting too long in the same constricted position. They're in deeper darkness now, with no moon to throw light through the cracks in the horse's sides – a moonless night was selected for the attack. Now and then a bunch of drunken revellers staggers past and their blazing torches cast tiger stripes over the faces of the men who wait inside. The light glints on helmets and breastplates and the blades of their drawn swords. Still, they wait. Out there, far out in the darkness, the black, beaked ships will be ploughing white furrows through the heaving grey sea as the Greek fleet returns. He imagines the ships entering the bay, their sails furled as the rowers take over, and then the scrape of keels on shingle as they drive hard on to the land.

Gradually, the singing and shouting die away; the last drunks have crawled home or passed out in the gutter. And Priam's guards? Is it likely they'll have stayed sober, now the war's over, now they think they know they've won and there's nobody left to fight?

At last, at a nod from Odysseus, four fighters at the far end draw back bolts and remove two segments of the sides. The cooler night air floods in; Pyrrhus feels his skin tingle as the sweat evaporates. And then, one by one, in a steady stream, men start to climb down the rope ladders and gather in a circle on the ground. There's a bit of jostling at the front because each man wants the honour of being the first out. Pyrrhus doesn't care about that; he's one of the first, that's enough. As his feet hit the ground, he feels the jolt all the way up his spine. People are stamping their feet, trying to get the circulation back because any minute now they'll have to run. He grabs a torch from a sconce on the temple wall and in the glare of red light turns and looks back as the last fighters drop heavily to the ground. The horse is shitting men. Once they're all out, they turn and stare at each other, the same half-waking expression on every face. They're *in*. Slowly, the realization floods through him: an unstoppable wave. Now, at this moment, he's standing where his father never stood, inside the walls of Troy. There's no fear now. Everything light, everything clear. Over there, in the darkness, are the gates they've got to open to let the army in. Pyrrhus tightens his grip on his sword and breaks into a run.

2

An hour later, he's on the palace steps in the thick of the fighting. Seizing an axe from a dying man, he starts hacking his way through the door. The press of fighters pushing up the steps behind him makes it hard to get a good swing – he shouts at them to get back, to give him room, and four or five blows later there's a gap just wide enough to get through – and after that it's easy, everything's *easy*. Hurtling down the corridor, he feels his father's blood pounding through his veins and shouts in triumph.

At the entrance to the throne room there's a solid wall of Trojan guards, the Greek fighters already grappling with them, but he veers off to the right, searching for the secret passage that leads from Hector's house – where his widow, Andromache, now lives alone with their son – to Priam's private apartments. This is the information Odysseus tortured out of his captive prince. A door in the wall, half hidden by a screen, leads into a dimly lit passage shelving steeply downwards – the cold smell of musty, unused places – and then a flight of stairs takes him up into the bright light of the throne room, where Priam stands in front of an altar, motionless, expectant, as if his whole life has been a preparation for this moment. They're alone. The sounds of Greeks and Trojans battling on the other side of the wall seem to fade away.

In silence, they stare at each other. Priam's old, shockingly old, and so frail his armour weighs him down. Pyrrhus clears his throat, an odd, apologetic sound in that vast stillness. Time seems to have stopped, and he doesn't know how to make it start again. He moves closer to the altar steps and announces his name, which you must do before you fight: 'I am Pyrrhus, son of Achilles.' Incredibly, unforgivably, Priam smiles and shakes his head. Angry now, Pyrrhus puts one foot on the bottom step and sees Priam brace himself – though when the old man finally throws his spear it fails to penetrate the shield, just hangs there for a moment, quivering, before clattering to the floor. Pyrrhus bursts out laughing, and the sound of his own laughter frees him. He leaps up the steps, grabs a handful of Priam's hair, drags the head back to expose the scrawny throat and –

And nothing . . .

For the last hour, he's been in a state of near-frenzy, feet scarcely touching the ground, strength pouring into him from the sky – but now, when that frenzy is most needed, he feels it draining from his limbs. He raises his arm, but the sword's heavy, heavy. Sensing weakness, Priam twists out of his grasp and tries to run, but trips and falls headlong down the steps. Pyrrhus is on to him at once, clutching the mane of silver hair, and this is it, this is it, now, *now*, but the hair's unexpectedly soft, almost like a woman's hair, and that tiny, insignificant detail's enough to throw him. He slashes at the old man's throat, misses – *stupid, stupid* – he's like a ten-year-old boy trying to stick his first pig, hacking away, cut after cut and not one of them deep enough to kill. With his white hair and pale skin, Priam looked as if he hadn't a drop of blood in him; oh, but he has, gallons and gallons of it, he's slipping and slithering across the floor. At last, he gets a grip on the old bugger, kneels on his bony chest and, even then, he can't do it. He groans in despair, 'Achilles! Father!' And, incredibly, Priam turns to him and smiles again. 'Achilles' son?' he says. '*You? You're* nothing like him.'

A red mist of rage gives Pyrrhus the strength to strike again. Straight into the neck this time, no mistake. Priam's hot blood pumps over his clenched fist. That's it. Over. He lets the body slip to the floor. Somewhere, quite close, a woman's screaming. Bewildered, he looks around and sees a group of women, some with babies in their arms, crouched on the far side of the altar. Drunk with triumph and relief, he runs towards them, arms spread wide, and shouts 'BOO!' into their faces – and laughs as they cower away.

But one girl stands up and stares back at him – goggle-eyed, face like a frog. How dare she look at him? For a moment, he's tempted to strike her, but pulls back in time. There's no glory to be gained by killing a woman, and anyway, he's tired, more tired than he's ever been in his life. His right arm dangles from his shoulder, as lifeless as a spade. Priam's blood tightens on his skin, stinking, that fishy, ferrous smell. He stands for a moment, looking down at the body, and then on impulse kicks it in the side. No burial for Priam, he decides. No honour, no funeral rites, no dignity in death. He'll do exactly what his father did to Hector: strap the old man's spindly ankles to his chariot axle and drag him back to the camp. But first, he needs to get away from all the screaming and sobbing, and so, blindly, he stumbles through a door on his right.

Dark in here, cool and quiet; the cries of women sound fainter now. As his eyes grow accustomed to the gloom, he sees a rack of ceremonial robes and, beside it, a chair with the vestments of a priest draped over the back. This must be Priam's robing room. Standing just inside the door, he listens, feeling the room shrink away from him, just as the women did. Everything's silent, empty. But then, suddenly, he catches a movement in the far corner. Somebody's hiding, over there in the shadows, he can just see the outline of a shape. A woman? No, from the glimpse he had, he's almost sure it was a man. Pushing aside the rack of clothes, he edges forward – and then almost laughs aloud with joy, with relief, because there, straight ahead of him, stands Achilles. It can't be anybody else: the glittering armour, the flowing hair – and it's a sign, a sign that he's been accepted at last. He walks confidently forward, peering into the dark, and sees Achilles coming towards him, sheathed in blood; everything's red, from his plumed helmet to his sandalled feet. Hair red too, not orange, not carroty, no, red like blood or fire. At the last moment, face to face, he reaches out and his tacky fingers encounter something hard and cold.

Close now, close, almost close enough to kiss. 'Father,' he says, as his breath clouds the mirror's shining bronze. 'Father.' And again, less confidently now: '*Father?*'

3

We're going
We're going
We are going home!

I'd lost count of the number of times I'd heard that song – if you could call it a song – in the last few days. Groups of men staggering around the camp – drunk, slack-mouthed, fish-eyed – bellowing out the simple, repetitive words until their voices grew hoarse. Discipline had almost completely broken down. All over the camp, the kings were struggling to regain control of their men.

Crossing the arena one morning, I heard Odysseus shout: 'If you don't bloody well get that ship loaded, you won't be going any-where!' He'd come out of his hall and was standing on the steps of the veranda, confronting a group of twenty or thirty men. It was a sign of the general mood that, even there, in his own compound, he carried a spear. Most of the singers began to edge away, but then a voice shot out of the crowd. 'Aye, an' what about you, yer conniving bastard? Don't see *you* lifting much.'

Thersites, of course. Who else? He hadn't exactly stepped for-ward; it was more a case of the others stepping back. Odysseus was on to him immediately, spear raised high above his head. Using the butt end as a cosh, he struck Thersites repeatedly on the arms and shoulders and then, as he lay curled up and groaning on the ground, delivered several more blows to his ribs before finishing him off with a kick in the groin.

Clutching his balls, Thersites thrashed from side to side while the other men crowded round, roaring with laughter. He was well known as a shit-stirrer, a gobshite; if there was any work to be handed out, you'd always find Thersites at the back of the queue. Oh, they might get a vicarious thrill from his challenges to authority, but they'd no love for the man, no respect. So they left him lying there and wandered off, possibly to load the ship but more likely to look for fresh supplies of booze, since the goatskins slung across their shoulders appeared to be empty. A few yards further on they began singing again, though with every repetition the song sounded more and more like a dirge.

We're going
We're going
We are going home!

The truth? Nobody was going home. Nobody was going anywhere. Only four days ago, they'd been within an hour of departure – some of the kings, including Odysseus, had already gone on board – but then the wind suddenly veered round and started blowing at near-gale force off the sea. You'd have had to be mad to leave the shelter of the bay in that. 'Oh, don't worry,' everybody said. 'It'll soon pass.' But it hadn't passed. Day after day, hour after hour, the freak wind blew, and so, here they all were, the victorious Greek fighters, penned in – and the captive Trojan women with them, of course.

Meanwhile, Thersites. I bent over him, trying not to recoil from the reek that blasted out of his open mouth. It pained me to think ill of a man who'd just called Odysseus a conniving bastard to his face, but really there wasn't much to like about Thersites. Still, there he was, injured, and I was on my way to the hospital, so I put my hand under his arm and helped him to his feet. He stood doubled over for a moment, hands on knees, before slowly raising his head. 'I know you,' he said. 'Briseis, isn't it?' He wiped his bloody nose on the back of his hand. 'Achilles' whore.'

'Lord Alcimus' *wife.*'

'Yeah, but what about that brat you're carrying? What does *Lord* Alcimus think about that, then? Tekking on another man's bastard?'

I turned my back on him, aware all the time as I walked away of Amina trailing along behind me. Did she know the history of my marriage? Well, if she didn't before, she certainly did now.

A couple of days before he was killed, Achilles had given me to Alcimus, explaining that Alcimus had sworn to take care of the child I was expecting. I knew nothing about this until the morning it happened. Dragged out of Achilles' bed – a semen-stained sheet wrapped round my shoulders, breadcrumbs in my hair, feeling sick, smelling of sex – I was married to Alcimus. A strange wedding, though perfectly legal, with a priest to say the prayers and bind our hands together with the scarlet thread. And, give credit where it's due, Alcimus had been as good as his word. Only this morning, he'd insisted I must have a woman to accompany me whenever I left the compound. 'It isn't safe,' he'd said. 'You've got to take somebody with you.'

This girl, Amina, was the result.

We made a ridiculous little procession, me a respectable married woman, heavily veiled, Amina trotting along a few paces behind. All nonsense, of course. What protected me from the drunken gangs roaming around the camp was not the presence of a teenage girl, but the sword arm of Alcimus, as once, only five months ago, it had been the sword arm of Achilles. The only thing, the *only* thing, that mattered in this camp was power – and that meant, ultimately, the power to kill.

Normally, I found a walk along the shore pleasant, but not today. The wind had become a hot, moist hand pushing you away from the sea, saying: *No, you can't go there*. I say 'moist', but so far there'd been no rain, though an anvil-shaped cloud towered high into the sky above the bay and, at night, you could see flickers of lightning deep inside it. Everything suggested a storm was about to break, and yet it never came. The light, a curious reddish brown, stained every bit of exposed skin bronze, until men's hands and faces seemed to be made of the same hard, unyielding metal as their swords.

Under the celebrations – the drinking, the feasting, the dancing – I detected a current of uneasiness. This wind was beginning to saw at everybody's nerves, like a fractious baby that just won't go to sleep. Even at night, with all the doors shut and barred, there was no escaping it. Gusts insinuated themselves into every crack, lifting rugs, blowing out candles, pursuing you along the passage into your bedroom, even into your sleep. In the middle of the night, you'd find yourself lying awake staring at the ceiling, and all the questions you'd managed to ignore by day gathered round your bed.

What does Lord *Alcimus think about that, then? Tekking on another man's bastard?*

My pregnancy was public knowledge now. The change seemed to have happened imperceptibly, rather like the drawing-in of the nights. Evening after evening, you see no real difference until suddenly there's a chill in the air and you know it's autumn. People's attitudes to me had shifted with the swelling of my belly and that in turn made my own feelings about the unborn child more difficult to deal with. Achilles' child. Achilles' *son*, according to the Myrmidons, who apparently could see inside my womb. At times, I had the feeling that what I carried inside me was not a baby at all, but Achilles himself, miniaturized, reduced to the size of a homunculus, but still identifiably Achilles; and fully armed.

As we neared the gate of Agamemnon's compound, I looked down, determinedly following the movements of my feet – *in, out*; *in, out* – as they appeared and disappeared under the hem of my tunic. I'd been so unhappy in this place, I always dreaded going back, but I reminded myself that the shame of being a slave in Agamemnon's huts, in Agamemnon's bed, belonged to the past. I was a free woman; and so, once inside the gate, I lifted my head and looked around.

We were in the main square of the compound. When I'd lived there, this had been the parade ground where the men mustered before marching off to war; now, it was occupied by a hospital tent, moved there from its original, exposed position on the beach. In its new setting, the tent looked even shabbier than before, its canvas covered in green stains, foul-smelling from long storage in the hold of a ship. This was one of the tents the Greeks had lived in for the first months of the war when they'd been arrogant enough to think Troy would be easily defeated. After their first miserable winter under canvas, they'd cut down an entire forest to build their huts.

I ducked under the open flap, pausing for a moment while my eyes adjusted to the green gloom. I thought I'd heard every sound the wind could make, but the snapping and bellowing of canvas was new. The smells were the same though: stale blood from a basket full of used bandages; a tang of fresh herbs: thyme, rosemary, lavender, bay. When I'd worked there, the tent was so overcrowded you'd had to step over one patient to reach the next. Now, it was half empty: just two rows of five or six ox-hide beds, their occupants for the most part sleeping, except for two at the far end who were playing dice. These would be men who'd been wounded in the final assault on Troy. None of them seemed to be seriously injured, except for one at the end of the front row who looked to be in a bad way. I wondered why I was even bothering to assess them; it had nothing to do with me now.

Ritsa was standing by the bench at the far end, wiping her hands on the coarse sacking apron round her waist. She smiled as I approached, but I noticed she didn't run to meet me as she used to do.

'Well,' she said, as I reached her. 'Look at *you*.'

I wondered what was different about me. My pregnancy, which was beginning to show, or the rich embroidery on my robe? But neither of these was exactly new. Then I realized she must be referring to Amina, who'd followed me in and was hovering a few feet behind me.

'Who's this, then? Your maid?'

'*No*.' It was important to make this clear. 'It's just, Alcimus doesn't want me going around the camp on my own.'

'He's right there. I've never seen so many drunks. Come in, sit down . . .'

She picked up a jug of wine and poured three cups. After a moment's hesitation, and with a glance in my direction, Amina accepted one. Annoyingly, she was behaving exactly like a maid.

I sat down at the long table and turned to Ritsa. 'How are you?'

'Tired.'

She looked it. In fact, she looked haggard, and I couldn't understand why because these men, apart from the head injury in the front row, all had slight wounds.

'I'm sleeping in Cassandra's hut.'

That explained it. I remembered how frenzied Cassandra had been when the Trojan women were waiting to be shared out among the kings – how she'd grabbed torches and whirled them round above her head, stamping her feet, shouting for everybody to come and dance at her wedding . . . She'd even tried to haul her mother to her feet, forcing her to dance and stamp her feet too.

'Is she any better?'

Ritsa pulled a face. 'She varies – mornings are pretty good; the nights are bloody awful . . . She's obsessed with fire, it's amazing how she gets her hands on it, but she does – and every single time, *I*'m in trouble, *my* fault. I'm surprised she hasn't burned the whole bloody place down. I daren't go to sleep – and then I've got to work in here all day. It's no life.'

'You need somebody to help.'

'Well, there is one girl – she's pretty useless though. I couldn't leave Cassandra with her.'

'I could sit with her – let you get some sleep.'

'I don't know what Machaon would say about that.'

'We could ask. *I* could ask.'

She shook her head. Machaon was the Greek army's chief physician. He was also – and rather more relevantly – Ritsa's owner. I could see she was reluctant to let me approach him, so I had to let it go.

'Nice wine,' I said, to fill a silence.

'It is, isn't it? Not bad.'

She was just pouring us another cup when a great blast of wind bellied the canvas above our heads. Alarmed, I looked up. 'Aren't you worried? I'd be scared it was coming down.'

'I wish it would.'

I looked at her, but she just shrugged again and went back to grinding herbs. You might think it strange, but I envied her the cool feel of the pestle against the palm of her hand. It was a long time since I'd worked beside her at this bench, but it had been my happiest time in the camp. I could still identify every one of the ingredients she had lined up in front of her – all of them sedative in their effects. Mixed with strong wine, you'd have a draught capable of knocking out a bull. 'Is that for Cassandra?'

She glanced at Amina, then mouthed, 'Agamemnon. Can't sleep, apparently.'

'*Ah*, the poor soul.'

We exchanged a smile, then she jerked her head at Amina. 'She's quiet.'

'Still waters.'

'Really?'

'No, I don't know. But you're right: she doesn't say much.'

'*Is* she your maid?'

'No, she's one of Lord Pyrrhus' girls. Suits both of us, I suppose. I need somebody to walk with, she needs to get out.'

This was all rather awkward. I'd known Ritsa since I was a child. In those days, she was a person of some standing, a respected healer and midwife. She'd been my mother's best friend – and after her death Ritsa had done her best to take care of me. Then, years later, when Achilles sacked and burned our city, we'd been brought to this of Lyrnessus camp together as slaves. She'd been an immense help to me then, and to many of the other women. But now I was a free woman, the wife of Lord Alcimus, whereas Ritsa was still a slave. Oh, it's easy to say changes in status, in fortune, shouldn't put a strain on friendship, but we all know they do. Not *this* friendship though. I'd lost so many of the people I loved; I was determined not to lose Ritsa.

So, instinctively, I began reminiscing about our life in Lyrnessus, reaching out to her through shared memories of a happier past, before Achilles destroyed everything, before we first heard his terrible battle cry ringing round the walls. Even so, the conversation was hard going, guttering like a candle at the end of its life – and I was aware all the time of Amina, avidly listening. After another pause, I said: 'Well, I suppose I should be getting back.'

Ritsa nodded at once and pushed her mortar to one side. We hesitated over kissing, making ineffectual pecks and bobs in each other's direction before finally achieving an awkward bumping of noses. Amina watched. As we set off, she once more lagged deliberately behind. I dropped back, wanting to walk beside her, but the minute I slowed down, she did too, so the distance between us was maintained. I sighed and struggled on against the wind. This girl was on my conscience and I rather resented the fact, because I felt I was doing everything I could. Remembering my own first days in the camp, how much other women had helped me then, I'd tried to reach out to her before, on my visits to the women's hut, but so far, she'd rejected every overture of friendship. Of course, I was trying to support the other girls too, but Amina particularly, probably because she reminded me so much of myself – the way I'd watched and listened and waited. Friendship's often based on similarities, the discovery of shared attitudes, shared passions, but the resemblances between Amina and me weren't having that effect. If anything, they simply increased the

23

doubts I felt about myself. But still, I wanted to make contact. I kept glancing back at her, but she was walking with her head bowed and neatly avoided my gaze.

A group of men had gathered in the arena and were kicking a pig's bladder around. At least, I hoped it was a pig's bladder. The day after Troy fell, I'd come across some fighters playing football with a human head. This lot seemed harmless enough, but I wasn't taking any chances. I turned round, put my hand on Amina's arm and nodded towards the beach. I was beginning to think Alcimus had been right all along and it was just too dangerous to leave the compound.

The beach was deserted, except for two priests wearing the scarlet bands of Apollo who were whirling bullroarers above their heads, perhaps thinking if they made enough noise, the wind would be cowed into submission. As I watched, a gust caught one of them off balance and dumped him unceremoniously on to the wet sand. After that, they gave up, trailing disconsolately away in the direction of Agamemnon's compound. All over the camp, priests like these were trying everything they knew to change the weather: examining the entrails of sacrificed animals, watching the flight patterns of birds, interpreting dreams . . . And still the wind blew.

After the priests had gone, we had the whole vast beach to ourselves, though we had to hold our veils over our faces to be able to breathe at all; talking was impossible. Neither of us could have stood alone against the blast, so we were forced to cling to each other – and those few minutes of shared struggle did more to break down the barriers between us than my offers of friendship had ever done. We staggered about, laughing and giggling. Amina's cheeks were flushed; I think she was probably amazed to discover that laughter was still possible.

At first, we kept to the edge of the beach, where the cradled ships provided some protection, but I can never resist the pull of the sea – and anyway, I told myself, the wet sand at the water's edge would be firmer. Easier to stay on our feet. So down the slopes of mixed sand and shingle we went, to find ourselves confronted by a wall of yellowish-grey water that seemed to be intent on gobbling up the land. On the shoreline, there were stinking heaps of bladderwrack studded with dead creatures, thousands of them, more than I'd ever seen before: tiny, grey-green crabs, starfish, several huge jellyfish with dark red centres, almost as if something inside them had burst, and other things whose names I didn't know – all of them dead. The sea was murdering its children.

Amina turned to look back at the smouldering towers of Troy, her face suddenly tense and wretched. I felt I was failing her and that somebody else, older, more experienced – Ritsa, perhaps – would have been better able to reach out to her. So we walked in silence until we drew level with Pyrrhus' compound. Once inside the gates I knew we'd be safe, but we weren't there yet. Hearing a burst of braying laughter, I approached cautiously, keeping to the shadows, trying to work out what lay ahead of us. It wasn't dark exactly, but in those days the sky was often so overcast that even at midday it was scarcely light.

Immediately outside the gate was a big open space where the Myrmidons used to muster before marching off to war. Here, another group of fighters had gathered, but at the centre of this scrum was a girl. Blindfolded. They were spinning her round the circle, each man sending her careering off into the arms of the next. She didn't scream or cry for help; probably she knew by now that nobody would come. *Amina mustn't see this.* I grabbed her arm and pointed back the way we'd come, but she just stood, transfixed, and so, in the end, I had to drag her away. Stumbling, she followed me along the wall, but still looked back over her shoulder at the spinning girl and the ring of laughing men.

In my first weeks in the camp, when the sea had been both a solace and a temptation – I say 'temptation' because I so often wanted to walk into the waves and not turn back – I'd explored every inch of the beach, and that knowledge served me well now. I knew there was a path through the dunes that led to another entrance into the stables, so I headed straight for that. Reaching the first sheltered place, I flopped on to the sand to gather my scattered thoughts and, after a moment's hesitation, Amina sat beside me, stretched out on her back and stared up at the sky.

Lying down like that, we escaped the full force of the wind, though the sharp blades of marram grass tossed wildly above our heads. I closed my eyes and put my arms across my face. I was afraid Amina would want to talk about the incident we'd just witnessed, and I didn't know what to say to her. Tell the truth, I suppose – but it was a difficult truth to tell. On my second night in the camp, I'd slept in Achilles' bed. Less than two days before, I'd seen him kill my husband and my brothers. Lying underneath him as he slept, I'd thought nothing worse could ever happen to me, or to any woman. I thought this was the pit. But later, as I walked around the camp, I began to notice the common women, those who scrabbled for scraps around the cooking fires, who went without food to feed their children, who crawled under the huts at night to sleep. It hadn't taken me long to realize there were many fates worse than mine. Amina needed to know that, she needed to understand the realities of life in this camp, but I couldn't face the brutality of telling her. And anyway, I told myself, she'd learn soon enough.

When I opened my eyes, I saw that she was watching some crows which were circling a hundred yards or so further on. I thought she looked puzzled, and after a while she stood up, shielding her eyes to see better. With her black robe flapping around her, she looked like a crow herself. Reluctantly, I got to my feet, wondering how I was going to get her past the spot, because I knew – or rather suspected – what was there. When Pyrrhus had returned in triumph after his exploits in Troy, he'd been dragging a bag of blood and broken bones behind his chariot wheels: Priam. The action was both horrific and drearily predictable. Achilles had dishonoured Hector's body by dragging it behind his chariot, so obviously Pyrrhus must inflict the same fate on Priam. I remembered Achilles coming back to the camp that day, how he'd stridden into the hall and plunged his head and shoulders into a vat of clean water, surfacing, a minute or so later, dripping wet and blind. The crows had been circling that day too.

'Come on.' I tried to force a little energy into my voice. 'Let's get going.'

Wrapping my veil tightly round my face, I set off. There was a taint in the air that I hoped she hadn't noticed, though she seemed alert to everything. Sliding down slopes of loose sand, we came out into a clearing, and there it – *he* – was. No way of telling whether this place had been deliberately chosen or if Priam's body had been simply abandoned where Pyrrhus' mad ride had come to an end. But, whether by accident or design, he'd been left propped up against a slight incline so that he seemed to be half rising to greet us. Somehow that made everything worse. Nothing much left of his face: his eyes and the tip of his nose were gone. Crows always go for the eyes first, because it's easy and they need to work fast. Many a hungry crow has lingered a second too long and ended up in a fox's jaws.

There was no way round the body: we had to walk past. Close to, the stench became a physical barrier that you had to push against. I breathed through my mouth, keeping my eyes down so I'd see as little as possible. What I hadn't expected was the buzzing of flies, thousands of them, covering the body like a fuzz of black bristles. As my shadow fell across them, they rose up, only to settle again the moment I was past. The noise filled my head till I thought it was going to split open. Sometimes, even now, so many years later, I'll be sitting outside enjoying the warmth of a summer evening, and I'll become aware of the buzzing of bees fumbling the flowers, of countless other insects seething in the green shade – and it's unbearable. 'Where are you going?' people ask. And I say – convincingly casual, because I've had a lot of practice – oh, believe me, a *lot* – 'It's too hot out here, don't you think? Why don't we go inside?'

That day, there was no escape. I tried to focus on trivial things – what we were having for dinner, whether the women would remember to have a hot bath ready for Alcimus' return, though I'd no idea when he was coming home, or if he'd come home at all. I thought about anything and everything except what was lying there in front of me – the pitiful ruin of a great king.

Amina was some way behind. I turned, meaning to chivvy her along, and found I couldn't speak. Sickened by the stench, she'd raised her veil to cover her nose and was staring at the body. That mane of silver hair, laced with blood – not much else was recognizable – but still enough for her to say: '*Priam?*'

I nodded and beckoned her on, but she stood rooted to the spot, staring, staring, her eyes so wide they seemed to have swallowed the rest of her face. And then she turned aside and retched, her whole body convulsed by the effort. A few moments later, she was dabbing her mouth delicately on the edge of her veil.

'Are you all right?'

No reply. Well, fair enough, stupid question. Using the edge of her sandal, she was scraping up enough soil to cover the vomit. Taking her time. Fastidious as a cat. When, finally, she turned to face me, I was startled. I don't know what I'd expected. Revulsion? Yes. Shock? Yes. Even full-blown hysteria, perhaps; anything but this cool, calm, calculating stare. It made me nervous. 'Come on, let's get you home.'

'*Home?*'

Too late to choose another word, and anyway, whether she liked it or not, the women's hut *was* her home now. I walked on, hoping she'd follow, but she didn't, and when I glanced over my shoulder, I found her still staring – not at Priam, now, but at the small mound of earth she'd raised to cover her sick. She looked up. 'The soil's very loose. Be easy to dig.'

At first, I didn't understand. Then: 'No. *No!*'

'We can't just leave him like this.'

'There's nothing we can do.'

'Yes, there is. We can bury him.' Then, like a child repeating a lesson she'd learnt by rote: 'If a dead person isn't given a proper burial, they're condemned to wander the earth. They can't enter the world of the dead where they belong.'

'Do you honestly believe that? Priam's being punished because Pyrrhus won't let anybody bury him? Doesn't say much for the mercy of the gods, does it?' Every word of that was false. Nothing in my life up to that point had inclined me to believe in the mercy of the

gods. 'The point is, Pyrrhus doesn't want him buried and what Pyrrhus says goes.'

'There's a higher power than Pyrrhus.'

'Yes,' I said, deliberately misunderstanding. 'Agamemnon. Do
you think *he* cares whether Priam's buried or not?'

'I care.'

'You're a girl, Amina. You can't fight the kings.'

'I don't want to fight anybody. And anyway, I wouldn't be – I'd
just be doing what women have always done.'

She was right, of course. Preparing the dead for burial is women's
work, every bit as much as childbirth and the care of the new-born.
We are the gatekeepers. In normal times, the women of Priam's
household would have prepared his body for burial, but things were
different now, and she seemed to have no grasp of how fundamen-
tally her life had changed.

'Look, Amina, if you're going to survive, you've got to start living
in the real world. Troy's gone. In this compound, whatever Pyrrhus
wants, Pyrrhus gets.' What I really wanted to say was: *You're a slave.*
Learn to think like a slave. But I couldn't do it. She was so young, so
brave. And I was a coward, I suppose; I just let it go, hoping the reality of her situation would sink in without me having to hammer it
home. 'Let's get you back to the hut. Have something to eat.'

Reluctantly, she nodded. I set off, striding out as fast as I could,
though on this sheltered ground behind the dunes, grasses and weeds
grew almost waist high; it was a struggle to get through them. Ahead
of us was the cinder path that connected the stables with the grazing
pastures on the headland. A groom was coming towards us, leading a
black stallion. Disturbed by the high wind, the horse was tossing his
head and side-stepping so often the man walking on the other side of

him was barely visible. Ebony. I recognized him because he was one half of Pyrrhus' chariot team. I stopped on the edge of the path and raised my veil, aware of Amina standing tall and straight-backed beside me. At first, I was so absorbed in watching Ebony's constant pirouetting that I didn't see who the 'groom' was; but then I caught a glimpse of wind-blown red hair, jarring against the horse's sleek black neck. *Pyrrhus.*

What on earth was he doing, bringing his own horse back from pasture, when he had a dozen or so grooms to do the job for him? But then I remembered that when Pyrrhus first arrived in the camp, ten days after Achilles' death, Alcimus had more than once remarked on how many hours he spent in the stables. 'Brilliant with horses,' he'd said, in a tone that implied Pyrrhus was rather less brilliant with men. 'Strange lad.' This was the closest he'd ever come to voicing the doubts I knew he had. Sometimes I wondered if any of those initial doubts remained, despite Pyrrhus having done so well at Troy. A short war, but a good one – that seemed to be the general verdict. ('Doing well at Troy' and 'a good war' are phrases that blister my tongue.)

So, there we stood, both of us discreetly veiled, waiting for horse and man to pass by. Perhaps Ebony could smell death or perhaps he just didn't like the huge black birds still circling overhead, their sharp, angular shadows slicing the ground beneath his feet. Dragging on the lead rope, he reared, then bucked three or four times in quick succession, letting out a string of explosive farts. Pyrrhus did well to hold him. He had a real fight on his hands, but he stayed calm, speaking quietly, gently, reassuringly, until at last the horse was steady, though sweating heavily. Pyrrhus moved to the other side of him, keeping his head averted so he didn't have to see the dreadful birds.

And they were dreadful – they seemed so even to me who had no reason to fear them – cawing raucously in the fading light, their flight feathers like outstretched fingers beckoning the night. Only when he was well past Priam's body did Pyrrhus ease the rope and let Ebony move his head freely again.

I breathed out, though I hadn't known till then that I was holding my breath. I waited till Pyrrhus was well ahead of us before I stepped out on to the track and, with a carefully expressionless glance at Amina, set off for the camp, aware all the time of her trailing reluctantly behind.

4

Entering the compound via the stable yard, I noticed the Trojan women had been allowed out of their hut. They were sitting in two rows on the veranda steps, looking, in their long black robes, rather like swallows about to migrate – the way they line up on ledges and parapets in the days before they fly away. Except swallows keep up a constant twittering whereas the women were silent. I say 'women' but they were girls really, not one of them over seventeen – some a lot younger than that. They clung together, too frightened even to whisper, staring towards Troy where columns of black smoke hung over the citadel, pierced now and then by jets of red and orange flame.

Amina ran to join them. They shuffled along the step to make room for her, but they didn't greet her.

I walked on to Alcimus' hut. As I lifted the latch, a fresh gust of wind sent the door crashing against the wall. I wrestled it shut behind me and stood in silence for a moment, gazing around at what was now my home. A table, four chairs, a bed pushed hard against the wall, several rugs and, in the corner, a carved chest containing Alcimus' clothes. A comfortable room: cushions on the chairs, a tapestry on the wall, lamps, candles – but nothing in it felt as if it belonged to me. I'd come to this hut the day after Achilles died, Alcimus prostrate

33

with grief, the whole camp in turmoil. That was five months ago, and yet the room still felt strange. I forced myself to move, do something, anything, and decided I'd go outside and check on the preparations for dinner.

The cooking fire was at the back of the hut where there was a small enclosed space that gave some shelter from the wind. I had women to help me now, slaves. There's a saying that the worst mistress a slave can have is an ex-slave. I tried at least to make sure that wasn't true of me. Alcimus' slaves had a safe place to sleep and I made sure they were well fed.

Once I was sure the meal was well underway, I went back inside and picked up a basket of raw wool, grey-black, with lumps of dung bulking out the fibres. I don't suppose teasing wool is anybody's favourite job; it certainly isn't mine. Within minutes, my hands were slick with grease, but I persevered, though the monotonous repetition of the task was sucking me into a tunnel of shapeless fears. Once again, I heard Amina say: *Be easy to dig*, and I shifted a little to stretch my aching back. Of course, she hadn't meant it; she wouldn't be mad enough to do anything that dangerous – and anyway, the women's hut was guarded at night. No, it was all right. There was nothing to worry about.

But then, floating between me and the wool, I saw Priam's hand, with the gold thumb ring he always wore glinting in the sun. Back, back, I went, hauled back helplessly into the distant past. When I was twelve years old, not long after my mother's death, my father had sent me to live with my married sister in Troy. Helen, who was – unaccountably – my dumpy sister's best friend, took a fancy to me. Everybody remarked on it: I was always 'Helen's little friend'. She used to take me with her when she went to the citadel, which was almost every day. She'd lean over the parapet and avidly – there was something unpleasant about the fixity of her gaze – watch the battle raging far below. The first time we went, Priam was there, and in the midst of all his troubles – war going badly, sons quarrelling, coffers emptying, a generation of young men dying – he found time to be kind to me. Taking out a silver coin, he put it on the palm of his hand and, muttering some magic words, passed the other hand rapidly across it – and the coin vanished. I stared at his empty hand, inclined to stand on my twelve-year-old dignity – I was too old for magic tricks – but mesmerized too, because I couldn't see how it had been done. Priam patted himself all over, pretending to search inside his robes. 'Where's it gone? Oh, I do hope I haven't lost it. Have *you* got it?' I shook my head vehemently. Then – of course – he reached across and 'discovered' the coin behind my ear. In spite of myself, I laughed. Bowing courteously, he presented the coin to me – and then, I remember, turned aside to watch the battle, his face settling into its lines of habitual sadness.

Now, years later, I remembered that hand – and saw the same hand lying dishonoured on the filthy ground. Pushing my fingers hard into my eyes, I banished the image, letting my head fall back against the chair. No more wool-teasing, I decided, it was too depressing. Squeezing my eyes tight shut, I simply sat and listened to the wind.

When, eventually, Alcimus came home, he had Automedon with him. That was no surprise – they often dined together – but then a third man followed them in. Pyrrhus. I bowed deeply and went to fetch cups and wine. Because I knew it would be expected, I selected the best wine and served it undiluted, with only bread and olives as an accompaniment. They sat round the table and talked. Alcimus was keeping pace with Pyrrhus' drinking, but he had a good head and his speech was no more than slightly slurred. Automedon, though he seemed to drink as much as the others, appeared to be entirely sober. Pyrrhus was unequivocally drunk. I fetched a second jug, set it on the table beside Alcimus and retreated to the shadows round the bed. Nobody so much as glanced at me.

They were talking about Alcimus' plan to organize games against teams from other compounds. The men had to be found something to do, Alcimus said. Idleness would only breed discontent and already there were rumours flying round the camp that the weather was unnatural, that Agamemnon or one of the other kings must have offended the gods. Fights between rival tribes and factions had begun to break out, and that was dangerous. The Greek kingdoms had a long history of festering border disputes, blood feuds passed down the generations, ceaseless conflict – and now that the Trojans had been defeated, there was nothing left to unite the warring bands. The coalition that had won the war was crumbling, each individual king-dom jockeying for position. The brother kings, Agamemnon and Menelaus, who'd led the expedition, had quarrelled because Mene-laus, in defiance of honour, decency and common sense, had taken that bitch Helen back into his bed. Thousands of young men had died so Menelaus could get back to humping his whore. And so, Alcimus went on, they had *somehow* to seize control of the situation, bring the divided factions together. Pyrrhus said 'Yes' and 'No' and drank and offered the opinion that what the men really needed was a bit of *fun*. The games will be fun, Alcimus insisted. 'Until they start killing each other over the results,' Automedon said.

They were well into the second jug – and I still didn't know if Pyrrhus would be staying for dinner. Now *very* drunk, he began talking – boasting, rather – about the part he'd played in the fall of Troy. I saw Alcimus and Automedon glance at each other. Myrmidons were – are – a stocky, dark-haired, dark-skinned race, as agile as their own mountain goats, deeply sceptical, slow to trust, taciturn to a fault. Neither Alcimus nor Automedon looked comfortable during Pyrrhus' slurred ramblings; Automedon, in particular, stared into his cup, his sallow, aquiline face expressionless. I wasn't enjoying it much either. I didn't want to dwell on what had happened inside Troy; I certainly didn't want be told what Alcimus had done. I had to spend the rest of my life with this man; it would be easier if I didn't know. But I needn't have worried: Pyrrhus' account featured nobody but himself.

He was describing – reliving – the moment he'd hacked his way through the doors of Priam's palace. I'd never thought of Pyrrhus as an eloquent man, but on this subject the words flowed. I was forced to see everything through his eyes: the long corridor, doors opening off on either side, glimpses of rugs, tapestries, gold lamps – all the fabled wealth of Troy – though he'd only looked just long enough to make sure there were no fighters hiding there. Then on he ran – feeling, he said, Achilles' blood coursing through his veins – towards the door at the far end. Finding it heavily guarded, he'd veered off in search of the secret passage that linked Hector's house with Priam's apartment. The existence of this passage was one of the crucial pieces of information Priam's son Helenus had revealed under torture. The briefest of searches had led Pyrrhus to it. By now, he'd left the other Greek fighters far behind, so when, finally, he burst into the throne room and saw Priam, in full armour, standing on the altar steps, the two of them had been alone together.

All this was painful to me, though no different from my own

37

involuntary imaginings. I tried not to hear what came next, but it was no use, I had to go on listening. He spoke of how proudly he'd announced his identity: Pyrrhus, son of Achilles. How, at the mere mention of that name, Priam had gone white with terror. How he'd leapt up the altar steps, dragged the old man's head back and quickly, cleanly, deftly, easily, cut his throat. One blow, he said. Like sticking a pig.

I looked at him and I thought: *You're lying.* I don't know how I knew, but I did. The death of Priam had been nothing like that. And nobody would ever be able to contradict Pyrrhus' account, because nobody else had been present. Eventually, he lapsed into silence, staring at his cup as if he couldn't remember what it was for. I watched him, searching, I suppose, for some resemblance to Achilles, whose unappeasable anger had caused hundreds, if not thousands, of deaths. People kept telling Pyrrhus he was the spitting image of his father, but I couldn't see it. To me, he looked like a portrait of Achilles done in coarse red clay by a competent but mediocre sculptor. So? *Yes,* there was a resemblance; and *no,* he was nothing like Achilles.

As if made uneasy by my gaze, Pyrrhus straightened up and looked around. 'You know what I really regret?' he said. 'Giving Hector's shield to that fucking woman to bury her brat in. *You —*' jabbing his finger at Automedon — 'should've stopped me.'

'It was very generous,' Automedon said, stiffly.

'It was very bloody stupid.'

'You've got the helmet,' Alcimus said. 'You've got everything else.'

'S'not the point though, is it? My father stripped that armour from Hector's dead body, the minute after he killed him. I should have the full set — not bits missing.'

Abruptly, he lurched to his feet. Alcimus put out a steadying hand, but Pyrrhus ignored him, grabbed the edge of the table and then launched himself at the door. Alcimus followed him out on to the veranda. I could hear them talking, though their words were broken up by gusts of wind. After a few minutes, Alcimus came back to the table, bringing the cool night air on his skin. He pulled out his chair and sat down.

'Well,' he said.

Automedon shrugged. They were used to waiting in ambush, these two, where one whisper might betray them – and so over the years they'd developed a method of communication that hardly seemed to rely on words. I sensed that this particular conversation had been going on, unspoken, for much of the past hour.

'He's very young,' Alcimus said.

'Not young enough.'

Not young enough for drunken boasting to be excusable?

'He just wants to prove he's as good as Achilles. And he can't.' Alcimus glanced in my direction. 'Nobody can.'

A fraught silence. I'd never told anybody my marriage was unconsummated, not even Ritsa, and until that moment I'd always taken it for granted that Alcimus wouldn't have spoken about it either. Now, suddenly, I felt Automedon knew – or, more likely, guessed.

'More wine?' I asked.

'Better not,' Alcimus said. 'Fact, I think we should be going.'

I nodded, regretting yet another uneaten dinner. At the door, he hesitated. 'I don't know when I'll be back.'

And I felt he resented even that small concession to the obligations of domestic life. This was at the root of all my uneasiness. I knew – I thought I knew – that Alcimus had loved me once – or been infatuated with me, at least. I'd noticed the way he'd looked at me, whenever we were together in a room, though of course he'd never said anything. As Achilles' prize of honour, I'd been as far beyond his reach as a goddess – but, then, perhaps he'd preferred it like that? Perhaps the real love had been for Achilles.

5

As Alcimus' wife, I led a much more isolated and restricted life than I had as Achilles' prize of honour. I no longer served wine to the men at dinner in the hall, and the lawlessness of the camp meant it was harder to see my friends. There weren't many hours I didn't spend alone. Alcimus came and went, busily organizing the work of the compound; we barely spoke. In the evenings, when I was always alone, I sat spinning wool, letting the thread lead me down a labyrinth of memory. I found myself thinking a great deal about my sister, Ianthe – the daughter of my father's first wife. I had no memories of her from my childhood: she'd already been a woman on the brink of marriage when I was born. It was only later, after my mother died and I was sent to live with her in Troy, that I got to know her. I thought of her now, because I felt as lonely as I'd ever felt since arriving in the camp, and she was my only living relative. *If* she was still alive.

After Troy fell, as the captive women were being herded into the arena, I'd gone in search of her. Since she'd been married to one of Priam's sons, I'd looked for her first among the women of the royal household, who were being housed in an overcrowded hut on the edge of the arena, waiting to be allocated as prizes of honour to the various kings. Some of the women had spilled out of the hut and were sitting or lying on the dirty sand. Hair stringy with sweat, faces bruised, eyes bloodshot, tunics torn: their own families would have struggled to recognize some of them. As I walked through the crowd, I'd stared hard into every face, but Ianthe wasn't there.

Later, I looked for her among the common women I'd seen being forced down the muddy track into the camp, stumbling, sometimes falling over like cattle driven to the slaughter. Those who fell were 'encouraged' to get on their feet again by blows from the butt ends of spears. No pregnant women among them, I noticed – and though some of the women were leading little girls by the hand, there were no boys. Once again, I looked from one terrified face to another, but fear made them all look alike and it took me a long time to establish that my sister wasn't there. I learnt later that several hundred women had thrown themselves from the citadel, and as soon as I heard that I felt sure Ianthe would have been one of them. It was in her to do that – as it was not in me.

Gradually, over the intervening days, I'd learnt to accept that she was dead. But I couldn't be sure and, now more than ever, I needed certainty. The only person I could ask was Helen, who'd been Ianthe's friend – though it wasn't a friendship that many people had understood. So, one morning, I rose early, dressed myself in my darkest clothes, and set off, creeping between the huts as unobtrusively as I could, nervous and alone. I couldn't take Amina with me on this trip because she'd have told the other girls and I didn't want this visit to be generally known. I wasn't sure I'd be able to get to Helen – she was known to be heavily guarded – but the sentries at the gate of the compound waved me through. Women were not considered a threat.

I'd never been in Menelaus' compound before, so I had no idea which door to knock on. After looking around for some time, I noticed a young girl sitting on the steps of one of the huts, grinding corn. She was skinny, with dark shadows under her eyes and an open sore at the corner of her mouth – only too clearly one of the women who scratched a miserable living round the cooking fires. When I asked for directions, she pointed at one of the huts. 'You want to see Helen?' she said. And then she spat to clean her mouth after saying the name.

I climbed the steps, waited a few moments – wishing I hadn't come – and then knocked. My hand was still raised, my mouth open to ask the maid if I could see her mistress, when I saw there was no need. Because there she was. I detected no change in her, none at all. She looked my age – even a little younger, perhaps – though she had a daughter old enough for marriage. Her hair was unbound and so tousled I thought she must just have tumbled out of bed.

'I'm sorry to get you up.'

'You didn't. I was working.'

I noticed there was a loom in the far corner, with lamps lit all around it. Helen and her weaving. I remembered a cruel story I'd heard when I was a girl. People believed – or at least affected to believe – that whenever she cut a thread in her wool, a man died on the battlefield. I wondered, now, if she'd known that's what people were saying – and, if so, whether it had frightened her as much as it ought to have done. Every death in the war laid at Helen's door.

She was staring at me, not stepping aside to allow me into the room. I realized she didn't recognize me, so I pushed my veil away from my face. 'Briseis.'

Instant delight. 'Well, look at you!' She caught my hands. 'You're as tall as I am.' She sketched the air between our heads. 'And so beautiful. I knew you would be.'

'Then you were the only one. Everybody keeps telling me what an ugly duckling I was.'

She shook her head. 'Eyes, cheekbones – you don't need anything else.'

Said the woman who had everything else. She pulled me towards a chair and sat opposite me. There were two pink spots on her cheeks; she was warm, friendly, excited. There was no doubting the sincerity of her welcome.

'*You* haven't changed.'

I meant it as a compliment, I suppose, or a simple observation. Nobody ever really complimented Helen on her looks – what would have been the point? But the words lingered on the air, sounding slightly accusatory. And yes, I did feel that some sign of grief or regret, some external mark, would have been welcome – a few faint lines around the eyes and mouth, perhaps? Would that have been too much to ask? But no, there was nothing.

If there was an edge to my voice, Helen didn't appear to notice. She was busy mixing wine and pouring it into cups. As she handed one to me, she said, 'Pregnancy suits you. Achilles' child?'

I nodded.

'A great, *great* man. Menelaus always speaks well of him.'

I didn't know how to answer that. Obviously, the past had been wiped clean. Helen was Greek again, no longer Helen of Troy – that was over, finished. She'd gone back to being Helen of Argos. Queen of Argos. *So many thousands . . .*

I cut the thought off. 'I was wondering whether you know what happened to my sister?'

Immediately, Helen's expression changed. 'I saw her that day – she came to the house, we had a cup of wine sitting out in the courtyard, in

44

the shade. She was happy, I think – or as happy as she ever was. And then there was this great outcry, shouting in the streets, I couldn't think what was going on – the slaves were all running around gabbling something about a horse, so we went outside to see. I knew it was a trap. I know it's easy to be wise after the event, but I really did know. I felt there was something living inside it, and that could only be men. And Cassandra was there, of course, screaming her head off: *Don't let them in!* Until Priam told her to shut up and go home. After it was dark, I went back. I walked all the way round it, singing Greek songs.'

Love songs. I'd been told about this, though there was something strange about the story. Some of the men hadn't heard her singing at all – Automedon hadn't; Pyrrhus hadn't – and even those who did remember her singing could never agree on the song. It was as if every man had heard the song that meant most to him.

'Why?'

'Why did I sing? Oh, I don't know, I suppose it was a way of – reaching out?'

'You weren't trying to get them to reveal themselves?'

'*No.*' She was shaking her head so vigorously she might have been trying to dislodge a wasp that had got caught in her hair. 'I wanted to go home.' Her voice broke on the word. Raising her hand, she dabbed the corner of one perfect eye.

'Helen – you could have left at any time.'

'Could I? You've no idea how difficult it was.'

Somehow my sister had disappeared from the conversation, but that was Helen all over. I saw something at that moment that I'd never been aware of before. You couldn't imagine a more feminine woman than Helen nor a more virile man than Achilles, and yet in every way that mattered, they were alike. It was always about them.

'*Ianthe*,' I said, firmly.

'Oh, yes. I was told – I don't know if it's true – she threw herself down a well. Apparently, a lot of women did. There was a whole group of them who used to meet in the temple of Artemis – widows, you know . . . She did become *very* religious after her husband was killed. No children, I suppose, nothing to hang on to . . . A bit of a temple mouse, I'm afraid . . .' Helen looked at me. 'As I say, I don't know for sure.'

'Well. Better than the slave market, I suppose.'

Because that was the only other possibility. My sister was much older than me, and women nearing the end of their child-bearing years are routinely sent to the slave market – and in many ways it's a worse fate. Older women can be picked up cheap and worked to death. Why not? You can always buy another. I made my mind up at that moment to believe that Ianthe was dead.

The business of my visit was over, and yet I lingered. We stayed silent for a while, though not awkwardly. Rather to my surprise, something of the old intimacy had returned.

'You were such an odd little thing,' she said.

'I wasn't very happy.'

'No, I could see that.'

There had been genuine affection between us. Poor woman, she'd had to find her friendships where she could. Her real friends were Priam and Hector, who'd always treated her kindly, but in the nature of things she'd seen very little of them. Like all women, she lived her life largely separate from men – and every woman in Troy (except my sister) hated her. And she them. Oh, in public she was always respectful, but in private it was a different story. Andromache was 'the child bride', Cassandra 'the mad woman', and Hecuba . . . What had she said about Hecuba? I couldn't remember. Perhaps Hecuba had been spared. I could imagine that inside the walls of the women's quarters Hecuba would be a formidable opponent, too intimidating even for Helen to take on. We lapsed into silence again and let the tides of memory wash over us.

At last, hearing voices outside the hut – the compound was starting to come to life – I stirred. 'May I see your weaving?'

She brightened. 'Yes, of course.'

Jumping to her feet, she caught my arm and almost dragged me across the room. Helen's weaving was unlike anybody else's. Most women use motifs that are common in the culture – often stylized flowers and leaves, or incidents in the lives of the gods – but Helen's designs were nothing if not original. She was weaving a history of the war, telling the story in wool and silk just as the bards sing it in words and music. I assumed she'd still be doing that and, sure enough, taking shape on her loom was a gigantic wooden horse. Inside its belly were two long rows of curled-up foetuses; man-babies lying in a womb.

I stood there taking it in, my silence probably a better compliment than any words would have been.

'This is for Menelaus' palace, I suppose?'

'Who knows?'

Something in her voice made me turn to look at her. The light from the lamps she'd been working by fell full on to her face, but it wasn't that familiar perfection which caught my eye; it was the necklace of circular bruises round her throat. Many different shades, I noticed – being, I'm afraid, something of a connoisseur in such matters – from angry red fingermarks all the way through blue and black to the mottled yellow and purple of old injuries. All of them on

47

her neck and throat – he hadn't touched her face. He'd throttled her as he was fucking her. As you would.

Instinctively, she started to wrap the blue shawl more tightly round her neck, but then let her hand fall, meeting my gaze with that too steady, *skinned* look I'd seen so many times before – and since. She was ashamed, while knowing she had no reason to be ashamed. She wanted to hide the bruises – and yet, at the same time, she wanted me to see.

'Oh, Helen.'

'Well, you know, he gets drunk and . . . It's just one long list of names.'

'Names?'

'People who've died. Patroclus, Achilles, Ajax –'

'But that was suicide.'

'Doesn't matter, he still blames me. Nestor's son – what's his name? Antilochus. Agamemnon –'

'*Agamemnon?* Last time I looked he was very much alive.'

'Yes, but it's got very bad between them. He says he's lost his brother – and what did they fall out over? *Me.*'

Poor Helen. All that beauty, all that grace – and she was really just a mouldy old bone for feral dogs to fight over.

'Oh, I know, it's just grief and it's natural, but it's all the time – relentless. And, of course, it's all my fault. All of it, every single death – *my* fault. When I was first returned to him after Troy fell he said he was going to kill me. Sometimes I wish he had.' She choked on a laugh. 'Except I don't, of course.'

'I'm sorry.'

'I need to get my hands on some plants.'

'Not *poison*?'

'*No* – I'd never get away with it. But there are drugs that make people forget – even if somebody they love dies, they don't feel it, they don't cry, they don't mourn . . . They don't get angry. It's all just –' She swept her hand from side to side. 'Smoothed away.'

'I don't know where you'd get your hands on something like that.'

'Machaon?'

'Well, you could always ask. He'd certainly give you a sleeping draught.'

'No, that's no good, he'd see through that straight away. I need him awake – but calm.' She hesitated. 'There's masses of stuff in Troy. In the herb garden there.'

I knew what she was asking. 'That's a long way away. I think Machaon's your best bet.'

I didn't blame Helen for wanting to drug Menelaus. When I looked at her, I didn't see the destructive harpy of the stories and the gossip; I saw a woman fighting for her life.

'He will kill me,' she said.

I shook my head. 'If he was going to do that, he'd have done it by now.'

'So, you won't help me?'

'Ask Machaon.'

That was that. In the end, everything done, everything said, we simply stared at each other. Then she touched me lightly on the arm and led me to the door. As she opened it, the light revealed the full extent of the bruising, which went right down to her breasts. I sensed she wanted to leave me with that sight and I felt myself recoil from her.

'You can't blame me for trying to survive,' she said, closing the door till it was open no more than a crack. 'From what I hear, you're pretty good at that yourself.'

6

That night, once again, I ate alone. After dinner, instead of waiting up for Alcimus, I went straight to my own room. This was easily the smallest in the hut, just large enough to contain a bed and – recently acquired from the looting of Troy – a cradle. The cradle was so finely carved, so lavishly embellished with ivory and gold, that it could only have belonged to an aristocratic or royal family. Lying down on the bed, I stared up at the roof beams while the baby inside me – who'd been restless all day – settled slowly into its own version of sleep.

Flat on my back like that, I didn't have to see the cradle. Alcimus had presented it to me with such pride, I knew I couldn't get rid of it, or even suggest moving it into one of the storage huts, and yet I loathed it. I couldn't stop thinking about Andromache's son, the little boy whom Pyrrhus had hurled to his death from the battlements of Troy. I had no logical reason to believe this was his cradle, and yet I knew it was. I felt his small ghost in the room.

It was difficult to sleep with that thought in my head, but I did at last manage to drift off. Only a few moments later, it seemed – though it might have been hours – I was jerked awake by a banging on the door. Getting up too quickly, I felt myself go dizzy, but managed to stumble along the passage. The banging had stopped, but then it started again.

'Coming!' Peering into the darkness, I saw one of the girls standing there, though I couldn't see which one, until she took a step closer. 'Amina. What's wrong?'

'He's sent for Andromache.'

She didn't need to say any more. I got my mantle and stepped across the threshold, a mizzling rain immediately dampening my skin and hair. We scaled along the wall, staggering a little in the gap between two huts where the wind blew with full force off the sea. Amina tapped on the door and one of the girls let us in. I didn't really know any of them yet, three or four by name, the others not even that. It didn't help that many of them were still mute. They'd got their pallet beds from beneath the hut where they were stored during the day and arranged them in rows across the room. Each girl had a small rush light by her pillow. As they turned to look at me, the pallid flames illuminated their faces from below — they looked like their own ghosts. A girl called Helle said, 'You're too late, she's gone.' She sounded spiteful, petulant — the way a small child might sound if her mother had failed to protect her.

'It's all right,' I said. 'I know where to find her.'

I did. I must have crossed paths with half a dozen past selves in the short distance between the women's hut and the hall.

As I approached, I heard singing, banging of fists on tables, the braying laughter of young men drinking hard to celebrate, or forget. Pyrrhus' voice rose louder than the rest. I walked along the veranda to the side entrance that led directly into his private apartments. Not much shelter there — as I opened the door, the wind blew me into the room. I looked around. A fire was burning, though the logs were green and smoking badly; my eyes stung. Two chairs faced each other across the hearth. The one opposite me had been Patroclus' chair. I could see him now, as always, with a couple of dogs asleep at his feet: hunting dogs, twitching and whimpering as they chased imaginary rabbits across dream fields. One of them yelped and its paws scrabbled on the floor. Patroclus laughed and the man in the other chair, whose face I couldn't see, looked up from his lyre and laughed too. And for a moment, I forgot Andromache waiting in the small room, Pyrrhus drinking himself stupid in the hall, and simply stared at the empty chairs – which in my mind were not empty at all. How powerful the dead are.

Another shout from the hall. More singing, louder now, accompanied by stamping feet. *Hold him down, you Argive warriors! Hold him down, you Argive chiefs! Chiefs! Chiefs! Chiefs! Chiefs!*

Hold him down? From what I'd seen of Pyrrhus, propping him up would have been more like it.

I knew Andromache would be in the room that opened off this one – the cupboard, I used to call it. I tapped on the door. 'Andromache? It's me – Briseis.'

Pushing the door open, I saw her face, pale, disembodied, floating on the darkness like the moon's reflection on water.

'How did you know I was here?'

'Amina told me.' I realized, even as I spoke, that I'd answered the wrong question. 'Oh, don't worry, I'm very familiar with this room.'

On my first night in the camp, Patroclus had given me a cup of wine. I couldn't understand it – such a powerful man, Achilles' chief aide – waiting on a slave. That simple act of kindness has haunted me ever since. Turning to the table on the left of the door, I filled two of the largest cups I could find and gave one to her.

She looked anxious. 'Do you think we should?'

'I don't see why not. It's Priam's wine and I don't suppose he'd begrudge us a cup.'

Uncertainly, she raised hers to her lips.

'Have you had anything to eat?'

She shook her head, so I went back into the other room, picked up a basket of cheese and bread and set it down beside her. I didn't expect her to eat, but at least now she could if she wanted to. I squeezed on to the bed beside her and we sat in silence for a while, listening to the singing in the hall.

'You'll be all right.' That sounded feeble, but anything said in this situation would have sounded feeble. 'It'll soon be over and then you'll be back in your own bed.'

'You know he killed my baby?'

Sometimes there are no words. I put my arm round her shoulders — she was so thin, birdlike, I almost expected to feel her heart fluttering against her ribs. At first, she was unresponsive, every muscle tense, but then, suddenly, she curled into my side and rested her head in the crook of my neck. I put my lips against her hair and we sat like that for a long time. My free hand rested on the coverlet. The pattern of leaves and flowers was so familiar I could trace it from memory without needing to see it. I was thinking about my friend Iphis, who'd so often waited in this room with me. After my first night in Achilles' bed, she'd had a hot bath waiting for me when I got back to the women's hut; she'd understood how you needed to feel clean, to immerse yourself in that all-enveloping warmth. I decided then and there that there'd be a hot bath waiting for Andromache whenever he let her go.

The shouting in the hall had died away to a low rumble with ripples of laughter running through it. Oh, they were pleased with themselves, these Greeks, celebrating the destruction of Troy. With their bellies full of looted beef, drunk on looted wine, their voices drowning out the roar of the wind, it was easy to forget they were trapped on the beach with no hope of launching their black ships. Only now the evening was drawing to a close – and the wind would whistle round their huts all night. Suddenly, they were singing the final song. I knew every word of it; I'd heard it sung so many times as I'd sat waiting in this room. It's a song about friendship; friends parting at the end of a good evening, a celebration of warmth and life, but tinged with melancholy too. As the last notes fade into silence, they tip the dregs of their wine on to the rushes as a final libation to the gods.

I squeezed Andromache's shoulder. 'I have to go.'

She nodded, bracing herself, knowing that the next time the door opened it would be Pyrrhus. And at that moment, all the protective numbness I'd built up over the last months vanished and I was back in this room, sitting where she was sitting, waiting for Achilles – experiencing all over again the terror I'd felt when the door opened and his huge shadow blotted out the light.

7

The hut was empty when I got back. I had no idea where Alcimus was or whether he'd be coming home. Probably not. I didn't know where he slept when he stayed out all night and I had no right to ask. Of course, he had other women – all men do – but I didn't know of anyone in particular.

It was too late to start carding wool, and yet I knew I wouldn't be able to sleep. Instead, I paced up and down, while the memories I'd become so good at suppressing bubbled away just beneath the surface and the baby boiled inside me. Spending time with Andromache and the girls was forcing me to relive my own early days in the camp. When I look back on that time, I think I must have been almost insane. Oh, outwardly normal, calm, smiling – always smiling – but moving my arms and legs about with no more feeling than a puppet. Whole days went by and towards evening I wouldn't be able to recall a single thing that had happened. Except, no, that's not quite true. I remembered – and still remember – the numerous small acts of practical kindness I received. I couldn't repay Iphis, but I could pass her kindness on – Andromache would have her bath.

But that was for the morning. I still had to get through the night. Perhaps I could have a small cup of the sleeping draught Alcimus kept by his bed, though I was wary of some of its effects – he had nightmares, the kind that don't stop when you open your eyes. I'd hear him sometimes moaning in his sleep. Still, I told myself, a few mouthfuls couldn't hurt. I tossed it back in a single gulp, twisting my mouth against the bitter taste, then went to the little room at the end of the passage, realizing as I did so that it was the exact equivalent of the 'cupboard' in Achilles' private quarters – the room where women sat while they waited to be summoned. I wondered who'd waited there for Alcimus in the years before his involuntary marriage.

My bed was hard and even on the short walk back from Pyrrhus' hall the cold had got into my bones. The sultry nights of summer were long gone; the year was turning towards the dark. I closed my eyes and kept them closed, though I was aware all the time of the empty cradle at the foot of my bed.

You know he killed my baby?

I did, though I'd only recently found out. At first, I'd assumed it was Odysseus who'd killed Andromache's son, simply because I'd heard him argue with such passionate intensity that every Trojan male must die, including babies in the womb. *All* of them, he'd insisted, but particularly the bloodline of Priam. There must be nobody left alive with any claim to the Trojan throne, nobody who could act as a focus for resistance and revenge. I'd discovered the truth accidentally through overhearing a conversation between Alcimus and one of the other fighters. Pyrrhus had been chosen to kill the baby as a reward for the part he'd played in the downfall of Troy. His exploits ran from mouth to mouth and no doubt grew in the telling. I'd even heard a rumour that he'd killed Priam by bludgeoning him to death with the body of his baby grandson. *That* wasn't true, or at least I hoped it wasn't true, though he had lied about the death of Priam – I was sure of that. So many hideous things had been done inside the fallen city that it was difficult to rule anything out.

The child inside me kicked again and I rested my spread fingers on my belly. I didn't know what pregnant women were supposed to feel; I had nobody to ask except Ritsa – and she always responded with the automatic cheeriness of an experienced midwife. So, what did I feel for this baby whose father had killed my husband and my brothers and burned my city down? I felt it wasn't mine. At times, it seemed more like a parasitic infestation than a pregnancy, taking me over, using me for its own purposes – which were *their* purposes. Kill all the men and boys, impregnate the women – and the Trojans cease to exist. They weren't just intent on killing individual men; they meant to erase an entire people.

I hadn't chosen this pregnancy; I didn't want it. And yet I knew it was my salvation. Without it, I'd have been given away – offered as a first prize in Achilles' funeral games. Instead, I had marriage, security, even a certain deference. I'd noticed a marked change as soon as the pregnancy started to show. Only the other day, a man I scarcely knew had placed his hand on my stomach, and not in a sexual, predatory way, but as a mark of his loyalty to the bloodline of Achilles. I was the casket that contained the crown jewels – at least, that's how the Myrmidons seemed to see me. As a person, I didn't count at all. If they ever thought about my feelings – and I was fairly certain they didn't – they'd probably assume I was glowing with pride at the thought of bearing Achilles' son. To be pregnant by the greatest warrior of his time – perhaps of all time – what more could a woman want?

I listened to the whimpering of the wind. At night, the roar that bullied and threatened all day sometimes died away to an inconsolable sobbing – like an abandoned child begging to be let in. By now, I knew every flaw in the hut. The gap beneath the door that allowed sand to blow in, so the floors were always gritty no matter how often they were swept. You had to be careful to place the lamps well out of the draughts, because if they happened to be blown over, they'd continue to burn. Candles were safer, since they'd probably be extinguished by the fall. You had the constant sensation that the wind was blowing darkness in through every crack. I'd have said that by now I knew every trick the storm could play, but then, lying there with my eyes closed, beginning to drift off to sleep, I heard a new sound: a knocking I'd not noticed before. Dragging myself awake, I opened my eyes and saw that the cradle had begun to rock. No human hand had touched it and yet there it was, creaking away, *moving* – inching its way across the floor. My mind scrabbled for an explanation, and as soon as I'd managed to shake off the pall of sleep, it was obvious enough. There was a gap in the wall at floor level – you could feel the draught round your ankles as soon as you entered the room – and since the floor sloped from the outer wall to the door, it was actually easy for the cradle to move. There was nothing remotely supernatural about this, and yet still the skin at the nape of my neck crawled. I watched the cradle rock and felt a stifling sense of dread. It was a long time before I managed to get back to sleep.

First thing next morning, still a bit dopey from the sleeping draught, I walked along to the women's hut, intending to wait for Andromache, only to be told – by Helle, who opened the door – that she'd already returned. 'She was only there a couple of hours.'

That was a bit odd. Normally, if you were summoned you expected to be there all night – but that was Achilles. I had no experience of

Pyrrhus. I went straight along the passage to Andromache's room, which in size and shape exactly mirrored my own. She was curled up under a blanket, tear-sodden and silent, though when I sat at the end of the bed, she rolled over and began wiping her eyes on the side of her hand.

'Well, that's done,' she said. 'And I'm glad it's over.'

I offered her a square of linen to blow her nose. She emerged from its folds sniffing, moist, pink-eyed, but a lot calmer than I'd been expecting. She jerked her head at the door. 'They keep asking me what it was like . . .'

Natural enough; they must all have thought it would be their turn soon. I remembered how important it had been to me that Iphis never asked questions. 'Look, why don't you come back with me?' I said. 'You can have a bath, there's plenty of hot water . . .'

She looked helplessly around the room, as if just getting off the bed was too daunting a task to be contemplated, but then she swung her legs over the side and stood up. Her hair was bedraggled, her tunic stained. I went back to the hut ahead of her, ordered a hot bath and set food on the table: cold cuts of meat from last night's dinner, warm bread, ripe apricots, white, crumbly cheese. I didn't for a moment suppose she'd be able to eat, but she surprised me. I can't say she ate heartily, but then I'm not sure she ever did. She did manage a cup of wine, though, and that brought some colour to her cheeks.

By the time she'd finished, the bath was ready and I took her outside to the back of the hut where she could bathe in privacy. Steam rising from the water, sweet-scented herbs floating on the surface, white towels warming on a clothes horse by the cooking fire . . . She did brighten a little at the sight. When she took off her tunic, I saw she was wearing a ring on a silver chain round her neck and wondered how on earth she'd managed to hang on to it. Usually, when a woman is captured, her jewellery's taken from her; many of the girls had arrived in the compound with torn earlobes where their earrings had been ripped out. I could see it was a man's thumb ring; but I didn't want to look too closely. More than anything else, she needed privacy. I knew how raw she'd be feeling – every inch of her body *raw* – as if she'd been skinned.

I turned away and began fussing with the towels. When I looked round again, she was lying stretched out in the bath with her eyes closed, shadows of passing clouds moving softly over her face. I let her take as long as she wanted, going back inside the hut and selecting one of my tunics for her to wear. It was fully twenty minutes before I heard her call my name. She stepped out of the bath into the embrace of warm towels. Then I helped her into the clean tunic and we sat on the step while I combed and braided her hair. There's something soothing about combing hair – for both the people involved. I kept trying to remember her as she'd been when I was in Troy. I was only twelve, so I'd have thought of her as a grown woman, though, looking back, I realized she must have been very young – not quite fifteen when she married Hector. That was unusually young, particularly since by all accounts she'd been a much-loved only daughter, but her father had wanted to get her safely married because he suspected (rightly) that his city was next on Achilles' list of targets.

I could imagine how difficult the early days of her marriage must have been. Preoccupied with fighting the war, Hector had postponed marriage till he was well into his thirties. By that age, he'd have had several concubines; some, at least, of the children playing round the dinner table would be his. But that's only to be expected; a young wife who makes herself miserable over her husband's concubines is a fool. No, the real problem was Helen. Hector was dazzled by her, though he was far too honourable a man to express in word or deed his infatuation with his brother's wife. For her part, Helen flirted outrageously with him, scarcely bothering to disguise her feeling that she'd married the wrong brother – and she was totally dismissive of Andromache, 'the child bride'. All women faded in Helen's presence, but Andromache – skinny, flat-chested and painfully shy – faded more than most. Hector always treated his wife with great respect on the rare occasions when they were obliged to appear together in public; and if, on such occasions, his eyes frequently strayed towards Helen . . . Well, that was true of every other man in the room.

Helen was well aware of the effect she was having. I remember one evening in particular when – tongue in cheek, as usual – she'd been complimenting the Trojans on how strictly they chaperoned unmarried girls. Helen was from Argos where things were done quite differently. 'Do you know,' she said, 'when I was a fully grown girl, ripe for marriage, I was still stripping to the waist and racing my brothers along the beach? I mean –' She gazed innocently around the table. 'Can you *imagine*?' Oh, they could, they could, they *definitely* could. One or two of Priam's more elderly counsellors looked as if imagining it might be the last thing they ever did. The women muttered and exchanged disapproving glances, while at the head of the table, Priam, his face alight with amusement, caught Helen's eye and gently shook his head.

Now, as I finished braiding Andromache's hair, I couldn't help smiling at the memory. In spite of everything, I've never been able to hate Helen – which, as far as Trojan women go, puts me in a minority of precisely one. I knotted a ribbon round the final braid and

Andromache, who'd drifted off into an almost trance-like state, opened her eyes and looked around.

'Thanks,' she said. 'I don't think I could have stood it a minute longer in there. They go on and on asking questions and I just don't want to talk about it.'

'No, of course not,' I said. I fetched a jug of wine and set it on the floor by our feet. We talked about this and that, but nothing held her attention for long and after a while she began telling me about Pyrrhus – as she'd been wanting to do since she arrived.

'He was so *drunk* – I've never in my life seen anybody that drunk. He kept knocking things over, and he'd say something and then forget he'd said it and say it again. I mean, Hector drank – well, they all do, don't they? – but *nothing* like that.' She paused for a moment, staring at the sparse grass around her feet. 'I think it helped in a way because I knew he wasn't going to remember anything – and that meant I needn't remember it either. Yes, I know, *mad* – I'm just saying that's how it felt.' She looked up. 'I thought when I was sitting in that room, you know, after you left, he was going to come in and just . . . pounce. But it wasn't like that at all. He sat me down and just . . . *stared* at me. I couldn't breathe, I couldn't speak . . . After a while he poured me a cup of wine – spilled most of it – then he jumped up and got a box off the table – and he tipped everything out and said: "Come on, choose." It was jewellery mainly – necklaces, brooches – from Troy, I suppose. If I'd been thinking straight, I'd probably have recognized a lot of it. And he kept saying: "C'mon, choose." Well, I knew the one thing I *didn't* want was to pick something to make myself look pretty – for him. So, I chose this.'

She fished underneath the neck of the tunic and brought out the ring I'd noticed earlier. Gold, with a big green stone – not an emerald – a pale, milky green, the colour of a calm sea. I looked at it; and a man's hand with a silver coin glinting on the palm rose up from the darkness of the past.

'*Priam*'s ring?'

'Yes, I didn't want him to have it.'

'But didn't he ask you why you wanted a man's ring? You'll never be able to wear it.'

'I *am* wearing it. No, he didn't ask. I think he was trying not to be sick.' She hesitated. 'I still don't know if he . . . You know. He kept having to . . .' Jarringly, she made a tossing movement with her closed fist. 'And it just went on and on.' She gave a little non-laugh. 'And then he threw me out.'

'You must know if he came inside you.'

For a moment, I thought she wasn't going to answer. Then: 'Yes. Yes, he did.'

She'd gone grey again; every bit of life seemed to be draining out of her as I watched. We sat in silence for a while, listening to the wind. And then, among all the other more familiar noises, I heard the grinding of rockers on a wooden floor. I hoped she wouldn't hear it, but she did. Immediately, she jumped to her feet, stumbling through the door, almost as if it were the middle of the night and she'd heard her baby crying. Once inside the hut, the sound was louder and she started to run. I caught up with her just as she reached my bedroom door and saw, over her shoulder, the cradle rocking. She fell on her knees beside it, peering into the emptiness under the hood.

'I'll give it back.' I was stammering, desperate to stop her being any more hurt than she was already. 'I can't do it now because Alcimus gave it to me, but don't worry, as soon as I can, I'll give it back . . .'

Her hand, clamped to the side of the cradle, had stopped the rocking. We stood in the sudden quiet, breathing. Then she looked up at me. 'Why would I want it back?' she said. 'I'll only have to put *his* child into it.' Her gaze slid from my face to my belly. 'How are we supposed to love *their* children?'

She was staring at me, almost as if she thought I might have an answer. Feeling sick, I put my hand over my mouth and turned away.

8

It hurt even to turn his head on the pillow. His mouth was dry; he must have been snoring like a fish all night – though what a bloody stupid saying that was. Whoever heard a fish snore? Eyes tight shut, he spread out his arms and found the other side empty. She'd gone, then. When had she gone? Dimly he remembered kicking her out of bed. No, not kicking – he wouldn't have done that. She was Hector's widow, after all – an important prize, like his helmet and his shield. Except that he didn't have the shield. Automedon should have stopped . . . Eyes open now, but the light burned like acid and he was glad to close them again. Something was niggling away . . . The ring, oh, shit, *yes*, the ring. He'd offered her necklaces, bracelets, brooches – and she'd chosen a man's ring. Why? Because it was Hector's ring. Because she'd recognized it? He should've stopped her taking it, and he would have done – if he hadn't felt sorry for her. If he hadn't been trying not to be sick.

How they'd managed to have sex he didn't know. But they had, the damp sheet underneath him was proof. He couldn't remember much, but he'd done it. Had he? Yes, of course he had. He can remember it now, though it's hardly worth remembering. Like sticking your dick in a bag of greasy chicken bones. He shouldn't have let her take the ring. Trouble is, he's too generous – people take him for a fool. *She* certainly will. Still, it hadn't helped her much, had it? The important thing is, it's over. The next time it'll be easier, and the next. And the next . . . Shit. It's a life sentence — time off if he gets her pregnant, but otherwise . . . He's got to stop thinking like this. The important thing is: he did what he had to do. The walls of Troy had been well and truly breached.

The momentary spurt of confidence enables him to sit up and look around. As always, the room seems to shrink away from him. It's extraordinary how alive these things are. The lyre, lying there as if Achilles had only just put it down; the mirror that had once held his reflection, but is now black; his shield propped up against the wall. All these things are his now, but they don't feel like his. He can't play the lyre, and he certainly isn't going to let anybody else play it. He can, and does, polish the shield. The mirror plays tricks. Sometimes he puts on Achilles' armour and stands in front of it, but his reflection doesn't always move when he moves. He's becoming detached from himself.

Enough. The only solution is to get out. He pulls on a clean tunic, thrusts his feet into sandals and bangs out of the hut. The wind snatches his breath, slams the door behind him, almost as if it's locking him out. Where to go? Nobody's up. The late-night-drinking session in the hall will have everybody groaning and nursing their sore heads much as he's been doing; apart from a few women stoking fires and grinding corn, the camp's deserted. The sea, then. He follows the path through the dunes, aware every time he puts a foot down that he's treading where great Achilles trod. Literally, there's nowhere on the beach or in the camp that he can stand without knowing that Achilles stood there before. Nothing he can touch: the table, the cup, the plates at dinner . . . Nothing. And, of course, it's a comfort to have his father so close. Except he isn't. He's not here at all. Coming out on to the beach, Pyrrhus experiences the vast expanse of sea and sky as one unbearable, aching absence.

Swim. As once Achilles swam – every morning, every night. But the sea's a wall of brown, churned-up sand. Even the thought of plunging into that makes him feel sick, but he's got to do it – there's no choice. There's never been a choice. So, he wades in; feels ice-cold water slap against his knees, sand slip away between his toes. The next wave slops into his groin, his chest, his mouth and then he's swimming, his head and tense neck raised above the waves. He tries to put a foot down, but there's no ground beneath his feet, and so he has to go on through the bubbling foam into the quieter space beyond, though even here the swells are tipped with white and seethe along their crests. A few more yards of shameful doggy paddle, becoming ever more frantic as the waves threaten to carry him away, and then he's ready to come out. Half walking, half crawling through the shallows, he feels no sense of achievement. The sea swallowed him; the sea's spewed him back, that's all.

Achilles, as Pyrrhus has been told over and over again, swam like a seal, as if the sea were his real home. Once, he'd stayed underwater so long that Patroclus ran into the sea to rescue him, only to see him surface a couple of hundred yards further out. That scene's one of the clearest images he has of his father: a man swimming far out to sea, another waiting anxiously on the shore. Now, for the first time, it occurs to him that the scene makes no sense. What had Patroclus been anxious about? The strongest swimmer in the Greek army, swimming in a calm sea?

There are so many things he doesn't understand.

Slowly, he puts on his damp tunic, pushes his feet into gritty sandals and turns to look at the camp. One or two lights in the huts now, but he has no desire to go back. He's better off out here, with the wind scouring his mind clean of the night's tawdry memories. Not her fault, poor cow. Not her fault at all. If only it wasn't so cold. If only the wind would stop. And at that very moment, just as the thought forms, there's a lull.

Silence. Nothing moves, not even a blade of grass. All over the camp, men who've slept soundly through the raging of the storm, will be awake, staring at each other. Is this it? Has it stopped? Can we go home? But before they even have the chance to speak, the wind starts picking up again; at first no more than a cat's-tail twitching of dead leaves and grass, but then with greater and greater force, till it's sweeping off the sea with every bit as much power and venom as it had before.

These unpredictable lulls, when, for a brief moment, leaving, going home, begins to seem possible, sap morale more than the worst blasts of the storm. And every time it happens, the common-sense view that the wind means nothing, that it's just, to use Machaon's contemptuous word, *weather*, loses ground a little. Because, in the aftermath of one of these lulls, it really does feel as if the gods are playing with them, holding out hope on an open palm only to snatch it away.

Pyrrhus feels his wet hair lift from the nape of his neck, feels his damp tunic being moulded yet more closely to the contours of his body, and trudges on. A hot bath? A bowl of stew? Last night's leftovers, but stews sometimes taste even better the second day. Or a visit to the stables? See Ebony, help the grooms turn the horses out to pasture. No, none of those things. Not now.

All the time he's been pretending to think about hot baths and food, his feet have been leading him to where he needs to be. He's reached the place now. Fingers pinching his nose, breathing loudly through his mouth, he follows the path until he sees what lies stretched out on the dirty sand. He needs this. He needs to confirm what he already knows, that the tongue that said those words – which he will not let himself repeat, no, not even in the buzzing vacancy of his own mind – is rotting now, inside a rotting skull. He stands, stares, takes in every minute detail, notices every change.

Enough. He won't need to come here again, possibly not for several days, but he will be back. Because this is his proof that he is who he claims to be: the man who killed King Priam. Great Achilles' son. The hero of Troy.

9

I thought about Priam a great deal over the next few days. Seeing his ring round Andromache's neck brought everything back. There was nothing I could do to prevent the dishonouring of his body, but at least I could visit his widow, Hecuba, and perhaps make her life more comfortable in some small way. So, one morning, I set off to see her, taking Amina with me. I could have taken one of the other girls, but I thought the walk might give me a chance to talk to her. I was still concerned about her; she seemed unable to accept the reality of her situation. In fact, she was steadily and dangerously defiant. But there was no possibility of speaking to her on our way to the arena. The wind was so strong it made speech impossible. I had to walk head down, muffled in my veil, while Amina trailed obstinately behind.

A group of men was raking the sand on the arena floor. Alcimus' idea of holding competitive games was proving popular and many of the events were to be held there. I stopped to watch them work, noticing little piles of offerings at the feet of the gods' statues: fruit, big bunches of purple daisies, as well as other more eccentric gifts: models of shields and spears, a pair of new sandals, a child's toy horse. Looking around the circle, I saw that some gods – Athena, in particular – were doing better than others and I realized this was a visual guide to what ordinary Greek fighters were thinking. *Why are we being kept here on this bloody awful beach? Which god have we offended?* Answer – or at least best guess: Athena. And why Athena? Because it was in her temple that Cassandra had been raped, and the rapist, Ajax the Lesser – Little Ajax – had not been punished as he ought to have been, which arguably made Agamemnon and the other kings complicit in his crime. Of course, it wasn't the rape that bothered them; it was the desecration of the temple. That was a violation Athena might well be inclined to avenge.

Amina was staring at the piles of offerings, her eyes darting from one statue to the next. I wondered what she made of them. They must have been splendid when they were first erected, but they'd fallen into a state of dilapidation over the years: rotten bases, flaking paint. Artemis, the Lady of Animals, goddess of hunting, was in a particularly bad state: her features half erased, barely a trace of paint left on her robes.

Since I was there, I thought I'd visit Hecamede, Nestor's prize of honour and, after Ritsa, my closest friend in the camp. I found her sweeping the hall, a stack of fresh rushes by the door waiting to be laid, though, as she pointed out after we'd hugged each other, the hall scarcely needed cleaning. There'd been no celebratory feasts in Nestor's hut; his youngest son, Antilochus, had been killed in the final assault on Troy. Antilochus: the boy who'd loved Achilles. His death had plunged the whole compound into mourning. You felt the stricken atmosphere the moment you stepped over the threshold of the hall – the loss of a young, promising life. Amina lingered by the door; I perched on a bench with my feet raised while Hecamede finished sweeping, then helped her lay the rushes.

'How's Nestor?' I asked.

She pulled a face. 'Not good.'

71

I couldn't believe Nestor was really ill. He was like an ancient tree that bends in every gale – you think at any moment it's going over, but next morning there it is, still standing, surrounded by acres of healthy saplings uprooted in the night. Though I could see why this illness, whatever it was, might be preying on Hecamede's mind. If Nestor died, what would become of her? If she was lucky, one or other of his surviving sons might take her, though sons don't normally inherit their father's concubines; more likely, she'd be awarded as a prize in Nestor's funeral games. Exactly what would have happened to me if Achilles hadn't given me to Alcimus.

We finished laying the rushes and sat on one of the benches. There was a smell of burnt sugar and cinnamon and further along the table were two trays of small cakes, scarcely more than a mouthful each, but utterly delicious. The popular name for them was 'come-again cakes', because nobody ever managed to stop at one. 'Can't be much the matter with him if he's eating those.'

'Oh, they're not for him – they're for Hecuba. I was just going to take them across if you'd like to come?'

'Yes, of course. I was on my way to see her anyway. I just couldn't resist coming to see you first.'

'Good, we can go together. I'll just need to check on Nestor first.'

Apparently, he'd been talking of sitting out on the veranda, but when we put our heads round the door, we found him asleep – snoring loudly, his upper lip pouting on every breath. Even at this distance, I could see his nose and lips were blue. 'It's the sharpness I don't like,' Hecamede said, touching the tip of her own nose. 'They get like that before they go.'

It was a relief to leave the room, with its smell of old, sick flesh. Outside, in the hall again, I took several deep breaths. Then,

Hecamede picked up one tray, I took the other, and with Amina lagging as usual several yards behind, we set off across the arena where long shadows cast by the gods' statues slanted over the freshly raked sand. Dazzled, we moved from light to shade to light again – a short, brisk walk in the gritty wind – and then, ducking our heads, emerged into the frowsty darkness of Hecuba's hut. One sickroom to another, I thought. There the resemblance ended: Nestor slept in a king's bed surrounded by all the trappings of wealth and power; Hecuba's hut was more like a dog kennel than a human habitation. Though at least she had it to herself – a rare luxury in that overcrowded camp. Odysseus did seem to be treating her reasonably well. When the royal women were shared out among the kings, there'd been a lot of joking at Odysseus' expense. Agamemnon and several of the other kings had got Priam's virgin daughters, Pyrrhus a sprightly young widow – plenty of go in that one, if she'd only cheer up a bit – whereas Odysseus was left with a scraggy old woman. Odysseus just shrugged, brushing the laughter aside. He knew he'd be taking home the only woman his wife, Penelope, would have accepted – and, with any luck, he might be able to convince her that he'd slept alone for the last ten years with nothing to while away his lonely evenings beyond the occasional game of skittles with his men. He was clever enough to make it sound convincing – and, from all accounts, Penelope was quite clever enough to pretend to believe it. Everybody you spoke to praised Penelope's wit and kindness. I could easily imagine Hecuba sitting in a warm room doing light embroidery and not, as so many older women were forced to do, scrubbing stone floors while being shouted at because they weren't working fast enough. Oh, it might be a life of misery, ravaged by grief, but at least she'd be physically comfortable, for however many weeks or months she might have left.

All nonsense, these imaginings. Hecuba never, from the minute she saw Priam killed, intended to live.

At first sight, she was a bag of bones, huddled under a dirty blanket. The one arm lying outside the cover was so wrinkled and brown-spotted it looked more like the pelt of an animal than human skin. She stirred when she heard our voices and started trying to sit up, blinking in the sudden light. I was horrified to see how frail she'd become; even in the short time since her arrival in the camp, she seemed to have shrunk. I wondered how much she was eating. Hecamede touched her feet and offered the tray of cakes. Hecuba thanked her profusely, but immediately set it aside and peered up at me.

'This is Briseis,' Hecamede said.

I too knelt and touched Hecuba's feet. I didn't expect her to remember me. We'd met often enough during the two years I'd spent in Troy, but I'd been a child then. I must have changed out of all recognition since – and she did look puzzled for a moment, but then reached up and laid one thin hand on the side of my face. 'I want to thank you, my dear.'

'*Why?* Hecamede baked the cakes.'

'You were kind to Priam when he went to see Achilles. He remembered you, he remembered Helen bringing you to the citadel. "Helen's little friend". You must have been quite a child back then?'

'I was twelve.'

'He talked about you when he came back. He said you'd been kind.'

I couldn't speak, I was so close to tears.

'Well, well.' Hecuba patted my arm. 'Let's have some cakes.' She was peering into the shadows where Amina stood, ostentatiously obliterating herself, as usual. I realized Hecuba couldn't see very well.

'Amina?' I said.

She came forward then, knelt and touched Hecuba's feet. To my surprise, Hecuba said, '*Amina*. My poor child. How are you?'

'All right.'

'You were given to Pyrrhus?'

'Yes – not what I'd have chosen . . .'

Hecuba made a curious sound midway between a snort and a laugh. 'No, well, I think choice is a thing of the past.'

Hecamede handed round the cakes while I poured the wine. Hecuba was too excited to eat, though I noticed she drank rapidly. Well, let her drink. In her position, I'd have drunk the sea dry. Within minutes there were two red spots on her cheeks, contrasting garishly with the general greyness of her skin and hair. At first, she concentrated solely on the wine, but then she began to talk about Helen. Did we know Menelaus was sleeping with her again? She had a whole hut to herself – 'not like this, *three* rooms!' – maids to wait on her, pick up after her. Oh, and a loom. Helen weaving again, like a spider waiting for the vibration that would tell her another fly had landed. Another victim sucked dry . . . Oh, the hatred in Hecuba's voice as she spoke of these things. I wondered how she knew about the loom, but gossip flew round that camp – and of course Helen's maids would be Trojans. Probably it all came from them. They'd be pressing their ears to the wall to hear Menelaus' grunts, Helen's ecstatic cries . . . And there'd be plenty of ecstatic cries; Helen was no fool. The whole camp resented his taking her back. Greek fighters and Trojan slaves united in one thing and one thing only: hatred of Helen. Menelaus had sworn so many times he was going to kill her – the minute he set eyes on her again! Then, that he was going to take her back to Argos and let the women stone her to death – and there'd have been no lack

of volunteers. So many widows, so many women who'd lost sons . . .
And yet there he was, back in bed with her. '*All night*,' Hecuba said.
'What's he trying to do – fuck her to death?'

I think I may have been shocked; I didn't know Hecuba as well
then as I did later.

'Oh, and the lies she comes out with! She was raped – *my son* raped
her? She couldn't get enough of him! Oh, and saying we kept her a
prisoner in Troy. Nothing of the sort; she could've gone home any
time she liked. Who did she think wanted her there? My idiot son –
nobody else! Any one of my girls would have taken her across the
battlefield if she'd been too frightened to go on her own. *I*'d have
taken her.'

And you could see it was true: she was dauntless. All this time, her
mouth had been working constantly – even after she'd finished
speaking, she actually had to pinch her lips together to keep them
still. She looked like a frail, gaunt old bird – a storm thrush, perhaps –
feathers ruffled by the blast, but still singing, still shouting defiance
from its perch. I was struggling to understand her. Every day, I saw
how erased by grief Andromache was – and I suppose I'd expected
Hecuba to be the same, or worse. But she was nothing like that. Hatred of Helen consumed her. Perhaps she felt the kings were too
powerful, too intimidating, to hate – or perhaps she'd always blamed
women and exonerated men. Some women are like that. But it was
making me rebellious.

I said: 'You can't just blame Helen! It wasn't Helen who killed
Priam – it was Pyrrhus. And who threw Hector's son off the battlements? Pyrrhus. And who sacrificed Polyxena? Not Helen – Pyrrhus.'

'And what are you going to do about it?' Hecuba asked.

Silence. I had no answer to that. I knew Pyrrhus was far beyond our reach. Instead, I looked around the walls of the hut, and I just wanted to be outside, filling my lungs with clean air – if you could call that scouring wind with its whipped-up grains of sand 'clean'. I wanted to be away from the stale smell that emanated from the dirty blankets on her bed; above all, I wanted not to have to hear that incessantly ranting, exhausted voice; and yet, at the same time, I felt pity for her, and a kind of awe.

At last she was silent. She actually ate one of the cakes, dabbing her mouth daintily with the edges of her veil. 'Delicious,' she said, waving away another. 'Do you know' – turning to me – 'I don't think I ever tasted cakes like that in Troy – and Priam had the best cooks in the world. Though I must say I still like the ginger cake best. Such a *strong* taste.'

Hecamede looked concerned. 'Was it too strong?'

'No, no, perfectly balanced. Not too spicy, not too sweet.' She turned to me again. 'And what about you, my dear?'

I wasn't sure what she meant. 'Do I bake? Well, yes, a bit – nothing like Hecamede.'

'But I'm sure you have other talents. They tell me you know quite a lot about herbs?'

'I wouldn't say a lot.'

'You see –' She paused, looking around the little circle. 'I've been thinking, about what we could do.'

I felt a prickle of uneasiness as I listened. She seemed to be asking Hecamede to bake a cake for Helen. A cake? *For Helen?*

And then she said, looking at me: 'I know where to find the plants.'

Of course she knew. Like every other great herbarium, the garden at Troy had a gated area set aside for poisonous plants, because – paradoxically – poisonous plants produce some of the most powerful medicines. Administered in minute doses, under careful supervision, these plants can actually save lives. Henbane, wolfbane, foxglove, sweet clover – it sounds so innocent, doesn't it? Sweet clover – snakeroot, castor-oil plant, strychnine tree . . .

Hecuba touched my arm. 'You'd know which ones to pick?'

I glanced across at Hecamede and saw her realize what we were being asked to do. She reached for Hecuba's hand. 'Why don't you leave her to the gods?'

'Because leaving things to the gods doesn't bloody well work! You need to grow up, my girl.'

'Only the gods can judge.'

'Huh! You think the gods care about justice? Where's the justice in what's happened to me?'

She turned away from us then, hunching her shoulders like a hawk in the rain. For a moment, there was silence. Then she said: 'Amina understands, don't you?'

Amina nodded. '*Yes.*'

'Fortunately,' I said, 'Amina isn't allowed out of the women's hut without me.'

The atmosphere had gone sour. I flared my eyes at Hecamede, asking: *How soon can we leave?* But then Hecuba turned to face us again and her whole demeanour had changed, almost as if the corrosive fantasy of poisoning Helen – which, I suspected, had been her sole companion during her long, sleepless nights – had fallen away and left her suddenly lighter. 'Do you know, I think I might manage another cake.'

There was only one left. When she'd finished, she moistened her finger and picked up the last crumbs from the plate. 'And now, I'd like to go for a walk.'

The three of us exchanged glances. We all thought it was non-sense: the wind would blow her away. I actually had visions of her being whirled up into the sky like one of those skeletal brown leaves you see in autumn, but I nodded and helped Hecuba to her feet. She draped her thin arms across Hecamede's shoulders and mine and then, awkwardly, like a six-legged freak calf, we shuffled towards the door.

Once outside on the veranda, Hecuba stopped dead and I felt a tremor run through her. She was blinking in the harsh light, as if daunted by her own temerity. I half expected her to change her mind, to turn back and say she'd try again another day, but no, she was determined. One or two women who were squatting on the ground grinding corn looked up as she embarked on her perilous journey down the steps. I was terrified she'd fall. In the end, we simply lifted her down – she was no weight at all.

'Where would you like to go?' I asked.

She thought for a moment. 'The sea. I haven't been to the sea for years.'

So, keeping as far as we could to the shelter of the huts, we set off. Several times, we had to stop so she could wind her veil round her mouth; the wind was snatching her breath – as it was ours, but she had less breath to spare. Though she might as well not have bothered, because as soon as we left the shelter of the huts, the veil streamed out behind her and she had to let go of me to stop it flying away. Crows circled, their ragged wings black against the white sky. 'Look at the buggers!' she said. 'Better fed than we are.' And she made a sound that in other circumstances might have been a laugh.

Slowly, very slowly, we got her down on to the beach. By now, we were almost carrying her, our arms crossed over her bent back as she tottered towards the sea. Once her veil came off altogether. Amina chased it across the sand and brought it back, knotting it securely round Hecuba's neck. On the shoreline, we stopped and watched the waves in their relentless assault on the land, each one failing, falling back, dislodging pebbles that peppered down the slope after it – then, the long, grating sigh of its defeat. But already, beyond the breakers, the sea was flexing its powerful shoulders for the next attack. Hecuba stared at the black, beaked ships that were lined up on the beach like a flock of predatory birds, seeing probably for the first time the forces that had destroyed her life. I was afraid she'd look along the beach to where crows and seagulls still squabbled over Priam's body, but instead she drew a shuddering breath and turned to face inland.

A group of women had gathered a short distance away, slaves who'd come running out of Odysseus' huts to see their former queen, but she looked over their heads at the ruined city. I followed her gaze and saw, through her eyes, Troy's black and broken towers, like the fingers of a half-buried hand pointing accusingly at the sky. I waited for Hecuba to speak, but she said nothing. Perhaps, confronted by this sight, words felt like such debased currency she couldn't be bothered to use them any more. Somewhere deep in her throat a wordless sound was forming. I didn't hear it; I felt it – running from her neck and shoulders down into my arm. And before I realized what was happening, she'd slipped from my grasp and fallen to her knees. She crouched on the hard sand and suddenly the grief burst out of her. She raised her face to the sky and shouted for Priam, and then for Hector and for all her other dead sons. And then again for Priam. *Priam. Priam.* She was pulling out chunks of hair, clawing her cheeks, beating the ground, as if she could make her cries heard in the gloomy halls of Hades. As if she could wake the dead.

I knelt beside her and tried to get an arm round her shoulders, made meaningless, soothing noises, desperate to calm her – as much for my own sake, I'm afraid, as hers. I couldn't bear it. And then she threw back her head and howled, and the howling went on and on – it seemed to have no end. The watching women moved closer, gathering round her where she knelt on the filthy sand, joining their cries with hers – until they turned from women into wolves, the same terrible howl coming from a hundred throats. And I howled with them, horrified at the sounds I was making, but unable to stop. Hecamede howled, and Amina, all of us, for the loss of our homeland – for the loss of our fathers, husbands, brothers, sons, for everybody we'd ever loved. For all the men carried away on that blood-dark tide.

Surely, if ever living voices could penetrate the world of the dead, it was then; but nobody answered us. After a while, Odysseus came out of his hall to see what the commotion was about and, a few minutes later, a couple of guards appeared and ordered the women roughly back to work.

IO

Somewhere along the beach, a pack of dogs has begun to howl. Calchas stops and listens as the howling fades first into whimpers and then into silence.

Looking around him, he's aware that something's changed. *What is it?* The sky still burns the same awful red, the air still tastes of iron, the waves still crash with that deadly monotony on the shore . . . He feels his lungs struggle to keep pace with the endless rise and fall; his chest seems to be full of swirling water. Resting his hand on the warty side of a ship, he tries to breathe deeply. For a moment he feels dizzy, his vision blurs, but then slowly, slowly, the beach swims back into focus. A smoke of fine grains is blowing across the hard sand and, as he watches, several balls of dry grass trundle past.

All this he's seen many times before, so why does it suddenly feel strange? He sucks his index finger and holds it up. Yes, that's it, the wind's changed. Not very much – it's still blowing off the sea – but at a slightly different angle. Perhaps it'll make walking easier; perhaps he'll be bowled along, like one of those balls of grass. Leaving the shelter of the ship, he sets off confidently, no longer the gawky boy who'd once knelt at Priam's feet, but Apollo's high priest, the chief seer in the Greek army, a man who enjoys the confidence of kings. Though when he turns to look back, his footprints scrawling across the wet sand are as erratic as a crab's. Nevertheless, he presses on, intent on reaching his hut before darkness falls. He decides that tonight he'll allow himself a cup of strong wine, perhaps with a small cake to dip into it. A man can't always be denying himself the good things of life; he's been worn thin by sacrifice. He thinks with some resentment of Machaon, who's never denied himself anything, and yet sees Agamemnon as often as he wants – every day, it's said – while he, who's given the king years of loyal service, *years*, spends his days waiting for a summons that never comes.

The light's fading fast now, but it's not the blue shadows of a normal evening that are lengthening across the ground, the creeping twilight that makes the flames of fires and lamps glow suddenly brighter, more inviting; no, these shadows are a sickly yellow, the bone-ivory of old skin. He remembers Hecuba's wrinkled neck, as he'd seen it when she was first led into the camp, and touches his own neck nervously. Men experience their own ageing in the bodies of women, even men like himself who've chosen a celibate life; not that he'd ever actually chosen celibacy – or stuck to it either, come to that. He walks on; but now he's back in Troy, a child again – white houses, black shadows, a little boy sitting on a doorstep, squinting up at the sun. Dimly, he's aware of the sky darkening, of his own narrow feet flashing in and out of the shallows, but he's lost in memories of the past . . .

And when he looks up again, Agamemnon's there.

At first, he doubts the evidence of his eyes. Agamemnon never leaves his hall; he hasn't been seen outside since the wind changed and pinned the Greek ships to the beach – he who was always giving feasts or attending feasts given by the other kings – but there he is, wrapped in a dark blue cloak, a gold circlet round his head to stop the lank, iron-grey hair blowing across his face. He hasn't noticed Calchas; he's gazing out to sea. Calchas looks around, but there's nobody else in sight. This is the hour when men wrap themselves in warm cloaks and gather round the cooking fires. When the serious drinking starts.

So, they're alone – with the wind making snakes of loose sand and sending them writhing across the beach. What to do? He daren't approach Agamemnon, who's obviously come out unattended because he wanted to be alone, but neither can he just walk past and ignore him. The slanting light discovers worm casts, little heaps of coiled sand, each with its own distinct shadow; he pretends to take a great interest in them, even kneeling down as if to examine them more closely. Next, he spends a few moments looking out to sea, where each crash and roar of waves pounding the cliffs emphasizes – as if emphasis were needed – the impossibility of a ship leaving the shelter of the bay. Is that why Agamemnon's here, to confirm the hopelessness of the situation, like somebody jabbing a broken tooth to check that it still hurts?

Calchas feels sharp granules of sand sting his bare ankles. The wind's colder now – and still he can't move. But then he hears a new sound, somewhere between a groan and a roar, and it seems to be coming from the ground beneath his feet. Singing sand. A recognized phenomenon, familiar to everybody who lives along this coast. The words 'recognized' and 'familiar' are comforting, because they seek to tame the experience, to bring it out of the realms of the uncanny and establish that it's merely part of normal life. Though it's not really 'singing' at all – it's a far more menacing sound – and it seems to be coming from deep inside the earth. As if the dead had found a voice at last – or perhaps recovered the voices they once had.

Agamemnon's staring all around him. At last, he kneels and puts both hands to the ground as if he needs touch to confirm what his ears are telling him. Everything about this situation – the failing light, the howling sand, the all-powerful, helpless king – combines to produce a rush of terror in him. Calchas would run away if there was anywhere to run to, but the roaring's everywhere. All over the camp there are raised voices, so the men around the fires must be hearing it too, but it'll be fainter there, and less frightening with other men for company. There, they'll be able to crucify the mystery with jokes and laughter, but out here, exposed on the darkening beach, two men turn to stare at each other, neither of them able to disguise his fear.

And then, as suddenly as it began, the roaring stops. Agamemnon straightens up, looks in Calchas' direction for a moment, and seems about to speak, but then, abruptly, turns and strides off towards his compound.

Calchas follows at a slower pace, mouth dry, heart thumping his ribs, but underneath it all he's jubilant, because Agamemnon can't ignore this. He's a man who craves signs and portents, who sees the action of the gods in even the most mundane events, and assumes, of course, that any message from the gods will be aimed exclusively at him. *Yes! He's got to send for me now.* Though, after a moment's further reflection, Calchas returns to his previous anxious state. Yes, Agamemnon will send for him, he'll be asked to explain why the gods are forbidding the Greeks to leave the site of their greatest victory – and he has absolutely no idea, no idea at all, what he's going to say.

I I

After a stormy night, I put bread and cheese and a jug of weak wine
on the table in case Alcimus came home for breakfast and then went
down to the beach. The wreckage left by yesterday evening's high
tide lay all around me. I'd grown used to finding large numbers of
dead creatures on the beach, but I'd never seen anything like the
carnage I saw that day. The sand was littered with pale greenish-grey
crabs, jellyfish, probably a hundred starfish blanched in death – the
latter a particular grief to me because I loved them so much. I hunted
about for anything still living, but found nothing. Picking my way
across the devastation, I felt I was on a battlefield in the aftermath of
one of Achilles' red rages, but it was the sea that had done this, the
sea that had cast these small, delicate creatures so far up on to the
land, where they had no chance of survival.

I'd been walking up and down the water's edge for ten or fifteen
minutes, perhaps, when I glanced up and saw a tall, thin man standing
twenty or so yards ahead of me, gazing out to sea. Calchas. Observing
him like this, the two of us alone on the desolate shore, I felt I was seeing him more clearly than I'd ever done before. He was immensely
tall – six foot five, perhaps, something like that – though the word
you'd choose to describe him was not so much 'tall' as 'long'. Long
feet, long hands, long fingers – even his neck was long, the larynx so

prominent that in certain lights it cast its own distinct shadow. Like all Trojan priests, he painted his face white and outlined his eyes in black, in effect putting on a mask, behind which his thoughts were impenetrable. If you add to this a slight speech impediment that turned any word beginning with 's' into a hiss, you can see why the Greeks found him both intimidating and ridiculous. He struck them as effeminate and that made them uneasy, so they laughed at him, but feared him too.

I was only a few feet away from him now, and still he hadn't moved. Curiosity made me stop and look out over the bay, trying to work out what it was that he found so fascinating. It didn't take me long. A huge black bird – though possibly it merely appeared black against the bronze glare of the sky – was soaring high above the waves. All along the beach, gulls were gathering and bursting apart like showers of spray, but this bird flew with precision and purpose, like an owl quartering a meadow. Suddenly it dived, at the last moment stretching out its gnarled yellow feet. A splash, a glint of silver, and then it was struggling to rise, powerful wings flailing to escape the water's drag. For a second, I thought it might be sucked under, but no – slowly, slowly – it fought its way into the air. It was so nearly there – when a gust of wind caught it. Blown off course, it crashed on to the wet sand only a few yards away from me. With a stab of pity, I saw it trying to get its breath back. Nothing else inspired pity. The shoulders were pure hunched muscle, the beak designed to tear still living flesh from bone, and the eyes – pale gold, gleaming, intent – were the eyes of Agamemnon.

Even as I watched, it was gathering itself together; the mighty wings began to beat, and at last, still grasping the flapping fish between its talons, it lifted off. Less than a minute later, it had become merely a black dot in the red furnace of the sky.

Excited, I turned to Calchas. 'Wasn't that amazing?'

I didn't just mean the sea eagle itself – though it was amazing – I meant the mistake that had seen it blown off course. There'd been something shocking about that – like watching Achilles throw a spear and miss.

Calchas stared at me. I expected him to share my excitement, but I saw only calculation in the black-ringed eyes. He was a bird seer – so naturally a large part of his time would be spent observing them, though I suspected an even larger part would be spent observing men. Who was currently most powerful? Who was climbing the rickety ladder? Who had to be placated? Who could safely be ignored? Above all, what did this woman, asking this particular question, at this particular time, want to hear? I could see him trying to work out who I was, whether I was worth bothering with. Remember, until recently I'd been a slave, as far beneath his notice as a slug. Eventually, after a lengthy pause, he nodded. 'Yes, most unusual.' Stiff, stilted, pompous – altogether typical of the man. I was misjudging him – badly. But that's what I thought at the time.

'What do you think it means?' A slightly mischievous question.

'*Ah*. The interpretation of omens requires many hours of thought and prayer.'

Once again, stiff – how could he possibly be unmoved by the experience we'd just shared? But I bowed to acknowledge his superior wisdom – and watched him walk away towards Agamemnon's compound, noticing how his steps slowed as he approached the gate. The gossip was he'd fallen out of favour, that Agamemnon no longer bothered to consult him, and, seeing him dawdle like that, almost literally dragging his feet, I had no difficulty believing it.

Ever since the fall of Troy, I'd been living from hour to hour, without energy and without hope. Now, suddenly, I felt alive again – more than excited – *elated*. Somehow the encounter with the eagle changed everything. I'd come face to face with one of the lords of life, and the experience lifted my mood beyond recognition – even though the impression I took away with me was one of pure savagery. As a woman living in this camp, I was navigating a complex and dangerous world, but the eagle – everything he saw was his by right. Because he was perfection: every feather, every curve of that hooked beak, every glint of his sunlit eyes – they were all exactly as they ought to be. He was older than the gods. And for a moment, just for one moment, I'd been up there with him, gazing on the wrinkled sea and the earth-bound creatures toiling far below. When he looked down, he saw . . . *dinner*. Nothing else – nothing complex, nothing difficult, nothing that could possibly be a threat – just dinner. There was a grandeur in the simplicity of it – and I hated the idea of Calchas rubbing his smeary fingers all over it, trying to extract a 'meaning'. The eagle was its own meaning.

That night, I lay awake, thinking about Helen and Hecuba, about my sister, who I had to hope was dead, and my lost brothers. The same thoughts that preoccupied me every night. But when eventually I slept, I dreamt about the eagle – as I did on many of the nights that followed. When, just before dawn, I woke, I lay in darkness, listening to the wind, and I thought of Calchas, who was also, I felt sure, lying awake staring into this same darkness, remembering the eagle and trying desperately to work out what this 'sign', this portent, this 'message from the gods', might mean.

12

The blaze of energy I felt after seeing the eagle stayed with me. I started looking for ways to make things better for the captive girls. So far, they hadn't been able to use the yard behind their hut because a section of the fence had been blown flat. Now, with a great deal of help from Alcimus, I managed to get the fence repaired and the ground cleared. It wasn't easy because the Greeks resented spending time and effort on huts they were always about to leave, but once they started on the job, it took them less than an hour. It gave the girls privacy and some shelter from the wind. That afternoon I baked cakes and two huge trays of sweetmeats and set them aside to cool. I was tired of the loneliness of my hut and looking forward to an evening with the other women.

As soon as night fell, three of the girls helped me carry trays of food and jugs of wine into the yard and we spread them on rugs around the fire. Wary at first, the other girls emerged from the hut like animals let out of a pen, sniffing the air. One or two of them actually looked back at the hut as if they'd felt safer indoors, but most seemed to enjoy the extra freedom. The fire was sulky, but they crouched round it, blowing on twigs, feeding handfuls of dry grass into the flames, finally whooping with triumph when a big log started to burn.

I'd been hoping Andromache might join us, but she stayed in her room. I tapped on her door and asked if she was all right, but got only a grunt in reply. Going back outside, I saw the fire was roaring now, sparks whirling up into the sky, shadows flickering across the girls' faces. The air was clear, but chilly; we gathered close round the flames, our toes only inches away from the hearth stones. I'd brought drums and pipes – Alcimus kept a great collection of instruments in his hut. I thought one or two of the girls might know how to play the pipes and the rest of us could surely manage to beat time on the drums. I'd also brought Alcimus' lyre – with his permission, of course – though I'd need to be careful with that and wipe off any sticky fingerprints, because it was a good instrument, valuable. Not the equal of Achilles' lyre, but better than most – and it was kind of him to lend it to us. Amina, it turned out, could play the lyre – rather well, in fact – but the real find was Helle, who could play not only the lyre but the pipes as well. In her previous life, she'd been a public entertainer, a dancer, musician and acrobat, her experience as far removed from the sheltered existence of the other girls as you could possibly imagine. She'd been a slave, as such performers generally were, though the best of them were famous throughout the city.

At last, we were all settled. Amina and Helle nodded to show they were ready. 'Nothing sad,' I said. The girls began calling out their favourites – and many of them were happy, even jolly, songs; but as soon as the singing started, they all sounded sad. Perhaps all songs do when they're sung in exile. Soon, many of the girls were in tears. Maire – a lumpish girl whose eyebrows met in the middle – positively wailed. But still, they went on singing; even the two girls who still couldn't speak at all, sang. And that amazed me. I hadn't realized till then that people who've been shocked into muteness can still sing.

Helle, who was far from sympathetic, stared incredulously at the sobbing girls, and began playing something so fast and furious they struggled to keep up, clapping and gabbling until, with a final flourish of the drums, they collapsed into helpless giggles.

'Again!' I stood up, raising my arms to encourage them to do the same, and one by one they got to their feet. The music started again – only now there was foot-stamping as well, and our shadows, thrown by the flames, leapt over the walls that fenced us in and escaped into the night.

As we all sat down again, I glanced across at Amina, but she was busy adjusting the strings on the lyre and neatly avoided my gaze. This was becoming a pattern and she was very good at it. She never seemed to be avoiding me, but somehow, she always happened to be on the other side of the room or, in this case, the fire. It made me uneasy, but I brushed it aside. I didn't want anything to spoil this evening.

When she'd finished fiddling with the strings, she began singing a love song. She had a high, clear voice, like a boy's before it breaks; you don't often find that quality in a woman's voice and it's heartbreaking when you do. Many of the girls were crying again; I wondered how many of them had been promised in marriage to young men whose bodies now lay rotting inside the walls of Troy. They needed to grieve, but after a while I began to feel the weeping had gone on long enough. I looked at Helle, who pulled a face and shrugged: *What can you do with them?* But then, a moment later, she was on her feet and dancing, clapping her hands above her head in time with the stamping of her feet. I picked up a drum, as did several others, and the rest started clapping. Soon, all of us, in various ways, were carrying the beat.

I've never seen any girl dance the way Helle danced that night. At weddings and religious festivals, girls do dance, but always modestly, covered from collar bone to ankle in flowing robes, careful not to let their gaze stray beyond the movements of their feet. Helle was wearing a sleeveless tunic, the hem well above her knees – basically, a man's tunic. Her oiled skin gleamed in the firelight, her elaborately braided hair swung around her shoulders, as the stamping and clapping gathered pace.

Of all the girls – well, apart from Amina – Helle was the one who stood out. There weren't many in the camp who hadn't lost all their male relatives and, since older women were sent to the slave markets, the younger girls had lost their mothers as well. Only Helle showed no sign of grief. She'd seen her owner speared in the throat, flapping on the floor like a landed fish, the life choked out of him in front of her eyes. When I murmured some tentative words of sympathy, she'd laughed out loud. 'Oh, don't worry,' she said. 'I'd been wanting to do that for years.'

She'd been bought when she was very young, no more than six or seven years old, and she had no memory of her life before that day in the slave market, so, in effect, she'd been born into a life of physical pain. Her owner selected her by forcing her thumbs back till they touched her wrists and then making her lie on her back while he twisted her legs round and round in their sockets. He'd trained her as an acrobat, a singer, a dancer, a musician; she'd been the star performer in a troupe that regularly appeared at Priam's court. Of course, her owner made her available for other services too, but only to the most prestigious clients, and even then, at an exorbitant price. Poor Helle. She was, in some ways, the most pitiable of all the girls – though she would certainly not have said so! – free from grief, yes, but only because her previous life had been devoid of love.

The drumbeats and clapping were getting faster, keeping pace with Helle's dancing feet. I wondered why she was putting so much effort into this performance for an all-female audience when she'd always treated the other girls with such contempt. For the sheer joy of it, perhaps? Her dance had become a flirtation with the fire. She'd approach close enough to draw *oohs* from the girls, then retreat a little, only to flutter back like a moth drawn to a flame. The firelight gleamed on her arms and legs, which were slender but muscular. She looked like a boy – graceful, even beautiful – but still a boy. And this was a warrior's dance.

Outside the circle of light, her shadow kept her company, flickering along the fence. The fire lit up the faces of the watching girls, who were entirely lost in the music. One or two of them even stood up and began to stamp their feet too, though that just served to throw Helle's grace and power into sharper relief. I looked around the circle, and then again at Helle's dancing shadow. I was aware of something on the fringes of my vision. At first, I couldn't think what it was, but then a movement from inside the hut caught my eye. I hoped it was Andromache, that she'd decided to join us, after all – but a second later, peering into the darkness, I recognized Pyrrhus. He had a perfect right to be there, since he owned the hut and everybody in it. Except me. I nursed that thought, cradling it against the dark. *Except me.*

The drums were pounding now. Seeing Helle measure the height of the fire, I tried to shout *No!* but she was already running and, before I could say anything, she'd leapt high in the air and landed lightly on the other side. The flames whirled in the wind of her passing, as if they were reaching out to get her, but she just stood there, laughing, punching the air, as men do after they've won a race. 'Are you all right?' I asked. By way of reply, she extended one beautiful leg towards me. At first, I couldn't see anything, but then I noticed a shiny, red patch above the ankle.

'A fire-kiss.' I must have looked concerned because she laughed again. 'It doesn't hurt.'

Her gaze slid to the door of the hut, but Pyrrhus had withdrawn into the shadows. So, she'd known he was there. She'd known all along.

A whiff of smoke from her braided hair, as she sat down to cheers and a cup of wine. Only Amina looked unimpressed; positively disapproving, in fact. Helle stared straight at her and lifted her cup in a mocking toast. I sensed that they hated each other, those two, and that was a pity, because both of them were strong characters, natural leaders. Together, they could have done so much, but neither of them seemed inclined to take on the role that should rightfully have been Andromache's. Amina, because she was following the straight and narrow path of religious purity; Helle, because she was focused exclusively on her own survival. And the other girls were just lost. All of them – lost. So, it fell to me, I suppose. I knew they looked up to me, they trusted me – simply because I'd survived in this nightmarish place to which the loss of their homes and families had brought them.

Not long after that, Pyrrhus sent for Helle; almost immediately, in fact, while we were still sitting in the yard. He'd scarcely have had time to get back to the hall. 'YES!' Helle shouted, raising both arms above her head.

I thought that was the last we'd see of her till morning, but when, finally, we tore ourselves away from the fire, we found her curled up on her pallet bed with the blanket pulled up to her chin.

'What happened?' I asked.

'*Nothing* happened. He just wanted me to watch him wank.'

The girls looked at each other and I realized not one of them knew what the word meant.

It was odd, and this wasn't the first time I'd been aware of the oddity. Pyrrhus was a young man, not fully grown, and yet he showed very little interest in these girls. Until he'd sent for Helle, no interest at all. And he seemed to regard sleeping with Andromache as more of a punishment than a pleasure. Alcimus hadn't said anything about it. Perhaps he just wasn't aware of it, though I did wonder whether it formed part of that wordless conversation he and Automedon carried on for so much of the time.

Half an hour later, safe and warm in my own bed, I looked back over the evening and thought it had been a great success. Obviously, it would have been better if Andromache had joined us, but even without her the girls had come together as a group in a way they'd never done before. I was pleased. I kept telling myself how pleased I was, because I was aware of a growing uneasiness and I couldn't put my finger on it. Because Helle had been summoned by Pyrrhus? No, it wasn't that. Better her than one of the other girls. Anyway, she couldn't wait to get into the hall; she was nakedly ambitious. No, it was no use, I couldn't pin down why I felt that something was wrong, but I wasn't going to lie awake worrying about it.

Blowing out the candle, I pulled the covers up and stared into the darkness, my eyes smarting from the smoke of the fire. I could smell it on my skin and in my hair. *Bath, tomorrow, first thing*. All the time, involuntarily, my brain went on sifting through the events of the evening. What was it? Something didn't fit. And then, on the edge of sleep, I realized: that moment, right at the end, when the girls had gathered round Helle's bed, their faces full of curiosity and fear, I'd looked around the circle, noticing how bewildered and ignorant they all were. Now, I closed my eyes, trying to recreate that scene because I needed to be sure, and slowly, one by one, the faces swam into focus, even the two mute girls whose names I still didn't know. All of them – except Amina. Amina hadn't been there.

I told myself it didn't matter, that she'd probably just stayed behind in the yard, gathering up the cups and dampening down the fire. That would have been like her; she was always tidying up the mess in the overcrowded hut, and becoming tetchy and frustrated when the other girls didn't keep it that way. Still, I was a bit concerned. I even wondered if I should get up and check to see if she was all right, but they'd all be asleep by now. No, it could wait till morning. I tossed from side to side, while the baby turned somersaults as it always did if I was upset. At last I found a position that suited both of us, but even so it was a long time before I got to sleep.

13

Calchas is dreaming, as he often does now, about his childhood in Troy, long before he became a priest, back in the days when he was, nominally at least, his father's apprentice in the blacksmith's shop. A skinny, pasty-faced kid, all thumbs, slow to move in response to his father's barked orders and not nearly fast enough to dodge his fists. Inclined to slope off into the house where his mother is baking in the kitchen – smells of warm bread and cinnamon, the rush of heat as she takes loaves from the oven, sticking her bottom lip out to blow strands of hair away from her flushed face. She pauses for a moment as he bursts in, presses his swollen face against her hot side, but she daren't say too much; she's even more frightened of his father than he is. Calchas stirs and briefly wakes, remembering his mother. A mouse-like little woman, she seems to him now, who had once been his entire world. Always praying, every feast day at the temple, a little in love with the priest, perhaps? A bruise here and there, though nothing her husband didn't have a perfect right to inflict, she wasn't complaining, only she did wish he wouldn't be so hard on the boy. And then, one day, the obvious solution presented itself. Calchas remembers it as a day of talk behind closed doors, his father's rumble going on and on, and then the priest's voice, reedy but authoritative, rising above it – and suddenly his few possessions are being bundled together and he's following the priest, a respectful three paces behind, along the narrow, winding alleys, the congested streets, which till now are all he's ever known, to the sunlit squares and splendid temples near the citadel. Different smells here: flowers, incense, the ferrous smell of blood from the sacrifices. And meat, always meat, so much meat. He's leaving behind the awful smells of the tannery, the glue factory and the knacker's yard, though they linger on his skin till he's had the ceremonial bath – and then they're gone, along with the smell of baking bread and cinnamon.

Once a month, he's allowed to go home, and at first he longs for that day, even marks the days on the ground with a piece of chalky stone, but then increasingly with every visit he ceases to belong in the neighbourhood and even in his own home – as if he were in a fast-moving ship and his mother was just a tiny figure waving from the shore.

After a night of confused dreams, he wakes with a dry mouth, his eyelids stuck together; he doesn't often drink strong wine but last night he had – his head's pounding. He's spent the last days and nights waiting for a summons from Agamemnon that he knows must be coming soon; but when, at long last, there's a knock on his door it's not the imposing figure of the king's herald he sees standing there, but Lord Nestor's slave girl: his 'prize of honour' as the Greeks say. He remembers this girl vaguely from the times he'd dined in Nestor's hall, though it takes a few seconds to recall her name. Hecamede, that's it. His first thought is that Nestor's dead – there've been rumours about his health ever since his youngest son was killed – and Calchas feels his brain bulge with the effort of calculating what Nestor's death will mean for the already fragile balance of power within the camp, but a moment later he realizes it's all nonsense – news of a king's death is proclaimed by heralds, not carried by slaves. He's still struggling to wake up, to shake off the last vestiges of sleep. When, at last, the girl speaks, she says, in a remarkably sweet, modest way, 'Hecuba would like to see you.'

'*Hecuba?*'

Instant outrage. Is he really so reduced in status that he can be summoned by a slave to see a slave? Because that's what Hecuba is now – no matter that she'd once been queen of Troy. But then he starts to remember her as she used to be. She – Priam too, of course – always attended the temple on days that were especially sacred to Apollo. The first time he saw her he must have been . . . what, fourteen, fifteen years old? A little more, perhaps. As he'd knelt to offer Priam the first cuts of meat from the sacrifice, he'd stolen a sidelong glance at her, where she sat in a gold-embroidered robe with diamonds flashing in her hair. How old would she have been? Not young; even as long ago as that, she couldn't have been young. And she wasn't beautiful, not in the way many of Priam's concubines were beautiful; but she did have the most extraordinary voice, deeper than women's voices generally are – and with a rasping quality that might have been unpleasant, but wasn't. He'd thought about her later, lying on his pallet bed trying to get to sleep with all the sights and sounds of the feast day revolving inside his head, and her voice had made him think of a woman's nails being dragged down a man's back, all the way from the nape of his neck to the cleft in his arse – but gently, very gently, leaving only the faintest score marks on the skin. Sixteen, he'd have been. An age when really all you think about is sex.

'What does she want?'

'I don't know, Sir, she didn't say.'

'Well, tell her —' He bites the words back.

The girl stood, breathing softly.

'Tell her I'll come when I can.'

There is no business to detain him in Agamemnon's compound, and yet he can't bear to leave. He waits in his hut all day and still the summons doesn't come; so, in the late afternoon, his shadow stretching far ahead of him along the beach, he sets off for Odysseus' compound. Frustrated, bad-tempered – yes, but curious too. He's astonished to realize there's still a slight undertow of attraction – but she's an old woman now, too old to arouse feelings of that sort.

He finds her lying on a pallet bed, her head raised on two pillows – so evidently some effort has gone into making her comfortable, though the blanket she lies under is far from clean. When she pushes it to one side, it exhales a breath of sickness, of old flesh. He wishes he'd remembered to bring the half-lemon stuck with cloves that he always carries whenever he's obliged to visit the more malodorous parts of the camp.

'Hecuba.' No title; what's the use of pretending?

She peers up at him. 'For god's sake, man, *sit down*. You always were a streak of piss.'

That same warm, dark, rasping voice. It jolts him out of his pre-determined reactions. He looks around the squalid little kennel of a hut, licks his lips like a confused dog – and then, unexpectedly, involuntarily, sits. He's surprised himself, though not her – she'd taken his obedience for granted. He looks at her, sees the wrinkled neck and the age spots on her skin, sees it all, but none of it matters. She turns her head and he's a boy again, kneeling at Priam's feet, gazing sidelong at her.

She reaches for a jug. 'Pour yourself a cup. It's rubbish, but if I can drink it, I'm bloody sure you can.'

'No thanks, not just now.'

He hears himself: stilted, prissy, constipated. His eyes stray to the cake that's sitting on a platter beside her bed.

'Go on, help yourself, I won't get through it.' She pushes the platter towards him. 'Hecamede's. You won't get better than that anywhere.'

'I saw her this morning.'

'Well, yes, of course you did, I sent her.'

She's as imperious as ever. He remembers her as she was when he first saw her: a small, thin, brown-skinned woman with high cheek-bones and a curious habit of sucking in her cheeks as if she'd just tasted something unexpectedly sour. Perhaps, in old age, it actually helps a woman not to have been too beautiful? Hecuba had kept Priam interested, amused, exasperated, frustrated and utterly beguiled through fifty years of marriage. God knows how she'd done it – no tits to speak of either. And she was outrageous; some of the things she came out with. *Streak of piss? Really?* What kind of language is that for a queen? And she'd been equally outspoken in Troy. He has a distinct memory of Priam with his head in his hands, saying, '*Hecuba!*' Can't remember the occasion – some reception for a foreign ambassador.

'Are they treating you well?' he asks, using his index finger to scoop up a blob of cream and pop it on to his tongue.

'Oh, yes. I want for nothing.'

It's not clear how she means that to be taken. Compared with the palace in Troy, this . . . *hovel* – you couldn't call it anything else – obviously lacks a great deal.

'I get food, I get wine – bloody awful wine, but . . .' She shrugs.

'Odysseus wants me kept alive. He wants me as a coming-home present for that wife of his.'

'Penelope does have an excellent reputation.' God, he sounds so pompous. How has he turned into this person? 'I do think she'll be kind to you.'

'Oh, yes, I know, I know. *Faithful* Penelope, *loyal* Penelope, *wise* Penelope . . . I was all those things – fat lot of good it did me.'

Faithful, yes; loyal, yes. *Wise?* Suddenly, he's impatient to be gone, to get back to his hut, to wait for the real summons – the one that actually matters – but she holds him there, by sheer force of will, it seems, and he's tired of it, he's tired of the arrogance of these people who believe they're born to rule and then, when fate turns against them, can't – or won't – adjust. Lying there in her filthy rags on a slave's bed, she's still, in her own mind, a queen. Once, he might have found that admirable, but not now. *Wise* people trim their sails when the wind changes; they don't sail headlong into a gale. He makes a move to rise, but then looks at her again and recognizes in the sharp cheekbones and hollow temples a different kind of authority. He sees that she's dying and that she knows she's dying. It's this, not some delusional idea that she's still a queen, that gives her strength. He sees that she fears nobody, because she has nothing left to lose – not even her own life.

'Well, you certainly enjoyed that.'

Looking down at the platter, he sees to his horror that the cake has disappeared. All of it.

'Moderation in all things,' Hecuba says, piously. 'Mind, you never were very good at moderation, were you?'

He feels himself blushing underneath the paint. He knows exactly what she's referring to: one particular, rather unfortunate, incident.

Why is she referring to it? That's the question. She still hasn't said what she wants – and he wonders now whether she might be capable of blackmail. Well, if she is, it's not going to get her anywhere. It's all too long ago, nobody cares – and anyway, who's going to listen to a slave? His mind whirrs on, automatically calculating risk and probability, planning his next move . . . There's no emotion involved now – he can't afford emotion – but then he looks at Hecuba once again; the light falls on her face and he's back in Troy again. All the years between, the years of plotting, dissembling, keeping quiet when things were said that violated everything he believed in – all those years have been erased, leaving him stranded, as naked as a hermit crab without its shell.

'We had fun, though, didn't we?' Hecuba says.

'Now and then.'

'Oh, come on, you know we did.'

Yes, it was fun. It was tremendous fun. He remembers hot summer evenings in Priam's orchards, moonless nights when you could barely see the person you'd bumped into. Good, while it lasted, but his position at court had become increasingly precarious. Not long after the unfortunate incident, it had been gently suggested that perhaps a celibate priesthood might not be his true vocation. He'd taken the hint and packed his bags, telling himself he'd welcome a change of scene, though in fact he'd been deeply hurt. Perhaps they were right, he'd thought. And here he is, twenty years on, still a priest, still celibate; though admittedly the celibacy is rather more strictly observed now.

'How's Agamemnon?' Hecuba asks.

'What makes you think *I* know? I haven't seen him since –'

'Since you officiated at my daughter's death.'

'That wasn't just me, it was –'

All of us. Every priest in the camp had been there. He'd closed his eyes as Pyrrhus raised the sword, and kept them closed till it was over. Sheer cowardice, and even so the attempt to spare himself had failed. At night, in dreams, he still hears the silence, the gasp from the crowd as the blade fell.

'She died bravely.' He swallows to dislodge the lump in his throat. 'Do you know the men put flowers on her grave?'

'The *Greeks* do?'

'Yes. She was brave, they respect that. And you've got to remember it was quick. Seconds. She was dead before she hit the ground.'

'I suppose I have Pyrrhus to thank for that. Well, yes, I suppose I have – he could've made a mess of it. God knows he made a big enough mess of Priam. You wouldn't kill a dog like that.'

'You were there?'

'Yes, I saw it all.'

She throws back her head, exposing her wrinkled neck and throat and a new sound comes from her mouth, a whimpering, like a dog that's about to howl. He can't bear it; he has to look away. When he turns back, she's put her fingers round her mouth; she is actually holding her lips together to stop the dreadful sound getting out. He waits while she brings herself back under control. At last, she straightens up.

'She was a good girl, Polyxena. She'd have taken care of me.' A shuddering breath. 'We'd have taken care of each other.'

'They say he's mad.'

'Agamemnon?'

'Yes – apparently he sends for Machaon every night. Can't sleep. Downs a whole cup of Machaon's sleeping draught, still can't sleep.

You know, you're not supposed to take it with strong wine – try telling that to Agamemnon! Oh, and apparently, he's started seeing things.'

'What sort of things?'

'Achilles.'

'Oh, I know about that. That's why Polyxena had to die. Give him a girl, he might stay underground.'

'He's livid with Menelaus. Apparently, they don't speak. You know, he's back sleeping with Helen?'

'Yes – and I'm not surprised. I warned him . . . I said: Don't let her anywhere near you – send her home on a different ship. I knew she'd worm her way back – I knew. Oh, well, there you are. Grab a man's dick, you can lead him anywhere.'

He is inclined to bridle a bit at that, which does seem to imply an unduly low opinion of his sex. She'd been married to Priam, for god's sake – what did *she* have to complain about? Not like his own poor mother, fastened to a man who'd been stingy with his money and generous with his fists.

'Has he sent for Cassandra?' she asks.

'Now that I can't tell you.'

'Can't – or won't?'

'We-ell, she did foretell his death . . .'

'Huh, they think she'll set fire to the bed, do they? Mind, she did do that once. Set fire to the bed.' Her voice softens. 'How is she?'

'Calmer – so I've been told; I haven't seen her.'

'Surely you could ask to see her?'

'*No.* I don't know who Agamemnon listens to these days, but it certainly isn't me.'

'Why do you think that is?'

'I don't know.'

'Oh, come on, you must know, clever man like you?'

'He quarrelled with Achilles once – and my advice to the assembly went against him.'

'Backed the wrong horse, didn't you?'

He says, stiffly: 'I was telling the truth.'

'I want to see my Cassandra. I've lost one daughter. I don't want to lose her.'

Suddenly, she looks completely exhausted. It is extraordinary how rapidly the colour drains from her face. Even her lips have gone white.

'I can't help you.'

He hates saying it, though it's no more than the truth. Agamemnon's women are kept in close confinement, and his own influence in that compound is close to zero.

'Well, then.' She sets the wine jug aside. 'Off you go.'

Dismissed, he stands up, bows – and from sheer force of habit begins to back out of the room; but then catches himself up, sharply. *She* might suffer from delusions about her status, but that's no reason for him to share them. He turns on his heel and marches straight out of the door, trying not to hear the chuckle that pursues him down the steps.

14

The next time I went to see Hecuba, the arena was being prepared for an archery competition and I stopped for a moment to watch the targets being set up: crudely painted faces of Trojan warriors left over from training sessions during the war. As many events as possible were being held in the arena because it was comparatively sheltered. Some games – archery and spear-throwing among them – would have been impossible at the training grounds up on the headland where the wind blew even more fiercely than it did down here. I'd turned away and was edging through the outskirts of the crowd towards Hecuba's hut when the door opened and Calchas came out. We bowed to each other. I was astonished he'd bothered to visit Hecuba; he'd always seemed so totally focused on cultivating powerful men. For a moment, I thought he looked as if he wanted to stop and talk, but then he appeared to think better of it and strode off.

As soon as I entered the hut, I could see that Hecuba looked brighter. Her blankets were folded neatly at the foot of her bed and she was walking, though rather unsteadily, up and down the hut.

'Well,' I said. 'Look at you.'

She actually smiled. 'I'll be glad to sit down though.'

I helped her back on to the bed. Not wanting to arrive

empty-handed, I'd brought figs, grapes and white cheese and I was pleased to see Hecuba force a little down. There was a jug of wine already on the floor beside her. She was used to the fine wines of Priam's court, but I noticed again that this rough, peasant stuff went down easily enough, bringing a slight flush to her cheeks.

'What did Calchas want?'

'Oh, what does he ever want? You can't always tell, can you?' She seemed to be considering whether to say more. 'That's the second time he's been. We had a good laugh – well, I did. You won't credit it, but as a young man, he was really beautiful. You know, not just a bit good-looking – absolutely *stunning*.' She sighed. 'Ah, well, some people should just die young, I suppose.'

I think I was rather shocked by her flippancy. The fact is, I couldn't keep pace with her changing moods. One day she was on the beach, howling for Priam; the next, she mentioned him quite casually, as if he'd just gone ahead of her into the next room. I was nineteen. I knew nothing. It's taken me nearly fifty years to be able to say: I understand Hecuba.

But I could see she was enjoying herself: drinking wine, eating cheese, gossiping . . .

'Everybody was chasing him – men *and* women. Not that he ever ran very fast.' Her voice sank to a whisper. 'There was one night, Priam and I were coming back from dinner, and Priam spotted somebody ahead he didn't want to see – one of his counsellors – oh, I can't remember his name – never mind, nice man but my god he could go on! So, we did a detour through the bedrooms, and you know how they open off each other? Well, the door of one of them was thrown open and there was Calchas on all fours between two lords . . .' She giggled. 'Plugged at both ends.'

'What did you do?'

'Oh, somebody had the presence of mind to slam the door. Priam laughed about it, but it was a bit much really. I mean, Calchas was supposed to be celibate. God, he was trouble . . . And yet you look at him now . . . Did you ever see such a *stick*?'

She was enjoying herself, regaling me with gossip from the Trojan court. 'Holy Ilium' Troy used to be called, because of its profusion of temples – but it did have another side. I'd been dimly aware of that even as a young girl. So, Hecuba and I ate, drank and laughed – but I felt all the time there was something else, something she wasn't getting to. We lapsed into silence for a moment, and then she said: 'I want to see Cassandra.'

Perhaps because I'd lost my own mother at such an early age, I've never been able to bear the thought of mothers and daughters being separated. 'All right,' I said, cautiously. 'Though it won't be easy. I doubt she's allowed out of her hut.'

No reply. Hecuba was sitting with her head turned pointedly away, in her sulky, moulting-bird-of-prey mode. I was remembering Cassandra's prophecy that her marriage to Agamemnon would lead directly to his death, to the fall of the royal House of Atreus and the destruction of the kingdom that had destroyed Troy.

'Do you believe her? I mean, about Agamemnon being killed?'

Hecuba shrugged. 'She gets carried away. People always say it's divine frenzy, but I could never see it. I think she just makes things up to suit herself.'

Difficult to believe your daughter's a prophet: the little girl you potty-trained and sang to sleep at night.

'It's all very precise, though, isn't it? She says his wife's going to throw a net over him while he's in the bath and then hack him to pieces with an axe. Why would she do that?'

'Because he sacrificed their daughter to get a wind for Troy. They were all stuck there waiting, starting to fight among themselves – same as they are now – the whole thing was falling apart . . . So, he sacrificed her.' She'd been staring into space, but then suddenly she turned and looked straight at me. 'I'd kill the bastard, wouldn't you?'

'She says she's going to die too.'

'I know what she says.' Her expression softened. 'She was always frightened of nets when she was a little girl. We used to put nets over the children's beds at night to stop insects getting at them, but she'd never let me put one over hers; she always used to scream and pull it down. I gave up in the end. Of course, she got bitten to bits. She was riving at herself all the following day. I just said, "Serves you right." I actually made her sit down and count the bites – forty-seven, *forty-seven* – but it didn't make any difference, she still wasn't having it.'

Such a mixture of emotions flitting across her face: regret, love, guilt, exasperation . . . Mothers and daughters have their battles, I knew that – though my own mother had died before I reached the awkward age and I had only happy memories of her. But the impression I was getting from Hecuba was of a really troubled relationship in which nothing had ever been put right.

'I need to see her.'

What could I say? 'All right, I'll do my best.'

The archery contest was well underway now; our conversation was being punctuated by roars and groans from the men outside.

When I left, I was confronted by a solid wall of backs. There was a tense silence as one of the contestants took aim, then a thud as the arrow hit the target, followed by a buzz from the spectators. Peering between the rows of backs, I saw the targets standing in a line and the painted faces of Trojan fighters torn to shreds. So much hatred; you felt it must've soaked into the ground beneath our feet.

I turned away and walked on.

15

On my way across the camp, I promised myself I wouldn't burden Ritsa with my problems, but as I ducked under the flap and stood blinking in the green gloom, I couldn't help but remember that the last time I'd been here I'd brought Amina with me – and that reawakened the niggling uneasiness that was never very far from my mind. And the tent was not a welcoming place. I still had the sense of being inside a diseased lung that was struggling to breathe, but as soon as I hugged Ritsa and sat down at the bench beside her I started to feel better.

'No maid today?'

'She's busy,' I said. 'And she's not my maid.'

'Just asking.'

I reached for a pestle and mortar and began grinding some of the herbs she'd laid out in front of her. She made no comment and for a few minutes we worked in silence.

'Actually, I was wondering if I might see Cassandra?'

'I don't see why not. Perhaps leave it a bit though. She was asleep when I left.'

I looked around the tent. 'Bit busier?'

'Huh – silly young idiots tearing chunks out of each other. Fighting over the games – we had one lad in here the other night, his ear had been nearly torn off. "Oh, you think this is bad, do you?" he says. You know, all cocky – "You should've seen *him*." Machaon gave him a right bollocking.'

Poor Alcimus, I thought. So far Automedon had been proved right. Every result was disputed; every friendly contest ended in a fight.

'How is Cassandra?' I asked.

'Oh, you know, up and down. Nights are still bad.'

'No better, then?'

'She is a bit. You can have a conversation now, whereas before . . .'

'Hecuba wants to see her.'

'Well, of course she does, poor woman, but I'm afraid there's not much chance of it. Cassandra's not allowed out of the hut. You know what he's like.'

'That's what I thought. And Hecuba's too weak to walk all the way here . . .'

'And mightn't be welcome even if she did. I've heard Cassandra say some pretty awful things about her mother. There's no love lost there.'

We'd been working for perhaps half an hour when there was a commotion at the entrance and two men came in half carrying, half dragging a third man between them. They dumped him unceremoniously on the ground and left. We got up and went to see who it was: Thersites. At first, I thought he'd been beaten up, but then I noticed his eyes were unfocused, or rather, focused on a point only a few inches away from his face; he kept making odd little snatching movements in the air as if trying to catch something only he could see. Drunk? His breath stank, but I didn't detect wine particularly, or no more than usual.

'Best get him into bed,' Ritsa said. 'Let him sleep it off.'

There were several cowhide beds already made up and vacant, so it was largely a matter of dragging him across to the nearest and persuading him to crawl on to it. He was covered from head to foot in what looked like goose shit – god knows where he'd been. 'He'll have to be washed,' Ritsa said. 'Machaon'll go mad if he sees that.' She looked exhausted; she even held on to my arm as she spoke.

'You go and sit down; I'll do it.'

'Briseis, you *can't*.'

I knew what she meant: *You're Lord Alcimus' wife*. It was all very well for a lady to bathe the sick in her own home – that was perfectly right and proper – but to perform the same menial task in a hospital, to choose, actually choose, the work of a slave? It was only what she'd been wanting to say ever since I pulled the pestle and mortar towards me.

'Go on,' I said. '*Shoo*.'

I fetched a bucket and some rags and set to work, stripping off the stinking tunic and loincloth, rubbing the wet rag in great sweeps across his body. The water in the bucket changed colour rapidly as I worked. Overhead, the canvas flapped and strained, but I was getting used to that; I no longer feared the entire tent was about to take off. Once or twice, Thersites cried out – more, I thought, from the frustration of not being able to catch the invisible objects in front of him than from any real pain. His body was covered in bruises, some purple, some yellow, some blue around the edges with a pale cream centre – taken together they formed a visual record of the last few weeks of Thersites' life. He kept up a constant gabbling; the few snatches of speech I understood were typical of the man, foul-mouthed, aggressive, obsessed with shit, filth, blood and pus. It was extraordinary how many of his insults involved boils: boils, blains, blebs, wens, pustules, chancres and sores. Where did it come from, I wondered, this preoccupation with diseased skin? But then I rolled him over. One glance at his backside and I wondered no more.

I straightened up and beckoned Ritsa; I wanted to ask her advice about a poultice for after I'd cleaned the boils. Wiping her hands on the sides of her apron, she joined me at the foot of the bed.

'What do you think we should do?' I asked.

Still lying face down, Thersites twisted round and peered over his shoulder. 'Oh, you. Thrown you out, has he?'

I ignored him while Ritsa and I considered how best to bring the boils to a head.

'Oi, *you*!' Drunken arrogance, spoiling for a fight. 'I'm talking to *you*. Has he thrown you out?'

It was a waste of time getting upset by anything Thersites said. He hated women, especially the young, pretty girls that the kings reserved for their own use. He particularly resented women like me – the prizes of honour – because we were as far out of his reach as goddesses. Though even with the common women round the cooking fires he must often have found himself elbowed aside by stronger men. I wondered how many of his bruises came from those encounters. But any sympathy I'd ever felt for him was long gone. I added salt to the water and gave his arse a good scrub.

'*Ow!* Fucking bitch!'

'It's for your own good.'

'Fucking hurts – and I can't lie on me back.'

'Lie on your belly, then.'

When I came back an hour later, he was curled up on his side, dozing, though he jerked awake when I set the platter down beside him. Ignoring the food, he went straight for the wine, only to spit the first mouthful out. 'Is this the best you can do? Virgin's piss.'

'If you don't want it there's plenty who will.'

He went on grumbling, but eventually settled down to eat. The food was good. Machaon insisted on that.

Machaon himself came in a few minutes later, examined the boils and asked about the snatching movements. 'White things,' Thersites said. 'Little white things flitting about.'

Machaon turned to Ritsa, reeled off a list of instructions for tackling the boils, then looked down at Thersites. '*And no strong wine.*'

'Fat chance of that in here. Cows.'

'You keep a civil tongue in your head.'

After a few more instructions about salt-water washes and the various poultices Ritsa might try, he bowed low to me and left. The bow amused me. The first time I met Machaon, I'd been a slave in Agamemnon's compound, sent to help in the hospital because it was overcrowded, the nurses barely able to cope with each day's influx of wounded. Within minutes of meeting me – and it had been a warm welcome – Machaon, quite unselfconsciously, had hitched up his tunic and given his balls a good scratch – exactly as he might have done if he'd been alone. Because he was alone. A slave counts for no more than a bed or a chair.

But now, he bowed.

Following Ritsa back to the bench, I thought perhaps it was time I went to see Cassandra.

'Yes, of course,' Ritsa said. 'Just let me finish this.' She was working on a kaolin poultice. 'You'll have seen them all soon, the Trojan women.'

I nodded. 'Yes, I suppose so.'

'Including Helen.'

'Now who told you that?'

'Oh, one of the girls.'

Ritsa went out of her way to help the common women; her goose-fat jar came in useful after many a rough night, and I've no doubt she helped in other ways as well. I'd noticed the hospital kept a very large store of pennyroyal, and there were whole beds of it growing in patches of rough ground behind the huts, though as far as I knew it was of no use whatsoever in the treatment of wounded men, but properly prepared it could end an unwanted pregnancy.

'You don't approve,' I said. 'Me seeing Helen.'

'Not my business.'

I explained about my sister – and then I mentioned Helen's bruises.

'She's not your responsibility,' Ritsa said. 'Anyway, let him kill her, it's no more than she deserves.'

Ritsa: the kindest of women, and yet she shared the universal hatred of Helen.

'She was kind to me after my mother died – when I was in Troy and I didn't have you.'

She nodded, though her mouth remained hard. Neither of us wanted this meeting to end in a pointless argument over Helen, so we chatted, laughed and joked, as she finished making the poultice for Thersites' backside. 'There, that can go in the oven now.' She wiped the kaolin from her hands on the sacking cloth round her waist. 'Let him have his sleep out first.'

'What do you think's wrong with him?'

'Wickedness.'

There was no answering that. We checked to make sure he was still asleep, then I followed Ritsa across the small yard at the side of Agamemnon's hall. Once, this area would have been full of tethered animals waiting to be slaughtered. Hens, geese, ducks too. I remembered particularly a flock of hens ruled over by a white cockerel with a blood-red comb whose crowing had woken the whole compound every morning an hour before dawn. Now, the chickens were gone, and in their place strutted half a dozen crows, naked eyes glinting as we approached. We were walking rapidly, talking as we went, and yet they scarcely bothered to lift their wings and flap out of the way. Crows were everywhere now, and they seemed so arrogant, so *prosperous* . . . Almost as if they were taking over.

Cassandra's hut was surprisingly large and – as I saw when Ritsa opened the door and ushered me inside – extremely well furnished. Rugs, cushions, lamps – and, on the wall facing the door, a very fine tapestry: Artemis, the Lady of Animals, hunting with dogs. No Cassandra, though. I glanced at Ritsa, who put a finger to her lips and led me along the passage to a room at the end. There, lying fast asleep on the bed, was Cassandra, her unbound hair spread across the pillow, and, lying beside her with his head on her breast, a really rather beautiful young man. My heart thumped with shock, but then I realized this must be her twin brother, Helenus. The man who under torture had betrayed the details of Troy's internal defences. Helenus was Trojan; he was male – so why was he still alive? Perhaps because his life was part of the bargain he'd struck with Odysseus. That was possible – or perhaps the Greeks just didn't see him as a man. His betrayal of his father and his city didn't seem to be weighing heavily on him. He was as deeply asleep as Cassandra, his upper lip making a little popping sound on every exhaled breath.

Ritsa pulled me back. 'He's always here, scrounging for food, but what can you do? I can't turn him away, he's her brother.' Back in the living quarters, she said, 'Do you want to wait? She shouldn't be long – they've been asleep hours already.'

'I'll give it half an hour.'

Under the tapestry of vengeful Artemis, we sat quietly. After a while, I noticed that Ritsa had nodded off – she was permanently exhausted, poor woman. My gaze fell on the tapestry again. It told the story of Acteon, whom Artemis changed into a stag when he tried to force himself on her – or, in another version of the story, stumbled upon her accidentally while she was bathing. As the cloth swayed in a draught, Acteon seemed to be fleeing in terror from his own hounds, though there was no hope of escape; he was only a foot away from their slavering jaws. Ritsa was snoring slightly, her head slumped forward on to her chest. I closed my eyes and settled back into my chair. Immediately, behind my closed lids, I saw Cassandra and Helenus entwined on the bed. They looked like lovers; perhaps that's what I found disturbing – though I suspect few lovers ever achieve that degree of intimacy. All those months before birth, aware, however dimly, of each other's presence . . . What a bond that must forge. And yet, as boy and girl, man and woman, the whole trajectory of their lives must have been pulling them apart.

A few minutes later, I heard the front door close and another moment later Cassandra came into the room, blinking and yawning, her hair still tousled from sleep. She took a step back when she saw me, but Ritsa struggled to her feet and introduced us.

'Oh, yes, I know who you are.' Cassandra had curiously bright, hyper-alert eyes and a habit of staring straight at you without blinking. She always seemed to be groping after the meaning of words. This had the odd effect of making her seem stupid, which was certainly not true. At last, after quite a long silence, she went on, 'My father told me about you.'

'*Priam* did?'

'Yes, when he came back to Troy with Hector's body. He said you'd been very kind.'

Once again, I was touched to think Priam had remembered me. For a moment, I was blinking back tears.

We sat at the table and Ritsa produced bread and some cheese. Cassandra ate very little. She was making small grey pellets with the bread, rolling them between her thumb and forefinger. I noticed she had rather masculine hands: the bones prominent, a network of raised blue veins like drowned worms under the skin. At last she looked up. 'So, what brings you here?'

I said I was trying to see all the women who'd arrived in the camp from Troy.

'Oh, you're the welcoming committee, are you?'

'Not exactly.'

'So, you'll have seen my mother?'

'Yes, she's very concerned about you.'

'Bit late for that.'

'She'd like to see you.'

'Not possible, I'm afraid. Nobody's allowed in, I'm not allowed out . . . I'm buried alive here.' The silence went on so long, I didn't think there'd be any more from her, but then she said, 'I just want this bloody awful wind to stop.' She put her head in her hands, peering at me through her fingers like a frightened child. 'You know what really scares me? They're going to ask me why they can't leave, and I won't know what to say . . . I don't know!'

'They won't ask you – they'll ask Calchas.'

'Will they?'

I did my best to reassure her, pointing out that Agamemnon had his own priests and seers – of whom Calchas was by far the most important – but I might as well not have spoken. Those unblinking eyes stared straight through me.

'Anyway, isn't it obvious why the gods are angry?' Ritsa said. 'Look at what happened. Temples desecrated, children murdered, women raped . . .'

Cassandra ignored her.

I said: 'Some people say it's because of what happened to you.'

'What about it?' Hostile now.

'Well, wasn't that an offence against the gods?'

'It was an offence against *me*. Anyway, I don't want to talk about it.'

She went back to making pellets out of bread. But then a minute later it all came bursting out of her. How she'd been walking home from the palace when she'd heard a clash of weapons in the streets and taken refuge in the temple of Athena, hiding behind a huge painted statue of the goddess. How Little Ajax had found her there and dragged her out. How she'd clung to the statue, bringing it crashing to the floor beside her. How all the way through what happened next, she'd stared into the owl-eyes of the goddess, refusing to admit that the body below her neck still belonged to her. I remember I did that, the first few times with Achilles.

'You know the worst thing?' she said. 'I was on my period. Made no difference, he just pulled the bloody clout off me and threw it away . . . I wouldn't have wanted my own sister to see that.'

I was struggling to find something to say.

Cassandra took a deep breath. 'Look, what happened to me happened to hundreds of women. As soon as they heard the fighting, they ran to hide in the temples, and the Greeks knew where to look for them. There wasn't a temple in Troy that wasn't desecrated.'

Bugger the temples, I thought. *What about the women?*

Out of the corner of my eye, I saw Ritsa shaking her head. I nodded to show I understood, but then Cassandra held out her hands towards me, slightly raised so her bracelets fell back to reveal the raw skin underneath.

'They tied me to the bed. They needn't have worried – I'm not going to kill him. It's his wife who'll kill him.' Her voice was dreamy, abstracted. 'She makes him a hot bath, she gives him a cup of the finest wine, tells the maids to rub oil into his back, and then when he's half asleep, dreaming and lulled and warm, she throws a net over him, she raises the axe and HITS HIM HITS HIM HITS HIM...' She banged the table with her clenched fists.

I tried to think of something to say to calm her down, but my mind had gone blank – and it was too late anyway. She was on her feet, pacing up and down, arms flailing, spit flying, bouncing off the walls. It was essentially the same rant I'd heard once already, in the arena, on the day the Trojan women were brought down to the camp.

'Let her be,' Ritsa said. 'She'll wear herself out.'

Gradually, Cassandra became calmer. At last, white-faced, she walked towards me. 'You must have seen my mother?'

'She's very concerned,' I repeated.

Her mouth twisted. '*Huh.* Do you know, whenever I look at my mother, I see hairs growing out of her heart?'

And with that she turned on her heel and left the room. As the door closed behind her, Ritsa shrugged, even managed a slight smile, though I felt she was being more tolerant of me than I deserved. 'I'm sorry,' I said.

'Not your fault.'

'Yes, it was.'

'All right, it was.' She patted my shoulder. 'You see why I turn a blind eye when she sneaks that brother of hers in? What else has she got?'

'I just hope she doesn't give you a bad night.'

She didn't bother replying to that. At the door, we hugged, and then I set off to walk home. As I reached the other side of the yard, I turned to look back, but Ritsa had already gone inside and closed the door.

16

It was too late to see Hecuba – and anyway, I had no good news to give her – so I went straight home. As soon as I entered the compound, I knew at once that something was wrong. Groups of men were huddled together in the yard, many of them looking over their shoulders, their eyes fixed on the door of Pyrrhus' hall. *What's going on?* I heard the question run from mouth to mouth, but nobody seemed to know the answer.

I didn't have one either. What I did have was a knot of fear in the pit of my stomach that twisted and tightened as I threaded my way through the crowd. Entering the hut, I found Alcimus and Automedon facing each other across the table. I put bread and olives in front of them and began to pour the wine, but Alcimus waved me away, so I went and sat on the bed. Neither of them said anything; though I got the impression they had been talking before I came into the room. A few moments later, a great hammering on the door began. Thinking there must be some crisis in the women's hut – Amina was still very much in the forefront of my mind – I ran to answer it, but Alcimus got there first and pushed me out of the way. Pyrrhus bulged into the room – there's no other way of describing it – and, once inside, seemed to go on expanding till he was taking up every available inch of space.

'I can't let it go!' he said, as he sat down.

I knew in my bones – in my water, as the old wives say – what 'it' was, and yet I listened avidly, needing to have my worst fears confirmed. Last night – but it might have been the previous night, or even the night before that – somebody had tried to bury Priam. Made quite a good job of it, actually – the grave, though shallow, was enough to keep seagulls and marauding crows away. A shovel had been found abandoned nearby, together with a jug of wine and a few scraps of stale bread. The jug was still half full, so it seemed likely the funeral rites had been interrupted, perhaps by somebody leading horses along the path between the pastures and the yard. Who could have done it? – that was the question.

Who would have dared?

'Nobody in this compound,' Pyrrhus said. In fact, he refused to believe any Greek fighter would have done it.

Automedon tried to point out that some people had strong religious objections to leaving the dead unburied, to denying them their rite of passage into the other world. 'Everybody deserves a proper burial,' he said.

'What, enemy fighters?'

'Ye-es.'

'My father didn't bury Hector.' Evidently, he felt any reference to Achilles was enough to settle an argument. 'No, it's a Trojan – got to be.'

Alcimus pointed out patiently that there were only two Trojans in the camp. Calchus, a priest and a seer, highly respected – even if he did wear make-up and traipse about in a skirt. Could they rule him out? Well, yes, they could – almost. Why would he suddenly risk his life to bury Priam? Surely any loyalty he might once have felt to

Priam was long gone; he'd worked for Agamemnon for at least the past ten years.

Alcimus was looking doubtful. 'Yes, but he's not in favour at the moment, is he? Hasn't been for a while.'

'Can't be him,' Automedon said. 'No integrity.'

'No balls,' said Pyrrhus.

Alcimus looked from one to the other. 'Well, then – that leaves Helenus.'

'Not him either,' Pyrrhus said. 'He betrayed his father.'

'Under torture,' Automedon said.

'What's that got to do with it?'

'None of us knows what we'd do under torture.'

'*Huh*,' Pyrrhus said, obviously thinking he did know.

'Mightn't that be precisely why he would do it?' Alcimus asked. 'A way of making good?'

They considered it.

'Ye-es,' Pyrrhus said. 'I can see that.'

'Right, then,' Automedon said. 'Let's bring him in. Though if he's any sense, he'll have buggered off.'

'Where to?' Alcimus said. 'He's nowhere to go.'

'He could live off the land, hunt. For that matter, there's plenty to eat in Priam's gardens.'

'*You* might do that,' Alcimus said. 'I doubt if Helenus would. And anyway, he can barely walk.'

This was true. I'd seen him hobbling around the camp, with blood-stained rags knotted round his ankles. Odysseus must have beaten the soles of his feet to pulp.

'Are we agreed, then?' Alcimus went on. 'We bring Helenus in and – Well, what about Calchas? We can't just drag him in – he's a priest.'

'Invite him to dinner?' Automedon said.

Pyrrhus groaned. 'For god's sake . . .'

'But you agree we need a different approach?'

'Yes. *Yes!* Just don't sit him next to me.'

Pyrrhus was already on his feet, obviously eager to get on with it. The others followed him to the door, both of them offering to find Helenus, but Pyrrhus insisted he had to go himself. In the end, all three of them set off together. I listened to their voices fading into the distance, and then it was quiet again, except for the buffeting of the wind.

I stared blindly at the bread and olives lying on the table, my brain scrabbling for a way of denying what I knew. I was remembering that moment by the fire when I'd glanced across at Amina and she'd lowered her eyes and pretended to adjust the strings of the lyre. I'd told myself it meant nothing; perhaps she just didn't like me, but that was only one instance in a pattern of avoidance. And then later, she'd been missing from the circle of girls who'd gathered round Helle. At least, I was *almost* certain she'd been missing; I still wasn't entirely sure. A large part of me just didn't believe she could be involved. The women's hut was guarded. Yes, but she could have climbed over the fence at the back. So, I paced up and down, wondering what to do, aware all the time of a mounting anger at the conversation I'd just heard. Only two Trojans in the camp? There were hundreds of Trojans in the camp; but they were women and women are invisible. An advantage, perhaps? If Amina had buried Priam, her best chance of getting away with it was that nobody would believe a girl capable of doing it. I needed to talk to her. No matter how many times I churned these thoughts round — and I did, for upwards of an hour — I always returned to that. I needed to talk to her — and away from the hut, away from the other girls. Whatever happened to Amina, the others mustn't be implicated.

Next morning, early, I fetched four wicker baskets from the yard and went along to the women's hut. The girls were still sitting on their pallet beds, even Helle, who was usually up early and practising dance routines in the yard. As I came in, Amina looked up and then quickly away. I tried to guess whether any of them knew about the burial; on the whole, I was inclined to think not. Amina wouldn't have tried to involve anybody else; she'd have been too proud of the fact that she'd acted alone. Yes, but she must have been gone hours . . . Some of them at least would have noticed that, and might have known what she was doing – or guessed. *If* she'd done it. They might all, including Amina, be oblivious to anything going on outside the confines of the hut.

Before speaking to Amina, I went along the passage to Andromache's room. I was worried about her. She was so white and thin and miserable, it occurred to me she might be one of those (rare) people who simply give up eating, who make up their minds to die. One of my mother's maids starved herself to death. I could see her quite clearly; she had a mole on her upper lip. I hadn't thought about that woman in years and I wondered why she came back to me so vividly now.

Andromache was in bed, apparently asleep.

'Andromache?' At the sound of her name, her eyelids fluttered. 'Andromache? *Wake up.*'

'What's wrong?'

'Somebody tried to bury Priam.'

Her eyes were wide open now. 'Helenus?'

'Perhaps. Actually, I think it might have been one of the girls.'

'Who? Which one?'

She did sound genuinely incredulous. Whatever had happened, it must have been without her knowledge. 'Amina.'

'Is she the one who danced?'

'No, that's Helle.'

For the first time, I felt impatient, resentful even, that she took so little interest in the girls, refusing to accept what should have been her role; hers, not mine. And then I felt ashamed, because I didn't know what it was like to have a child killed; I was afraid even to imagine it. And I certainly had no right to judge her.

'I'm going to take her out, see if I can get her to talk to me.'

'All right.' She sat up and wrapped her thin arms round her knees. 'I'm glad he's buried.'

'Yes, me too – as long as Pyrrhus doesn't kill somebody for doing it. They're going to question Helenus, but they won't stop there . . .'

Amina was folding her blanket when I went back into the other room. The air was full of the smell of young, unwashed bodies and their slightly sour, early-morning breath. Somehow or other I was going to organize baths for all of them. There was so little I could do. Suddenly, I was furious, almost to screaming point, at this confinement to one tight little space that was being imposed on us by the violence of wind and sea – and by the far more lethal violence of our captors. But then, I reminded myself, there was no 'us' now. No 'we'. I wasn't a slave any more – and perhaps that's why I suspected them of hiding things from me. I hoped they trusted me, but they must also have looked at my pregnancy, my fine clothes, my Greek husband – and wondered where my loyalties really lay. I could scarcely blame them, when I was so aware myself of all the possible conflicts. Trojan mother, Greek baby – how was that going to work out?

'Amina.' I heard my voice, sharper than I'd intended. 'I'm going to get some fresh herbs. I want you to come with me.'

I held out two of the baskets. Amina could have refused, but perhaps she didn't know that – or perhaps she was tempted by the thought of fresh air, a few hours away from the hut.

'Yes,' she said, simply. She turned to one of the other girls asking her if she could put her blanket and bed away. I'd already reached the door, glad to get away from the frowsty atmosphere. Even the wind snatching the door from my grasp and slamming it shut behind me was welcome. After a few minutes, when I was just about to go inside to fetch her, Amina joined me, muffled from head to toe in her usual black cloak.

'I didn't know there was a herb garden in the camp.'

Her tone was chatty. I thought she was trying for normality, hoping against hope I hadn't guessed.

'There is, just a small one, up on the other headland – but we're not going there. We're going to Troy.'

Her eyes widened. Perhaps she dreaded going back, and who could blame her? Though she needn't have worried; I had no intention of entering the city. Priam's orchards, the kitchen garden, the herb garden – all lay outside the walls. The orchards had been Odysseus' and Diomedes' favourite hunting ground for capturing prisoners, because people had to go there; they had to risk their lives to get basic supplies. Helenus had been captured in his father's orchards – and that fate had befallen more than one of Priam's sons.

We set off through the narrow gap in the trench. It had been dug to defend the camp in the time-before-time when it still seemed possible the Trojans would win the war – before Achilles, intent on avenging Patroclus' death, had returned to the fighting. Now the trench lay abandoned, wheelbarrows and spades stacked up against the sides. I wondered if that was where the spade used to bury Priam had come from; I glanced sideways at Amina, but she was staring straight ahead. At Troy, of course. At the ruined towers.

I knew there was a path by the river, but we'd have to cut across the battlefield to get to it. We walked in silence, Amina lagging behind, which was mildly irritating but I managed not to say anything. The ground was so uneven, I had to plan where to put my feet. Deep ruts scarred the surface, old wounds inflicted by chariot wheels and the tramp of marching feet – like memories carved into the land. This plain had once been farming land: the soil heavy, black, too good to pasture cattle, made for growing grain. That's how it was meant to be and how it had been for hundreds, perhaps thousands, of years – until the black ships came.

The day was overcast, though by now we'd given up expecting rain. It was heavy going stumbling across the churned-up ground; I felt sweat prickling in my armpits; my back and thighs ached. At last, I was forced to stop. Amina, still following along behind, her gaze, like mine, fixed on the ground, cannoned into me. We stood getting our breaths back, looking around. I'd seen this battlefield from the ramparts of Troy when it was thick with struggling backs, men grappling each other to the death, while, high above them, the kings rode in their glittering chariots. Now it was empty, desolate.

Perhaps pausing for breath had been a mistake, because having once looked up I found I couldn't go back to staring at my feet. So, as we walked on, I was alert to everything. There was something eerie about this silence; it was like the silence you hear in empty rooms when somebody you love has died – toxic. The trees had been cut down to build the Greek camp and without them the land looked naked, indecent, with not a shred of cover to hide its disfigurements. In some places, water had seeped up from the earth, from the clayey depths, filling dips and craters to the brim. Now and then, bubbles broke the surface from god knows what decomposition going on below. We had to splodge through several of these miniature lakes before we reached the path that ran beside the river. Here, at least, there was sound — water rippling over the stones — but this only served to heighten the silence of the battlefield.

Rounding a bend in the river, we came across a corpse, several weeks dead, bloated inside its battle shirt, the lower regions pitifully exposed. Neither the water nor the land had claimed him and so he lay there, his face mercifully turned away. I saw Amina put her veil to her mouth as if she were afraid of being sick, but when I reached out to touch her arm, she shook her head violently and moved away.

As we got closer to the city, there were sounds loud enough to fracture the silence: the strident cries of crows circling above the smouldering citadel. Crows are ferociously intelligent birds. I used to watch them gather as the men set off for another day of war. Drums, pipes, trumpets, the rhythmical pounding of swords on shields — to the fighters, this music meant honour, glory, courage, comradeship . . . To the crows, it only ever meant food. They didn't care who won or lost; their day always ended well.

We stopped again, looking at the city's smoking towers. I wondered if Amina was thinking of brothers or cousins lying dead inside the walls. I'd lost four brothers when my city, Lyrnessus, fell — and the thought of their unburied bodies tormented me for months after their deaths. And it still did — on the rare occasions I allowed myself to think about it at all. But they were dead — there was nothing I could do to help them — she was still alive.

'Come on,' I said. 'It's not far.'

'I know where it is.'

A path ran all the way round the city walls. As we began to walk along it, I had a sudden memory from my time in Troy, of how, in the shadow of the high walls, the flowers would close long before night-time. There were banks of pale, starlike flowers around us now and some of them had already begun closing, their petals puckering like lips. I saw Amina glancing repeatedly over her shoulder, perhaps hoping some Trojan guerrilla band, men who'd miraculously sur-vived the massacres, would appear and rescue her, but there was only the cawing of the crows that went on circling the black towers, as if fragments of charred wood had taken off and lifted into the air. At first, their cries were the only sound, but then I heard another, an insensate buzzing of flies from inside the walls, worse by far than the calling of the crows.

I'd been worried we might find the garden locked, but no, the gates stood wide open – it gave me a curious sense of being expected. No doubt the gardeners had gone to help drag the horse through the streets, and then perhaps been caught up in the celebrations, and never returned. Once we were through the gates, the high walls pro-tected us and the wind was abruptly cut off. The tops of the orchard trees were tossing but at ground level once we were away from the open gate there was no more than a slight breeze. I felt we were being watched, not by human eyes but by the flowers that seemed startled by our presence. Masses of birds, the small, multicoloured, flickering kind who prefer seeds and ripe fruit to rotting carrion. They were enjoying a feast of their own with no gardeners to chase them away. Two whole rows of goldfinches lined up cheekily on the arms of a scarecrow – and seemed to know there was nobody left to fear.

We walked along the path between two huge plots of vegetables to the herb garden at the far end. Immediately, I started picking handfuls of coriander. Out of the corner of my eye, I saw Amina, who'd been staring at the burnt-out towers, kneel down and begin gathering herbs too – though I noticed she started at the other end of a row, too far away for conversation to be possible. Never mind, I could wait. I knew she was expecting to be interrogated, but I didn't intend to oblige – not yet.

The humming of bees, the mingled scents of apple mint, thyme, rosemary, oregano, bay, the heat, like a hand pressing hard on the top of my head, sweat stinging my eyes . . . I lifted a hand to wipe it away and felt myself go dizzy – the garden was revolving around me. Carefully, I stood up and managed to get myself to a bench where I could sit in the shade. This wasn't like me, but perhaps pregnancy made you more likely to faint? I closed my eyes and wished for water.

When I opened them again, Amina was standing over me. 'Are you all right?'

'Yes, fine.'

I was feeling slightly better, but I can't have looked it because she sat beside me. 'Take deep breaths.'

I did as I was told, focusing my eyes on a clump of foxgloves until, gradually, the spinning stopped. I felt exhausted, empty. Looking around, I realized that everything here – every herb, flower and vegetable – had been planted by men who expected to see the next season, the next spring. Everywhere, there were signs of a normal day disrupted. A spade, its blade crusted with dry soil, lay at the end of a freshly dug row. On the bench, there was a square of red-and-white cloth wrapped round somebody's half-eaten lunch: a hunk of bread and a slab of mouldy pale-yellow cheese with a bite taken out of it. Whoever it was, he must have been just starting his meal when the gates opened and the wooden horse was dragged inside – and he'd left, just like that, carelessly, without a second thought, expecting to return. He'd vanished into the shouting, celebrating crowds . . .

Nothing that I'd experienced that day, not on the battlefield, not seeing the dead fighter, not even hearing the buzzing of flies from inside the walls, had broken me; but this did: an unknown man's teeth marks in a slab of smelly old cheese. I put my face in my hands and cried for the destruction of Troy, for the death of Priam and the ruin of his people.

I was only dimly aware of Amina as a blur of face and staring eyes, but then I felt her arms round me. She held me, rocking me, stroking my back, as tears and snot dripped out of me. 'I'm sorry, I'm sorry,' I kept saying, until at last I was hiccupping and sniffing and wiping my nose on the back of my hand. After a while, I picked up the red-and-white cloth and used that instead. 'Oh, god,' I said. 'I don't know what came over me – I don't cry, I never cry.'

'There, there.'

She took off her veil and used it to dry my face – and then we just went on sitting in the shade. The ground around the bench was littered with mushy brown apples with a myriad dozy bees zigzagging drunkenly over the feast. Now that the storm of weeping was over, I felt flat again, desolate; but then, gradually, my mood began to lift. I gazed around at all the colours in the garden – the purples, blues, reds, greens, yellows, many of them so bright they even survived their immersion in the tainted light, for though we were sheltered from the wind the grey clouds had parted to reveal the usual orange glare. *One day*, I thought, *I'm going to have a garden like this*. I felt a stirring of hope, almost painful, like blood flowing back into a numbed limb. Amina was quiet beside me, looking up into the tree, at the moving leaves and branches. She'd made no attempt to console me except for that meaningless *There, there* – and I was grateful to her for that. Perhaps I should have spoken then, when we were momentarily close, but I was feeling too vulnerable. So, after a while, with no more than a glance at each other, we simply went back to gathering herbs.

At the centre of the garden was a built-up bed in the shape of a wheel, the spokes designed to contain the more prolific plants, those that would otherwise run wild and choke the rest. We worked our way round the circle, coming from opposite directions. The intimacy we'd achieved on the bench was ebbing fast, the tension between us growing as we got closer, until at last we met.

'Well,' I said. '*Was* it you?'

The lie she'd been about to tell died on her lips. 'Why do you want to know? Wouldn't it be better if you didn't?'

I brushed that aside. 'The thing is, he's not going to suspect the women. At the moment, he's thinking about Calchas – you know, the priest? – or Helenus, because they're the only two Trojans in the camp –'

'I'm a Trojan.'

That stung. '*So am I.*'

'Yes, but it's different for you, isn't it?' Her gaze slid to my belly. 'You've made your choice.'

'A *choice*? What *choice* do you think I had?' Deep breath. 'Look, I'm trying to help. If you keep a low profile and don't do anything silly, there's every chance it'll blow over. We can get through this.'

'We?'

'Yes! *We.*'

She gave an irritating smirk and I wanted to slap her. 'You know he's had the body dug up again?' I was watching her closely – and I could see that hurt.

'He tells lies.'

'Who does?'

'Pyrrhus. He told Andromache Priam died painlessly – he said it was quick – and it's just not true. You wouldn't kill a pig the way he killed Priam. And the awful thing is, Hecuba saw it. She begged Priam not to put his armour on, but he would do it – there was no way he wasn't going to fight.'

'He did what he had to do.'

'Yes – so did I.'

What was becoming steadily more apparent as I listened to her was how stubborn she was, how impervious to reason. She reminded me of two women I'd known when I first came to the camp. Sisters. Every day at dusk, they'd set off for a short walk, arm in arm, heavily veiled, looking neither to right nor left, but always, modestly, down at their feet. And then, after about two hundred yards, without even needing to glance at each other, they'd turn round and walk back. On the surface, nobody could have been less like Amina than those two *timid* little women. And yet I saw the same inflexibility in her: the same refusal to accept that life has changed. It made her unreachable, and yet I felt I had to go on trying. 'He'll kill anybody who tries to bury Priam again now.'

'I know.'

I had to leave it at that. 'Come on,' I said. 'We may as well get some fruit while we're here. It's a shame to let it go to waste.'

The orchard was at the other end of the garden, a shady, rather mysterious place full of listening trees. The cherry trees had been covered in nets to keep out marauding birds but, standing on tiptoe, we were just able to reach one of the nets and pull it off. Amina climbed the tree and threw cherries down to me. I remember how they cascaded on to my face and arms, leaving red stains like splashes of blood. I was begging her to come down, I was frightened she'd fall, but she just went on pelting me with cherries – laughing, full of fun. They were ripe, overripe, we couldn't resist eating them and they were delicious. I turned to her, and noticed she had two red ticks at the corners of her mouth, pointing her lips in the direction of a smile.

We were so nearly friends.

The journey back was a hard slog. The baskets were heavy, and now we had the wind blowing directly into our faces. I realized looking ahead of me that the wind was invisible on the battlefield: there were no trees to be uprooted; no plants to be flattened. We struggled on across the dead land. I'd misjudged how long it would take and dusk was falling before we were halfway across. The evening roost was just beginning. In the failing light, the birds were almost invisible against the black soil until, late and reluctantly, they moved. I put the baskets down, waving and clapping my hands, but nothing frightened them. They cawed their triumph, the conquerors – and conquerors they certainly were with their crops crammed full of human flesh. We skirted round them as best we could, but it was a relief to reach the trench, to see lights and hear voices. I was so desperate for the warmth and relative safety of the compound that I almost ran the last hundred yards.

17

The hut was dark and silent when I got back. I groped my way into the living quarters, which at first I took to be empty, but then I noticed an oblong of deeper darkness by the bed. With shaking fingers, I lit an oil lamp and Alcimus' shadow leapt across the floor.

'You've been gone a long time.'

'We're running short of herbs, I –'

'I was worried.'

'I'm sorry. Is there anything I can get you?'

'I'll have a cup of wine – and pour yourself one too. We need to talk.'

I poured two cups and set them down on the table. We sat facing each other, but despite what he'd just said he didn't immediately speak. I knew I mustn't ask questions about Priam's burial – it might be rash even to express an interest – but I couldn't help myself. 'Did you find Helenus?'

'Yes, he was with his sister.'

I made myself wait.

'He just looked Pyrrhus in the face and said he wished he *had* buried Priam. He said he was ashamed somebody else had had to do it – it should have been him.'

'Was he . . .?' *Tortured*, I wanted to ask. That was my great fear:

that somebody else would pay a terrible price for what Amina had done. I forced myself to say the word.

Alcimus was staring down into his cup. 'No, no need, he's a broken man. Once a man breaks like that, betrays everything, there's no way back.'

Silence. I watched the shadows creating hollows in his cheeks. 'What did you want to speak to me about?'

'Oh. Andromache. Pyrrhus wants her to serve wine at dinner tonight.'

'*No* – she *can't.*'

The words were out before I could stop myself. Pyrrhus was entirely within his rights: she was his prize of honour, why shouldn't he show her off to his men? Not so long ago, Achilles had displayed me at dinner in exactly the same way; but I'd grown used to it, even learnt to value the access to information it gave me. But Andromache, in the state *she* was in . . .? I couldn't see how she'd even begin to cope.

'I thought you might like to do it with her,' Alcimus said. He'd always shown great gentleness to Andromache – he and Automedon had buried her baby son – but nevertheless, I was surprised he was willing to permit this. 'If you don't mind?'

'She can't do it alone.' I made to stand up. 'I'll go to her, unless there's something else . . .?'

He hesitated. 'Be careful around Pyrrhus. You know I said Helenus wasn't tortured? Well, he wasn't . . . but Pyrrhus did do something a bit strange. He stuck his dagger into Helenus' stomach, not very far, just a cut, but he dabbled his fingers in the blood – and I think he enjoyed knowing Helenus was afraid.'

On the scale of the blood-letting in the camp, that seemed absurdly trivial, but evidently it had disturbed Alcimus – a man not easily

141

disturbed. 'There was no need for it,' he added. 'Helenus was falling over himself to tell us everything he knew – which was nothing!'

I waited, but there was no more. 'If that's all . . .?'

'Yes, yes, you go.'

I went first to the store room and fetched an embroidered tunic from the chest where I kept my clothes, and then to my own room to brush my hair. So long now since I'd done this, though for months, when Achilles was alive, it had been my nightly routine. When I'd finished dressing and brushing my hair, I opened my mouth several times as wide as it would go, hearing the click of my jaws, then stretched my lips in a rictus of a smile. All the old nervousness, the old tension, was back. I let myself out and crossed the short distance to the women's hut. The men had already begun to gather outside the hall. A smell of roast meat drifted out through the open door; I felt a gush of saliva, but I knew I wouldn't be eating until much later – if indeed I ate at all.

Inside the hut, I went straight to Andromache's room. She was up and dressed, but standing rather helplessly beside the bed, her hair still tousled from sleep. The tunic she was wearing wouldn't do at all. I went back to the living quarters, selected two girls at random and told them to fetch hot water and clean clothes. Under my direction, they helped Andromache to wash – a bath would have been better, but there wasn't time for that – and brushed her hair until it shone. Much to my surprise, Amina came in carrying a wreath of purple daisies – the kind that grow in abundance at this time of year. She placed it on Andromache's head, pinned it into position and stood back to admire the effect. The colour suited Andromache, that glowing purple against the darkness of her hair, though there was no escaping the contrast between the freshness of the flowers and her

142

ravaged face. 'You'll be all right,' I said, fiercely, chafing her arms.
'I'll be there – you won't be on your own – just pour the sodding
wine and hope it chokes them.'

She stumbled twice on the short walk from the women's hut to the
hall. As we stepped over the threshold, I felt a blast of hot air open the
pores in my skin. Smells of roast beef, spices, warm bread, sweaty
men, resin from the walls, tar from the torches – but also, sharper,
greener smells from the rushes rustling under our feet. Oh – and the
din! Singing – ragged at first, rising to a roar, subsiding into laughter
and jeers. Banging of fists on tables, sometimes keeping time with the
music, sometimes protesting when the food didn't arrive fast enough.
I took Andromache across to the far corner where there was a sideboard with jugs of wine lined up. I put one in her hands, hoping to god
she wouldn't drop it, then picked one up myself and started to work
my way up the nearest table. Andromache kept pace with me on the
other side. The Myrmidons greeted me with every sign of affection;
one or two of them even patted my stomach. I could never have imagined being touched below the waist by so many men with so little
sexual intent. I saw two other women, common women from around
the fires, working their way up the other table – and they were being
pawed constantly, their breasts and groins grabbed. One of them happened to look across at me and her expression, unhappy, still, and far
away, haunts me to this day, though I can't remember her name.

Until all the men were eating and drinking, I had no leisure even to
glance at the top table, where Pyrrhus, Alcimus and Automedon sat.
Calchas was there too, in full priestly regalia though the white paint
on his face was flaking in the heat. Did he realize he was only here to
be interrogated, that the men sitting on either side of him were not his
friends? Alcimus was staring down at his plate. Sometimes, when you

see somebody you know well from a distance, it sharpens your per-
ception of them. He was thinner than he'd been when I first knew
him; older. When he looked up from his plate, his eyes ran up and
down the tables, assessing the interactions between the men, alert for
the moment when banter turned to real insult and old injuries, chafed
raw, resurfaced and demanded revenge. These were men who'd been
living on their nerves for years and now, when things should have
been easy, they were frustrated because the longed-for journey home
was continually postponed. Every day began in hope, every day
ended in disappointment. They'd just won a war. How could it be that
this victory, the greatest in the history of the world – and it was,
there's no denying it – had started to taste like defeat?

So, Alcimus was constantly alert for signs of trouble, and when I
turned and looked around, I thought I could see why. Pyrrhus had
brought a group of young men with him from his mother's island of
Skyros. They were drinking heavily, shouting, pestering the serving
girls – none of this was exactly unusual, but I could see that in the
eyes of the Myrmidons, this behaviour showed a lack of respect for
older, more experienced men who'd borne the brunt of the fighting.
A lot of shouted remarks passed between Pyrrhus and this group. He
was flushed – though admittedly his pale skin flushed easily – and
obviously very much the worse for wear. Far from setting an example,
he seemed to be a large part of the problem. None of this had been
apparent to me, sitting alone in my hut, carding wool, supervising
the preparation of dinner, waiting for Alcimus to come home, but I
saw it very clearly now. This hall was packed from floor to ceiling
with kindling; one spark would be enough to set it alight.

Andromache looked wan and wretched, but at least she was still
on her feet, and that was more than I'd expected. I whispered to her

to start collecting jugs; we needed to fill them up one more time, set them on the tables and then wait for the signal to withdraw. At least, that's what used to happen when Achilles was alive. I'd always been allowed to leave before the real, serious drinking started. We set the jugs at intervals along the tables and then I went to fetch some of the best wine for the top table. Andromache took up her position behind Pyrrhus' chair and, without so much as a glance at her, he held out his cup. As she poured, I thought I glimpsed a steeliness in her that I hadn't seen before, and it gave me hope.

Most of the men had had enough to eat by now; they were just picking at the meat or mopping up the juices with hunks of bread. Here, on the top table, Pyrrhus was talking about the attempt to bury Priam. Whoever had done this had been interrupted before he could finish the job, Pyrrhus said. So, the body had been dug up and guards posted to make sure it didn't happen again. Everybody at the top table knew this already. This explanation was directed at Calchas, who seemed bewildered by the turn the conversation was taking. I could see he was already deeply offended by his reception. He'd not been asked to lead the company in prayer, nor to pour a libation to the gods. Now, Pyrrhus was needling him; there was real aggression in his manner and no sign at all of respect.

I filled their cups – silently, invisibly – listening. And suddenly, looking down the hall, I thought: *I've missed this!*

As the eating ended, the singing began. Pyrrhus had secured the services of a notable bard, of whom there were several in the camp. The bard sang alone, although there were choruses in which the men could join. Every single song was about Achilles, his short life and glorious death, his courage, his beauty, his frequent, terrifying rages. I remember one of the songs was called simply 'Rage'. I happened to be standing in the shadows at the side of the top table, so I could see Pyrrhus' face. It must have been a source of pride to him to hear his father's achievements extolled in words and music – and these were some of the best words and greatest music I'd ever heard, but looking at him I did wonder whether there were other, more painful, emotions at work. In some parts of the camp – and not just in the Myrmidon compound – Achilles was worshipped as a god. There must have been times when Pyrrhus felt like a weedy little sapling struggling to survive in the shadow of a great oak. Did he ever doubt himself? I think he must have done.

The last song faded into silence. The men were on their feet, clapping, banging the tables, shouting their appreciation, while the singer took his seat at the top table and accepted a cup of wine.

Not long afterwards, Alcimus suggested to Pyrrhus that it was time for Andromache and me to withdraw. Pyrrhus looked blank for a moment, but then nodded. We retreated to the small room – the 'cupboard' – and sat on the bed where we ate hunks of bread and some very dry figs. Andromache kept taking deep breaths as if she'd been half suffocated up till then.

'Cheer up,' I said, as I got up to go. 'With any luck, he'll pass out.'

I crossed the yard to Alcimus' hut, but I wasn't ready to go to sleep yet. So I brought out a chair and set it down in the most sheltered part of the veranda. The hall was in uproar. It was always noisy towards the end of the evening, before the men spilled out in search of other forms of fun, but there weren't usually so many raised voices. I wondered if I ought to go across to the women's hut and warn Amina about the guards, but the girls would have settled down for the night, and anyway, I couldn't believe she'd take such an insane risk. Not a second time. We can all be brave once.

My head was buzzing with the sights and sounds of dinner, snippets of overheard conversation that meant nothing in themselves but together formed a pattern. Pyrrhus, the young men from Skyros whom he couldn't, or wouldn't, control. Alcimus' watchful face as he looked up and down the tables, doing for Pyrrhus exactly what Patroclus used to do for Achilles – heading off trouble. But Patroclus had enjoyed Achilles' total trust, whereas I suspected Pyrrhus secretly resented Alcimus, who'd fought beside his father; who'd known the man he would never know. I understood the pressures Alcimus was under much better now.

The uproar was getting louder, though I couldn't hear what they were shouting. We were in for a rowdy night. I stood up and was about to go inside when there was a commotion at the entrance to the hall and Pyrrhus appeared on the veranda with Calchas, the two of them obviously arguing. The quarrel seemed to be about Apollo and the part Pyrrhus believed the god had played in Achilles' death. It was self-evident, he said, that no mortal man could have destroyed Achilles – it had to be the work of a god and everybody knew Apollo hated Achilles, who'd rivalled him in strength and beauty. From Calchas' point of view, Pyrrhus was spewing out blasphemies. He raised his hand, to protest, I thought, but perhaps Pyrrhus saw it as a threat. At any rate, he caught Calchas by the wrist and shoved him violently towards the steps. I don't think he meant to do him harm, but unfortunately, Calchas caught his foot in the hem of his robe and fell headlong down the steps on to the yard, where he lay spread-eagled, every bit of breath knocked out of him.

After a few seconds, Calchas raised his head. Blood was oozing from a deep cut on his cheekbone, turning the white paint to a pink mess. Pyrrhus gaped at him, at first in horror, but then burst out laughing. He might have left it there – and that would have been bad enough – but the young men from Skyros came crowding through the door behind him, laughing and egging him on. By now, Calchas had managed to get himself up on to all fours. Confronted by that tempting backside, Pyrrhus simply couldn't resist. He leapt down the steps, planted his foot squarely on Calchas' arse and knocked him flat again, before turning to his followers, yelling and punching the air. They, of course, clapped him on the back, ruffled his hair and pulled him back into the hall, shouting at the women to bring more wine.

My first impulse was to rush across to help, but instead I retreated further into the shadows, watching, as Automedon lifted Calchas to his feet and dusted him down. Often, those who witness a man's humiliation are resented almost as much as the person who inflicts it – and I had no desire to make an enemy of Calchas. Perhaps, as everybody said, he was out of favour with Agamemnon, but he was still a clever and powerful man. So, I looked on as Automedon supported him as he hobbled a few trial steps. I knew Automedon was a devoutly religious man and he'd deplore the insult he'd just witnessed. Some of the men around the campfires sniggered or openly jeered as the priest limped past. It wasn't even that they disliked Calchas; they were bullies, ready to turn on anybody they perceived to be weak, like weasels sniffing blood. Others, though, were obviously appalled. One or two even made the sign against the evil eye as Calchas, with his arm draped across Automedon's shoulders, shuffled slowly to the gate.

I think Automedon must have helped the priest all the way home because although I lingered on the veranda for a while, I didn't see him return.

18

The day following that incident, Pyrrhus ordered the men to muster in the yard and spoke to them from the veranda steps. It was an ill-judged performance. After telling them that an attempt had been made to bury Priam (they knew) he went on to say that anybody who tried that again would face the death penalty. He concluded by haranguing them on the subject of loyalty, though the Myrmidons were the most fiercely loyal to their leaders of any contingent. They raised a cheer for him at the end, but it was muted, and as the crowd dispersed, I saw glances being exchanged, though nothing was said.

I kept busy; the hut had never been so clean. But as soon as I sat down and closed my eyes, my mind again filled with images, like the tide tumbling into a rockpool: Amina pinning a wreath of purple daisies in Andromache's hair; Pyrrhus' flushed face and braying laugh; Calchas spread-eagled in the dust. One thing I did – and this may strike some people as treacherous – I asked Alcimus to get the guards to patrol the area around the women's hut. Whether he remembered to tell them or not, I don't know. Later that evening, I went with Andromache to the hall where we served wine at dinner, and the atmosphere there was tense.

Somehow Pyrrhus' speech seemed to have increased the bad feeling that had developed between the young men he'd brought with him from Skyros and the Myrmidons, a division that Pyrrhus appeared to encourage. I had no sense that these young men were his friends – I'm not sure Pyrrhus had any friends – but he seemed to feel a need to ingratiate himself with them. Towards the end of the evening, a fight broke out between one of the Skyros ringleaders and an older Myrmidon. He wasn't generally known as a quarrelsome man; he'd simply had enough. Alcimus intervened, followed by Automedon, but Pyrrhus gave them absolutely no support. If anything, he was undermining their authority, even though his own position depended on their ability to control his men. The meal ended with the lads from Skyros jumping on the tables in what amounted to a victory dance, applauded loudly by Pyrrhus. I had to keep reminding myself he was only sixteen.

That night, I slept badly, jerking awake long before dawn and staring into the darkness, knowing that a new sound had woken me. I sifted through the various noises the wind was making: it was running through its usual repertoire of moans, groans, sobs and whistles. The cradle at the foot of my bed creaked. Nothing new in any of that, but then it came again: an urgent hiss from the other side of the wall. Somebody determined to wake me, but not wanting to attract attention by banging on the door. I put my lips to a gap between the planks and asked: 'Who is it?'

'Maire.'

I was so drugged with sleep it took me a moment to bring her face to mind. She was the heavy, lumpen girl whose eyebrows met in the middle, who was always shrouded in a loose black robe – even inside the hut. Excessively modest; not even Amina went as far as that.

'What is it?'

'Amina's gone.'

'Gone? What do you mean – *gone*?'

But I knew what she meant. Without waiting for an answer, I grabbed my mantle and felt my way along the passage. She was turning the corner of the hut as I opened the door, her pale moon-face looming out of the blackness. 'You go back,' I said. 'I'll go and look for her.'

She nodded and was about to set off, but I caught her arm. 'How long's she been gone?'

'I don't know – we were all asleep.'

'All right, you go back now. Tell them not to worry.'

How much did the others know? One of my fears was that Amina was capable of dragging the other girls into her crazy crusade, though I didn't think she would. She was too proud of her isolation, her solitary, joyless rectitude. She'd be in no hurry to share the credit for the risk she was taking, though as I left the hut, part of me was still thinking: *No, she won't do it*. Not now, not with guards posted near the body, and Pyrrhus hell-bent on finding the culprit. She must have heard his speech; everybody in the compound had heard it. But there was another possibility – that she'd simply run away. Perhaps I might even – inadvertently – have encouraged her. She'd seen how much food there was in the abandoned Trojan kitchen gardens. She might think she could hide there, though what future would there be in that? With marauding crows, feasting flies, burnt-out houses, ruined temples – winter just round the corner? For months, at least, she'd be facing total isolation – and, in the end, vegetables rot in the ground, fruit on the trees. The supply of food that now looked so plentiful would rapidly run out.

I imagined her running across the battlefield, not because I thought she had, but because I knew she hadn't, and the alternative was so much worse that I couldn't bear to contemplate it. What I actually thought was evident in the movement of my feet, which were taking me to the stable yard. My mantle was made of blue wool, a blue so dark it could easily be mistaken for black, and I'd wound it tight round my head so that everything was covered except my eyes. I crept along the side of one hut, waited until I was sure I wasn't being observed, and then dashed across the open space into the shadow of the next. Through the wooden walls, I heard groans, murmurs, now and then a cry. Very few of the men in the camp slept well. At night, in the dark, memories of what had happened inside Troy were not so easily erased. I peered ahead. Either my eyes were becoming accustomed to the dark or it was just beginning to get light. There wasn't much time.

Torches were burning in the stable yard, their lights wavering as they always seem to do in a high wind. I had to be careful, because I knew a boy-groom slept in the tack room at the far end, from which he sometimes emerged, slack-mouthed and vacant-eyed, with bits of straw stuck in his hair. I hesitated and the horses, sensing the presence of a stranger, began to weave from side to side. They were restless at the best of times because they hated the wind. One snorted and kicked the door; another whickered a reply. I made myself stay put, but none of them whinnied again, so I left the shadows and crept across the yard.

Soon, I was on the cinder path that led through the scrubland to the horse pastures. Here, I felt more exposed, with no walls to shield me, and somewhere in the distance I could hear men's voices. Thick black clouds were moving across the sky, but I knew that behind them the moon was full and might emerge at any moment. I crouched down, trying to locate the guards, straining my eyes until the shapes of trees and bushes began to move about. Finally, I located them, two hundred yards further on. They'd lit a small fire and were gathered round it, their shadows flickering over the coarse grass. I counted three, but then one of them leant forward to throw a log on to the fire and I saw a fourth man behind him. Glimpses of bearded, fire-lit faces under hooded cloaks; they'd be well wrapped up because the temperature was beginning to drop. They'd positioned themselves downwind from the corpse, about as far away as they could get, while still plausibly claiming to be guarding it. I wasn't so lucky. Already, I'd noticed a slight taint on the air.

The ground ahead of me, my own hands, suddenly became lighter. The wind had blown a hole in the cloud and the moon peered through it – an old moon, haggard, empty of everything but grief. I thought of Hecuba and shivered, but really there was no room in my mind now for anyone except Amina. Where was she? I'd heard no sound, detected no movement – I actually let myself hope the guards' voices had frightened her away. She'd be on the beach, I thought, walking up and down as I used to do, schooling herself to accept the unacceptable. If I went back that way, I might catch up with her. I started to walk through the dunes, moving swiftly and silently, every few paces crouching down again to make myself less of a target for the wind. Above my head, the blades of marram grass shone silver in the moonlight. I told myself I might just walk quickly past the body, check she wasn't there, and then slide down the slopes of sand on to the beach and go safely home. But, immediately, I remembered I couldn't go back that way because the entrance to the compound was guarded and, though the guards would recognize me, it might be a little difficult to explain what I was doing wandering about in the middle of the night. *Worry about that later.* I dropped to my knees and crawled in the direction of the smell, trying at the same time to hold my mantle over my nose and mouth – a curious, crippled, three-legged crawl through loose sand. I kept stopping, straining to hear the guards, but either the wind was drowning out their voices, or they'd gone quiet. Asleep? Probably. I couldn't imagine a more boring job.

But then, I did hear a noise: quick, shallow breathing. I thought of all the predatory animals that might be drawn to the body at night. I couldn't shout to scare whatever it was away because that would attract the attention of the guards, so I had to continue on the path. It was getting lighter; the slope of sand ahead of me gleamed white. Any minute now the grooms, who were always up before dawn, would be taking the horses to pasture. One quick look, I told myself, and then I'd go back home. As I got closer, the breathing became louder, the smell indescribably vile – and then I saw her, a huddled black shape scrabbling away with both hands.

'Amina.'

She spun around, her face sharp with fear, realized it was me and hissed, 'Go away.'

I crawled forward. The ground around the body was disturbed – her fingermarks everywhere like the claws of an animal. Forcing myself to look more closely, I saw the body was almost covered, but with one skeletonized arm still exposed. The hand seemed to reach out to me. I remembered that same hand with a silver coin glinting on its palm – only now there was no palm, no flesh left at all. The white bones pleaded with me to be covered up. Without ever making a conscious decision, I found myself scrabbling in the sandy soil, exactly as Amina had been doing. We didn't look at each other – we didn't speak – but two of us working together got the job done fast. I wiped my hands on my tunic and started to stand up. But then, to my horror, she began saying the prayers for the dead. Light perpetual, rest eternal . . . '*Amina!*' I said, struggling to keep my voice down. There seemed to be a blockage in my chest that stopped my breathing – not some irritating little impediment like you sometimes get with a sore throat or a cold – *big*, like a man's clenched fist. 'Look, you've done what you came out to do. We've got to go back now.'

She shook her head. 'Not till I've finished the prayers.'

'You can do that in the hut.' I saw something on the ground on the other side of her, a hunk of bread and a jug of wine, both of them needed to complete the ritual. 'You've done this once already.'

'No, I didn't, somebody walked past, I had to stop. I've got to do it properly this time.'

'Do you think the gods care? You've done enough.'

But she wouldn't listen. And I couldn't leave her. So, we knelt there, gabbling the prayers for the dead: a safe crossing, a quiet sea, peace at the last . . . All the hopes we cling to, as we send those frail vessels out into the dark. I've never in my life heard the burial prayers rattled through as fast as we said them that night – and I've sat through some perfunctory funerals in my day. When we'd finished, Amina broke off a lump of bread and handed me the jug. The crust was hard, the wine sour – by the time I'd forced it down tears were streaming over my cheeks – and they weren't tears of grief either. Amina managed to swallow her crust, though she almost choked, and then poured the last of the wine on to the sand as a libation to the gods. The ground was so parched the drops bounced, before puckering the surface and sinking in. I noticed Amina had a red stain at the corner of her mouth and, in noticing that, I became aware of how light it had become.

Abruptly, I was furious. 'Now come *on*,' I said, seizing her thin arms and dragging her to her feet.

She was staring at me. I couldn't understand why she didn't move or speak, but then realized she was looking not at me but at something behind me. At the same moment, a hand grabbed the back of my neck. I felt a jolt run through my body; the baby inside me kicked. The other guards were coming up behind him. I twisted round, wanting them to see who I was, knowing the Myrmidons wouldn't hurt me. But when I looked from face to face there were no smiles, no hint of recognition. These were the young fighters from Skyros, Pyrrhus' men – and I knew I had no influence with them. Pulling our arms roughly behind us, they forced us ahead of them down the steep path to the camp.

19

We were led away from the grave and marched through the stable yard. By now, the sun was climbing steeply above the horizon, throwing a harsh light on the faces of the grooms who turned to watch us pass. Through the stable yard and on to Pyrrhus' hall, where there were more guards, Myrmidons this time, who recognized me as Lord Alcimus' wife.

'We should fetch Alcimus,' one of them said.

'No,' said the guard holding me. 'Lord Pyrrhus was quite clear. They're to go straight to him.'

And so, they pushed us up the steps on to the veranda, where they hammered on the door – and went on hammering for some considerable time before Pyrrhus himself came to answer it. He'd draped the purple-and-silver coverlet from his bed loosely round his shoulders but was otherwise naked. He peered from face to face, bleary-eyed from sleep, foul-tempered and bewildered by the sudden intrusion. 'What's this?'

'We found them burying Priam.'

Pyrrhus stepped aside and the guards pushed us ahead of them into the hall.

'*Women?*' Pyrrhus said, staring at us incredulously. 'Are you sure?'

'We all saw them, Sir – and heard them. They were saying the prayers for the dead.'

Many of the Myrmidon fighters had followed us into the hall. One of them coughed and pointed to me. 'That's Lord Alcimus' wife.'

'Is it?'

Pyrrhus had no reason to know I was married to Alcimus. Even if he'd noticed me on one of his rare visits to Alcimus' hut, he'd probably have assumed I was just another slave girl.

'*She* was there?'

The young men looked at each other, uneasy now, but then the one holding me nodded.

'Well, I suppose you'd better find Alcimus, then.' Pyrrhus, obviously feeling he had to seize control, jabbed his finger at one of the guards. '*You* – stay here. Rest of you, get back there – DIG THE BUGGER UP!'

I saw Amina flinch, but when Pyrrhus looked directly at her she met his eyes defiantly. I stared at my feet, dreading the moment when Alcimus would appear.

'I'll get dressed,' Pyrrhus said. 'Keep an eye on them.'

He strode out of the room. Feeling suddenly faint, I looked longingly at the bench by the table. I knew there was no point appealing to the Myrmidon fighters; they had no power to set against Pyrrhus. They just gawped at me in astonishment. God knows how long it would take to find Alcimus; he could be anywhere in the camp, feasting, drinking . . . Or in some other woman's bed. So, I simply stared around the hall, which, as always in the aftermath of the previous night's feasting, looked desolate and slightly mad. Smells of rancid fat, resin from the walls, smoking oil lamps – the rushes, though freshly laid the day before, were too tired to sweeten the air. Feeling dizzy, I started to edge towards the bench, but at that moment Pyrrhus came back into the room, his face knotted in anger. '*Why?*' he said.

Amina stared straight at him. 'I buried my king. I don't have to explain that.'

Immediately – no pause for thought – he hit her. The sound of the slap echoed round the room.

'You knew I said the body wasn't to be buried?'

'Yes, I knew. Only you can't do that – you can't just overrule the laws of god. Nobody can – I don't care how powerful they are.'

I thought he was going to hit her again, but there were footsteps on the veranda and that distracted him. Alcimus came into the room, dishevelled, tunic blotched with wine. He bowed to Pyrrhus, though his gaze was fixed solely on me. 'What on earth possessed you?'

His voice was low, urgent, not much above a whisper, but Amina heard it.

'She didn't do anything.'

Pyrrhus said: 'The guards caught them at it. *Both* of them.'

'Yes, but she wasn't burying him – she was just trying to stop *me*.'

This was both true and untrue. I closed my eyes, wanting to shut them all out, and saw Priam's skeletal hand reach out to me from the ground. I had helped bury him, not in obedience to the gods, but as a simple act of respect for an old man who'd been kind to me when I was a child in desperate need of kindness. For a moment, I was tempted to accept Amina's offer of a way out, but then I said – heard myself say – 'That's not true. I did help her bury him.'

Amina spun round. 'You did *not*!'

At that moment, I glimpsed the full extent of her pride. There she stood, chalk-white, Pyrrhus' fingermarks red on her cheek, glittering with pride. She wasn't trying to save me; she wanted them to believe she'd acted alone. Perhaps by now she'd managed to convince herself.

Silently, I held out my hands to Pyrrhus. They were covered in dirt; every fingernail was black.

Pyrrhus turned to Alcimus. 'I can't overlook this. I don't care whose wife she is.'

'I didn't know,' Alcimus said.

'She *didn't* help,' Amina insisted. 'She was just trying to drag me back to the hut.'

Alcimus ignored her. '*I*'ll deal with my wife.'

'No, you won't,' Pyrrhus said. 'They were in it together. You've only got to look at her hands!'

'What are you going to do?'

'I don't know – lock them up, I suppose.' Pyrrhus was shaking his head like a bewildered bullock. 'There's got to be somebody else behind it – can't be just women.'

Amina cut in. 'I keep telling you – there was nobody else.'

Suddenly, I realized she actually *wanted* to die. And that she very probably would die – and me with her.

Alcimus said, 'Well, there's the laundry hut – that's got a lock. And there's the armour storage hut. I don't think you should put them in together.'

I couldn't bring myself to look at him; he was betraying me – *and* Achilles. That was the real surprise.

'All right,' Pyrrhus said. 'We can decide what to do with them later.' He nodded to the guards, who stepped forward to escort Amina from the hall. One of them grabbed her by the scruff of the neck and shoved her along.

'*Hoy* — no need for that,' Alcimus said.

A hand closed round my arm. Amina and the guards had almost reached the door, when there was a noise outside and the guards who'd been sent to uncover the body — no 'digging up' would have been required; it was the shallowest of shallow graves — burst into the room. One of them, a skinny youth with blank eyes and odd, dislocated movements, was pushed to the front. I recognized him. When not required to guard corpses, he worked in the stables and was generally the butt of the other men's jokes, a sort of village idiot, though he could quieten a nervous horse better than anybody.

'Go on,' the other guards said, pushing him to the front. 'Go on, show him.'

The poor lad, dimly aware that he'd been chosen to take the hit, stood at the centre of the group and stared desperately from face to face, but Pyrrhus was surprisingly patient with him. Of course, he'd know this boy from the long hours he spent at the stable yard, doing — or so it was said — quite menial jobs, wiping sweaty horses down, cleaning tack, even mucking out the stalls . . . Work that men of his rank simply didn't do. Now, he leant in and asked, gently, 'What's that you've got?'

Reluctantly, the boy opened his hand, and there, catching the light, was a man's thumb ring — the one I'd last seen hanging from a chain round Andromache's neck. Alcimus and the guards had no idea whose ring this was — or why it mattered. Instinctively, I turned away, hiding my face — I don't quite know why — almost as if I felt my own recognition of the ring would somehow transfer itself to them.

But Pyrrhus had recognized it. 'I gave this to Andromache.'

'And I stole it,' Amina said, quickly. 'She was having a bath and she took it off and . . . and I stole it. She was devastated, searched everywhere – she more or less had us ripping the floorboards up . . .'

She was gabbling. Closing my eyes, I willed her to stop.

'Why?' Alcimus asked.

'Why did I steal it? To pay the ferryman.'

Normally, when you're laying out a corpse, you finish by putting coins on the eyes. They keep the lids closed, but the devout believe they're also used to pay the ferryman who rows the departed spirit across the River Styx to Hades, the land of the dead. Amina had no coins, no jewellery, nothing of any value at all; none of the women did. Except Andromache, who had Priam's ring. Was Amina telling the truth? When Andromache had taken a bath in my hut, she hadn't taken the ring off, but that didn't mean she never did. It was possible Amina had seized an opportunity to steal it. Just about.

The silence dragged on. Pyrrhus was looking around the room and I could sense he was beginning to see us all differently. Alcimus, me, Amina, Andromache . . . It must have been starting to feel like a conspiracy to him. Abruptly, without taking his eyes off us, he yelled: 'Andromache!'

She appeared so promptly she must have been listening at the door. As she walked towards him, I noticed her mouth was pinched with fear.

Pyrrhus held out the ring. 'Did you give her this?'

Andromache looked from his face to his hand and back to his face and said nothing at all – a rabbit mesmerized by a stoat.

'I stole it!' Amina shouted.

Pyrrhus spun round and hit her again. This time, she put her hand to her nose and brought it away covered in blood.

Turning back to Andromache, Pyrrhus said: 'We-ell – *did* you?'

162

'I don't know what happened. I had it in the morning, and in the evening, it was gone. *Sorry*.' She was sobbing. 'I'm sorry, I'm so sorry.'

Andromache was looking at Pyrrhus as she spoke, but I felt the words were meant for Amina.

Amina said, 'She didn't give me the ring. I stole it.' Blood still dripping from her nose, she stared straight at Pyrrhus. 'Neither of them helped. I did it – and I don't regret it for a minute.'

She turned away from him then and, of her own accord, walked to the door, while the guards followed along behind her, transformed into what looked more like a royal escort. There was silence after the door had closed after her.

Alcimus picked up one of the oil lamps and handed it to me. 'Make sure she keeps that.' The guard, a Myrmidon, nodded.

'All right.' Pyrrhus was speaking to Alcimus. 'We'll talk later. And you –' jabbing his finger at Andromache – 'GET OUT!'

20

Outside the storage hut, the guard stopped and began unlocking the door. Three locks, an indication of the value of the armour kept inside. When he'd finished, he stood aside and politely indicated to me that I should go in. I recognized him as one of the men who'd touched my belly as I'd served wine in the hall, a sign of loyalty to the bloodline of Achilles. Well, gestures like that weren't going to help me now. And it was Achilles' son who'd sent me here.

I stepped over the threshold. The guard closed the door behind me and fastened the locks. They didn't really need locks to keep me in. Where would I go? The lamp cast a circle of pallid light around the hut and I caught the gleam of polished bronze. At first, I squatted down next to the lamp and gazed at the thin line of light under the door. My hands were trembling; I put them up my sleeves to warm them, but I couldn't stop them shaking. All around me was the cold, heavy smell of metal and oiled cloth that seemed to settle on to my stomach and lie there like a stone. I think, at that moment, I understood how fragile my position really was. As Alcimus' wife, I'd started to feel secure in my new status, but standing there in a storage hut with a locked door behind me, I knew I'd never been more than an inch away from slavery.

My whole life, years, weeks, days, hours, had led me to this moment in this place. And one day in particular: the day my own city, Lyrnessus, fell. I'd gone up on to the roof of the citadel to watch the battle raging far below. I'd watched Achilles kill my youngest brother with a spear thrust to his throat. Before pulling the spear out, he'd turned and stared up at the citadel. I knew I had the sun behind me, I knew he couldn't see me – or only as a dark smudge looking down – and yet I felt he was looking straight at me. Gradually, in twos and threes, the other women had drifted up from the floor below and together we'd waited for the end. As the Greek fighters had pounded up the stairs, Arianna, my cousin on my mother's side, had grasped my arm, saying without words: *Come*. And then she'd climbed on to the parapet and, at the exact moment the fighters burst in, she'd leapt to her death, her white robes fluttering round her as she fell – like a singed moth. It had seemed to be a long time before she hit the ground, though it could only have been seconds. Her cry had faded into a stricken silence in which, slowly, stepping in front of the other women, I turned to face the men who'd come in.

Arianna said: Come . . .

But I chose to stay – and everything else, everything that had happened between then and now, had followed on from that choice. From my first hours in the camp, I'd been wary, alert, single-mindedly focused on survival – right up to the moment when I saw Priam's hand lying dishonoured on the filthy sand. Did I regret helping to bury him? Yes. *Yes!*

And, no.

It seemed to me, crouched by the door of the storage hut, that I'd merely blundered into it. I *had* gone out to try to stop Amina, I *had* tried to persuade her to come away, to leave the task unfinished, but then I'd seen Priam's hand and suddenly there I was scrabbling like a dog in the sand. I'd said the prayers, I'd drunk the wine, forced the stale bread down my throat . . . I'd buried Priam – and less than twenty-four hours after I'd heard Pyrrhus say the penalty for doing so was death. I'd thrown away all the gains I'd made in the past dreadful year. I really thought it possible that Pyrrhus would kill me, or have me killed. Amina would go on lying to save me – or to save her concept of herself as the only person brave enough to defy Pyrrhus and obey the gods. But I didn't think they'd believe her. Why would they? When I'd shown Pyrrhus the dirt under my fingernails.

I closed my eyes, and gradually – this was a slow process – I felt a presence growing in the darkness behind me. 'Presence' is the wrong word, but I don't know what the right word is. Opening my eyes, I forced myself to lift the lantern high above my head – and cried out with shock. Because there, lined up along the far wall, stood Priam, Hector, Patroclus, Achilles. The cry died on my lips – because of course they weren't there. Of course not. What I was seeing were suits of armour, not stacked in corners, as I'd thought they would be, but fastened to the walls, each piece in its proper place, so that together they formed the shapes of men. Men, instantly recognizable. Here was Priam's armour, which Hecuba had begged him not to put on. Blood all over it – you never wipe off an enemy's blood. Beside it, Hector's armour, his famous plumed helmet glittering in the light – but no shield with it. Andromache had begged Pyrrhus to let her baby son be buried inside his father's shield – and he'd agreed, though he'd regretted his generosity later. I could imagine how furious he would be, every time he looked at the empty space. Finally, Achilles' armour. The shield was missing from this too, but only because Pyrrhus kept it close by him in the hall, polishing it obsessively, as Achilles himself had done.

Raising the lantern higher, I looked up at the helmet. Whenever I moved my hand, light and dark chased each other across the metal, creating – or revealing – movement behind the eye-holes in the mask. I heard two people breathing where only one had breathed before. No words spoken; none needed. I don't know whether this meeting – and it did feel like a meeting – lasted minutes or hours, but it changed me. On the day Polyxena died, I'd stood by Achilles' burial mound and told myself that Achilles' story had ended at his grave, and that my own story was about to begin. The truth? Achilles' story never ends: wherever men fight and die, you'll find Achilles. And as for me – my story and his were inextricably linked.

A sound of somebody outside the door. It opened and a widening arc of daylight cut a slice out of the dark. The light hit me like cold water, bringing me out of my trance. Alcimus said, 'Briseis!' and as I walked towards him, he stood aside to let me out. All the way across the yard, I felt him rigid with fury at my back. Evidently the moment of reckoning was upon me, and that was confirmed when I entered the living quarters and found Automedon waiting there.

Alcimus sat down at the table. 'All right. Let's start at the beginning.' He pointed to a chair and I sat down. The light was dim, so he lit a candle and set it down beside me, close enough for me to feel the warmth on my skin. Automedon slipped into the chair at the head of the table – and I remember thinking that was odd because Alcimus always sat there. So far, Automedon hadn't even glanced at me. I resented his presence, while at the same time knowing I had no right to resent anything. But I felt I couldn't have a proper conversation with Alcimus with him sitting there. I wondered – for the first time, which is stupid, I know – if Achilles had hesitated over which he should give me to – and how long it had taken him to decide. I knew what he thought of them; he'd never made any secret of it. Alcimus was a decent man, kind-hearted, a good fighter, but young for his age and a bit of a fool. Automedon – you could trust him with your life, totally honest, no sense of humour, a self-righteous, intolerant prig. But both brave, both loyal – both completely devoted to him.

Alcimus cleared his throat. 'There's something I should say before we start. I told Pyrrhus you're expecting Achilles' child.'

'What did he say?'

'Not much.'

'It won't necessarily help you,' Automedon said – and I felt he enjoyed saying it. 'I think he's quite attached to the idea of being great Achilles' *only* son. Difficult to know how he'll react.'

'No doubt it'll become clear.'

I saw them exchange glances. Perhaps *I* wasn't reacting in the way they'd been expecting either.

'Right,' said Alcimus. 'Let's start at the beginning. Where were you when the men found you?'

'By the grave.'

'Standing up?'

'No, kneeling. I –'

'And you had soil on your hands?'

I nodded. He seized my wrists and pulled them closer to the candle. There was soil under my fingernails and a dusting of grit on the palms of my hands. Alcimus glanced at Automedon and the atmosphere in the room subtly changed. I felt a ripple of cold air across my skin, though the room was airless and thick with the smell of candle-wax.

Automedon leant forward. 'What about the first time? Were you there then?'

'No.'

'She'd not said anything?'

I hesitated and caught a glint in his eyes. This was an interrogation. I looked to Alcimus for some warmth, some acknowledgement of the relationship between us, but I got nothing back. If we'd been alone, I'd have tried to be honest with him about the confusion in my mind, the unintended switch from trying to stop Amina to helping her. I'd have told him about meeting Priam on the battlements and how kind he'd been. But there they were, the two of them, and I didn't think Automedon had ever been confused in his life.

He was still waiting for me to speak.

'Only that she was horrified Priam hadn't been buried.'

'Did she tell you what she was going to do?'

'No.'

Alcimus said, 'So, when you found out he'd been buried what did you think had happened?'

'I didn't know.'

He was leaning in closer. The table was between us, only it didn't feel like that; he seemed to be breathing into my face. And he looked different: older, leaner, more focused. The infatuated boy – and I did think he'd been infatuated with me once – was gone, and in his place was somebody altogether more formidable. This was the man who'd taken part in the final assault on Troy and done nameless things inside its walls. No longer 'young for his age'; no longer 'a bit of a fool'. I felt I was seeing him for the first time.

After a pause, I said, 'Well, you were saying it must be Helenus or Calchas, so I suppose I thought it was one of them.'

Automedon thumped the table. 'No, you didn't! You *knew* who it was.'

169

'Look, she just said Priam deserved a proper burial. It's only what any Trojan would have said.'

'Any Trojan *fighter.*'

'Do you think women have no views? No loyalties?'

'A woman's loyalty is to her husband.'

Alcimus got up and fetched a jug of wine from the sideboard. He poured two cups and then, after a fractional hesitation, a third for me.

'Right,' he said. 'Last night. Did you know what she was going to do?'

'I had absolutely no idea.'

Not an outright lie, but not exactly the truth either. They sat in silence, staring at me. United. At that moment, I felt I'd lost my husband, while at the same time suspecting I'd never really had one. I wanted to ask what they thought Pyrrhus was going to do, but I didn't dare; I was too afraid of the answer.

Automedon: 'So when did you find out?'

'One of the girls knocked on the door. Don't ask me which one, I don't know all their names. Some of them still can't speak.' *Careful. Don't let the anger show.*

'Well, evidently this one could. What did she say?'

'That Amina wasn't in the hut. That she'd gone.'

'So, what did you think had happened?'

'I thought she'd run away. I certainly didn't think she was burying Priam.'

Automedon was shaking his head.

'We'd just been to the gardens. There's shelter there, plenty of food. I thought she might have gone there –'

'But you didn't go looking for her there, did you? You went to where you knew the body was.'

There was no denying that. And looking back, the idea that Amina might have run away had never been more than a passing thought. Amina would never have run away from anything.

Alcimus: 'What did you find when you got there?'

'She'd almost finished. I just wanted it to be over, I wanted her back inside the hut. Safe.'

'So, you helped her bury Priam?' Alcimus barked a laugh. 'My god, woman.'

It was too late now for anything but the truth. 'Look, I *was* trying to save Amina. But you know what? You're absolutely right, I buried Priam. Because I respected him. Because it was shameful to leave him lying there. You both met him – when he came to see Achilles, you met him. You know what happened that night. Achilles made him welcome, he gave him food, he gave him a bed, he treated him with *respect* – he even gave him his own knife to eat with. Do you think *he*'d want this?'

They glanced at each other. I could see them reading the truth in each other's faces, but neither of them was going to admit it.

'You *know*,' I said. 'Both of you – you *know* Achilles would have wanted Priam buried.'

Alcimus said, heavily, 'Your first duty is to me.' He took a deep breath. 'Just as mine is to you.'

I laughed; I couldn't help myself. 'No, Alcimus, we both know your first duty is to *this*.' I pulled the loose fabric of my tunic tight across my belly.

'Shouldn't that be your first duty as well?'

I felt ashamed in front of him then: his single-minded commitment to a child that wasn't his contrasted so sharply with my own doubts, my own ambivalence.

Automedon had been silent throughout all this, doodling with a spillage of wine on the table, turning it into a spider, giving it legs. 'I think we can find a way round this,' he said, at last. 'The girl says she acted on her own. Well, good, let her say it. All Briseis needs to do is keep saying she was trying to stop her. I think she might get away with it. Possibly.'

She. This was Automedon at his smoothest, his chilliest. 'Aren't you forgetting the guards?' I said. 'They know I was covering the body – they saw me.'

'You can leave the guards to us,' Automedon said. 'If we tell them they saw you trying to drag the girl away, that's what they'll say. As long as the girl doesn't change her story . . .'

'She won't,' I said. No, Amina would be where she'd always wanted to be: in a circle of blazing torches, every eye focused on her, and her alone. Perhaps I should have felt relieved, but I didn't. 'What's going to happen to her?'

Alcimus shrugged. 'It's nobody's business what he does with her. She's his slave.'

'But what do you *think* he'll do?'

'I don't know. I suppose if she's lucky he might sell her on. Anyway, it's got nothing to do with you. The less you have to do with her now, the better.' And with that he stood up, bringing the interrogation to a close.

'One more question,' Automedon said. 'Did you talk to Calchas? Or Helenus?'

Mutely, I shook my head.

'Well, that's a relief. Did she?'

'No – how could she? They're not allowed out of the hut.'

At the door, Alcimus turned. 'Look, while I'm out, don't open the door to anybody, right? Say you're ill or something. Don't let anybody in.'

Alcimus went out first – I couldn't help thinking he was glad to get away – but Automedon lingered. When he was sure Alcimus was out of earshot, he said, 'Be careful, Briseis. You *might* get away with it this time, pleading your belly, but you won't always be as lucky.'

He might as well have punched me. I thought of the women in Troy who'd been stabbed in the stomach or speared between their legs on the fifty–fifty chance their baby might be a boy. No amount of 'pleading their bellies' would have helped them. Of course, I didn't dare mention that. What happened in Troy had already become a sinkhole of silence.

But I wasn't going to let that go entirely. '*I* didn't plead my belly,' I said. 'Alcimus did. And you know what, Automedon? If you'd been there, you'd have done exactly the same.'

Then I turned away, without waiting for his reply.

21

I spent the rest of the day alone. Once, I went out and sat on the veranda, but I thought one or two of the fighters who walked past were staring at me, so I went back inside. I cooked, I changed the beds, I swept the floor. I didn't allow myself to sit down until late afternoon and then I think I must have dropped off because when I next became aware of my surroundings somebody was knocking on the door. Alcimus had told me not to let anybody in, but the door was pushed open before I'd even got out of my chair. I couldn't see anything clearly, only a bulky shape and a gleam of pale eyes. Pyrrhus. I stood up, remembering, though only just in time, to bow.

He came a little further into the room.

'I'm afraid Alcimus isn't here,' I said.

'No, I know, he's gone to see Menelaus. I suppose I should have gone too, but I just didn't feel like it.'

I pulled a chair away from the table and waved him towards it. 'Please . . .'

Without needing to be asked, I went to the wine store in the sideboard and poured him a cup of the best wine, realizing as I took it across to him that, for the first time ever, I was seeing Pyrrhus sober. He more than filled his chair, meaty thighs spread wide apart — massive; and yet there was an adolescent gawkiness about him that suggested he hadn't yet grown into his full strength – god help us. I remembered my brothers at that age, how clumsy they'd been, scarcely able to get across a room without bumping into furniture. He looked up as he took the cup, and smiled. I didn't find the smile reassuring. It occurred to me that when Alcimus warned me not to let anybody in, he might have been thinking of Pyrrhus, but hadn't been able to bring himself to say it outright.

This visit was unconventional, to say the least – men don't normally visit women when their husbands are known to be absent – but Pyrrhus didn't seem to think there was anything odd about it. To say he was retarded would give entirely the wrong impression, and yet there was something lacking. He didn't seem to know how people normally behaved, how relationships worked, and so he was always breaking the rules, not because he was driven to rebel against them, but simply because he wasn't aware that they existed. Or perhaps he thought they didn't apply to him.

'Won't you have a drink with me?' he said.

So, I poured myself a cup – still in silence – and sat down opposite him. I was too wary to speak.

'Alcimus says you're expecting Achilles' child?'

'Yes, I thought you knew?'

He shook his head.

'The Greek army gave me to Achilles as his prize of honour after he sacked Lyrnessus – and then, when he knew he was going to die, he gave me to Alcimus. He thought Alcimus would be a good protector for the child.'

'Well, he was right there. Good choice.'

I sensed he hadn't come to talk about Priam's burial and I think the relief of that made me a little mad. At any rate, I drank half a cup of strong wine much too quickly, and when I looked up again, I saw he was holding out his hand.

'Look.'

I leant forward. Realizing I still couldn't see, he got up and came towards me, his huge bulk blotting out the light. I felt him put something into my hand, and then he stepped aside to let the lamplight fall on it. I was holding Priam's ring.

'Do you know what that is?'

'Yes, it's Priam's ring.' I tried to hand it back.

'Definitely Priam's? Not Hector's?'

'No, Priam's – he always wore it. I think it was Hecuba's gift on their wedding day.'

'But you've seen it since then?'

'Yes, Andromache showed it to me, she said you'd given it to her. She said how kind it was.'

'*Huh.*'

He returned to his chair. For a moment, I thought that was it, but then he said, 'Sometimes I think people mistake kindness for weakness.'

'I'm sure some people do – but not Andromache. She's not like that.'

'I offered her a whole tray of jewellery – bracelets, necklaces . . . All of it fit for a queen. And she chooses a man's ring?'

'Well, she wore it round her neck.' I couldn't think of a single good reason why he'd be pursuing this. I was being asked to implicate Andromache in Priam's burial.

'Do you honestly believe that girl stole it?'

That girl. Poor Amina, she didn't even have a name. To put off answering, I took a sip of my wine and tried to think. Any lie I told to help Andromache would make things worse for Amina – but then, they couldn't be much worse. Perhaps I should try to save the one person who could still be saved? 'Look, all I know is Andromache was frantic when she lost it. She was; she was really, *really* upset.'

'You're a loyal friend.'

Was I? I felt that was the last thing I was. 'Have you spoken to Andromache?'

'No, I want to get the truth out of the girl first.'

I tried to close my mind to what 'getting the truth out of the girl' might involve. His huge hands lay on his thighs in the lamplight. If he'd inherited nothing else, he'd inherited Achilles' hands. I found it hard to look away.

'Anyway.' He slapped his knees and stood up. 'Tell Alcimus it's all right.'

All right? 'Yes, of course I'll tell him.'

I escorted him to the door, relieved that this strange, unsettling meeting was over – but then, just as he was about to step outside, he held out Priam's ring, as if he were offering it to me. I took a step back.

'No, go on, I'd like you to have it. For . . . you know . . .' He pointed at my stomach.

'I couldn't possibly,' I said, firmly. I was remembering how he'd given Hector's shield to Andromache – and how bitterly he'd regretted it. He was a man who couldn't answer for himself for two hours together. 'No, you took this from Priam's hand, the day you killed him. It belongs to you now.'

He tried to push it into my hand, but once again I backed away. Finally, I managed to convince him that I wasn't going to take it. Immediately, he put it on his thumb, and I thought I saw relief flit across his features. The offer had never been real. He was always acting out some idea of himself, as if he were living his whole life in front of a mirror.

I remembered to say: 'Thank you. Please, don't think I'm not grateful, it's extremely generous of you – I just don't think it would be right to take it.'

As I spoke, I felt a rush of blood to my face. I just wanted him gone and, after a few further awkward words, he did finally leave. I watched him walk across the yard towards the hall. On the way, he stopped to greet somebody – one of the young men from Skyros – and they talked for a while. A burst of laughter, a bit of back-slapping, then Pyrrhus ran up the steps into the hall, and the darkness swallowed him.

22

Automatically, I picked up Pyrrhus' cup and took it across to the sideboard, though I was almost totally unaware of my surroundings. Again, I saw Pyrrhus put Priam's ring on his thumb: the destruction of Troy summed up in that one casual action. But something strange seemed to be happening: I discovered I could still feel the ring on the palm of my hand – I had held it, briefly – as if, somehow, that fleeting contact had left a permanent trace. I know it sounds trivial, but it wasn't. Not to me. It was one of those moments that I think everybody experiences – and they don't have to be dramatic – when things begin to change; and you know there's no point ruminating about it, because thinking isn't going to help you understand. You're not ready to understand it yet; you have to live your way into the meaning.

I lit several more lamps, then stood in the middle of the room, aware that I was casting multiple shadows. It must have been about mid-evening – certainly no later – and Pyrrhus had told me something I needed to know: that Alcimus had gone to see Menelaus. Menelaus was famous for his love of good food and wine and his dinners tended to go on far into the night. So, I was free to leave the hut and go to see Amina. I took food and wine with me and also, after a moment's thought, a lantern, because I wasn't sure she'd have a light in the laundry hut. Probably I shouldn't have gone – Alcimus had said the less I had to do with Amina now the better – but she was frightened and alone. I had to go.

Climbing the fence wasn't difficult. At that stage of my pregnancy I was still reasonably agile and there was a barrel on the other side to help me down. Getting the food across was easy – I simply tucked it into my girdle – but I had to abandon the lantern and the wine. Quickly, I crossed the yard. Men rarely came into the laundry since washing clothes and laying out the dead were both women's work. Most of the fighters probably didn't know the yard at the back existed. I tried the door, but even putting my shoulder and hip to the job I couldn't make it budge. Feeling sick with disappointment, I stood back. I'd been so sure this would work, that I'd be able to get in; but there was a lock and, evidently, they'd used it. Either that, or the door was hopelessly jammed.

I heard a movement from the other side of the wall and put my lips to a gap between the planks. 'Amina?'

'Briseis? You shouldn't be here.'

'I've brought you some food.'

'Well, thanks for the thought, but –'

'No, look, if you go along the wall to your right, about five paces . . .' I was trying to visualize the room as I spoke. 'There ought to be a gap. Can you see it? About shoulder height.'

I heard her fingers scrape along the wall. 'Yes, I see it.'

'I'll pass you something.' Slices of cold meat and bread. I'd brought apples too, but there was no way I could get them through the gap. 'Have you got enough water?'

'Gallons. There's something soaking in it, mind.'

'Has anybody been to see you?'

'Yes, they've all been asking questions.'

'But they haven't hurt you?'

'Not yet. I think Pyrrhus might come.'

'Well, look, if he does, just be honest with him . . .'

'Why shouldn't I be? *I*'ve got nothing to be ashamed of.'

'You could say . . . Oh, I don't know. Say you knew Priam – he was kind, and –'

'I don't mind saying that – it's true. Though if I'd never met Priam, I'd still have buried him.'

'And then – sorry, Amina, I know you're not going to like this – plead with him, get down on your knees, *grovel* if you have to. Whatever it takes.'

'Is that what you'd do?'

'*Yes*, if I had to.'

'Do you really think he'll take pity on me?'

'No, but he's a vain man, and he'll like the *idea* of being merciful – you can use that.'

'*You* could.' She sighed. 'Go back to your husband, Briseis. Live. Be happy.'

'I won't be able to bear it if you die.'

'*Ah, come on*, you don't even like me!'

(Which was also true.) 'At least, *try* to live.'

I wished I could see her face, reach out and take her hand. But there were only our two voices whispering in the darkness through a crack in a wall. It wasn't enough. I felt her slipping away from me, sliding through my fingers like mist.

'*Why* do you want to die?'

'I don't! That's a stupid thing to say . . .'

From outside the yard came a burst of laughter. A group of fighters walking past.

'Because I can't bear the thought of him touching me.'

'He hasn't shown much sign of that . . .'

'No, but he could. Any time – and I wouldn't be able to stop him. People are made differently, Briseis. Andromache can bear that. I don't know how, but she can. I know I couldn't.'

More shouts, more laughter. The fighters were gathering round the cooking fires, settling down to a hard night's drinking. I couldn't risk being seen. 'I have to go.'

I wriggled my hand in between the planks as far as it would go and felt her fingertips touch mine.

'I'll try to bring you some food in the morning,' I said.

Then I went back to my hut, wondering if I'd ever see her again.

23

Coming in from the darkness, there's always a moment when he remembers the room as he saw it when he first arrived in the camp. Five months ago, now, nearly six. Then, it had seemed rich, bright, welcoming, full of his father's presence, though Achilles had been dead ten days: his funeral games over, his body burned, his burial mound raised. Now, the living quarters just look bleak – so bleak Pyrrhus is tempted to go straight out again. There'll be any number of drinking sessions going on. He could walk across to Menelaus' compound – he'd certainly be welcome there – or anywhere else in the camp, for that matter. He's the hero of Troy, his reputation guarantees him a welcome wherever he goes. Except this room. Except this room.

What more do I have to do? He struggles to suppress the question, but up it bobs again. *What more do you want?*

Nothing to look forward to, that's his problem. No more battles to fight, no more glory to be gained. If the games get off the ground, he supposes he might win the chariot race – and that produces a momentary spurt of excitement, but no more than momentary. Absent-mindedly, he picks up a cloth and begins polishing Achilles' shield. Not everybody can lift it, but he can – easily. He props it up against the wall, places a lamp on either side, the flames warm on his naked thighs. By now, the design's as familiar as the lines on the palms of his hands, and yet so complex he always finds something new. Encircled by Ocean, the whole of human life plays out in front of him: two men settling a blood feud, a law suit, a war, a prosperous city, a city in flames – and a herd of cattle grazing by a river, a crowd of people with torches on their way to a wedding, young men and girls dancing, holding garlands of flowers above their heads . . .

A shield forged by a god. You can't put a price on this – because there's nothing like it in the world, nothing to compare it with – and he owns it; he owns every inch of it, all of it, it's all his. Except the meaning. Though it's not the shield he needs to understand, it's the man who once knelt in front of it, as he's kneeling now, polishing the metal until the flames in the lamps find other flames hidden deep inside the bronze. Once, Achilles' breath had misted this shield, as now his own breath does, and another hand, long since reduced to fragments of charred bone, had rubbed the mist away.

After a while, the sheer monotony of the polishing sets the mind free. Is that why Achilles used to do it? What *he* needs to decide – and he really can't put it off any longer – is comparatively trivial. What to do about that bloody girl. He still can't believe it was just her – there's got to be somebody else. Not Helenus, that was obvious the minute he hobbled into the room. Calchas, then – now he could easily have done it. Though, as Automedon said, why would he start being loyal now when the Trojan cause is lost? It's a good point – but still he feels it must have been Calchas. Awful creature, *awful* – but it looks as if he's got away with it. It's the girl who's been left to face the consequences.

Which brings him back to the original question: what are the consequences going to be? It's entirely his decision – she's his slave, he can do what he likes with her. He's no stomach for killing her. It's not that he thinks there's been too much killing – quite the reverse; there hasn't been nearly enough. He doesn't feel his reputation's secure. He fought bravely at Troy – without any boasting, he knows that. At the gates, and again on the palace steps, he'd faced dozens of Trojan fighters – not green boys who scarcely knew one end of a spear from the other, no, battle-hardened veterans who'd known bloody well they were fighting for their lives. He'd fought them and he'd won – but nobody seems to remember that. They remember him killing Priam – and he remembers too, bursting into the throne room and seeing Priam, on the altar steps, holding a spear he could barely lift.

And that's the problem. Just there. That's it. He's famous for killing Priam, and Priam's little grandson, and Polyxena, Priam's youngest daughter, whom he'd sacrificed at Achilles' tomb. An old man, a baby and a girl. Oh, the deaths were necessary: he doesn't regret them. Only, sometimes, at night, he feels a child's chubby legs kicking against his chest, and struggles awake, relieved to find it's no more than the pounding of his own heart. Heroic deeds, atrocities – who's to say where the line is drawn?

It's just not *fair*. If he could've waved a magic wand and transformed Priam into a young, strong man, the greatest fighter of his generation, he wouldn't have hesitated for a second. He'd have preferred it to be like that.

So, no – getting back to the present moment – he doesn't want to kill the girl, and yet he's got to make an example of her. If you once start tolerating disobedience in slaves, you may as well give up altogether. Flogging, that's the obvious answer – and make sure the other women hear the screams. *Or* – sell her to slave traders, save himself the bother. Actually, that's not a bad idea – there's a group of slave traders in the camp now, working their way from compound to compound, haggling over slaves not needed on the voyage home. She's young, admittedly not much of a looker, but strong, probably fertile; she'd fetch a good price. And that'll be the end of her – done and dusted, he'll never have to set eyes on her again.

But first, he needs a drink. Wine's the only thing that drowns out the dreadful silence in this room. Throwing down the cloth, he goes to the table and pours himself a generous cup. As he crosses the floor, he's careful not to catch sight of his reflection in the mirror because recently it hasn't been behaving exactly as it should. Once or twice, it's gone on moving after he's stopped. One cup, thrown at the back of his throat, two, slower – he hesitates over the third, but then decides against it. Better get the business with the girl over first, then he can relax.

Minutes later, he's striding down the path that leads to the laundry hut. This is where dead fighters used to be prepared for cremation. You carried them there, heaved them up on to the slab, left clean clothes, coins for their eyelids – and then you backed out of the room, leaving the laundry women with their pale, moist, fungoid faces to start on their work. Outside the laundry, there used to be a whole row of troughs overflowing with piss. You'd see the women, skirts kilted up round their waists, treading blood-stained battle shirts. Apparently, urine gets blood stains out better than anything. Sometimes you'd see men stop and pee into the troughs, now and then directing a jet straight at the women, who'd shriek and try to get out of the way. All good-natured fun, of course – the Myrmidons are a good bunch. No blood-stained shirts in the troughs now, though the smells still linger: the ferrous tang of blood, the sickly sweetness of stale piss. Something else too. Fuller's earth? Is that the name? Anyway, the stuff they use to whiten the sheets.

On the threshold, he stops to look around. The troughs are empty now. Since Troy fell, the laundry work must have got a whole lot easier: no blood-stained shirts, no bandages. God knows what they're doing now to earn their keep . . .

Since Troy fell . . . Those words still have the power to amaze. That night, cooped up inside the horse, he'd told himself that things had got to change – and change they had. Complete success, from his point of view. Oh, he might doubt himself at times, but nobody else doubts him. Odysseus has given him Achilles' armour – no more than his due, but still nice to have it, and, almost certainly, Menelaus is about to offer his daughter's hand in marriage – and what a brilliant match that will be: Helen's daughter, Achilles' son. Just have to hope she doesn't get her looks from her father. Everywhere, he's listened to, consulted; he dines on equal terms with all the kings. Nobody in this camp dare defy him now.

Except this girl. This slave.

Taking a torch from a sconce on the wall, he enters the porch and kicks the inner door open. A breath of fresh herbs, not strong enough to cut the stench of soaking wool. Somewhere in the shadows, he hears a scratching sound, the same noise a rat might make, but it's not a rat, it's the girl. Lifting the torch high above his head, he sends a tumult of shadows fleeing round the walls, but right at the centre of this chaos of light and dark there's a small, pale face.

Ignoring her for the moment, he looks around the room. At the centre, there's a long marble slab where dead fighters used to be washed and prepared for cremation. Above that, creaking and sway-ing in the draught, are two huge airing racks where damp shirts are put to dry. There are a few hanging there now, casting man-shaped shadows that swing from side to side as the racks move, an oddly disorientating experience, because the room seems to be full of fighting men – and yet it's silent. Ranged along the benches that line the walls, there are dozens of candles, all, to varying degrees, burned down, melted wax running down their sides like tears.

'Let's have these lit, shall we?'

No reply, but then he wasn't exactly expecting an answer. He lines up the candles, taking his time – not knowing why he's taking his time – and lights them, one by one. He feels her eyes follow him from flame to flame to flame. Not all the candles survive. Some flicker into life but immediately gutter and die. Still, by the time he's finished, the benches are crowded with tiny lights. The room's no longer a squalid, stinking hole where creatures barely identifiable as human eke out a miserable existence – no, it's a palace, a royal bedroom decorated for a wedding night.

Lighting the last candle, he waits to see if it will burn, then turns to face the girl. A plain, slightly masculine face, though striking. He must have chosen her, though he can't for the life of him think why. Perhaps he didn't? Perhaps she's one of the women allocated to him by lot. Thick eyebrows, protuberant eyes, square jaw; nothing there to get you going. She's certainly not a patch on Helle, the girl he saw dancing round the fire.

For a moment, he can't think of her name, but then it comes back to him. 'Amina.'

No response. She might as well be carved from wood. He moves towards her; with the marble slab behind her she can't back away. Spread out across the surface, there are swathes of fresh herbs, blocks of salt, scrubbing brushes, bowls full of soaking clothes whose sodden folds rise above the scummy water like rocks exposed at low tide. So many sources of light in this room now – all of them casting shadows – but at least they can see each other clearly. Going back to the door, he slots the torch into a sconce, then walks slowly back towards the slab, enjoying the creak of floorboards under his measured tread.

'You know,' he says, at last – and his voice sounds strange after the long silence. 'This really doesn't need to be a problem. If I tell the guards not to mention it to anybody they won't, simple as that. We can all forget about it. But, you see, a lot depends on how many other people know. Did you meet anybody else out there?'

'Only Briseis. And she was just trying to stop me.'

'So you keep saying. What about the other girls? Did they know?'

'No.'

'Oh, c'mon, you must've said *something*. I mean, there you are, leaving the hut in the middle of the night . . . Where did they *think* you were going?'

'I just said I had to get out. It was true – I hate being shut in.'

'This must be a real nightmare?' He sees her glance from side to side, as unsettled by the swinging shadows as he is himself. 'So, you didn't tell Andromache?'

'No.'

'She didn't give you the ring?'

'I stole it.'

It's only now when he hears himself asking these questions that he realizes this is what matters. He can't bear the idea of people conspiring behind his back – and he's still not convinced they didn't. The shadows are beginning to get on his nerves. Shadows and silence. Their voices – even her voice, which is a lot quieter than his – echo round the walls, and yet they seem to make no sound. There's the howling of the wind, but that's so familiar it hardly registers, any more than the sound of his own breathing. It's as if everything out-side this room – the camp, the cooking fires, the crowded huts – has ceased to exist, and there's only this moment, alone in this room, with this girl.

'But you knew whose ring it was?'

'Priam's.'

'Not Hector's?' That possibility still rankles.

'No, I knew it was Priam's. It was part of Hecuba's dowry – she gave it to him on their wedding day, and he wore it for fifty years. I hated stealing it, but then I thought: *Well, it's his really* – and anyway, he had to have something to pay the ferryman.'

'*Pay the ferryman?* Listen to yourself. Do you really believe souls wander about for all eternity just because they can't pay some fuck-ing ferryman who doesn't exist anyway? It's a story – it's not *real*.'

'I know what I believe, Lord Pyrrhus.' Staring straight at him. 'Do you?'

Too bold for a slave; slaves are trained not to look at you, they're trained to face the wall as you go past. He's not as firmly in control of this situation as he ought to be – she'd been terrified when he first came into the room. He'd smelled it on her – but she's not terrified now. Time to rattle her cage a bit.

'Briseis says she helped you.'

'She's lying.'

'Why would she lie about that?'

'She didn't help me. Nobody did.'

She's angry now. Watching her eyes flare like that, it's like he's seeing her for the first time; except it's not the first time. Something that's been gnawing at the edges of his mind ever since the guards pushed her into the hall finally crawls into the light. She was one of the women in the throne room who'd surrounded Hecuba. The more he looks at her the more convinced he is. The goggle eyes, the frog mouth . . . No, there's no mistake, it's not a face you'd ever forget – it's her all right. She's the one who stood up and stared him out when all the others ran away. It takes a moment for the implications to sink in. She'd seen it all: his desperation, his clumsiness, his repeated, cack-handed attempts to dispatch an old man who should've been as easily killed as a rabbit. She'd seen everything.

'You were there, weren't you?'

'Yes.'

She doesn't need to say anything more; he reads the contempt in her eyes. And now there's no stopping the torrent of memory: the slippery feel of Priam's hair, the shameful hacking-away at the scrawny old neck, Priam's stubbornness, his obdurate refusal to die. *Why wouldn't he die?* How close had the women been? Can't remember. He hadn't really been aware of them till it was over and their screaming started to get on his nerves. He'd seen them then, of course – and it's not as if he'd forgotten they were there, he's always known they were. Only he's never thought of them as witnesses, not in the same way that Greek fighters would have been witnesses. Nobody would listen to *them* . . . but that's not what matters. They *know*.

'Did you hear what he said?'

She smiles – actually smiles. 'Of course. He said: "Achilles' son? *You?* You're nothing like him." '

He punches her – no hesitation, no choice. Her head snaps back and now he's got her by the throat – her frog eyes are really popping out. He wants her to see his face; he wants his face to be the last thing she ever sees. Her hands are behind her, scrabbling for something on the slab – he doesn't see the knife, feels it though, sending a jolt of agony from his shoulder down his arm. For a second there he almost lets go. The whites of her eyes are veined with blood. One last squeeze, a twist, and finally the threshing stops.

He lets her drop. Stands, wipes his mouth, feels the silence flow through him, cool as water. She's dead. Is she dead? Still twitching, but no, she's dead. How small she is. He stares round the room at the candles that have gone on burning and are still burning, as if nothing's happened. Well, nothing much has. He looks down at his shoulder – just a scratch – and then at the candles again, only now they're turning into eyes, dozens of eyes, all staring, all watching. He doesn't want to leave her on the floor like that. Sweeping the rubbish from the slab on to the floor, he picks her up and lays her on the white marble. Still twitching a bit – her neck's crooked, but he doesn't want to straighten it, he doesn't like the feel of her, her sharp bones under the soft skin. Going to the door, he takes the torch from the sconce and turns to look back.

The candles are watching him. How many women were in the hall when he killed Priam? How many pairs of eyes saw him botch the job? How many ears heard what Priam said as he lay dying? Thirty? Forty? They'll be scattered all over the camp, those women. Do they whisper about it in the women's huts at night? He's got to get a grip on his thoughts. What does it matter what slaves think, or say? Their whispers can't hurt him. Oh, but they do. From now on, he'll hear them wherever he goes, little worms of sound gliding over every surface, everything he touches. He looks at the girl lying on the slab surrounded by flames that have become eyes and he just wants to run away, he who's never run away from anything in his life. *She's dead*, he tells himself, looking blindly round the room. *She can't hurt me now.*

24

After yet another night of shallow sleep and convoluted dreams, Calchas is woken by a peremptory rapping on his door. Still dazed, he crawls to answer it and finds, standing on his threshold, flanked by guards, one of Agamemnon's heralds.

'Come in,' he says, eagerly. Though even as he speaks, he remembers the bucket in the corner. 'No, no, wait, I'll come out.'

Fingers trembling, he reaches for his best cloak and wraps it round himself, feeling even in his agitated state a moment of reassurance as good-quality wool settles on to his shoulders. He is a priest, after all – a high priest being summoned to see a king. Yes, a powerful and mighty king – yes, yes, all that – but priests do have their own authority, even, or so he tells himself, in the presence of kings.

This burst of confidence carries him all the way to the steps of Agamemnon's hall. It's gloomy inside – only a couple of lamps lit; his feet, shuffling through the rushes, release a cloud of tiny, stingless insects. On the threshold of Agamemnon's living quarters, the herald holds up his hand and Calchas is obliged to stop. *Jumped-up little pipsqueak.* A man of no ability whatsoever, there are fish with more brains, given this job solely because of his impressive appearance and noble birth. Oh, and of course the right accent – let's not forget that! And yet his position gives him daily access to Agamemnon, access which, for weeks now, has been denied to Calchas. Feeling querulous and ill, he peers over the herald's shoulder into the darkness beyond, but can see nothing. There's no glimmer of light coming from under Agamemnon's door – no voices either. He strains to hear, but the only sound's a rustle in the rushes behind him. When he turns, he sees another herald and, behind him, red-eyed and bad-tempered, Odysseus. Calchas bows low, but receives only a grunt in reply.

What's Odysseus doing here? Obviously, he has great influence – the man who brought this interminable war to a victorious conclusion – and, if you can believe the gossip, he's more powerful now than he's ever been. Nestor's ill – some people say *very* ill – and Agamemnon's quarrelled with his brother, so he's probably leaning more heavily on his few remaining counsellors. A conference, then, rather than a consultation? A review of what's gone wrong, and why?

They stand there, each desperate to know why the other has been summoned, but reluctant to ask. It's dangerous to admit ignorance – though it can also be dangerous to claim knowledge you don't possess. Normally, in such circumstances, conversation turns to the weather, but that's scarcely an option here, since 'the weather' is precisely the point at issue. So, Calchas smiles vaguely at nothing in particular, while Odysseus paces up and down, and hums, irritatingly, under his breath.

At last, there's a movement in the darkness. Agamemnon's door opens to reveal a circle of lamplight and there, his back to the light, his face in shadow, but instantly recognizable from his decidedly well-rounded physique, is Machaon, the king's physician. Calchas' heart bumps. Is Agamemnon ill? Is that why they've been summoned? If so, that's a worse crisis even than the gale. Stepping to one side, he bows to Odysseus to indicate that he takes precedence – you

should always let your enemies precede you into trouble, and anyway, being last into the room might give him a few precious minutes
to assess the situation before he's called upon to speak.

Agamemnon looks ill, extremely ill. That's Calchas' first impression, but then that's what Machaon's presence has primed him to
expect. Deep shadows under the eyes, three rows of bags – he looks
as if he hasn't slept in years – and his skin's the creamy yellow of old
ivory. But he's certainly not presenting himself as an invalid. He's
fully dressed, wearing a gold torque round his neck, sitting on the
chair that serves him as a throne. Behind his head, the rich gold-and-
ivory inlay on the back gleams in the lamplight. This is clearly
intended to be a formal audience. Only Machaon, going around
lighting more lamps, seems at ease, but then, by all accounts, he
spends a lot of time in this room. Arguably, these days, he has better
access to Agamemnon than any of the kings.

Odysseus puts his hand over his heart and bows low. Calchus kneels
to touch Agamemnon's feet. He feels the great man's toes cringe, and
knows that behind his back Odysseus and Machaon will be exchanging
glances, despising the Trojan way of showing honour to a superior.
They don't like this, the Greeks, they think it's a sign of servitude,
whereas their own upright stature establishes them as splendid, worthy,
independent, virile men. What fools they are. He steps back into the
shadows and settles down to listen. He's desperate to hear what Odysseus has to say, but nobody can say anything until Agamemnon speaks.

While they wait, Calchas glances round the room, his tongue
flickering out to moisten his lips. He notices that the bronze mirror,
pushed well back against the wall, is draped in black, as mirrors often
are after a recent death. The custom springs from the superstition
that mirrors are a door through which the dead can re-enter the

mortal world. So, Agamemnon fears the dead? Well, there are plenty of them to fear – young men with all their lives ahead of them do not go down into the darkness reconciled. Is this what he fears – the anger of the defrauded young? No, probably not. It's more likely to be one particular man he fears.

'It would have been better to have died in Troy,' Agamemnon says, 'than live the way I live now. Priam sleeps better than I do.'

'Yes, but you wouldn't want to join him, would you?'

Odysseus' words come out jarringly upbeat, dismissive of Agamemnon's obvious distress. *Careful*, Calchas thinks.

'I have bad dreams,' Agamemnon goes on, addressing Calchas directly now, as if he's the only other person in the room – and though it's flattering to be the focus of the king's attention, it's dangerous too.

Calchas says, hesitantly, 'A lot of people seem to be having disturbed nights. I think perhaps we're all wondering what we've done to offend the gods . . .'

We, he says, though he doubts if anybody in this room regards him as 'one of us'. Once before, he'd angered Agamemnon, but then he'd had Achilles' protection. Nobody, then, would have dared touch him, not even the kings, not even Agamemnon himself. But now Achilles lies under the earth and Calchas is alone. Flustered, he begins to tell Agamemnon about the sea eagle, caught by a rogue wave, unable to take off with its prey, but he tells the story badly, his fear making him stumble over the words, and long before he's finished speculating – cautiously – about what the sign might mean, Agamemnon's waving it aside.

'But we know all that! We know we can't leave. Fuck's sake, man, tell me something I don't know.'

'We-ell,' Calchus says, 'I do have one or two ideas, but it's going to take time and . . .' *Stop gabbling*. 'Do *you* have any thoughts? Sometimes the gods speak directly to a king.'

'Huh, I've had plenty of time to think, lying here night after night – and my first thought was: it's *him*.'

He gestures towards Machaon, who looks alarmed – as well he might – but Agamemnon's eyes are staring straight through him at the shrouded mirror. 'Cloth's bloody useless,' Agamemnon says. 'Need more than cloth to keep *him* out.'

'Who is it you mean?' Odysseus asks.

'Achilles, of course.'

Agamemnon says the name reluctantly, and indeed, at that moment, Calchas feels a chill run round the room: the fear of the supernatural, the uncanny . . . Or is it, perhaps, the fear of madness?

'Do you still see him?' Machaon asks.

But, like Odysseus before him, he gets the tone wrong: this is the jolly-the-patient-along voice of an experienced physician. In response, Agamemnon simply stares at him until Machaon's glad to look away.

Fear's thick in the room now, as unmistakable as the stink of rancid fat. 'How often does he appear?' Calchas asks, but deferentially; he's too wily a bird to make Machaon's mistake – and, in any case, he can't rule out the possibility that Achilles does actually appear.

'Every night.' A jabbing finger delineates the precise spot. '*There*.'

'Does he speak?'

Agamemnon shakes his head.

'Why do you think he can't rest?'

'Well, he never was much good at resting, was he?' Odysseus asks – only just not jeering.

197

Once again, he gets the tone wrong – Odysseus, who *never* gets the tone wrong. There's something almost reckless about him today – as if, after ten long years of navigating the quicksands of Agamemnon's whims, he simply can't do it any more. But he'd better start taking it seriously because however illusory Achilles' appearances may be, there's nothing illusory about Agamemnon's power.

'Isn't it obvious?' Agamemnon says. 'I promised him twenty of the most beautiful women in Troy – that's true, isn't it?' He stares at Odysseus, who reluctantly nods. 'Well, so far, by my reckoning, he's had *one*. The wind changed after Polyxena was sacrificed. Less than an hour after . . .'

'Yes,' Odysseus agrees. 'I'd only just gone on board.'

'Well, then? Don't you think that was Achilles saying, "Where's the other nineteen?" '

Agamemnon sits back in his chair and closes his eyes. For one horrible moment, he seems to be nodding off to sleep. Perhaps he really is ill. He certainly isn't speaking with anything like his usual authority; he isn't even projecting his voice properly. From where Calchas is standing, right at the back of the room, it's difficult to catch some of the words. This is the result of too many sleepless hours alone, following a thread of meaning though a labyrinth of fear. Of course, it's nonsense – worse than nonsense, blasphemous. As if any mere mortal – even great Achilles – could produce this disturbance in nature. It's so obviously the work of a god. But how to say so, without appearing to contradict Agamemnon, who may, at any moment, rouse himself from his drugged stupor and start insisting that more girls be sacrificed on Achilles' burial mound, that only by keeping his promises down to every last detail can he hope to appease that voracious ghost. How to stop him? Calchas knows he'll get no help from the other two. Odysseus thinks of nothing but his own self-interest, and Machaon can't assert his own faith in opposition to this madness, because Machaon has no faith. They're both rational men; they'll deplore the need for further human sacrifices – but they'll go along with it too.

Pushing Machaon aside, Calchas kneels and places his cupped hands round Agamemnon's knees – the position of a supplicant.

'What you've told us is deeply troubling, Sir. Perhaps I might be allowed to take a day or two to think about it – and to pray. I need to consider the signs. It may be some god is acting through Achilles' spirit. If I could just have a little more time . . .'

'Yes, yes.' Agamemnon swats his hands away. 'Take as long as you like. I'm not sure it's Achilles anyway. I said that was my *first* thought. I think we all know what's really going on here. My brother, taking that bloody woman back. Thousands of good men dead and all he can think about is fucking that whore. Do you know he's offered his daughter's hand in marriage to Pyrrhus? That girl was intended for *my* son. Right from birth.'

'Pyrrhus won't accept,' Odysseus says.

' 'Course he bloody will – he won't be able to resist it. Ungrateful little shite.'

Bewildered, Calchas stands up and backs away, wishing he dare risk a glance at Odysseus, but there must be no suspicion of collusion. Agamemnon's eyes are constantly darting from face to face and in his state of mind men readily begin to imagine conspiracies where none exists. He'd been so sure Agamemnon was blaming Achilles . . . Now, he has no idea what it's about.

Abruptly, Agamemnon stands up. 'Anyway, the other reason I

brought you here' – this is once again addressed to Calchas – 'is to marry me.'

'*Marry* you?'

'Fuck's sake, man, was your mother a parrot? *Yes*, marry me. And I want you two' – he nods at Odysseus and Machaon – 'to be my witnesses. We-ell?' He looks from face to face. 'Cheer up, everybody! This is supposed to be a joyful occasion.'

'Yes,' Odysseus says, hastily. 'Joyful, indeed.'

There's a rustle in the next room. A moment later, the door opens and Cassandra walks into the room. She's wearing a long blue tunic with silver bands woven through her hair. Behind her, comes a dumpy little woman with straw-coloured hair, evidently her maid. Cassandra looks dazed. Apollo's priestess, raped in Athena's temple – and the Greeks ask which god they've offended? There's two, for a start.

'Come on, then!' Agamemnon says. 'Marry us.'

Struck dumb, Calchas takes the scarlet band from his own head and winds it round their wrists, reciting the familiar prayers by rote, without needing to think about them – and just as well, because his mind's a perfect blank. As he ties the knot, he notices that the girl has bruises round her wrists – blue bracelets – and thinks, vacuously, that they match her robe. Vows are exchanged. She stumbles over hers; Agamemnon pronounces his loudly and clearly, with total conviction, though he must know the marriage is unlawful. He already has a wife and, though kings are allowed any number of concubines, it is the custom to have only one wife. Apart from anything else, this produces a clear line of succession, since it's always the queen's eldest son who inherits. Cake is produced, together with a dish of strong wine. They all break off pieces of cake, dip them in the wine and eat, though

Calchas' portion turns to clag and sticks in his throat. Odysseus swallows his with ease, but then he'd swallow anything Agamemnon handed out. And then it's over, a short, indecently casual ceremony.

As Calchas unwinds the band from round their wrists, he does what he's promised himself he won't do – he looks straight into the girl's face. A goat's eyes stare back at him, the same brilliant yellow, the same numbed look of a sacrifice – and then the moment passes and she's a girl again, a girl with bruises round her wrists. Now he looks more closely, he notices red marks on either side of her mouth, as if she's been gagged as well. Poor Cassandra, gagged one way or another all her life, most powerfully by other people's unbelief. No good will come of this impious, unlawful union. He only hopes the curse that follows will spare him. He was acting under orders, after all.

Odysseus proposes a toast. Agamemnon thanks him and then it's Machaon's turn. Cups are raised, congratulations offered and accepted. 'And now piss off, all of you,' Agamemnon says, waving them towards the door.

As they back out, they see him take Cassandra's hand and lead her into the next room.

In the hall, Machaon releases his breath with an audible *pouf*. 'What do you make of that, then?'

'What's in that stuff you're giving him?' Odysseus asks. 'He was half asleep.'

'Nothing wrong with my sleeping draughts. You're not supposed to take them with strong wine.'

'Yeah, like he's ever not going to drink!'

Machaon says, 'For a moment, there, I thought he was talking about more sacrifices. Girls.'

'And he'd do it too,' Odysseus says.

Calchas feels in equal measure alarmed and exasperated. Nobody seems to question why Achilles, who'd loathed Agamemnon when he was alive, who'd never voluntarily spent an hour in his company, should choose to spend the afterlife standing at the foot of his bed.

'Where's your thinking got you?' Machaon asked.

Calchas shakes his head.

'What about Little Ajax?' Machaon says. 'Raping a virgin priestess in the temple of a virgin goddess . . .? Isn't he the front runner?'

'Nah, he's too useful,' Odysseus says. 'If it comes to war with Menelaus, we're going to need all the allies we can get.'

War? Calchas still hasn't spoken and he's becoming ever more convinced that silence is his best option. Sometimes, at night, he lies awake and doubts his faith. In his darkest moments, it seems to him that all his agonizing over the will of the gods is no more than self-deception. Only now, listening to this talk of 'front runners' and the need for alliances, he knows it's not true. Without vanity, he knows himself to be a different kind of man. Not better, he doesn't claim that – but different. Somewhere in all this he thinks a real truth lies buried, and he won't be able to rest till he finds it.

'So,' he says, not bothering now to hide the sarcasm. 'Who's my best bet? Who do *you* think I should blame?'

'I'd stick with Achilles, if I were you,' Machaon says. 'At least he's dead.'

Odysseus pulls a face. 'No, I'd go for the "ungrateful little shite".'

'Pyrrhus?'

'Why not? Unless you enjoyed having his foot up your arse?'

They move off together, laughing. Calchas follows more slowly, bracing himself to face yet another tussle with the wind. The slight lull that often comes in the last few hours before dawn is already over. As he steps out on to the veranda, vicious little gusts blow specks of grit into face.

I'd go for the 'ungrateful little shite'. Unless you enjoyed having his foot up your arse?

Immediately after it happened, he'd consoled himself with the thought that very few people had witnessed it. With any luck, he'd thought, the gossip would be confined to Pyrrhus' compound – and might be a nine-day wonder even there. Of course, after all his years in the camp, he should have known better. The fact that nobody's mentioned it to him means nothing; they'd all have been sniggering about it behind his back. *Ignore it.* But he can't ignore it; it gnaws away at him, night after night, like a rat in his intestines. The damage to his reputation is real, and in this camp men live – and *die* – for reputation. Reputation is all-important. If people start to believe they can treat him with contempt, that's dangerous – and it doesn't just devalue him; it's an insult to the god he serves.

Calchas looks up at the stars. The wind's doing crazy things, making them swarm and dance like fireflies. After a few seconds he's so dizzy he's glad to look at the ground again. He wishes he could talk to somebody, but there's nobody he can trust. Hecuba? Yes, perhaps – though really a priest should derive his solace solely from his god – that's what he was taught, in the temple of Apollo in Troy. Though it had never really worked for him, even then. He'd always found his solace in the arms of strangers, at night, in Priam's orchards, under the trees. He'd so much like to be back there, just once, before he dies.

Out of some primitive impulse, he tries to pray, to ask for mercy, though he knows the gods have none – particularly not the god he serves.

> *Lord of light, hear me,*
> *Son of god, hear me,*
> *Slayer of darkness, hear me . . .*

But the long-familiar litany fails to soothe. He walks on, and on, wanting to tire himself out, before he goes back to the hut where he eats and sleeps alone. It's getting lighter now, the stars are beginning to fade, until finally, out of the heaving grey mass of the sea, the sun rises, as small and hard and cold as a stone.

25

Amina's death changed everything. I say that, and immediately I think: *How ridiculous!* No, it didn't – it changed absolutely nothing. For the first few days it seemed as though she had just sunk beneath the waves, unnoticed, leaving not a bubble behind. I went to the women's hut as usual, but I was aware all the time of that slim ghost flitting around the edges of the group. We still sat outdoors in the evening, but these were miserable gatherings. Then, one evening, about a week after Amina's death, Helle called for music. As always, the girls shouted out their favourites, but that night many of them asked for the song Amina had sung. I don't know why that song's so sad, because it's about a girl in love with a young man, a celebration of love with no shadow of parting. And yet sad it certainly is. When the music faded, we sat in silence for a moment, thinking about her. One or two of the girls openly wept, and even Helle looked suspiciously bright-eyed.

I was sleeping badly. After one particularly disturbed night, I got up and went out on to the veranda in my nightgown, with just a blanket thrown across my shoulders. Several of the fighters glanced at me curiously as they walked past on their way to the training grounds. The games were well underway now, the atmosphere in the compound tense, almost febrile, with excitement. I went back indoors and put

Alcimus' breakfast on the table. The bed was empty, but the covers had been thrown back so I knew he'd slept in it. He must have set off for the training grounds before dawn, as he often did these days. When, only a few minutes later, he came in, I saw his hair was stringy with sweat. After eating in silence for a while, he looked up. 'It must be lonely for you here.'

'Lonely?'

'Well, on your own . . .'

'It's quiet, but I'm all right – I don't mind.'

'I just wondered if you'd be happier living with the other women?'

Yes, I thought. *And then there'd be another woman waiting for you in the room at the end of the passage.* Because he had other women, I knew he did; all Greek men do. All Trojan men too, to be fair.

'I'll go if that's what you want.' I was afraid to raise my eyes. 'But it's very crowded in there.'

'Is it?' Of course, he didn't know. Only Pyrrhus was allowed inside the women's hut. 'I wouldn't want you to be uncomfortable.'

A glance at my belly where, as if in response to the attention it was getting, what felt like a tiny foot moved. 'How are the games coming on?'

Immediately, his face lit up. These games were the fighters' sub-stitute for war, and the training was going well, really well, though the men did sometimes get carried away with enthusiasm. One young idiot had just dislocated the shoulder of their best wrestler – in a training session! But at least everybody seemed to realize that if they wanted the games to continue, they had to stop fighting pitched bat-tles every time they lost.

I listened and admired and sympathized and by the end of the meal he seemed happy. I saw him off to the training grounds, and then I stood with my back to the door and shut my eyes. I *was* on my own too much – Alcimus was right about that – and visits to the women's hut didn't help at all, because everybody there leant on me. I had to watch every word, every change of expression, because I must never appear depressed or sad or frightened. I didn't mind, I accepted it, but it meant I could never be myself.

Ritsa, I thought. I needed to see Ritsa. But before I could allow myself to see her, there was another – overdue – visit I had to make.

Hecuba was quiet for a long time after I'd told her about Amina's death. This wasn't one of her better days. I thought she looked like an old mottled spider sitting there.

'Suicide?'

'Some people seem to think that's what it was.'

'But you don't?'

'I try not to think at all.'

She was rocking a little from side to side, more shaken by the news than I'd expected.

'She was Polyxena's friend, you know?'

'No, I didn't know.'

'There was only two months between them.' Her hands were perpetually pleating and smoothing the hem of her tunic. 'Ah, well. A sad end to a young life.'

Poor woman. She'd seen so many sad ends to so many young lives. I couldn't imagine what it must be like to survive your sons and grandsons – and then, when you thought nothing worse could happen, to lose your youngest daughter too. What was left to her really except grief and anger and the craving for revenge? A craving she had absolutely no hope of ever satisfying.

She looked at me, and her eyes were as sharp as they'd ever been. 'What *do* you think happened?'

'I think Pyrrhus killed her. Though I don't know why – he didn't have to do it.'

'Something else we've got to thank him for.'

I didn't know what to say to that, because there you have it: Pyrrhus, son of Achilles, my child's half-brother. The enemy. It doesn't get any starker than that.

After a pause, Hecuba said, 'Calchas came to see me. He'd not long left when you arrived.'

'What did he want?'

'That's a very cynical question.'

We smiled at each other.

'No, he came to tell me Cassandra's married.'

Again, I remembered Cassandra on the day she arrived in the camp: her triumph as she danced around the crowded hut whirling torches above her head, calling on her mother and sisters to dance at her wedding. Her absolute conviction that her marriage to Agamemnon would lead directly to his death.

Hecuba was shaking her head. 'I never thought he'd do it. I mean, I could see he was besotted, but I didn't think he'd actually marry her. He's got a wife already!'

'He obviously doesn't believe in her prophecies.'

'Obviously!'

'Do *you*?'

She shifted uneasily. 'I think a lot of it's completely random. People used to say it was Apollo speaking through her. I could never see it – I think she just made up things to suit herself. Anyway, it doesn't matter what I think – I need to see her.'

'Well, it's not easy,' I said. 'I lived in Agamemnon's compound, for a time – you were hardly allowed out of the hut.'

'Yes, but that's slaves. She's married now – he can't keep his wife locked up.'

I thought he probably could; but I could see how much the hope of seeing Cassandra meant to her, so of course I said, 'I'll try.'

She tried to speak, but choked and had to squeeze my hand instead.

'Was that all he wanted? To tell you about Cassandra?'

I was curious about these visits. I couldn't see what was in it for Calchas. At last, after a pause, she said, 'No, he was asking me about the time Priam went to see Achilles.'

'I wonder why he's interested in that?'

'Oh, he'll have his reasons.' She was sunk in thought, in memory. 'I didn't want Priam to go, I *begged* him not to, I was sure Achilles would kill him – I honestly didn't think he'd last five minutes once he was inside the gates – but he just said: "I've got to try. He's not a wolf, he's a man – and if he's a man, we can talk." *Talk? Talk?* I wouldn't have talked to him; I'd have ripped his throat out with my teeth before I'd have *talked* to him. He killed my son. And that wasn't enough, no, he had to drag him round the walls, tear him to pieces in front of everybody – killing him wasn't enough.'

'I hope you didn't see that?'

'No, Priam made them take me away. *He* saw it though – he saw all of it – and he still went to see him. There was nothing I could say that would change his mind.' Her fingers were busy with the hem of her tunic again. I was watching her hands because I couldn't bear to look at her face. 'I followed him into the store room. Torchlight, just him and me, none of the hangers-on, so I could say what I really thought. He was holding the Thracian cup. He absolutely loved that cup, and it's a beautiful thing, it is, but it didn't matter, it still went into the ransom for Hector. I told him he was a fool, I told him Achilles had no more compassion than a mad dog, but he wouldn't listen. In the end I just had to give up. I wanted him to have a proper send-off – because I didn't think I was ever going to see him again. I brought him a parting cup.' She laughed. 'He was sitting in a farm cart wearing a tatty old tunic – I thought he'd never looked more like a king. So, I prayed to Zeus to take care of him. He kissed me – and he was just about to drive off when he said, "Look!" And there were two eagles flying over the palace. Two eagles together, you never see that. He said it was a good omen and of course I went along with it. *I* didn't think it was. But there you are, you see, I was wrong – he did bring Hector's body back, and it was like a miracle. All those terrible injuries – they'd all vanished. He looked as if he was asleep.' She paused for a moment, remembering. 'And do you know, when we unwrapped the sheet, there were fresh herbs inside it. Somebody must have put them in.'

'That was me.'

'Was it?' She smiled. 'I thought it might be.'

We continued to sit in silence after that. I persuaded her to drink a little wine.

'Calchas wanted to know what Priam said when he came back. I told him to ask Cassandra. She ran out to meet him. I was too busy grieving for my son.'

A lot of bitterness there, and some jealousy too, perhaps. Cassandra had obviously been very close to Priam. I patted Hecuba's arm and stood up. 'I'll go to see her as soon as I can.'

Outside, a wrestling match had just started. A big crowd, quiet at the moment, were watching two men circle the arena, sizing each other up. Their oiled bodies gleamed in the bronze light. Everybody waited tensely for the bout to start, but the circling went on and on. 'Get a bloody move on!' somebody shouted. The men sitting round him laughed, but several other voices yelled: 'Shut the fuck up!'

In the arena, in their bubble of silence, the wrestlers made contact and grappled each other to the ground.

26

Cassandra and I got off to a bad start, which was neither her fault nor mine.

A maid answered the door and led me through into the living quarters, where I found Cassandra sitting in a carved armchair spinning wool. As she stood up and turned to greet me, I caught sight of her necklace: fire opals in a silver setting. I was too shocked to speak – though I don't think I gave anything away. The necklace had belonged to my mother, given to her on her wedding day as her bride-gift from my father. When Lyrnessus fell, it had gone to Agamemnon as part of his share of the booty. Now, I supposed, he'd given it to Cassandra as *her* bride-gift on *her* wedding day. As she moved her head, streaks of fire woke inside the milky stones. I couldn't take my eyes off them. Cassandra raised her hand to the necklace, but then seemed to mistake the direction of my gaze.

'Yes, I know,' she said. 'Looks awful, doesn't it?'

I was puzzled, until I realized she was referring to the rope burns on her wrists.

'People seem to think I was dragged kicking and screaming to Agamemnon's bed, but it wasn't like that at all.' She fixed her startling yellow eyes on me. 'I went willingly. Because I knew the sooner it happened, the sooner he'd be dead.'

'Did you tell *him* that?'

'No, I couldn't, they gagged me. It wouldn't have made any difference anyway. Nobody ever believes me.' Her hands were busy arranging sweetmeats on a plate. After finishing the display to her satisfaction, she looked up. 'His wife kills us, you know.'

'Is that right?'

'I mean, she has every reason . . . You can't blame her. You know what he did?'

I started to say 'Yes', but Cassandra ignored me and swept on.

'He sacrificed their daughter. It was a trap. He told her mother the girl was going to be married to Achilles and you know that would have been a brilliant match, so they all ran around making dresses and then they went to the camp at Aulis. She was sacrificed on the altar of Artemis to get the fleet a fair wind for Troy.' She smiled, and for a moment I saw a resemblance to Hecuba. 'I'd murder the bastard, wouldn't you?'

'Yes.'

'Oh, I'm glad we agree. I knew we would.'

I'd never met anybody like Cassandra, that curious mixture of the childlike – almost retarded, it seemed, at times – and the chilling. I wasn't sure how to respond.

She offered me the plate of sweetmeats. 'Try one of those, they're really good.'

I took one and then we sat back in our chairs, mouths full of a gooey mixture that made talking almost impossible. When she finally managed to un-clag her jaws, she said: 'I believe my family has reason to be grateful to you?'

I just shook my head.

'You tried to bury my father?'

'Not me, that was Amina,' I said, flatly. 'She paid the price for it too.' I had no desire to be thanked for an action I'd merely blundered into.

We went on chatting while she mixed the wine. There was something odd about this occasion and it took me a while to work out what it was. Cassandra seemed to have no recollection of our previous meeting. Perhaps it was the nature of the frenzy that she couldn't recall anything she'd said or done during one of her 'episodes' – or she may have remembered very well, but chose not to speak of it.

She handed me a cup of wine. 'I expect you've been to see my mother?'

'Yes, several times.' It would have been natural at this point for her to ask how her mother was, but she didn't. I said, hesitantly, 'I'm sure she'd love to see you.'

'I'm sure she would.'

'Well, then, why –?'

'I don't think so. I will go, I won't let her leave without saying goodbye – but not just yet.'

'*Why* is it so difficult?'

I didn't expect her to answer – in fact, I regretted asking the question almost before the words were out of my mouth – so I was surprised when she plunged straight in. 'It wasn't, to begin with. Not till Helen – that's when it really started to go wrong. You know, I watched them drive through the gates, Paris and Helen. I saw my father welcome her and I knew, I *knew* what was going to happen. It wasn't a vague premonition or anything like that – *I saw Troy in flames*. So, I clawed her face. I thought if I could stop her being beautiful, even just for a few days, Paris would come to his senses – and my father and everybody else – and they'd send her back to her husband where she belonged. Instead of that, *I* got sent away – that's when it all began. Apparently,

I attacked anybody who came near me, my mother came and tried to calm me down – and I attacked her too. So they locked me up. They had to force food down me, I didn't want to eat, I didn't want great big wobbly fat tits like Helen. I had women to look after me – guards really, but they weren't allowed to hit me. Didn't need to – Hecuba did that. With a hairbrush. I used to think she hated me – because I was the one stain on her perfect family.

'I got better, but by the time I went home everything, *everything*, revolved around Helen. Paris was besotted – Hector not much better – even my father! She could play him like a flute. There was some talk of marrying me off; I think they actually had some poor sucker lined up, but then it happened again. And again. And by this time, it was obvious nobody was going to marry me. Even being King Priam's son-in-law couldn't make up for the taint of madness. Who wants that in the family? So Hecuba decided I was going to be a priestess – a *virgin* priestess. Priam went along with it – he went along with almost everything she said – and I was packed off to the temple.'

'How old were you?'

'Fourteen.'

'You must have missed your family?'

'Not really. I certainly didn't miss my mother! I did miss my father, and Helenus. But, of course, from Hecuba's point of view – problem solved. Now, when I had fits of madness, she could say it was a frenzy sent by the god. Much more respectable. If I'd been religious, it might have made things easier, but I wasn't – not then, anyway. You must know the story? How Apollo kissed me and gave me the gift of prophecy, and then when I refused to sleep with him, spat in my mouth to make sure I'd never be believed?'

'I've heard the story. Is it true?'

'Of course it's true.'

I was starting to rebel against being the audience for an endless, self-justifying monologue. 'I'm not even sure I know what prophecy is.'

'Well, take a very minor example . . . I haven't moved from this chair since I got up, I certainly haven't looked out of the door, but I saw you walking along the beach and I knew you were coming here.'

'Hmm.'

'You don't sound convinced?'

'We-ell, I came to ask you a question – and I knew the answer before I arrived. Is that prophecy?'

'No, that's just intelligence.' She was looking intently at me, really seeing me, I thought, for the first time. 'You watch people, don't you?'

'Look, she's your mother. You've just got married – would it be so difficult to walk a few hundred yards?'

'You have no idea how difficult.'

I was beginning to glimpse the truth about Cassandra. Like Athena, who'd sprung fully armed from Zeus' head, she didn't owe her life to anything that had gone on between a woman's legs. So, Hecuba could be brushed aside as an irrelevance. She was – at least in that way – the opposite of me.

Anyway, I had my answer. I put my cup down – I'd barely touched the wine – and was about to stand up when there was a knock on the door.

Cassandra put a restraining hand on my arm. 'Don't go yet. That'll be Calchas – and he'll want to talk to you as much as me.'

I could hear the maid at the door letting him in. 'I can't think what he'd want to talk to *me* about.'

'Can't you? Clever girl like you – I'd have thought it was obvious by now.'

As Calchas came into the room, I smelled salt air on his skin, together with the rather less pleasant smell of the white paste he'd plastered on to his face. He was wearing a priest's robes and carried a staff festooned with scarlet bands. A compliment to Cassandra's new role as Agamemnon's wife? Or a visible reminder of their shared priesthood? They'd trained in the same temple, even slept in the same small room, though many years apart – Calchas must have been easily fifteen years older. Still, they had that experience in common. After he'd sat down and been given wine, they started reminiscing about the priest who'd trained them both, and then – with considerably more affection, I thought – about the ravens who'd been kept in the temple grounds, unable to fly away because their wing feathers had been clipped. These birds had been their childhood companions, their friends – and they'd been the same birds. Ravens live a long time in captivity. They all had a name, a personality, little tricks that they did. As I listened, a picture took shape in my mind of two very lonely children, each of them sent away from home before they were ready to leave. There was something incredibly moving about this – and it changed my attitude to both of them, but particularly to Calchas, whom I'd always thought a bit of a fraud. I wasn't so sure about that now.

After a short pause – Calchas was devoting his attention to the sweetmeats, getting through them at a surprising rate – he began talking about Priam's visit to Achilles, the night he went into the Greek camp to beg for the return of Hector's body. 'I believe you' – addressing Cassandra – 'spoke to him as soon as he returned?'

'Yes,' Cassandra said. 'I'd been on the battlements all night. I couldn't see a thing – even when it started to get light, I still couldn't see because there was a thick mist – but then suddenly there he was, driving that rickety old farm cart. I ran to meet him, I *made* them open the gates, and then I climbed on to the driver's seat beside him – and we drove into the city together.'

'In triumph,' Calchas said.

'Hardly triumph,' Cassandra snapped. 'We had my brother's dead body in the back.'

Calchas bowed slightly, an apology for his crassness, perhaps. 'Did Priam mention Achilles? I mean, did he say how Achilles had received him?'

'Oh, he was full of praise. He said Achilles walked beside the cart and saw him safely out of the camp. Apparently, the last thing Achilles said was, "When Troy falls, try to get a message to me – and I'll come if I can." And Priam said, "By the time Troy falls, you'll be in Hades with the dead." Achilles just laughed, then said: "Well, then, I won't come, will I? No matter how many messengers you send."'

I hadn't known about this final conversation until now, but I could hear Achilles saying that – and his laughter.

Calchas turned to me. 'Hecuba says you were there that night?'

'Yes, I was there. But before I answer any questions, I'd like to know where this is going.'

Did he look slightly taken aback? It was so difficult to read his expressions behind the mask of paint.

'I've spoken to Hecuba,' he said. 'And she told me how Priam died. She was there, you know? She saw it all. She said you wouldn't kill a pig the way Pyrrhus killed Priam.'

'I know. But can I just say in Pyrrhus' defence – Priam was armed, he was ready to fight, and he'd rather have died like that than be forced to his knees in front of Agamemnon.'

'Yes, that's true – but it doesn't stop me being angry. He was old, he could hardly stand up in his armour, he was butchered – and the man who did it was hailed as a hero. He's not a hero, he's a vicious little *lout*. And you can say a lot of bad things about Achilles – but he was never that.'

I saw his anger. I could scarcely avoid seeing it; it was literally cracking the paint on his face – and at that moment I forgot, or at least set aside, my instinctive dislike of Cassandra, my suspicion that Calchas tailored his prophecies to his own advantage. We were simply three Trojans talking together in a room at the heart of the enemy camp.

'Look,' Calchas said, 'the point we've got to establish is: what was the nature of the relationship between Achilles and Priam? Because, you know, it's perfectly possible they just did a deal. "Here's the ransom, check it out." "All right, good enough, here's the body." And that would have been the end of it. But if it was more than that, if Achilles accepted Priam as his guest, then a bond was forged between them. Guest-friendship. And that's a very different matter. Because there's no lawful way of killing a guest-friend. Even if you're on opposite sides in a war, even if you meet on the battlefield, you still can't kill a guest-friend. And the bond, once formed, descends from father to son – it's inherited. So, if Achilles and Priam *were* guest-friends, Pyrrhus and Priam were guest-friends too – and that makes Priam's death –'

'Murder,' Cassandra said.

I looked up – and found her staring at me with those brilliant yellow eyes.

'So, do you see now why it's important to answer Calchas' questions?'

I nodded, took a moment to organize my thoughts, and started telling them the story of that evening. But even as I spoke, another far more complex story was rising to the surface of my mind. That night was the most important of my life, the time everything changed. First there'd been the shock of seeing Priam, alone and defenceless in the midst of his enemies. And that was followed by a dizzying sense of possibility. I begged Priam to take me with him when he left, pleaded with him, but he steadfastly refused. He said the war had started when his son Paris, in defiance of the laws of hospitality, had seduced (some said raped) Menelaus' wife, Helen. So, he would not abuse Achilles' hospitality by stealing his woman away. There was my answer, but I couldn't – and didn't – accept it. I hid beside Hector's body in the cart as it trundled to the gates, aware all the time of Achilles walking beside it, only a couple of feet away. And then . . .

And then I thought better of it. Did it really make sense to go to Troy when everybody, including Priam, knew the war was lost? Did it make sense to endure the sacking of another city, a second enslavement? These were the reasons I gave myself for not escaping, for going back to Achilles' hall and Achilles' bed. I believe – though this is something no woman can ever be sure of – that my child was conceived that night.

Calchas didn't need to know any of that. He had no interest in me, except as a witness. So, as a witness I gave him exactly what he wanted, neither more nor less.

'We were just finishing dinner when the door opened and somebody came in. I looked up and saw that it was Priam. He was dressed like a peasant farmer, but I recognized him at once. Achilles didn't, he hadn't met Priam, and then, when he realized who it was, he was furious. He said, "How the bloody hell did you get in?" Priam said something like, "I was guided by a god" – and that made Achilles even more furious. He accused Priam of bribing the guards. And by this time other people had worked out who it was. They crowded round, and Achilles told them to back off. Priam was kneeling at Achilles' feet, clasping his knees. He said, "I do what no man before me has ever done, I kiss the hands of the man who killed my son." '

I looked from Calchas to Cassandra, wondering whether either of them could grasp the shock and power of that moment.

'Achilles could've killed Priam at any moment – he *chose* not to. Instead, he invited him through into his living quarters. Oh, and I remember he changed into a plain tunic, because obviously Priam was dressed like a peasant farmer. Then they sat down and ate together. Priam hadn't even brought a knife with him and so Achilles wiped his own knife and handed it across the table. I wasn't really waiting on them at all. Achilles poured the wine – I just put it on the table – and it was the best wine he possessed. He carved the meat for Priam; he even held the bowl for him to wash his hands. Then – well, Priam was obviously exhausted, so Achilles told me to make up a bed for him. I remember him saying: "Take the furs from my bed if you like, I don't want him to be cold." And then the following morning – I'd taken water for Priam to wash – Achilles was up early, in full armour. He told Priam the sooner he was out of the camp the better. He said he didn't want Agamemnon to find him there and Priam said something like: "But you'd fight for me?" And Achilles said: "Oh, yes, I'd fight. I don't need a Trojan to teach me my duty to a guest." '

Calchas leant forward: 'You're sure he said "duty to a *guest*"?'

'Exact words.'

'Did anybody else hear that?'

'I don't know. Alcimus and Automedon were on the veranda immediately behind him, but I can't say whether they heard or not. But they'll be able to confirm he walked to the gate with Priam and saw him safely out of the camp.'

When I'd finished, Calchas let out a noisy breath and sat back in his chair, looking across at Cassandra and then back at me.

'So,' I said. 'You're saying Priam's death was murder? Do you really think the Greeks are going to accept that?'

'I think it's possible. You see, people always say they want an explanation, but they don't – not really. They want somebody to blame.'

'I think they'd rather blame Menelaus.'

'Oh, of course they would – they want to see Helen stoned to death. But that would mean war.'

'So, you're going for Pyrrhus instead? The hero of Troy? Achilles' son?'

'I said I thought it was possible. I didn't say it would be easy.'

Calchas lapsed into silence, obviously thinking hard. He was a strange, difficult, complex, driven man – and yet I felt his loyalty to Priam was genuine. And with all his oddities, he was impressive. Though I didn't for a moment think he was going to succeed in this plan. Pyrrhus had so much power, so much prestige – the hero of Troy. There was no getting past that. And there was one major flaw in the case Calchas was building. He had Cassandra's account of Priam's return to Troy and my memories of what Achilles had said and done that night, but both of us were women – and a woman's testimony is not considered equal to a man's. In a court of law, if a man and woman disagree it's almost invariably his version of events that's accepted. And that's in a courtroom – how much more so in this camp where all the women were Trojan slaves and the only real law was force. Calchas would need to get Automedon or Alcimus to confirm everything I'd said, but for much of the time I'd been alone with Priam and Achilles, because Achilles thought Priam would be

more at ease with a Trojan girl than with heavily armed Greek fighters. I hoped, at least, Alcimus and Automedon would tell the truth
about what they knew, but I suspected their loyalty to Pyrrhus, as
Achilles' son, might override everything else.

Cassandra broke into my thoughts. 'I want to see my father buried,' she said. 'I want to see Pyrrhus crawl on his hands and knees
through the dirt.'

Suddenly, I wanted to get away from the fug in this room. Abruptly,
I stood up, and this time Cassandra didn't try to detain me, though
she did see me to the door. 'I will come to see my mother,' she said.
'Only not yet.'

I felt the promise was intended as a reward, a pat on the head for
being a good little girl. *Patronizing bitch.* She saw herself as being at
the centre of the web that was being spun around Pyrrhus, but I
thought she was deceiving herself there. Cassandra was so completely her father's daughter, so far removed in attitudes and
experience from almost all other women, that she was incapable of
appreciating the full extent of Hecuba's power. Calchas saw it. There
was something in his voice whenever he mentioned Hecuba, a soft-
ness that certainly wasn't there the rest of the time. Perhaps as a
young man he might have loved her, and perhaps somewhere underneath the face paint, the cynicism and the plotting, he still did.

27

That night, as was now usual, Andromache and I served wine at dinner. We arrived in good time and began pouring the first drinks. The torches were lit, fresh rushes laid, gold plate gleamed on Pyrrhus' table. I noticed he was drinking from the Thracian cup. I'd seen it before, of course, when Achilles was alive, in the last ten days before his death, but now I saw it with fresh eyes because I knew Priam had been holding it when Hecuba tried to persuade him not to go to the Greek camp, not to throw himself on the non-existent mercy of Achilles.

As the men ate and drank, as the torches blazed and the temperature soared, I kept glancing across the tables at Andromache. She looked so thin and pale – worse, I thought, since Amina died – but she seemed to be managing, though I noticed she still avoided looking at the men she served. They were talking about the games: which referee was blind (all of them), whose team was rubbish, who was favourite to win the chariot race. The games seemed to be going well. There'd been one pitched battle after a wrestling match that had left a contestant permanently disabled, but no other real disturbances. I was pleased for Alcimus, who seemed to be growing in confidence from one day to the next.

When the time came for us to leave, Andromache was told to

stay behind. She gave a despairing glance over her shoulder as she disappeared into the living quarters. I decided to go and visit the women's hut. By the time I got there, the girls had a meal ready: chicken with lemons and garlic, very simple, but delicious – the girls were becoming rather good at this. We sat outside to eat. One of the girls who still worried me was Maire; she was such a silent, depressed *lump*. Inevitably, we women tended to see each other through our captors' eyes, and I'm afraid I was as guilty of that as anybody. Why on earth had Pyrrhus chosen *her*? She was immensely fat, so fat she waddled when she walked – and she was obviously ashamed of her body because she'd been shuffling about in the same shapeless black robe every day since she arrived. Sitting beside her, Helle was slim, strong, firm, graceful, glowing with health – and yet, despite the stark contrast, they did seem to have struck up a friendship. At least, Maire spoke to Helle now and then – which was more than she did to anybody else.

At last, the dishes were cleared away, the fire built up and the drums and pipes came out. Alcimus' lyre had been returned to him – in pristine condition, I'd made sure of that – but he'd very kindly found another less impressive instrument for the girls to use. One of the quieter girls held up her hand and said she could play a little – 'but not as well as Amina'. A shadow – I could almost see it – passed over the group at the mention of her name.

Instantly, Helle was on her feet, clapping her hands for attention, announcing that they were all going to learn a new song. A drinking song. They looked at each other: women don't sing drinking songs. So, Helle went on, they all had to raise their cups and have a good long drink first.

It was, indeed, a drinking song: the kind sailors used to sing in Lyrnessus in taverns and brothels along the harbour front.

When a man grows old, and his balls grow cold,
And the tip of his prick turns blue.
When the hole in the middle
Refuses to piddle,
He can tell you a tale or two.
HE CAN TELL YOU A TALE OR TWO!

The girls giggled; some looked shocked – but they all seemed perfectly willing to learn the song. You heard versions of this song being sung all over the camp, no two exactly the same, though they all concerned a woman of gargantuan sexual appetites. A woman who could not be satisfied and only managed to reach a climax when somebody thrust a spear into her vagina. Needless to say, this woman's name was always Helen.

I hoped Helle would have the sense to stop before the final verse. There were plenty of women in Troy who'd died like that – I knew one of the girls had seen her pregnant sister-in-law dragged out of hiding and speared. But I never did find out what Helle would have done, because she'd only got as far as verse three when Maire vomited. Everybody turned and stared.

I knelt beside her, touched her forehead: she was sweating a little, but didn't feel too hot. I probed under her jaw: no swelling. 'Come on,' I said. 'Let's get you inside.'

The beds were already made up. I got her to lie down and covered her with a blanket. I noticed Helle hovering in the doorway. 'She'll be all right,' I said. I wasn't concerned at all; I just thought she had a stomach upset, which were extremely frequent in the camp. 'Maire? Try to get some sleep.'

I didn't particularly want to return to the group round the fire. I was tired after serving in the hall, my ankles were starting to swell, I needed my bed. The singing had started up again – a rather more appropriate song, I was glad to hear – so I thought I could slip away.

I'd actually got as far as the veranda when Helle burst out of the door behind me. 'You can't just *GO*! *I* don't know what to do.'

'She'll be all right. Just put a bowl by the bed in case she's sick again.'

She stared at me. 'You don't know, do you? How can *you* not know?'

And abruptly, like having a bucket of cold water thrown over me, I did know. Only of course, *you*'ve all got there before me, haven't you? Can I just say, in my own defence, that pregnancy in a fat woman, a first pregnancy, particularly when the woman's trying to hide it, is not as easy to spot as you might think. But all the same . . . I was pregnant myself. How could I not have seen?

'Of course, I'll stay. You go back to the others. Keep them out as long as you can.'

I went back into the hut and squatted down beside Maire. She was really sweating now; her face was a shining full moon in the flickering rush lights between the beds. 'Do you still feel sick?'

She shook her head. Her lips moved; I had to lean in to catch the words. 'I know how it ends.'

Pregnancy? Well, no prizes for that . . . But then I realized: she meant the song.

'That's not going to happen to you!' Though even as I spoke, I thought: *Why not? What's changed?* 'You're going to be all right,' I said, patting her leg.

I needed Ritsa. More than ever in my life, I needed Ritsa, but I could hear groups of drunken fighters walking past – and there'd be plenty of others, in every other compound, all over the camp. I couldn't go to get her, and I certainly wasn't going to send one of the girls. Somehow, we'd just have to manage. Thousands of women give birth every day, some with no more help than a whelping bitch. How difficult could it be?

I knelt beside Maire and asked if she was having regular pains. She nodded. When did they start? I asked. 'This afternoon.' So, she'd been in labour for several hours already and hadn't told anybody. The more I tried to understand her behaviour the more insane it seemed. Though I don't suppose she was thinking straight at all, poor woman.

Four or five of the girls came in to fetch their blankets, glancing sideways at Maire in a shy, curious, slightly embarrassed way. I could hear them chattering as they went back to the fire. They were so excited, staying up late, drinking wine under the stars . . . Children, really.

Maire was restless. I sat beside her watching as each pain seized her, reached a peak and ebbed. She arched her back when the pain was bad, and grunted, but made no other sound. She'd need something to bite on later. We couldn't risk the compound being woken by the unmistakable cries of a woman in labour. In the intervals between pains, she talked – more than she'd ever done before, at least to me. She'd been a slave in the kitchen of a great house; born into slavery. I'd assumed the baby's father would be her owner – slaves, even those as unattractive as Maire, are routinely used for sexual relief – but I was wrong. The father was a fellow slave, a man who worked on the farm and regularly brought supplies of vegetables and fruit to the kitchen door. 'And one day,' Maire said, 'he brought me flowers.' You could see the wonder of that moment on her face. After that, she'd slipped away to see him as often as she could. In the orchard, in the hay barn, even in the fields . . .

Do you know, I actually envied her? I'd been married twice, I'd been great Achilles' prize of honour, but no man had ever brought *me* flowers.

As she talked, I started to see why she and Helle got on. No two women could have been less alike, but they shared the experience of slavery. For neither of them did the fall of Troy mean a descent from freedom into bondage. They'd swapped one servitude for another, that was all.

After a while, the girls began drifting back in, bringing with them the smell of woodsmoke. Whispering quietly together, they undressed and settled down for the night. One by one, the rush lights were extinguished until the only light remaining was the lamp beside Maire's bed. In spite of all the excitement, most of the girls dropped off to sleep quickly. Hot food, wine and fresh air had knocked them out. Not all of them though. Looking around the room, I caught more than one glint of eye white in the darkness.

The night dragged on. If anything, Maire's pains got weaker and further apart; she even managed to doze off between them. I think I must have drifted off myself, because I jumped when Maire reached out and grabbed my hand. 'I need a pee.'

The bucket was at the far end of the room. *How on earth . . .?* Well, it would have to be done. Helle and I hoisted Maire into a sitting position and then on to her feet. I took the opportunity of stripping the black robe off her. Underneath, she was wearing only a thin white shift. My god, the size of her! Somehow, we managed to shuffle between two rows of beds, Helle pulling, me pushing from behind – and, in the process, waking everybody up. We supported Maire as she squatted over the bucket; Helle's face was screwed up with the effort – and Helle was a lot stronger than me.

What came out of Maire was no discreet ladylike trickle, but a gush like a pissing mare. For a moment, I was stunned, but then realized her waters had broken. It's the one thing everybody knows about labour, isn't it? The waters break. Helle and I looked at each other, then at the long road back to Maire's bed – only a few yards, yes, but that was a long, long way – and then Helle spoke to the nearest girl. 'Sorry, love, we need your bed.'

The girl looked shocked – she'd only just woken up, poor thing – but she stood up at once, and we lowered Maire on to her bed. Helle went to get the lantern and set it on the floor nearby. By now, all the girls were sitting up: I don't think anybody slept again that night.

After that, the pains got a lot stronger. Maire started to cry out; I tied a knot in my veil and gave it to her to bite on, but her mouth was dry and she kept spitting it out.

'You've got to be quiet,' I whispered.

I didn't need to say any more; Maire knew only too well why, but with every pain it became harder. The girls lit their rush lights and we all settled down to wait. As each pain started, Maire bit into the knot. You could see her fighting her way to the crest of every wave, then floundering down the other side. A few moments' peace, and the tightening started again. Helle kept giving her sips of water, but she couldn't keep it down, so we just moistened her cracked lips – all this in front of an audience of shocked girls who weren't able to help or do anything. Except be there.

I don't know how Maire managed not to scream, but she did – though some awful grunting sounds were coming from behind the veil. And then something new began to happen. I saw it first on Maire's face; she looked puzzled. I glanced across at Helle for confirmation, but she just shook her head. Maire, who'd been so grateful for everything we did, suddenly became bad-tempered, tetchy. Nothing we said or did was right. The next time Helle tried to moisten her lips, she pushed the cup away so violently it skittered across the floor.

'What do you want?' I asked.

She didn't know what she wanted. And then, with the next pain, she started to push. I thought it would soon be over, that we were only minutes away. Each in-drawn breath was expelled in a shriek of effort. 'Shush!' I kept saying, looking nervously at the door, but the shrieks were beyond Maire's control.

Helle stood up. 'Sing!' she hissed at the girls. 'Come on, don't just sit there – bloody sing!' And sing they did. I think they must have sung every song they knew – even the old man with the hole in the middle that refused to piddle got a second outing. 'Louder!' Helle cried. No doubt the fighters still drinking round the fires heard the singing and thought: *They're having a good time.* Under cover of the noise, Helle and I kept glancing at each other, frightened by the extent of our own ignorance. So, we hung on from one pain to the next – and were rewarded, at last, by the sound of Andromache's footsteps on the veranda.

She came in, head down, jaw clenched, not seeing anything or anybody. When, finally, she looked up and found everybody awake and a woman on the floor, moaning, she seemed bewildered. 'What's going on?'

Helle said, 'She's in labour.'

'*Labour?*' Andromache looked down at Maire and shook her head, the gesture saying: *I don't care.* 'I've got to get washed.'

And with that she walked through the frightened girls and out into the yard. A murmur ran around the room. Helle and I looked at each other and then I followed Andromache out into the night. The fire was still blazing; a cauldron of hot water stood on the grass beside it. Crouched over, splay-legged, Andromache was scrubbing herself viciously with a square of linen folded over to make a pad. Instinctively, I looked away – though she didn't seem to mind my being there. She had no need for privacy now, since her body didn't belong to her any more. I knew that feeling, and the angry words I'd been about to speak shrivelled on my lips. Face averted, I waited for her to be ready.

'Right, then,' she said, tossing the pad into the cauldron. 'Let's see what we can do.'

I followed her into the hut, wincing again at the overcrowding, the smells, the heat of all those bodies. Andromache knelt at Maire's feet, waited for the next pain and then, immediately, did what I hadn't felt able to do: push Maire's shift up round her waist and try to see what was going on. I was glad I hadn't done it, because it would only have made me panic. What I was looking at simply didn't seem possible. The pain ebbed; Maire gave that long grating shriek and let her head fall back.

'You're not trying,' Andromache said. 'You've got to push!'

'*I AM PUSHING!*'

'Not hard enough.'

That was harsh; but the roughness seemed to rouse Maire from her torpor and – whether coincidentally or not – the next pain was stronger. Andromache whispered to me, 'Under all that fat, you know, she's actually quite narrow.' She looked worried – and if she was worried, I was frantic. 'Come on, Maire,' I said. 'You can do it.'

Maire shook her head. Andromache slapped her, not hard, but any slap at that time was brutal. 'Look at me, Maire. *Look at me* – we've lost everything – homes, families, everything – but we are *not* going to lose you.'

Poor Maire. We must have sounded like demons urging her on to do the impossible. She turned to Helle, who took her hand and said, 'Come on.' And then, half laughing, trying for a joke: 'What am I going to do without you?'

Maire shook her head; the next pain had already started.

'*Good!*' Andromache said. 'I can see its head – lovely long black hair, just like you.'

All I could see was a bloody ball, but the words seemed to encourage Maire.

'Come on, it'll soon be over,' Andromache said.

We were all urging Maire on, unconsciously holding and blocking our breaths to the same rhythm as hers. Nobody heard her shrieks of effort now – we were too intent on the next pain. Andromache, who had her hand on the hard mound of Maire's belly, nodded. 'Make the most of this one. Go on, deep breath. Hold – *and push.*'

And there was the baby's head. As we watched, it turned – as if it were trying to help. As if it knew how to be born.

'Shoulders now,' Andromache said. 'Come on, just one more pain, and it's over.'

A gush, a flop. And there was a new person in the room, a person who'd never been there before. I've been present at so many births since then, and had children of my own, but nothing ever prepares you for that moment. Just as when somebody dies – that lengthening silence after the last breath always comes as a shock, no matter how long the death has been expected.

Andromache picked him up and chafed his chest until he produced a thin, bewildered wail. To begin with, he was the bluish purple of ripe plums, but gradually, as he went on wailing, he began to change to a healthy-looking red.

Picked *him* up.

Chafed *his* chest.

He began to change.

The room was very quiet, no sound except for the baby's reedy cry. I realized what was missing: the shout of triumph that follows the birth of a boy. I thought this might be the first time in the whole history of Troy that the birth of a healthy male child had been greeted with nothing but dismay. Andromache had still not given him to Maire to hold, and Maire was beginning to look anxious. Suddenly – even though only a moment before she'd been too exhausted even to raise her head – she reared up, snatched the baby from Andromache's hands and put him to her breast. Her nipple was so big, I didn't see how he could possibly get it into his mouth, but after a few frustrated cries he managed it, and his cheeks began working vigorously. After a little grunt of surprise – obviously the sensation wasn't what she'd been expecting – Maire heaved a sigh of contentment and relief.

Mechanically, Andromache went on attending to what else needed to be done, emerging from between Maire's legs with what looked like a sheep's liver in her hands. Mercifully, the girls were all craning to admire the baby. 'Look at his fingernails!' I heard one of them say.

Andromache gripped my arm. 'We need to talk.'

Helle and I glanced at each other, both of us, probably, thinking: *This is a nightmare.* We followed Andromache out into the yard where, under cover of burying the afterbirth, we could have a few minutes' private conversation.

'You should have killed it,' Helle said. 'It'll only be worse for her if *they* do it.' She jerked her head to indicate the Greek fighters who were shouting on the other side of the fence.

'No, it wouldn't,' I said. 'They're the enemy. We're supposed to be her friends.'

'It's too late now anyway,' Andromache said.

'Is it?' Helle said.

There was a moment when we looked into the abyss.

Then: '*Yes,*' I said. 'She's fed it.'

Many newborn children are killed or left to die: deformed boys, obviously, but also a great many perfectly normal girls. The rule is it must be done before the mother feeds the child. In snatching her baby out of Andromache's hands and putting him to her breast, Maire had saved his life.

For now. As far as any of us knew, the edict that all Trojan boys must be killed was still in force. Pyrrhus had killed Andromache's son: we had no reason to trust him. I didn't know whether he'd have the stomach to kill a newborn baby, now, when the heat of battle had passed, but I certainly didn't intend to find out.

'Let's get him swaddled,' I said.

A Trojan baby was bound in swaddling bands for the first few weeks of its life, and strapped tightly to its mother's chest. Nothing much was visible except for its face and hands – and even these were hidden in the folds of its mother's shawl. Could we get away with hiding the baby's sex? I thought we could, as long as the girls remembered to call the baby 'it' or – better still – 'she'.

Speaking with complete authority, Helle said: 'They'll remember.' Did I detect the faintest trace of '*or else*'? We-ell, what if I did? I'd wanted her to be a leader – and a leader she was turning out to be.

So that's what we decided. I fetched a sheet and a pair of scissors from my hut and together Andromache, Helle and myself set about making swaddling bands. Once the baby had been wrapped, all three of us spoke to the girls. They nodded and murmured assent; nobody seemed to need convincing – many of them would have seen sights in Troy that nobody their age – or any age – should ever have to see.

From that moment on, Maire's baby became a girl. The following day, I mentioned the birth casually in passing to Alcimus, who showed absolutely no interest. At dinner, one or two of the men commented on the singing. I said: 'Yes, we were celebrating. Maire had a baby girl!' Once again, no interest. A slave giving birth to a slave is nobody's idea of news.

Except in the women's hut. There, it changed the atmosphere completely. The girls had a new focus; Maire basked in being the centre of attention. After dark, when they gathered round the fire, the baby passed from one pair of arms to the next, like a good-luck charm. Maire looked on, smiling, though I noticed she was always relieved to get him back. Something fierce in that love. *Mine*, she seemed to be saying. *Not yours. Mine.*

Would *I* feel like that when my time came? Oh, I'm sure many women would tell me: 'Don't be silly – of course you will!' 'They bring the love with them.' I wish I had a gold coin for every time I've heard somebody say that.

It's not true – and I know it's not true. The love doesn't always come, not if the baby's the result of a forced union – and especially not if it's a male child who resembles his father. I've seen many such boys grow up, well cared for, well fed – or as well as their mothers can afford – but hardly ever touched, not cuddled, not loved. And believe me, they don't thrive. So, every time I looked at Maire with her baby, I wondered how it would be for me. Oh, I laughed when the Myrmidons patted my stomach and talked about Achilles' *son*, but I too thought it was a boy.

The exception to this welter of baby worship was Andromache.

Her detachment surprised me, a little – I'd expected her to adore the baby, but instead, she rarely looked at him. One evening, when we had a few minutes alone, I asked her why. She said: 'After Hector died, Hecuba went a little bit mad. She used to call the baby "Hector" – and not just once or twice, she did it all the time. Oh, she always corrected herself, but then a minute or two later, she'd do it again. I think she was genuinely confused. And then one day I came into the nursery and I found her trying to shove her little wizened tit into his mouth. I grabbed him off her and shouted: "*GET OUT!*" Top of my voice – the whole palace must have heard. Imagine that, telling Hecuba to get out! But he was *my* baby – he was all I had left. So, that's why I don't want to . . .' She shook her head and I saw she was trying not to cry. 'He's her baby, not mine. I've had my go.'

As for me, I was astonished at how strongly I felt about that little boy. He was nothing to me, really – and yet I was fiercely determined to keep him alive. I thought he'd be safe while we were still in the camp. Maire rarely left the hut except to sit on the veranda, and none of the Greek fighters showed any interest in her child. The sea voyage would be more of a challenge, but he'd still be in swaddling bands and I thought the women would probably be kept in the hold. Anyway, I couldn't worry about that now. I kept telling myself it was going to be all right. Given a reasonable amount of luck, I thought we could make it work.

28

Three or four days after the baby's birth, I awoke to the sound of
Alcimus moving around and got up at once to attend to him. As I set
fresh bread and wine in front of him, he asked me how I was. We'd
scarcely seen each other since Amina's death, though that was mainly
because he'd been so busy organizing the games. That's what I liked
to think anyway. Now, there were only two events left: boxing – a
bloody sport guaranteed to produce serious casualties, but popular –
and the grand finale of the games: the chariot race. That was to be
held at the training grounds on the headland where much time and
effort had gone into improving the track.

'Why don't you come to see it?' he asked.

I was slightly taken aback – he'd never suggested anything like
that before – but of course I said I would, I'd love to.

'Look out for me though, won't you? I don't want you standing
around on your own. There's been a lot of heavy betting – I think it
could get a bit rough.'

'Who do *you* think's going to win?' I had absolutely no interest in the
chariot race, or any race, but we were talking again – that's what mattered to me. I wanted him to feel I cared – and I did care – about him.

'Diomedes, I expect.' He was pulling a face: Diomedes won every
chariot race. 'Pyrrhus is in with a chance though.'

'Pyrrhus? Not Automedon?' Automedon had taken over as Achilles' charioteer after Patroclus was killed, and he was generally regarded as the best rider in the compound.

'No, Pyrrhus. He's far and away the best – and Automedon would be the first to tell you too.' He drained his cup. 'Of course, he's got next to no experience . . . but, I don't know. He's probably got the best team.'

I knew the team, everybody did – Ebony and Phoenix, the black stallion and the bay. I'd watched him drive them back from Troy, Priam's bloodied corpse bumping along behind. *Bastard*, I thought, smiling, as I followed Alcimus to the door and waved him goodbye.

I would go to watch the race, I decided, and try to persuade Andromache to come with me. As Pyrrhus' prize of honour, she ought to be there, ready to garland him if he won – and to mop his brow, or anything else that needed mopping, if he didn't. Either way, there'd be really heavy drinking in the hall that night – and I'd have to be there, because Andromache hated it so much, walking up and down the tables rigid with distaste, a king's daughter forced to play the part of a common serving woman. *Poor Andromache*, I thought – and then, rebelliously: *Poor me*. I'd had to do it.

Andromache was up and dressed. The girls were in the yard at the back, watching Maire bathe the baby. It was always rather touching to see how that little scrap of humanity with his dreamy, black-bubble eyes had the power to draw everybody in. I wished I could take them all to see the chariot race – the outing would have done them good: a brisk walk to the training grounds, something to distract them from their grief – but nobody had given them permission to leave the hut, whereas it was self-evidently right that Andromache should be there.

We walked up the steep track without talking much. She was still reserved with me – with everybody – but I thought she had slightly more colour this morning and had taken some care with her dress. The higher up we went the more fiercely the wind blew, but it didn't seem to be bullying us along, as it so often did – even though we kept breaking into little involuntary runs whenever a sharper gust caught us. I felt as I used to do, as a very young girl, that the wind was the breath of a god filling me with life. How full of hope and possibility the future had seemed then. It didn't seem so now – and yet the wind and the brightness of the day somehow still suggested the possibility of a larger, freer life beyond the confines of the camp.

Crowds of Greek fighters passed us on the road and we pulled to one side to give them room. The main influx would come after the boxing ended, but there was already a sizeable crowd, men who'd preferred to turn up early and secure a good vantage point. Alcimus had said there'd been heavy betting – and you felt the tension of that. The added excitement. The Greeks gambled on everything – I'd once heard a group of fighters placing bets on two raindrops running down a shield. Admittedly, they were laughing, but it hadn't been entirely a joke.

The competitors were already gathering. The whole scene was bathed in lemony-yellow light that became richer in tone, less acidic, as the sun rose higher. The chariots glittered; the horses' backs gleamed. The grooms would have been up well before dawn making sure everything was as perfect as it could be. At the end of the race, ash-grey men driving dirty horses would emerge from the clouds of dust, but they set off each of them looking like Phoebus Apollo driving the chariot of the sun. Among the crowd at the starting line, I spotted Pyrrhus' red hair and Diomedes' glossy black curls. Menelaus was there too, evidently intending to compete – which surprised me a little: in recent months, he'd become red-faced and fat, looking suddenly much older than his years.

Agamemnon was there, richly dressed, sitting on his throne-like chair, talking to Odysseus. Behind him, the red-and-gold standards of Mycenae snapped in the wind. Agamemnon had agreed to donate the prizes: a racing horse for the winner; a huge bronze cauldron for the runner-up. I looked carefully, and was relieved to see there was no slave girl dragged out of Agamemnon's weaving sheds and forced to stand shivering by the finish line. I was remembering the chariot race at Patroclus' funeral games when Achilles had given my friend Iphis as first prize. She'd disappeared into Diomedes' compound and, since his women were rarely, if ever, allowed out of their huts, I hadn't seen her since. But I did my best to shake off the memory, because this event, the chariot race, with its richly dressed spectators and waving flags, was as close to a splendid occasion as the camp could manage.

Nestor appeared in a chariot driven by his eldest son; he was the last of the kings to arrive and there was a great burst of cheering as he greeted Agamemnon. Meanwhile, I was scanning the group behind them for Calchas, who I felt sure would be there. Eventually, I spotted him, right at the back of the crowd, a tall, white-faced figure, carrying his gold staff of office. To my surprise, I saw that he was being jostled by some of the young men from Skyros, who were openly jeering at his dress. This lack of respect was something I'd never seen before, and it disturbed me. Calchas was a proud man and, quite possibly, underneath all the paint and the posturing, sensitive. He was surrounded – and nobody was helping – but just then a braying of trumpets announced that the race was about to begin, and the lads from Skyros surged forward to support their hero.

At a signal from Alcimus, the drivers climbed into their chariots. When they were settled, he went along the line holding up a helmet, and they cast lots into it. After giving the helmet a good shake, he presented it to Agamemnon, who drew the lots and called them out. His voice was considerably weaker than I remembered; I noticed that one or two of the men around me looked surprised. Diomedes was well placed, which was a shame, since it made the outcome of the race even more of a foregone conclusion. How many of the men here would've had the confidence to bet against him? The few that had must be feeling rather depressed now. Though I remember Alcimus saying Diomedes didn't have the best team – Ebony was probably the single best horse in the field – but, on the other hand, Diomedes was infinitely more experienced.

The charioteers raised their whips and at a signal from Alcimus set off, their horses' manes streaming in the wind, their wheels churning up clouds of dust. In places, the chariots bumped wildly over ruts in the ground, but somehow the riders clung on, racing away from us across the plain. In the far distance, you could just see the turning point, a dead tree flanked by granite boulders. Here, the track narrowed, forcing the chariots to bunch together, a potentially dangerous situation: if they clipped each other's wheels, there was a real chance they'd overturn, inflicting serious, possibly even fatal, injuries on men and horses alike. All the skill was there, at the turning point, where it was possible to overtake, but only by taking an enormous – though calculated – risk.

Menelaus was in first place as they went into the bend, but Diomedes, only a few yards behind, looked poised to overtake. In third place, Pyrrhus was driving like a madman, as if he thought he and his horses were immortal. And then, infuriatingly, the clouds of dust rising from the trampling hoofs hid them all from view. A groan from the crowd, followed by a tense silence as everybody strained to see who would be in the lead as they came off the bend. Shadows of chariots and drivers wielding whips appeared in a roiling cloud of red dust. Directly in front of me, a man shouted: 'Diomedes!' ' 'Course it's not,' the man standing next to him said. 'It's Menelaus. Are you blind?' And then, in true Greek fashion, they started quarrelling about it, each insisting he was right, though neither of them could see anything. They might have come to blows if the men around them hadn't sworn at them to shut up.

The murmurs died down, as everybody waited, dry-mouthed, for the riders to appear. I expected Diomedes; I think everybody expected Diomedes – even those who were cheering for somebody else – and when the first shadowy shape finally emerged from the cloud, Diomedes' contingent raised a ragged cheer. But the charioteer's face was caked in dust, unrecognizable. People peered instead at the horses: one black, one bay . . . Or were they? Both were so covered in red dust nobody could be sure what colour they were. But then, as the chariots hurtled towards us, the lead driver pulled off his helmet to reveal a mane of flaming red hair.

Alcimus, who was supposed to be neutral, just about managed not to cheer, but from the mouths of all the Myrmidons around me came a full-throated roar. Could anybody catch him? That was the next question. Less than a minute behind him was not Diomedes, as everybody had expected, but Menelaus. Pyrrhus was whipping his team, shouting – pulling ahead, if anything – and then he was over the finish line. The Myrmidons erupted and ran to congratulate him, swarming over his chariot like bees in a hive. But instead of letting himself fall into their outstretched arms, Pyrrhus climbed over the rim of his chariot on to Ebony's back and from there jumped to the ground, where he threw his arms round Ebony's neck. 'My boy,' he kept saying. 'My *boy*.' He pressed his face against the horse's head – and closed his eyes; in all that tumult, a moment of peace. Everybody felt it, and envied it too, I think: the perfect union of man and horse. Then Pyrrhus reached across and patted Phoenix, perhaps wanting to make sure he didn't feel left out; but you could tell his real passion was for Ebony.

At that moment, I happened to glance round and see Calchas, his face paint cracking in the heat, watching Pyrrhus. He must have been five or six yards away from me, but even at that distance, I could feel the hatred coming off him.

At the finish line, the usual post-race wrangling had begun. Diomedes came in third, furious because Pyrrhus had driven him off the track. 'Stupid young idiot,' he said, loud enough for everybody to hear. *He* wasn't hurt, but his pride certainly was. 'Don't rise to him,' Alcimus told Pyrrhus. 'It's just sour grapes.' With his hand on Pyrrhus' shoulder, he was steering him firmly towards Agamemnon, who was waiting to bestow the prizes. Meanwhile, Automedon leapt into the chariot and knotted the reins round his waist, ready to drive it back to the camp. Pyrrhus embraced Agamemnon, then turned to the crowd, both arms raised, fists punching the air. With a great cheer, the Myrmidons surged forward, lifted him shoulder high and carried him down the path in the wake of his chariot, like a colony of ants, I thought, carrying a particularly juicy larva back to their nest.

I turned to Andromache. She pulled a face and I read her thoughts. 'Oh, don't worry,' I said, wearily. 'The way they'll be drinking tonight, he'll have passed out long before that.'

29

Pyrrhus gave a great feast to celebrate his victory. Goats and sheep roasted on spits, wine flowing like water . . . Menelaus was guest of honour, though the other kings took their cue from Agamemnon and stayed away. Pyrrhus made a speech praising Menelaus to the skies: his courage, his wisdom, his horsemanship – and apologized, or very nearly apologized, for attempting to drive him off the track. When Menelaus stood up to reply, he was cheered to the rafters – everybody likes a good loser – and though he couldn't resist one or two barbed remarks about hot-headed young men getting away with murder, it was on the whole a gracious speech. He concluded by saying that he hoped in future the two kingdoms would be even more closely allied since Pyrrhus had accepted Menelaus' offer of his daughter's hand in marriage.

Well, the hall erupted. You'd have thought they were all getting married too. I stood at the back and watched, thinking how secure Pyrrhus was, how lauded, how glorified – and a little blind worm of anger deep inside my brain reared its head and swayed from side to side.

Once the speeches were over, the serious drinking began. Everybody sang, everybody clapped, everybody danced – and somewhere in the middle of all this Automedon indicated to Andromache and me that we should withdraw. I walked Andromache back to the women's hut; rather to my surprise she stopped at the foot of the steps and hugged me. She wasn't sent for that evening and neither was Helle – though I suspect the women round the campfires had a rough night. I just hope they got a share of the wine.

When I woke next morning, the compound looked abandoned. Gradually, over the next few hours, first one man and then another surfaced, gathering round the fires, shouting for breakfast, though few of them managed to eat very much. Some just groaned at the sight of food and went straight back to bed.

Hour by hour, the sky darkened until, by noon, it was almost black. Everything looked jaundiced, including people's skin – as if the only colours in the world were yellow and black. Warning colours they are, in nature – and indeed there was an increasingly threatening feel to the day. Several men pointed to the anvil-shaped cloud that hung over the bay, but others said that was a good thing. A storm was just what they needed. Thunder – a good heavy downpour – and then, at last, the wind would change.

Dinner that night was a subdued affair. Nobody felt like eating much and, although some of the younger men were going for the hair of the dog, the majority drank very little. The wind keened round the hall; the absence of the usual shouting and singing made it sound louder than before. Everybody felt like an early night. Some of the men were already on their feet, getting ready to depart, when there was a noise at the door. We all turned to look, as Agamemnon's heralds entered and processed down the central aisle. Pyrrhus seemed surprised, but immediately stood up to greet them. They bowed low, then indicated they had something to say to him in private. Summoning Alcimus and Automedon to follow him, he left the hall, and although people lingered for a while, curious to know what was going on, he didn't return.

I left Andromache at the door of the women's hut. The air was oppressively humid, and yet to me it didn't feel like thunder. Normally, before a storm breaks there's a period of threatening stillness, but there was no stillness that night: just the same constant moaning of a wind that couldn't rest, and wouldn't let anybody else rest either. I was glad to go inside and shut the door.

Alcimus came in an hour later. 'Agamemnon's called an assembly,' he said. 'Tomorrow, at noon.' He sat down on the bed and began unbuckling his sandals. 'I suppose it's surprising he hasn't done it before.'

Remembering Agamemnon's ravaged face, I wondered if he'd been in any state to take decisions. 'Isn't that a good thing?'

'If it brings people together, yes. But the risk is, it'll just make the divisions public.'

'Aren't they public already? I mean, Agamemnon didn't come to the feast.'

'Well, he couldn't really, could he, with Menelaus there? Can you imagine him sitting there, with Menelaus announcing the marriage? She was supposed to marry his son.'

'Poor girl,' I said.

He looked blank. He'd thrown his tunic off now. As I bent to pick it up, he caught my arm. 'Are *you* all right?'

'I'm fine.'

He let go of me, but perhaps reluctantly. For a moment it had seemed briefly, infinitesimally, possible that we might spend the night together. I felt suddenly that I had to speak, say something, anything . . . 'Do you regret marrying me?'

'Why would I regret it?'

'It wasn't your choice.'

'But I'm married to the second-most-beautiful woman in the world – how could I possibly regret that?'

What sort of man gazes deep into his wife's eyes and tells her she's the *second*-most-beautiful woman in the world? Well, Alcimus, of course. You mightn't always like what he said, but you could be fairly certain it was the truth as he saw it. I don't think I've ever known a more honest man. And, of course, that's why Achilles chose him. I remember Achilles saying he hated the man who thought one thing and said another 'as he hated the gates of death'. Well, nobody could ever have accused Alcimus of that.

He was still sitting on the edge of the bed, apparently trying to think of something else to say. 'I was pleased you came to see the race.'

'I enjoyed it.'

And that was that. I turned at the door and looked back, but he was already pulling up the sheets, so I picked up a candle and took my second-best beauty off to bed.

A narrow bed, and hard. Alcimus' bed was bigger, but no bed could ever be wide enough, as long as Achilles lay between us.

Great Achilles. Brilliant Achilles, shining Achilles, godlike Achilles . . .

We lived our lives in that vast shadow. That's what was wrong with my marriage – and I saw no way of putting it right. Perhaps after the baby was born Alcimus might see me simply as a woman? Or acquire some faith in himself; faith that he was not always and irredeemably second best? Perhaps.

The crux was that Alcimus believed – or rather assumed – that I'd loved Achilles, and still loved him. He certainly wasn't alone in that belief. Then – *and now* – people seem to take it for granted that I loved Achilles. Why wouldn't I? I had the fastest, strongest, bravest, most beautiful man of his generation in my bed – how could I not love him?

He killed my brothers.

We women are peculiar creatures. We tend not to love those who murder our families.

But there's another dimension to this and from my point of view a much less comfortable one. The night Priam came to the Greek camp, to ask Achilles to give him Hector's body, I hid in his cart as it trundled to the gate, aware all the time of Achilles walking beside it. I could have stayed in the cart, I could have gone all the way to Troy, but then I'd have been facing the sack of another city, a second enslavement. There were good reasons to abandon my attempt to escape, but when Achilles asked why I'd come back I said, simply: *I don't know*. And he just nodded. Because the extraordinary thing is that he'd known all along what I was doing – and he'd done nothing to stop me. I came back. He'd been prepared to let me go. So, when we met again, it was no longer, in any simple sense, a relationship between owner and slave. Some of the ties that bind people together are deeper than love. Though if you wanted to be cynical you could say that right from the start I'd been determined to survive and that I knew my chances were better in the Greek camp, under Achilles' protection, than they would ever have been in Troy.

Where did all this thinking get me? Nowhere. Still lying in a narrow bed listening to the wind, aware of the cradle that was just beginning to rock. In my early days in the camp I'd sometimes prayed for things to change. I didn't pray for that now. There was no need; the growing baby would bring change enough and, good or bad, there'd be no hope of stopping it. You might as well have tried to hold back the tide.

30

The wind blew at gale force all night. At noon, as each group of men entered the arena, they were faced with visible signs of storm damage. The statue of Artemis, which from its position in the circle was the most exposed of all the gods, had toppled over in the night, forcing the fighters to climb over it, or – out of some confused sense of respect – to go the long way round. Its fall was not entirely unexpected: for months now, it had been leaning away from the wind, rather like the warped trees on the headland. Nevertheless, in the sallow light, its fall appeared ominous; I saw more than one man make the sign against the evil eye as he shuffled past.

I was on my way to Lord Nestor's hall, hoping to watch the assembly from his veranda. By the time I arrived, Nestor had already left. I saw him making his way through the crowd, leaning heavily on his two older sons, taking his arms from their shoulders only long enough to acknowledge the cheers of the crowd. Hecamede greeted me at the door. As I stepped over the threshold, I smelled burnt sugar and sweet cinnamon. There were so many trays lined up on the long tables in the hall, I thought she must have been baking all morning. Not long afterwards, Cassandra arrived, attended by Ritsa, I was glad to see – though I didn't like the way Cassandra treated her. I sensed that a complex relationship had grown up between them. Ritsa had witnessed the worst moments of Cassandra's madness, had helped and supported her through them, and this made her somebody Cassandra depended on, but also resented – and even feared. Ritsa knew too much, had seen too much. When I saw how roughly Cassandra ordered her about, how contemptuous she sometimes seemed, it made me frightened for Ritsa – and it certainly didn't improve my opinion of Cassandra. I noticed she took sweetmeats from Hecamede's tray with barely a word of acknowledgement, and I reacted by thanking Hecamede so effusively she took a step back in surprise.

After a few minutes' stilted conversation, we carried our plates on to the veranda. The arena was filling up fast. Whenever one of the kings entered, there were ragged cheers from his followers, rising to a roar as he took his seat. Eventually all were present, and every eye turned towards Agamemnon's empty chair. He arrived last at every assembly, his entrance always formal, always dramatic, preceded by heralds and accompanied by a fanfare of trumpets. Leaning over the rail, I could see how old and ill he looked, though his dress was splendid, his manner imperious, and I doubt if many people saw beyond that. You've got to remember I'd seen Agamemnon at very close quarters. Too close. Sometimes, at night, I still felt his sweating bulk on top of me.

Ritsa touched my arm. 'Are you all right?' I put my hand over hers, but didn't speak.

I watched the greetings. Odysseus and Diomedes walked across the arena to meet Agamemnon, who then, in a rare moment of grace, heaved himself to his feet and went to speak to Nestor. What was conspicuously absent was any greeting between the two brothers. Menelaus, whether deliberately or not, was always looking the other way. Pyrrhus was sitting directly opposite Agamemnon, too far away for easy contact, but it would have been natural for Agamemnon to acknowledge him in some way – he'd presented him with first prize in the chariot race only two days before – but I saw no sign of it. Little Ajax was nibbling his beard – a bit scraggy at the best of times – and glancing nervously from side to side. He'd raped Cassandra in the temple of Athena, and here he was, tethered like a goat selected for sacrifice. He greeted nobody – and it was striking how few people greeted him.

At last, Agamemnon stood up and cleared his throat, gazing around the assembly with his sombre, heavy-lidded eyes. 'By now,' he said, 'we should all be home.' With those few words he caught the attention of every man there. 'Even you, Idomeneus, given a fair wind, should have been at home with your dear wife and children. Even Odysseus would have reached faraway Ithaca by now. Yet, here we still are, prevented from leaving by the will of the gods. And we don't even know what it is we've done to offend.'

Really? I thought.

'But it's in the nature of the gods that punishment often precedes knowledge of the offence. So, I have asked Calchas, a renowned seer who has often in times past guided our counsels, to speak to us again today. To all of you, I would simply say: listen carefully. Ponder his words.'

Calchas, in full priestly regalia with the scarlet bands of Apollo fluttering from his staff, emerged from between two rows of huts. Immediately the buzz that had followed Agamemnon's speech subsided. He was a familiar figure in the arena, not much liked, perhaps, sometimes sniggered at – but nevertheless, as a seer, respected. Many of those present would remember that when the camp had been visited by plague, he'd spoken out against Agamemnon, saying it was his disrespectful treatment of a priest that had provoked Apollo's anger and caused him to send his plague arrows flying into the camp, killing beasts and men alike. Agamemnon had hated Calchas for it, but he'd been right, hadn't he? As soon as Agamemnon sent the priest's daughter back to her father, there hadn't been a single new case of the plague – and there were some miraculous cures of men already infected. He'd stood up to Agamemnon then, he'd told the truth. So, they were prepared to listen to him now.

But Calchas didn't ask them to listen.

'*Look*,' he said, 'look at the statues of the gods.'

All over the assembly, heads turned.

'They've been here for ten years – as long as any of you. One of the first things Lord Agamemnon did after the ships disembarked was to order the clearing of a space where the gods might be honoured; these statues were carved and raised and ever since then all debates in the army and between the various kings have taken place under their gaze. We've all grown used to their presence. Perhaps you walk across the arena and never look at them. Two days ago, the boxing tournament was held here, and before that, the wrestling, but how many of you bothered to look up at the gods? How many of you noticed how faded and decayed their statues have become? Last night, the statue of Artemis blew over in the gale. Many of you will have stepped over it to get to your places in the assembly. It's a shock, isn't it? That gap in the circle – and yet the base of her statue must have been rotting for years.'

Like everybody else, I looked at the statues: flaking paint, rotting wood, Poseidon's nose missing, Athena's owl-like eyes dimmed, Apollo tilting dangerously to one side, as if bending in concern over his fallen sister.

'Now, I'm not saying the neglect of their statues has so incensed the gods that they've sent this wind as a punishment. I'm saying that the neglect of the statues is a sign of a much greater offence: a failure of the respect we all owe to beings so much greater than ourselves.'

Calchas was sweating in the heat, his face paint flaking, the dark lines round his eyes beginning to run – that, and his immense height, made him look like a decaying statue himself. A sort of thirteenth god.

'Friends,' he said. 'We all know that when a great city falls, things are done which in an ideal world would not happen. It's nobody's fault – I'm not blaming anybody. The harsh necessity of war, which the gods themselves have imposed on the Greeks, makes such actions inevitable – but still, the facts remain. The temples of the gods *were* desecrated. Women who'd taken shelter behind the altars *were* dragged out and raped. Even virgin priestesses were not spared.'

Calchas was careful not to look at Ajax, but everybody else turned in his direction. I was suddenly aware of Cassandra standing beside me; glancing down, I saw the whiteness of her knuckles as she gripped the rail.

'And then,' Calchas continued, 'the temples were set on fire. Many of them burned to the ground. Is there anyone among you who can say this was not a cause of deep offence? But the gods are merciful. They don't require the rebuilding of their temples. They'll be content if their statues are repaired and the kings make sacrifices in front of them – after every man in the camp has purified himself.'

That was the lightest of light punishments. A team of skilled carpenters – and there were many such in the camp – could repair the statues in a week. Ajax looked relieved – as well he might – and there was a general stir, an easing of tension.

But Calchas hadn't moved. He waited for his audience to settle again, and then said: 'In revealing the will of the gods, I run the risk of offending a great leader, a man pre-eminent for his courage and skill in fighting.' He turned to Agamemnon. 'I must ask for your protection, Lord Agamemnon.'

Agamemnon raised his hand. 'You have it. Speak without fear, as the gods direct.'

'Friends,' Calchas said, again. (Did he have a single friend in that whole vast assembly? I doubted it.) 'Friends. We all know that Zeus in his mercy gave laws to mankind that a wise man will be careful to obey, if he wishes to see his children and grandchildren prosper. Above all, Zeus gave us the laws of hospitality, guest-friendship, the sacred tie that binds host and guest together – for life. And we also know that this bond, once forged, overrides all other loyalties. Guest-friends are not permitted to kill each other, even if they're fighting on opposite sides in a war. Some of you will remember that Diomedes encountered his grandfather's guest-friend on the battlefield and *very properly* refused to fight him. Nobody blamed Diomedes for walking away from that encounter, because the killing of a guest-friend is never justified, not even in a war.'

The assembly had gone very quiet. They couldn't see where this was leading. Diomedes had been mentioned, but only to be exonerated. Ajax, everybody's favourite for the role of chief offender, seemed to be off the hook . . . 'Now I come to the difficult part,' Calchas said. 'You all know that when great Achilles walked among us, he killed Hector, the son of Priam, and so great was his desire for revenge that he dragged Hector's body back to the camp, inflicting countless injuries upon it. King Priam came to Achilles by night, alone, and was received by him with every mark of courtesy and respect. When Priam left the camp, with Hector's body in his cart,

Achilles saw him to the gate, fully armed, and prepared to defend him even against his fellow Greeks. There is no possible doubt that the bond of guest-friendship had been forged between them. That bond descended to Achilles' son, Lord Pyrrhus, who killed Priam on the altar of Zeus in Troy. He killed his father's guest-friend on the altar of Zeus, the god who gave mankind the laws of hospitality.

'Could there be any greater insult to the god than that? My friends, it's Zeus himself, the father of gods and men, who keeps us imprisoned on this beach.'

All eyes were on Pyrrhus now. He looked bewildered, staring blankly from side to side. It was obvious he hadn't thought for a moment that this might be the outcome of the assembly. I saw Automedon lean forward and put a steadying hand on his shoulder.

Calchas went on, 'Now you may say Lord Pyrrhus didn't know of the bond between his father and Priam, and that may well be true, but an offence committed in ignorance is still an offence. So now I come to the punishment that Zeus demands. Priam must be buried with all the honours due to a king, but before the pyre is lit Lord Pyrrhus must sacrifice his black stallion, one of the team he was driving when he won the chariot race.'

Pyrrhus leapt to his feet. '*NO!* No – you stinking heap of dogshit, I'll see you in hell first.'

Alcimus put out a hand to restrain him. Pushing him aside, Pyrrhus hurled himself across the arena, pulling his sword as he went. Agamemnon's guards were rushing forward to protect Calchas, who shrank back against the statue of Zeus with both arms raised to protect his face. At the last moment, Pyrrhus seemed to hesitate, long enough for Automedon to grab him by the hair and yank his head back. Alcimus stepped in front of Calchas, holding up his hands to show he was unarmed, and at a word from Agamemnon, the guards fell back. By now, the Myrmidons were closing around Pyrrhus, who had to suffer the humiliation of being disarmed by his own men and dragged away.

Uproar. All over the arena, men were out of their seats, waving their arms and shouting. Agamemnon called for order several times before he managed to make himself heard. When the assembly was finally quiet, he thanked Calchas for his words of wisdom, said that Pyrrhus was understandably upset – he was a very young man and, as they all knew, young men lacked judgement and had to be guided by those who were older and wiser . . . And so on. He was sure that when Lord Pyrrhus had had time to reflect, he would see sense – and obey the gods.

And with that, Agamemnon's procession re-formed and left the arena, leaving Menelaus to contemplate the fact that his sole remaining ally in the camp, the man to whom he'd just promised his daughter's hand in marriage, was in disgrace. Meanwhile, the Myrmidons, in total disarray, moved off in a great huddle with Pyrrhus' red hair at the centre, almost as if they were carrying a wounded comrade from the battlefield. I went back inside the hall, sat at one end of a bench and rested my arms on the table. Cassandra, who'd followed me in, sat opposite.

'We-ell,' she said. 'What did you make of that?'

I didn't need to ask what she'd made of it: her pupils were so widely dilated her eyes looked black. I wondered how much she'd had to do with Calchas' speech – which in many ways was uncharacteristic of him. No interpretation of dreams; no reference to the flight of birds – not a stranded sea eagle in sight. 'How much of that was you?'

She shrugged. 'Does it matter? I've learnt not to be too attached to my own prophecies. They've only ever been believed when I could get a man to deliver them.' She drummed her fingers on the table. 'I'm still waiting to hear what you thought.'

'I don't know. Of course, I want to see Priam buried . . . I just wish Calchas hadn't mixed it up with personal revenge.'

'*Personal* . . .? Oh, you mean the horse.' She was staring at me, her yellow eyes brighter than I'd ever seen them. 'It's not enough, not nearly enough – but I'll take it.'

Ritsa and Hecamede followed us in. Hecamede immediately began bustling around with preparations for dinner. Nestor would be back soon.

I stood up. 'I think we should go.'

The crowd was thinning by the time we left the hall, but I decided to walk along the beach anyway. I knew there was no hurry. Alcimus would be in the hall with Pyrrhus and Automedon, trying to pick up the pieces. I didn't envy him the task. Essentially, Pyrrhus had to be persuaded to obey the gods – and sacrifice the only creature he seemed capable of loving. Except himself. And I wasn't even sure about the exception.

31

I dawdled along the beach and when I reached the compound went straight to the women's hut. Most of the girls were in the yard at the back, where Maire was getting ready to give the baby a bath. Free from swaddling bands and nappy, he lay on a blanket, making little contented cooing sounds and kicking his legs. One of the girls was holding up a linen sheet to shield his eyes from the sun. We were so lucky in his temperament: he fell asleep at the breast, woke up, suckled, slept again. He never attracted attention by screaming with colic for hours on end as so many first-born babies do. Mind you, we were a bit less lucky in his appearance. Most babies you see could be either sex, but not this one: he was a right little bruiser, even his curled fingers looked like fists.

Andromache came out and sat beside me, while I told her what had happened in the arena. We speculated about what Pyrrhus might do, and agreed we'd probably not be required to serve wine at dinner that night. The baby was no more than a few feet away from her, but she never once looked at him and shortly afterwards went back into the hut.

After a while, I lay back, closed my eyes and lifted my face to the sun. The black clouds had vanished, though the wind still blew as fiercely as ever; still, it was more sheltered here than anywhere else in the camp. The chattering of the girls faded into the distance; I think I must have drifted off to sleep, but then suddenly I jerked awake, aware of a scrambling all around me as the girls struggled to their feet. Opening my eyes, I saw Pyrrhus towering over me, over everybody. And there was the baby, cooing and gurgling and trying to get his fist into his mouth. Pyrrhus glanced down at him, and I saw his expression change; though I doubt if he really took in what he was seeing – a naked, and very obviously male, child – but that didn't mean he wouldn't remember it later. This was a disaster. Slowly, I got to my feet. He bowed, and asked if he could have a word. Of course, I agreed, and we went into the hut together. It was cool inside, but somehow that only served to underline how groggy and disoriented I was feeling. I should never have let myself go to sleep.

There were several girls sitting on their beds, talking, one girl brushing another's hair. They turned as we came in, looking thoroughly alarmed at the sight of Pyrrhus. I jerked my head to one side and they ran outside.

Pyrrhus said: 'Alcimus suggested I should talk to you.'

Then: silence. Nothing. I waited, desperately trying to think of something, anything, to distract him from what he'd just seen.

'Shall we go across to the hall?' Pathetic, but the best I could do. 'It's so crowded here.'

That was even less impressive, since we were standing together in an otherwise empty room, but he didn't seem to question it, just moved automatically towards the door.

We walked across the yard and up the steps of the veranda into the brightly lit hall. Fresh rushes had already been laid and the tables set for dinner. Preparations would have been well advanced by the time Pyrrhus cancelled. He started walking down the middle aisle and, of

261

course, I followed. I expected to be taken through into his living quarters, but at the last moment he seemed to change his mind. Instead, he sat at the top table in Achilles' chair, curling his fingers into the lions' snarling mouths. Beside his plate was the Thracian cup with its frieze of horses' heads with flowing manes. He reached for it, entwining his thick fingers round the stem.

'Alcimus says you were there the night Priam came.'

'Yes,' I said. 'I was there.'

He asked the same questions Calchas had asked. I gave the same answers. It was harder this time for me to remain detached, because I was sitting in the room where those events had happened. Then, I'd been standing behind Achilles' chair – tired, my feet aching, longing for the evening to be over; but Achilles, though he'd given up pretending to eat, still sat slumped in his chair. Nobody could leave until he left, but he seemed almost torpid, as he so often did in the days after Patroclus' death. Once a day, sometimes twice, he roused himself to fasten Hector's corpse to his chariot and, yelling his great battle cry, dragged it three times round Patroclus' burial mound, returning to the camp with lathered horses, his face caked in filth. There, he abandoned the body in the stable yard, flayed, every bone broken, scarcely identifiable as a man. Sometimes, when Achilles staggered back into the hall, his face was disfigured by the same injuries he'd inflicted on Hector. He saw them; I know he did – I watched as he peered into the mirror, lifting his hands uncertainly to touch his skin.

Pyrrhus was listening intently as I came to the end of the story. 'Achilles said, "Oh, yes, I'd fight. I don't need a Trojan to teach me my duty to a guest."'

'You're *sure* that's what he said?'

'Exact words.'

'Yes, but do you think he'd *really* have done that? Fight the other kings – for Priam?'

'I think he would, yes. He wasn't a man to say one thing and do another.'

'Well, then. I suppose I've got to accept it. They were guest-friends.' He was slapping the table top with both hands, an oddly restrained gesture that did nothing to conceal the violence within. 'I'm just sorry for Ebony. Why does he have to die? He did nothing wrong.'

Did he actually expect me to sympathize *with his horse*? But the strange thing is, I did sympathize. I never, at any point, wanted to see Ebony destroyed.

'I have to be going,' I said.

He stood up at once. 'I'll see you back to your hut.'

'Oh, no need – it's still light.'

He stood on the steps and watched me cross the yard. I was glad he hadn't insisted on escorting me to my door. As it was, I waited for him to go inside and then slipped along to the women's hut where I found the girls huddled around Maire, who was looking terrified, as well she might. I had a brief urgent conversation with Andromache and Helle. We agreed we had to get the baby out. It was good to talk to them. Left to myself, I think I might have been paralysed by a fear of overreacting, of creating one problem in the course of solving another. By running away, Maire would expose herself to all the punishments visited on runaway slaves – and they were savage. It was a relief to know that the others agreed on the dangers. Pyrrhus was an angry, vengeful man – capable of great generosity, yes, and brave, but brutal, too. Killing Andromache's baby – that had been done in the immediate aftermath of battle, and under direct orders from Agamemnon. The pressure to comply would have been immense. But Amina . . .? What excuse was there for that, really? No, we had no reason to trust him. If he was forced to sacrifice Ebony – and I couldn't see how he was going to get out of it – his reaction would be to spread the pain around to as many people as possible. Having been publicly humiliated, he'd want to stamp his authority on his men – and on the slaves who'd lied to him, *again*, and defied him, *again*. I didn't think we could expect any mercy from him at all. Somehow, we were going to have to get the baby out – and it had to be done tonight while everybody in the compound was preoccupied with the practicalities of burying Priam. So, we agreed and then parted. Helle went to break the news to Maire, and I went back home to wait, since nothing could be done before dark.

32

After watching the woman, Briseis, walk across the yard, Pyrrhus turns back into the hall. Lamps and candles cast circles of light over empty plates . . . He ought to be hungry by now – in fact, he should be famished, he hasn't had a bite to eat since breakfast; but he isn't. If anything, he feels slightly sick. *Move*, he tells himself, but his feet have taken root. Peeling familiarity from his eyes, he notices shadows struggling in the rafters, the same battle they fight every night, creating a sense of conflict, however convivial the gathering going on below. Not that they always are convivial. He's thinking these trivial, scum-on-the-surface thoughts so he doesn't have to think about . . .

He must be standing almost exactly where Priam stood that night, gazing up the hall at a man who sits slumped in his chair, torpid as a lizard on a cold day. Still dangerous, though: lethargy to murderous rage in seconds. How much courage it must have taken to begin that walk up the aisle between the tables, a wall of muscular backs on either side.

Pyrrhus starts walking in Priam's footsteps down the hall towards the empty chair at the end, though he doesn't seem to be moving at all, it's more as if the chair is coming towards *him*. He stops in front of it – contemplates the impossibility of kneeling as once Priam had knelt. He'd held Achilles knees – the position of a supplicant – and said: 'I do what no man before me has ever done, I kiss the hands of the man who killed my son.'

And that's where Pyrrhus loses it. Totally. Up to that point, he thinks he understands. Priam had shown immense courage in driving, alone and unarmed, into the Greek camp – and Achilles would have responded to that. He would always have responded to courage. But are those really the words of a brave man? It sounds more like giving in. And yet, it's at that point that Achilles' behaviour begins to change. Suddenly, he's inviting Priam into his private quarters, bringing out the best wine, waiting on him at dinner, apparently, like a common serving man. Why didn't he call Alcimus and Automedon into the room – let them do it? It was their job to wait on a royal guest. And there it is, the word 'guest'. He wasn't a guest! He was an interloper – he'd just walked in off the yard. And yet Achilles himself had used the word 'guest' . . .

That was one thing everybody seemed to agree on, that Achilles and Priam had begun the night as enemies and ended it as friends – guest-friends – to the point where Achilles had been prepared to fight his fellow Greeks to defend Priam. How could a single encounter send a man spinning off on to a different path from the one he'd been pursuing, with such undeviating resolution, up till then? Pyrrhus doesn't get it. He's talked to Alcimus, to Automedon, and now to Briseis: he knows exactly what happened that night, but he understands none of it. How could his father, who'd been the scourge of the Trojans for the last nine years, have made a friend of Priam? Even offering to help him when Troy fell. In the deepest, darkest corner of Pyrrhus' mind is the thought that – if he'd lived – Achilles would have defended Priam on the altar steps.

Anyway, where *is* everybody? He looks round the empty hall, then remembers he cancelled dinner. Just as well . . . Tonight's a time to be alone, because tomorrow . . . Tomorrow . . . Everybody says it's what the gods require. *No, it fucking isn't.* It's what Agamemnon requires. Not even that – it's what Calchas requires. *Should've killed the bastard, not just kicked his arse. Ah, well, too late now . . .*

The hall with its indecipherable echoes is intolerable, so he goes into his living quarters where, as usual, somebody has set out cheese and wine. He pours himself a cup, gulps it down, reaches for the jug – and feels the mirror stir into life behind him. Refusing to pay it any attention, he pours himself more wine, and –

Bor*ing*! Bor*ing*!

Slowly, he puts down the cup.

No, go on, go on, do what you always do!

He can't ignore it any longer. So he turns and walks towards the mirror but, instead of his reflection becoming bigger as he approaches, it dwindles till it's scarcely more than a point of light. Once, not so long ago either, he used to dress up in Achilles' armour and stand in front of this mirror, narrowing his eyes until the image in front of him blurred and it was possible to believe the man standing there was Achilles himself. He's the model of his father; everybody says he is. Now, though, what he sees is a taunting homunculus. He knows perfectly well this isn't Achilles – or any other manifestation of the afterlife. It's *him* – a sheared-off sliver of his own brain.

No running to Daddy now, is there?

There never was.

Oh, it must be tough, being an orphan. Of course, there aren't any other fatherless children in Greece, are there? God's sake, man, get a grip.

He stares at it, this gibing homunculus whose face is a caricature of his own. Abruptly, he remembers something horrible – it's one of the things this creature does best, dredging up memories from the sediment at the bottom of your mind, and they are never good memories. After the first attempt at burying Priam, Helenus had been brought in for questioning. The man had been tortured before, by Odysseus; he was falling over himself to tell them everything he knew – which was nothing. And yet, Pyrrhus had still pulled out his dagger, and turned it thoughtfully over and over, the movement finding a blue light on the blade. He'd noticed – without appearing to notice – the fear on Helenus' face, the tension in his muscles. There'd been no need to use force, but still he'd pressed the dagger into Helenus' belly, only a little way in, just far enough to make a thin rivulet of blood trickle down. No real damage, minimal pain – but there'd been no need for it. He's ashamed of the action now, ashamed of the excitement he'd felt – and feels again, remembering the involuntary sucking-in of Helenus' breath. A small, mean-spirited thing to do, altogether unworthy of great Achilles' son.

That's you all over, though, isn't it? Nasty little boy pulling wings off flies. Do you remember doing that? . . .

I don't have to listen to you.

Oh, but you do listen, don't you? And you always will.

Summoning up all his strength, he turns his back on the mirror, grabs his cloak and crashes out into the night.

Outside, breathing the cool night air, he pauses. The stables? No, though he craves time with Ebony, he's too afraid of the pain. Later, perhaps – or tomorrow morning, first thing, then he'll go, oversee the making of the drugged mash – better still, make it himself – groom Ebony, plait his mane . . . But not now, not tonight. Tonight, he wants . . .

What does he want? Punishment. A surprising answer, since he doesn't know what crime he's supposed to have committed and doesn't accept that he's actually to blame. How was he supposed to know about the guest-friendship between Priam and Achilles? An offence committed in ignorance is still an offence. No excuses, no allowances, no mercy – the gods are nothing if not relentless. Punishment, then. But it should be for him – not for Ebony.

He doesn't want company, and anyway, there aren't many places in the camp he'd be welcome now. He'll go to the sea. Setting off down the path through the dunes, he's aware once again of following in Achilles' footsteps, as he does wherever he goes in the camp. What would it be like to choose his own path . . .? That's never been possible. Coming out on to the beach, he sees a huge wave burst in thunder and clouds of spray – and beyond that, other waves already gathering. At the water's edge, he kicks off his sandals, lets his tunic fall round his ankles and braces himself for a few minutes of extreme cold before the sea spews him back on to dry land. No dolphin-like cavorting with the waves for *him*. He wades a little way in, feels the shock of the rising swell against his knees and then as it retreats the slipping-away of sand between his toes. Would even great Achilles have swum in such a sea? Oh, yes, of course he bloody would – and enjoyed it too! Pyrrhus edges an inch or two further out, as the sea flexes its muscles for the next assault . . .

'I wouldn't if I were you.'

A cool, amused voice. Pyrrhus spins round and nearly topples over as the next wave catches him. Can't see a bloody thing. Ridiculously, he raises a hand to his eyes as if shielding them from the sun – though it's the moon that's bleaching the wet pebbles at his feet. The shadowy figure looking down from the top of a steep bank of shingle seems to have absolutely gigantic feet. Pyrrhus shivers a little, though a second later, he realizes it's only Helenus with his feet still bound in several layers of rags. It's a strange coincidence seeing him so soon after remembering sticking a knife in his belly (though only a little way in – it can't have hurt, or not very much) and the strangeness makes him go quiet. He waits for Helenus to speak, but Helenus, perhaps finding the silence threatening, is already backing away.

'No, don't go,' he says. Instantly, Helenus stops. 'What are you doing out here?' That sounds like the beginning of another interrogation – the last thing he intends.

'Actually, I came to wash my feet.'

'Really?'

'Yes, well, you know . . . Salt helps.'

'I suppose it does.'

Warily, Helenus sits down and begins unwinding the rags. After hesitating a while, Pyrrhus climbs the slope towards him, but slowly, not coming too close. 'Might be better to let the air get to it.'

Helenus flexes his toes. 'Yeah, I think you're right.'

Skin heals; the mind doesn't. Pyrrhus knows it's time to bring this awkward encounter to a close, though he tells himself it was Helenus who started it – he needn't have spoken at all. But now, he's curious to know why he did. So, against his better judgement, he watches as Helenus wades in, wincing as a wave foams round his ankles. He's not steady on his feet, though he does go a little further before turning round and struggling towards the shore. On impulse, Pyrrhus reaches out and offers his hand. Helenus clasps it, laughing in embarrassment at his weakness, and lets himself be hauled on to dry land. Breathless from the effort, he rests his hands on his knees. He's very dark-skinned with a lot of hair on his legs that the water's swirled into half-moons and circles, rather like the pattern seaweed makes on rocks. Exactly like the patterns some kinds of seaweed make on rocks. Somehow, seeing that similarity clears a space in Pyrrhus' head and he begins to relax, to open up a little.

'They do look a lot better.' A ridiculous comment, since it's the first time he's seen them. Nothing he says seems to come out right.

'I'm walking a bit better.' Helenus looks out to sea and then back at Pyrrhus. 'Are you going to swim?'

'No, I think I'll give it a miss.'

'Very wise.' A slight hesitation. 'Big day tomorrow.'

Trying to keep his voice neutral, Pyrrhus says: '*You* must be pleased.'

'It's the right thing to do.'

'I don't need a Trojan to –' He bites the words back. 'It isn't easy, you know, being Achilles' son.'

Helenus snorts. 'You think it's easy being Priam's son? At least you didn't betray your father.'

'Didn't get the chance, did I? Never met the fucker.' But that's altogether too brutal, too honest; it frightens him back into his cave. 'I'd better be going. There's a lot to do still.'

Pyrrhus picks up his tunic and sandals and starts to walk past Helenus, who puts a hand on his chest to stop him.

'I'm sorry about the horse. They were a great team.'

Bugger the team. It's Ebony. The pain's unbearable. He nods brusquely and strides off, though he's only gone a few yards when Helenus calls after him: 'When great Achilles was alive, he defied even the gods.'

Not bothering to turn round, Pyrrhus shouts over his shoulder: 'How would *you* know?'

'Everybody knows.'

Pyrrhus just shakes his head and walks faster. He has to get away from the sea and the sand and the drifting black clouds that are making a widow of the moon, back into *his* world: straw and hay, smells of leather and saddle soap, the warmth of Ebony's shoulder, the strong curve of his neck. Reaching the stables, he finds them deserted. Where are all the grooms? Up on the headland probably. All of them? How many men does it take to build a funeral pyre? Only it won't be the building that's taking the time, it'll be the hauling of the logs. He notices the carthorses' stalls are empty. Anyway, it doesn't matter that the men aren't here; the horses have been fed and watered, they're all settled for the night – and he'd rather be alone anyway. Though even as he thinks that, the idiot boy comes rushing out of the tack room, spit flying, stuttering his eagerness to help. Pyrrhus waves him away and walks along the row of stalls. Ebony whickers a greeting. Pyrrhus selects a few wizened apples from a bag by the door, and gives one to Phoenix first, as always pretending an equality of love he doesn't feel. It's a mystery why some horses are special, and others not. Rufus was. Ebony is.

Crossing the narrow aisle, he holds out an apple on the palm of his hand and gently, delicately, Ebony takes it. Much chewing, a foam of green saliva at the corners of his mouth, followed by several nods and shakes of the great head: *More!* 'Just one, then, but that's the last. You've got your hay.' There can't be too many extra treats, because Ebony's routine must be kept as normal as possible right up to the moment Pyrrhus raises the sword. Ebony mouths the next apple off his palm. There's green slobber all over Pyrrhus' fingers now; he wipes it off on the side of his tunic, picks up a handful of clean straw and begins to rub Ebony down. It's not necessary – Ebony's coat gleams, as it always does – he's better looked after than many a child – but Pyrrhus enjoys doing it. His body bends into the strokes and he gives himself up to the pleasure. Something hypnotic about this; Ebony feels it too – little twitches and flickers run across his skin. *He* doesn't regret the past or dread the future, but at the back of Pyrrhus' mind, there's always the thought of what the morning will bring.

Only hours left now.

Even as he runs his hand over Ebony's neck, he's estimating the precise angle and force of the cut – because this time there mustn't be any shameful, cack-handed bungling. Ebony mustn't die the way Priam died.

At last Pyrrhus throws down the straw and stands back. He'd like to spend the night in the stables, to sit with his back against the wall and snatch whatever sleep he can, but he can't let himself do it. He needs to be rested and Ebony needs his normal routine. Tomorrow morning, early, he'll come and supervise the making of the drugged mash, though he does wonder whether that's really necessary. Seeing crowds of people gathered on the headland, Ebony might think it's the start of another race? He loves racing and, because he's never been ill-treated, he won't be afraid, even when Pyrrhus raises the sword.

When great Achilles was alive, he defied even the gods. He wonders what Helenus meant by saying that, whether he'd really been suggesting that Ebony didn't have to die. If so, he's a fool. Only madness and ruin await a man who defies the gods. *Achilles did*. Resting his head against Ebony's, Pyrrhus blows gently into his flaring nostrils, as once, long ago, he used to do with Rufus. 'Sorry, Ebony,' he says. 'Sorry, sorry, sorry. *I am not that man.*'

A few minutes later, stumbling blindly up the veranda steps to the main door of the hall, he fails to notice a man huddled in the shadows, so it's a shock when he moves. Helenus, of course. No time for that now; no patience. 'What do you *want*?'

'Our fathers were guest-friends. That means we are too. The least you could do is offer me some food.'

Pyrrhus, mouth already open to refuse, looks down at Helenus and sees that he's cold, hungry, frightened and alone. Then he remembers the emptiness of his living quarters: the gibing mirror and the tongueless lyre. Really, what else is he going to do? So, he steps to one side, opens the door a little wider – and lets the future in.

33

Outside, it was dark at last. Before leaving the hut, I filled a bowl with blackberries and added a dollop of the claggy porridge the Greek fighters were inexplicably addicted to. I found Maire sitting on her bed with the baby guzzling at her breast. Helle was hovering behind her.

'Just hold still for a minute.' I crushed a few blackberries against the side of the bowl, mixed them into the grey gloop and began sticking them on to her face and chest. Not too many, but enough to persuade the curious to take a step back.

'What's that supposed to be?' Helle asked.

'Plague.'

'*Plague?* Doesn't look anything like it.'

'Have you got any better ideas?'

Maire handed the baby to me while she spread the shawl to wrap him in. I felt the warm weight of him in my arms and a slight dampness against my chest. Looking down, I saw his eyes beginning to close. Sleep, eat, sleep again. There were thin blue veins on his lids and a small grey milk-blister on his upper lip. When Maire was ready, I handed him back and felt a chill emptiness where his warmth had been. The girls clustered round Maire to say goodbye, peering into the folds of the shawl for a last glimpse of the baby's face. One or two

275

of them were crying; they'd invested so much hope in that child – far, far, far too much. We all had.

When Maire was shrouded in her black robe, I told her to say a final goodbye and went to wait by the door. Andromache came over and wished me luck. I wondered if she was secretly pleased that Maire and the baby were going. The surprise, as so often, was Helle, who followed Maire and me out on to the veranda. 'I'm coming,' she said, in a tone that brooked no argument. 'Oh, not to stay, I know I won't be able to stay. But there's safety in numbers – and anyway, I've got this.'

She pulled back her cloak and I saw she was holding a knife – a wicked-looking thing with a bone handle and a long blade. She must have stolen it from the hall on one of the evenings she'd danced after dinner. I didn't find the sight of it at all reassuring. Helle was strong, but no match for a Greek fighter; I thought she'd just be handing them a weapon – and she was a striking figure, likely to attract the attention of anybody walking past. I felt Maire and I would be safer on our own. But she wanted to come, and I couldn't deny her the chance to spend a few more minutes with her friend.

'All right,' I said, reluctantly. I could see they were waiting for me to lead the way. They hadn't been outside the hut since their arrival, except for Helle's short trips across the yard to the hall, so they'd have no idea of the layout of the camp. 'We'll go along the beach,' I said. 'C'mon, this way.'

'Where are we going?' Helle said.

'I'm taking them to Cassandra.'

'You trust her, do you?'

'No, but I think she'll agree to help. And she does have a certain amount of power.'

I'd thought about this long and hard. Ritsa and Hecamede would have helped if they could, but realistically what could they hope to do? It had to be Cassandra.

Keeping to the shadows as far as we could, we scaled round the edges of the yard. I was tense with fear that the baby would wake up suddenly and howl. As we passed through a circle of torchlight, I noticed he was awake, but he didn't move and he made no sound. Perhaps the walking movement soothed him, or perhaps, like so many young animals, he knew to keep quiet when there were predators around. Soon we left the torchlight and the cooking fires behind, setting off along the path that led to the beach. The moon kept disappearing behind black clouds, but the darkness didn't bother me. This was one of the paths I'd often followed before dawn and sometimes late at night during my early days in the camp. Not usually at this time, because I'd been required to serve wine in the hall.

When we came out on to the beach, I started to relax a little, but then immediately froze because there were two men standing at the water's edge. One of them had waded a little way in and seemed to be getting ready to swim. I heard their voices between the crashing of the waves, but I couldn't make out the words. One of them looked a bit like Pyrrhus, but I couldn't be certain because in the moonlight his hair looked black. I didn't dare move, for fear of attracting their attention, but we needed to take a break anyway: Maire was gasping for breath. She wouldn't have been a fit woman at the best of times, and she'd lost a lot of blood after the birth. Turning to my right, looking up at the headland, I saw dark shapes of men with torches moving around, their huge shadows flickering on the grass. They'd be building the funeral pyre for Priam. On my left, peering cautiously out of the shadow of the dune path, I saw the ground was clear. One of the men at the water's edge had picked up his tunic and was striding off. After a while the other got up too and followed him.

Maire was breathing more easily now. 'Come on,' I said. 'Let's keep going.'

Feeling that the shore was too exposed, I led the way along the line of cradled ships that circled the bay. We moved in quick bursts, darting from one patch of shadow to the next. From the moment I arrived in the camp, the constant thrumming of the rigging against the mastheads had haunted my dreams. It struck me then as the sound of a mind at the end of its tether, but I was stronger now, and focused solely on getting Maire and her baby to safety – or what passed for safety in that camp. There were no guarantees for anybody.

As we drew level with the arena, a whole bunch of fighters, many of them carrying torches, erupted from between the ships and spilled out on to the beach. Most of them set off at a run, probably on their way to the next compound for a drink, but three stragglers happened to notice us standing in the shadow of the hulls. One of them lingered for a moment, but then shrugged and moved off.

'Hello, girls!'

The man facing me was thin, sweaty and very, very drunk. Not nasty, not threatening – or not yet. There was no way round him – no way back either. In effect, we were trapped in the narrow space between two ships. I put my arm round Maire and made a great show of supporting her. Helle did the same, but I felt her stiffen and hoped she wasn't reaching for the knife. 'We're on our way to the hospital,' I said. 'She's got a fever. I wouldn't come too close.' He peered at Maire, who was sweating and panting. No acting required – half an hour of floundering through loose sand had tested her to the limit. 'I think it might be the plague.' Taking her cue, Helle pulled Maire's mantle away from her face and neck, while I clutched the shawl to make sure the baby stayed hidden. Seen by torchlight, in the shadow of the ships, the purple crusts that had been so unconvincing in the hut looked absolutely terrifying. Fear of the plague was a constant feature of life in the camp; less than a year ago there'd been a really bad outbreak and most of the men would have known somebody who'd died of it then. The man stopped dead in his tracks. 'C'mon!' the man behind him shouted. 'Leave it.'

He turned and fled, though when he'd reached a safe distance he stopped and wished us luck. Out of the corner of my eye, I caught the glint of Helle's knife. 'Will you put that bloody thing away!'

Though I have to admit, I felt better with her there. It would have been harder managing Maire and the baby on my own. As it was, I ended up carrying the baby, while Helle supported Maire. Fortunately, we didn't meet anybody else. We heard shouting and singing coming from men drinking round the cooking fires, though I thought they were rather more subdued than usual. Nobody knew quite what to expect the following day. At last, we reached Agamemnon's compound. For once, I had no time to dwell on the feeling of desolation that always hit me the minute I passed through the gates. The hospital lay straight ahead, the lamps inside making the canvas glow. Leaving the others outside, I ducked under the flap and looked for Ritsa. Two women at the bench filling jugs with wine, but no Ritsa. She must be with Cassandra – I couldn't think of anywhere else she might be.

Sounds of eating and drinking, sporadic singing, laughter and a clattering of pots and plates came from Agamemnon's hall, but the yard outside was quiet. I knocked on Cassandra's door. A maid answered and was obviously reluctant to let us in, but then I heard Cassandra asking, 'Who is it?' I called out my name and a moment later the maid invited us in. Maire and Helle stood, uncertainly, just inside the door while I went through into the living quarters to talk to Cassandra. I found her with her hair unbound, wearing a yellow robe that didn't suit her – and my mother's necklace.

'What is it?' She didn't meet my eye and I got the impression she was ashamed to be seen like this: dressed to titillate and seduce, and from sheer lack of practice not doing it very well. Of course, dinner in the hall would be over soon; she'd be expecting a summons to Agamemnon's bed. I wondered how she felt about that. All very well to see yourself sweeping through the gates of Hades, crowned with laurels, being hailed as a conqueror by all the Trojan dead – but there was a lot of lying on her back while Agamemnon puffed and sweated on top of her to be got through first. But perhaps she didn't mind? Perhaps she might even enjoy it. She hadn't chosen to be a virgin priestess; Hecuba had made that choice on her behalf.

I was about to explain why I was there, when Ritsa, who must have heard my voice, came in carrying a diadem and veil. Cassandra snapped at her to put them down. 'Well?' she said, turning back to me. 'What can I do for you?' Her tone was only just not hostile.

I explained the problem and, thinking that the baby might be his own best advocate, called for Maire and Helle to come in. Maire had tried to rub off the blackberry 'sores' and so her face was now entirely purple. Helle was looking truculent. Cassandra glanced at them, placing them instantly in a category far beneath her notice. Maire pushed the folds of her shawl away from the baby's face, obviously thinking the sight of him might move Cassandra to pity. Her gaze did flicker across him – briefly – but her expression was difficult to read. She must have given up hope of motherhood years ago – and since she obviously believed her prophecy that she and Agamemnon were soon to die, there was no prospect of it in the future either. What could a baby be to her other than a source of pain and, perhaps, regret? I thought it might even harden her against us. But, in fact, she simply turned away, picked up the diadem and began fiddling with it, distractedly. 'Oh, well,' she said, at last. 'I suppose she could work in the kitchen.' She looked at Ritsa. 'Will you see to it?'

Ritsa glanced at me and then, spreading her arms wide as if she were herding geese, swept Maire and Helle out of the door.

Perhaps Cassandra expected me to leave with them, but I sat down facing her instead. I wanted to give Helle plenty of time to say good-bye to her friend. I waited till I heard the front door close. 'You don't serve wine at dinner, then?'

'I'm his *wife*.'

'Oh, yes, of course,' I said. 'Quite different.'

There we were, two women who'd shared Agamemnon's bed. We had to talk, because good manners required it, but the conversation merely limped along, weighed down by the things we were not say-ing. She couldn't bring herself to look at me. I doubt if Cassandra had ever had an intimate conversation with another woman. At last, after an awkward pause, she said: 'What was it like for you?'

'Brutal.'

She darted a glance in my direction.

'He was angry with Achilles. He took it out on me.'

'Every time?'

I laughed. 'It only happened twice. And then he stood up in the arena and swore by all the gods he'd never laid a finger on me.'

'Did Achilles believe him?'

281

'*No!*' I looked across at her. 'You're his wife – you're right, it's not the same.'

'Calchas says the marriage isn't lawful.'

'It is if Agamemnon says it is. He *is* the law.'

I was trying to give Ritsa plenty of time to settle Maire in. I only hoped it was going to succeed, that the cook in Agamemnon's kitchen wouldn't object – but they always seemed to be short of staff and Maire had experience of kitchen work. Agamemnon wouldn't even know she was there. I was more concerned about Helle. She wasn't a woman to make friends easily; this wouldn't be a trivial loss. But really, I was finding Cassandra in this prickly, defensive mood rather hard to take. It was a relief when the door opened. I looked up expecting to see Ritsa, but it was the maid relaying the summons from Agamemnon. Cassandra stood up, looking rather helplessly at the diadem and veil. I picked them up and began pinning them into place. She seemed agitated: the red lights inside the opals stirred with every breath. Our faces were only inches apart, but she endured my fingers in her hair, my breath on her skin, and managed to get through the whole awkward business without once meeting my eyes.

'I'm sure Ritsa will be back soon,' she said, retreating to a more comfortable distance. 'You're welcome to wait.'

After she'd gone, I sat alone in the lamplight until Ritsa and Helle returned – without Maire. 'Don't worry about them, they'll be all right. I'll keep an eye on them and the cook's not a bad sort.' I hugged her, wishing we'd had more chance to talk, but feeling the pressure of getting Helle safely back to the women's hut. Ritsa came with us to the door and waved us goodbye.

We walked along the beach, keeping as far as we could to the shelter of the ships. The moon came and went on the surface of the water.

Helle still hadn't spoken. If it had been one of the other girls, I'd have put my arm round her, given her a hug perhaps, but you couldn't do that with Helle. The body she trained so hard and displayed with such complete arrogance was not for touching. It was armour, I thought, rather than flesh.

We said goodbye at the door of the women's hut. I didn't feel like going in, and Helle would be able to tell them what had happened. At the last moment, as she was about to step across the threshold, she looked back and raised a clenched fist. *We did it*, she seemed to be saying. *We got them out.*

She obviously thought they were safe now. And perhaps they were, safer anyway than they would have been if they'd stayed in Pyrrhus' compound.

34

Women don't normally attend funerals, so I didn't expect to go to Priam's. From early morning, the camp was buzzing with expectation. The Myrmidons had built a huge pyre on the headland near the horse pastures. Priam's armour had been brought out of storage and polished till it shone. For me, sitting alone in my hut, this should have been a day of real – if meagre – consolation, but instead, I felt increasingly frantic. I didn't know where I wanted to be, and so, in the end, I decided I'd simply get out and walk along the shore. Think about Priam. And Amina too.

Normally, at that time of day, the beach would have been deserted, but today it was black with crowds of men gathering at the water's edge to purify themselves. Most of them were rubbing oil into their bodies. Usually, after a hot bath, that's a pleasant thing to do, but out here, the wind blowing sand everywhere, sand that stuck to the oil and had to be painfully scraped off, followed by immersion in a cold sea dotted with scuds of dirty yellow foam . . . Not so pleasant. Somebody started singing a hymn to Zeus, but the singer's voice was drowned out by a cacophony of yelps as salt water slapped against abraded skin.

I sheltered near the ships and watched, but after a while my deliberate self-isolation began to seem selfish. There were others in the camp who had more reason for grief than me. Hecuba, for one. Hecuba, above all. So, turning my back on the beach, which by now was more crowded than the camp, I made my way to her hut. She was out of bed, wearing a clean tunic, two hectic spots on her wasted cheeks. Only recently, I'd sometimes thought she wouldn't live another day, but I'd reckoned without the sheer force of will that carried her on. I knelt to touch her feet; as I stood up, she pulled me into her arms and embraced me. The top of her head scarcely reached my chin.

'I've sent for Odysseus,' she said, smoothing her hair to make sure it was tidy.

Sent for? She was his slave. Looking at her feverishly bright eyes, I thought her mind must have gone at last – only a mad woman talks like that. I said, as soothingly as I could, 'Well, you know, he mightn't come . . .'

She patted my arm, almost patronizingly. 'He will.'

She was too excited to keep still; she kept making little forays up and down the hut, like a small girl who's been given new clothes for her birthday and isn't allowed to put them on yet. At last, I persuaded her to sit down and conserve her energy. 'It's a long way,' I said. 'You don't want to wear yourself out.' I didn't believe she'd be going any-where. I gave her a cup of diluted wine, but she pushed it away after only a few sips. When the doorway darkened, she looked up, obvi-ously expecting to see Odysseus, but it was only Hecamede, bringing bread and cheese, moist, crumbly white cheese made with herbs, bread warm from the oven, but Hecuba couldn't eat anything, and it seemed disrespectful for us to eat without her.

'Nestor's going to the funeral,' Hecamede said. 'Calchas says all the kings have to be there.'

Hecuba brightened. 'Well, if that decrepit old git can get there,

I'm bloody sure I can. I'll walk if I have to. Or ask one of those young men to give me a piggyback.'

'You will *not*!' I said. It wasn't often I managed to be firm with Hecuba, but really this was too much.

A few minutes later, another shape darkened the open door. Once again, Hecuba looked up. I actually heard her breathe Odysseus' name; but it wasn't him this time either. It was Cassandra – tall, young, strong, richly dressed, very much the future queen of Mycenae. She might only enjoy the status for a few days, or weeks at most, but evidently, she meant to make the most of it. Hecamede and I scrambled to our feet to greet her. Hecuba had gone very still.

It didn't feel like a meeting between mother and daughter. I'd spent so much of my life missing my own mother that I expected tears, embraces, reconciliation . . . but there was nothing like that. Cassandra stepped forward – reluctantly, I thought – knelt and touched her mother's feet before offering her cheek in an awkward, arm's-length embrace. She was wearing a green robe with a yoke of fine embroidery and looked as exotic as a tropical bird in the squalid little hut. After the embrace was over, Hecuba sat back on her heels and looked at Cassandra with bright, sceptical eyes. A lot of pain there, but she was keeping it well hidden.

'Cassandra,' she said, taking in the dress, the elaborately styled hair, the necklace, the rings . . . 'You look well.'

'I'm as well as I'm going to be.' A tense pause. 'You know I'm married?'

'*Yes*. So, he actually did it . . . I must say, I never thought he would. What do you think his wife's going to say about that, then?'

'I imagine she won't be pleased.'

Without bothering to hide her distaste for her surroundings,

Cassandra sat down, tucking her legs underneath her as neatly as a cat. Whatever attempts at a real connection these two might be inclined to make could only be hindered by the presence of other people, so I jerked my head towards the door and Hecamede and I left them alone. Out on the veranda, I was delighted to see Ritsa's broad back and mop of straw-coloured hair. I sat beside her – we hugged and cried a bit, and then turned to watch the men repairing the statues in the arena.

'So, you're Cassandra's *maid* now?'

'Looks like it.'

'Do you ever go into the hospital?'

'Not often. There's less work than there used to be. Few young idiots tearing chunks off each other . . . but that's all.'

All the same, Ritsa was a healer. Cassandra could have had any woman in Agamemnon's compound as her maid.

Hecamede touched my arm. 'I'll have to go. Nestor's going to need a lot of help getting ready.'

We watched her walk away across the arena, threading her way between the fallen gods.

'How is she?' I asked, meaning Cassandra.

'Still a bit up and down. She's like a child sometimes. But, you know . . . I saw her when she was at her worst, pissing herself some-times. And she's a proud woman. Some days, she can't stand the sight of me.'

'She should be bloody grateful.'

'Ye-es – but we both know it doesn't work like that.'

We watched a team of men lower the statue of Athena to the ground, two of them hauling on ropes, others reaching up to steady her in case she suffered even worse damage from a too abrupt descent.

'Anyway,' Ritsa said. '*You* must be pleased. Priam cremated.'

'Not yet!'

'No, but he will be. And as for that little squirt . . . I thought Calchas could have made a lot more of that. I'd like to see him following Priam's body on his hands and knees. Still, at least he'll lose the horse. Not much, though, is it – a horse, for a child's life?'

I wondered which child she meant. Andromache's baby? Polyxena? Amina? The girls must have seemed like children to her. I was about to make some comment, but at that moment a shadow fell across us. I looked up and there, incredibly, was Odysseus. We shuffled along the step to let him pass and, ducking his head, he went into the hut.

Ritsa looked as astonished as I felt. 'Do you know she actually sent for him?' I said.

'Well, there you are. You're taken at your own evaluation in this life. In her mind, she's still a queen.'

A murmur of conversation from behind us. Odysseus: a low rumble; Hecuba: frail, breathless, resolute; Cassandra: a penetrating, ever so slightly nasal whine. 'How much did she have to do with Calchas' speech?'

Ritsa shrugged. 'I don't know. They thrashed it out between them, but they couldn't have done it without you. Apparently, Alcimus and Automedon weren't at all keen to talk – till they realized Calchas knew anyway.'

Movement inside the hut. A moment later, Odysseus came out, nodded to me, ignored Ritsa, and set off in the direction of his hall. Shortly afterwards, Cassandra also emerged. 'Go to my mother,' she told Ritsa. 'She'll need help getting down the steps.'

Pointedly, I got up and followed Ritsa into the hut. Hecuba was looking even more excited than before; dangerously so, I thought.

'He's sending a cart,' she said. 'He said I could have his chariot, only then I'd have to stand, so I said, "No, no, a cart's good enough for me. I'm not proud."' There she stood, in her poky little dog kennel: the epitome of pride.

I found a comb and began sweeping back her long white hair, thinking it might help to soothe her, but nothing could have calmed her down that day. She was *euphoric*. I'd always struggled to understand her moods and this was no exception. I was too young to understand that elation is one of the many faces of grief. At the funeral, in front of the entire Greek army, she would represent Priam. More than that: she would *be* Priam. Because isn't that, ultimately, the way we cope with grief? There's nothing sophisticated or civilized about it. Like savages, we ingest our dead.

As I finished dressing her hair, I heard the cart pull up outside. Suddenly anxious, she said: 'You'll come with me, won't you?'

I'd been intending to walk, but of course I said I would. Odysseus had sent a team of horses – rather than mules, which would have been more usual – and, to drive them, a fresh-faced young man with a scattering of ginger freckles. He clearly felt driving the cart was beneath him – I thought I recognized him as Odysseus' charioteer – but he was all gentleness as he lifted Hecuba on to the seat. Hecuba was flustered and pleased and even a little flirtatious as he put her down. Once settled, she looked around her with great interest, at the arena, and the statues of the gods, and the crowds of men returning from the beach. We might have been setting off on a pleasure jaunt. Beside her, stony-faced, Cassandra stared straight ahead.

The journey to the cremation site was long and hard, the cart wheels jolting over ruts in the cinder path. More than once Hecuba had to brace herself against the side of the cart, but she stayed bolt upright from beginning to end. We were surrounded by men who'd only just emerged from their ritual purification in the sea. There was an overwhelming smell of wet hair, of dampness trapped in folds of skin. They looked surprised to see women – as I say, women don't normally attend funerals – but they stepped to the side of the path to let us through. Many of them openly stared at Hecuba, as if aware that they were seeing history pass.

Cassandra asked the driver where he was taking us and, when he pointed to the place, said, 'No, we need to be closer than that.' By now, Hecuba had seen the funeral pyre and was holding her lips together in the way she sometimes did when grief and anger threatened to overwhelm her. I wanted to reach out and touch her, but held back. There was an isolation about her now that no amount of love could breach.

Finally, at long last, the jolting stopped; the driver dismounted and went off to join his mates. We were on a slight incline, so we had a good view of everything. No grave, of course – that would be dug later to receive the bones. Instead, the Myrmidons had built a huge funeral pyre, towering ten or twelve feet above the crowd. The ground was filling up fast. Men were still streaming up the path, but the upper slopes of the headland were already densely packed. The cart had become an island in a sea of heads and shoulders. The kings had not yet arrived; they'd be waiting till all the men were assembled before they made their entrances.

Gradually, one by one, they began to appear: Odysseus, first; he shielded his eyes and scanned the slopes, looking for Hecuba, perhaps. At any rate, his gaze seemed to alight on us, before he turned to greet Ajax. Nestor received his usual roar of applause. I caught a glimpse of Hecamede walking beside his chariot. Agamemnon arrived last, as was his right, glancing at Menelaus and delivering a slight, dismissive bow. As he took his seat, silence fell, except for the frantic yapping of seagulls wheeling overhead.

Then, we waited.

At last, in the distance, came a sound of drums and marching feet. Nothing else, at first, just that single pounding note, and then, slowly, the funeral procession wound into view. Ritsa and I helped Hecuba climb on to the bench so that she could see, both of us holding on to her skirt, the way you do with a little girl who wants to walk along a wall. Only when I felt she was secure could I look towards the cinder path and the procession moving towards us. Priam's body, tightly wrapped in gold-and-purple cloth, was carried on the shoulders of six Myrmidon fighters. I thought I recognized the cover I'd used to make up his bed the night he came to see Achilles. As they came closer, the fighters started to bang their swords on their shields, as they used to do every morning before setting off for the battlefield. A solemn sound, but menacing too. And then, rising high above the clash of swords on shields, the pipes began to play Achilles' lament, the music that had haunted me – driven me to the verge of insanity, almost – in the weeks after his death.

Immediately behind Priam's body came Ebony, led by the slow-witted boy who was so good at calming horses, though even he must have been finding this a challenge. Excited by the crowds, Ebony kept tossing his head, pirouetting, dancing about . . . Perhaps, to him, this looked like the start of a chariot race; he had no way of knowing that he'd been garlanded for sacrifice. Pyrrhus, in full armour, his head bowed, walked a few paces behind the horse. In fact, all the Myrmidons were wearing full armour, though I suppose that was only fitting for the funeral procession of a king. As they left the path and began moving through the crowds of men in tunics and cloaks, they formed an alien, glittering stream. Myrmidons: ant-men. I'd always thought what a stupid name that was for men who were so sturdily independent, so ready to question authority, whose respect always had to be earned; but seeing them like this, hearing – and, in the vibration of the cart, feeling – the power and precision of those marching feet, I understood – for the first time, I think – the terror they inspired on the battlefield.

At last, they came to a halt at the foot of the pyre. The pall-bearers carried Priam up the steep slope and laid him on the bier while other men went round larding the logs with beef fat and oil. All this the crowd watched in total silence, though I could hear Hecuba whimpering a little beside me. Or rather, I thought I could – but when I turned to look, I saw that it was Cassandra making the sound. Hecuba neither moved nor spoke.

A solitary voice began singing a hymn of praise to Zeus. Gradually, one by one, other voices joined in until the whole assembly was singing:

I will sing of Zeus,
Chief among the gods and greatest,
All-seeing, Lord of all . . .

I've heard that hymn sung in temples all over the Greek world, but never as movingly as it was that day. Even as the singing continued, Calchas emerged from the knot of men behind Agamemnon and went to stand at the foot of the pyre. As the music faded into silence, he called to Priam. 'May it go well with you in the house of Hades. These, your enemies, salute you.' Immediately, at a signal from Agamemnon, the army gave three full-throated shouts for Priam – 'Priam! Priam!

Priam!' – and the seagulls that had begun to settle took off again and screamed overhead.

Calchas nodded to Pyrrhus, who glanced over his shoulder at the men standing behind him, but then stepped forward. The lad who'd been stroking Ebony's neck to steady him led him closer and, seeing Pyrrhus, the horse neighed a greeting. The crowd hushed, Pyrrhus drew his sword – and then turned to face Agamemnon and the other kings.

'Yesterday, Calchas said in front of all of you that I have to sacrifice my horse Ebony at the foot of Priam's funeral pyre.' A pause, during which he looked round at the circle of familiar faces. 'I've thought long and hard, and, in all honesty, I don't believe the gods require this of me.'

A sharp intake of breath. All around us, men were turning to stare at each other – their expressions ranging from surprise to shock and even horror. Pyrrhus raised his arms and waited for silence before he spoke again.

'So, I'm going to make another more personal sacrifice.'

He raised his sword, pulled his thick plait forward and hacked it off, as close to the scalp as he could get. This might seem an inconsequential sacrifice, but to the men watching it was no trivial matter. Greek fighters were – *are* – immensely proud of their long, flowing hair. It's almost as if they think their strength resides in it. A man will throw a lock of hair on to his father's or his brother's funeral pyre, but it's rare to cut off the entire length. Achilles did it for Patroclus – I can't, for the moment, think of anybody else. The hacking took no more than a few seconds, then Pyrrhus turned, threw his plait on to the logs at Priam's feet and, before anybody had time to react, seized a torch from one of the guards and lit the pyre. Immediately, men with more torches scrambled up the heap of logs setting fire to the kindling in as many different places as possible. Sometimes, however well larded with fat, a pyre will fail to light – it happened at Patroclus' funeral – but there was no danger of that today. Bone dry after the long drought, the logs blazed instantly. A fierce wind blowing straight off the sea fanned the flames, sending a column of black smoke and sparks whirling into the upper air. One or two of the men near the top of the pyre nearly got caught by the flames and had to leap to safety.

As soon as Hecuba saw the pyre begin to burn, she raised her voice in lamentation, a wordless ululation of grief. The vast crowd of men around us stayed silent. Pyrrhus and Calchas were still staring at each other. I was aware of Pyrrhus' drawn sword, of the ranks of helmeted Myrmidons massing behind him, fanning out on either side, so that he stood in a semicircle bristling with spears. Calchas glanced uneasily at Agamemnon, who shook his head slightly and waved at him to step back. At that moment, two of the sea eagles who nest on the headland flew over the pyre.

Pyrrhus pointed to the sky. 'Look!' he said. 'Zeus has accepted the sacrifice.'

It suited the Myrmidons to believe it. I doubt if anybody else did, but seeing the Myrmidons solidly behind their leader, obviously prepared to fight – and armed – nobody felt like arguing.

The pyre would burn all night. Normally, the sons, grandsons, brothers and nephews of the dead would keep watch beside it, but there was nobody left to do that for Priam. Perhaps Helenus might creep up to the headland after dark and perform this last service for his father – or perhaps not. He might be too frightened – or ashamed.

The gathering had started to break up. One or two of the men walking past our cart were inclined to complain. 'Calchas said sacrifice the horse. Nobody said anything about *hair*.' 'If it was one of us, *we*'d have had to do it.' A rumble of agreement. 'Yeah, well, that's it, though, isn't it? One rule for them – another for us. Always the bloody same.' The grumbling wasn't loud, but it was persistent. Pyrrhus wasn't in the clear, not yet. In the end, either the wind would change – or it would not.

I don't think Hecuba heard a word of it. She'd gone on staring at the blazing pyre, the wind lifting her white hair until it whirled round her head like flames. I was still holding on to her tunic, but even so was taken by surprise when she fell. I staggered, but caught her easily enough – she was no weight at all – and lowered her to the bench.

'That went well,' I said, gently, when she'd revived a little. 'They gave him every honour.' She nodded and seemed to take some consolation from it, but Cassandra said, sharply, 'He should have sacrificed the horse. Calchas made it perfectly clear.' It wasn't enough for her that her father's body had been cremated with all the honour due to a great king. She'd have thrown Pyrrhus on to the fire if she could, used his body fat to feed the flames. I was reminded of Achilles, who'd sacrificed twelve Trojan youths, the pride and hope of their families, on Patroclus' funeral pyre. They were alike in their insatiable desire for revenge. Once, only a few days after the fall of Troy, with Achilles' lament repeating endlessly inside my head, I'd thought: *We need a new song.* And we did. We do. But a song isn't new merely because a woman's voice is singing it.

Wanting to get Hecuba back home and into bed as soon as possible, I looked around for our driver. At last I saw him, striding up the hill towards us. When he saw Hecuba, he looked concerned. 'Don't worry, love,' he said to me. 'We'll have her back home in no

time. Just let this lot get clear first.' He waited for a bunch of stragglers to walk past, then we lurched forward, Hecuba all the time
twisting round to look back at the fire.

A little further along, I saw Andromache walking alone. She must
have got left behind when Pyrrhus and the Myrmidons marched off.
When I called her name, she looked round. 'Why don't you come with
us?' I said. 'There's plenty of room.' She agreed, and I helped her into
the cart. Cassandra greeted her sister-in-law rather coolly, I thought;
Hecuba was more welcoming and reached out to clasp Andromache's
hands. And so, jerking and swaying, we passed through the stables,
where I noticed Ebony's sacrificial garlands lying torn and trampled in
the dirt.

Andromache and I got down outside the women's hut, and
together we watched the cart trundle through the gates.

35

Later that afternoon, it began to rain. That's an understatement. The ground was too parched to absorb the sudden deluge: puddles grew out of nowhere; every hill became a river. Huge grey columns of rain swept across the camp, driven by a wind that blew with undiminished ferocity straight off the sea. I wondered if Calchas was beginning to feel nervous, but then I thought: *No, he doesn't need to be.* He could always blame Pyrrhus for not having obeyed the will of the gods. Despite the downpour, I still went for a walk, though before I'd gone a few yards, my hair was plastered flat against my skull. Blinking water from my eyes, I almost bumped into Machaon, who waved cheerily as he splodged past. 'What did I tell you?' he shouted over his shoulder, pointing both hands at the sky. '*WEATHER!*'

A deep uneasiness spread through the camp that evening as men grappled with the fact that the gale was still blowing, and that their situation had been made worse by the added misery of lashing rain. Alcimus came home briefly, but then left again immediately. He had to take a work party up to the headland, where they were struggling to keep the pyre alight. Holding my mantle over my head, I splashed across to the hall because food and wine would need to be sent up to them, and I didn't trust anybody else to organize it. On the way back, I called in on the girls and found them listless, bored and fractious. I decided that wasn't my problem, and went for another walk instead.

Everywhere you went you were greeted by smells of wet hair and wet wool. Men with their cloaks pulled over their heads huddled round the fires – fires that smoked and spat and threatened to go out altogether. The meat was half cooked, at best; wine was the only reliable comfort, and they were certainly downing plenty of that. No singing, no laughter, no conversation – and the little there was, mainly grumbling. Oh, they'd still have fought for Pyrrhus, even now, if they'd had to – but his claim to know the will of the gods better than Calchas, who was, after all, the army's chief seer, didn't sit well with them. Most of them would rather Ebony had been sacrificed.

The rain fell persistently all night. The groups round the fires broke up early, the men staggering off to find whatever comfort they could inside the huts. But in the past few weeks, a considerable amount of storm damage had been done and very little of it repaired. Consequently, leaking roofs added to the general discomfort. When I got back from my walk, I discovered three leaks had started in my own hut, so I fetched buckets from the yard and found a bowl big enough to catch the drips that were falling on to the sideboard. In the midst of all this chaos, I actually sat down and tried to spin, but the wool felt damp and it was full of those annoying little bobbles that are so difficult to get out. From where I sat, I could hear water plopping into the buckets and the bowl, but the plops came at unpredictable intervals, and each made a slightly different noise. That must sound like a very minor irritation but, believe me, after an hour of it I thought I was going mad, so I put the wool to one side and went to bed. The cradle creaked; the baby kicked. I thought I'd never get to sleep, and then, somehow, still listening to the rain, I drifted off.

Just before dawn, I jolted awake and lay, dry-mouthed and panicky, staring into the darkness. For a moment, I couldn't even remember where I was. I listened, straining to identify whatever it was that had woken me. Alcimus coming in? One of the girls knocking on the door? Then, very slowly, I began to realize that what I was hearing was silence. Of course, it was only the pre-dawn lull that for weeks now had tormented us with a daily renewal of hope – invariably dashed. With any luck, I might manage another hour of sleep before I needed to get up, so I turned on to my side and pulled the covers up to my chin, but I couldn't settle. The silence went on. And on. There was no sound at all except for the *tick-tick* of drops falling into the buckets. Even the cradle had stopped creaking.

In the end, I got up, reached for my mantle and went out. All over the compound, doors were opening, dazed-looking men staggering out, blinking at the light. Their movements seemed jerky, stiff, as if they were suits of armour learning to walk. I glanced to my right and saw the girls had tumbled out of the hut and were standing on the steps, looking around them as if they were seeing the place for the first time. The strange thing was, nobody spoke – as if we were all frightened of breaking this infinitely fragile silence.

Then, ripping the soft silk of the air, a man shouted – and instantly others joined in; they danced, they sang, they splashed in puddles until mud caked them to the thigh – and then they ran. Ran headlong to the ships, a stampede there was no stopping, though I heard Automedon yelling at them to stop, to go back. The ships weren't loaded, two of them needed repairing, they couldn't just leap on board and start rowing for home. After a while they started to show sense, if dancing and turning cartwheels on the sand is sense. Pyrrhus appeared, looking, with his short, jagged hair, rather like a half-fledged chick. Behind him stood Helenus, both of them red-eyed from the smoke. They must have done the night watch together. They might even have raked through the ashes to collect Priam's bones.

After talking to Automedon, Pyrrhus went inside to get dressed. Within minutes, all the action had shifted to the beach. The women were left alone in the compound, as we used to be every morning when the men set off for war. It was a strange experience, listening to those shouts of jubilation, trying to imagine what this meant for us. It was obvious what it meant for the Greeks: they were going home. Where were we going? I looked at Andromache. There was nothing for her here now, everybody she'd ever loved was dead, and yet I knew she wouldn't want to leave. She'd given birth here; her dead lay buried in this ground. That's *home*.

All the girls seemed subdued, facing up to the desolation of exile. I kept telling myself nothing was certain yet. And a part of me still expected the wind to start up again at any moment, though I didn't say that to the others.

In the end, we simply huddled together, listening to the men shouting on the beach. Watching the rain fall.

36

Odysseus was the first to leave. He'd always been the one chafing at the bit; the one most desperate to get home.

I watched Hecuba being led away. The women had all gathered on the beach to bid her farewell, though she scarcely looked up from the gangplank beneath her feet – and, even when safely on board, she stood in the stern gazing out over our heads towards the blackened towers of Troy. We shouted: 'Goodbye, good luck!' – waving her into the distance until that pinpoint of white hair was wholly swallowed up in mist.

As the women dispersed, I saw an immensely tall man stalking elegantly through the crowd, like a grey heron in a puddle of ducks. Calchas – it couldn't be anybody else – but Calchas as I'd never seen him before: no face paint, no scarlet bands, no staff of office. I was about to walk past when he called out a greeting. As I turned to him, I realized I was seeing his face for the first time, *meeting* him for the first time – that's how it felt. It was possible to see that he must once have been extremely beautiful, but what really struck me was how shy he was. I'd never noticed that in him before.

After the conventional enquiries had been stumbled through, he said, 'I'm going to miss her.'

'Yes, me too.'

We walked on together. Glancing down, I saw he was wearing the same short tunic the Greek fighters wore – which meant that I was also meeting his legs for the first time. They were spindly and pallid from their long confinement underneath ankle-length skirts – altogether, a disgrace to Trojan manhood. Helle's were better.

'Are you about ready to leave?' I asked.

'I'm not going.'

'Not going?'

'No.'

I looked around at Odysseus' deserted compound. 'But there'll be nothing here.'

'There's plenty of food in Priam's gardens. And I don't suppose I'll be here for ever – I expect I'll move on.' He smiled. 'See if I can find a city Achilles *didn't* sack . . .'

'But why?'

'Why am I staying? I want to go back to Troy. I was only – I don't know . . . twelve? – when I was taken to the temple. My parents were poor, I didn't get on with my father, it was a solution of sorts, I suppose – but *I* didn't choose it. And now I want to go back.'

'Actually *into* Troy?'

He shrugged. It wasn't necessary for me to point out what horrors he'd be facing there; he knew perfectly well.

'I just want to go home,' he said. 'Isn't that what we all want really? To turn time back . . .?'

'Ye-es, but it's not usually considered possible.'

'Well, then, I'll fail.'

We stopped and looked out to sea. At that moment, almost miraculously, the mists parted and we saw Odysseus' ships just as the men stopped rowing and began to hoist the sails.

'I hope she'll be all right,' I said.

'Penelope's kind – or so everybody says.'

'It's not freedom, though, is it?'

Glancing sideways, I saw that he was choking on tears. He turned to me, attempted to speak, but then just shook his head and, with a hurried bow, strode up the beach towards the huts.

I looked out to sea again, but the mists had rolled back and Odysseus' ships were nowhere to be seen.

And now I'm going to break my own rules. So far, in telling this story of my youth, I've tried to make no reference to facts I only learnt later; sometimes – as with the fate of Odysseus and his ships – many years later. But I think I'm justified in making an exception of Hecuba. After all, if the mist hadn't closed in again, I might well have seen what happened next.

At the precise moment the sails were hoisted, Hecuba, who'd been huddled in a corner out of the way, was transformed into a mad dog with slavering jaws and red-rimmed eyes and, before anybody could stop her, she climbed to the topmost mast, where she stood, snarling her defiance at the Greeks below – and then leapt to her death.

Nobody seems to know whether she burst open on the deck or fell into the sea. I like to think it was the sea.

No crowds came to bid Helen farewell. I went to see her off and stood alone on the beach, watching, as a dozen or more cylindrical rolls were carried carefully on to Menelaus' ship. A tall figure in a dark cloak was supervising the operation – a man, I assumed, until it turned to face me and I saw that it was Helen, making sure her tapestries were safely stowed. Nothing else, I think, mattered to Helen

303

in the end. Not her daughter – and certainly not any of the men who'd loved her. She lived solely in, and for, her work.

We stared at each other, across a great gulf of time and experience. She gave one wave of a small white hand – a barely noticeable gesture – and then went swiftly below deck.

Inevitably, the day arrived when Agamemnon was ready to leave. I walked across the almost deserted camp to see Ritsa, determined not to upset her by crying. I found her outside Cassandra's hut, supervising the loading of household goods on to a cart. She came towards me, wiping her hands on the sacking cloth she'd knotted round her waist – a painfully familiar gesture. She'd always done that whether her hands needed wiping or not. Our parting was, like all such partings, awkward. I think we both wanted it to be over – to have the relief of putting it behind us – and yet, at the same time, we clung to every passing second. I remember at one point a group of women walked past on their way down to the ships. I spotted Maire's bulky shape, the baby still tightly strapped to her chest and half hidden by her shawl. Even as I recognized her, she glanced back at us and smiled. A few moments later, she was out of sight.

I turned and found Ritsa watching me.

'They'll be all right,' she said. 'I told you, didn't I? I'll keep an eye on them.'

My resolve not to cry lasted till we had to say goodbye, and then I broke down and howled like a little girl: 'But I want you to be there!' – meaning when I went into labour.

'I would be if I could, you know that.' She patted my stomach, reassuringly. 'You'll be all right.'

On my way back to Pyrrhus' compound, I called in on Hecamede.

Nestor's ships were also ready to sail. Another goodbye. I felt more optimistic about Hecamede's future than I had for some time. Nestor's health seemed to be improving, and as long as the old bastard managed to hang on to life, I thought she'd be all right. We hugged each other, and then I had to let her go.

First Ritsa, now Hecamede. I walked away, knowing that in all probability I'd never see either of them again.

Wanting to dull the pain of parting from my friends, I made straight for the rock pools on the beach, where I squatted down, searching – though without much hope – for signs of life. Even with the anguish of leaving Ritsa behind, I felt some of the excitement I'd felt as a small child clinging to my mother's hand as she'd helped me over the slippery rocks. One starfish, that's all I found, and even that was dead. My mother used to love starfish – she loved all the life you see on the shoreline, but starfish in particular – and she passed that love on to me. I bent to examine the pallid corpse. It had been badly injured before its death, one of the limbs torn off and lying some distance from the body. As I leant forward, my shadow fell across the water, and immediately the starfish came to life and began inching towards a fringe of overhanging seaweed. Not only that, but the severed limb also began to move and make for shelter. I wanted to laugh, because now I remembered: *This is what happens*. I heard my mother's voice explaining it to me: the parent starfish grows a new limb, the amputated limb becomes a starfish – and so, from one damaged and mutilated individual, two whole creatures grow.

Seeing that gave me hope – and yes, I do know it's ridiculous. What could I possibly have in common with a starfish? And yet, suddenly, I found the strength to stand up, to look for the last time at

Achilles' burial mound, and to walk quickly back to the compound, where the Myrmidons were almost ready to sail.

The girls had put their few possessions into cotton bags and were clustered together on the veranda, waiting to be told where to go. Helle flared her eyes at me as I approached. Somehow, without ever talking very much, we seemed to have formed a friendship. I felt safe leaving the girls with her. I couldn't see Andromache in the group, and that worried me, so I went in search of her. My footsteps echoed round the empty room, which suddenly seemed much bigger. I was about to go along the passage to her bedroom, when I heard a movement in the yard at the back. She was picking purple daisies, the kind that grow as vigorously as weeds at this time of year. In fact, they probably *are* weeds. Now, I can see great clumps of them from my bedroom window. Weeds or not, I've never been able to pull them up.

'Andromache?'

Arms full of daisies, she turned to face me and said one word: 'Amina.'

'I don't know where she's buried.' Or *if* she was buried. More likely they'd just throw her body off the headland. Then I thought: *But I do know where she died.*

So, together, we wove the daisies into a wreath and took it along to the laundry hut, which looked much the same as it had always done: airing racks swaying in the draught, a row of tubs where bloodstained shirts were put to soak, and, right in the middle of the room, the big table with the marble top. I'd washed Patroclus' body on that slab, and Hector's, and Achilles' – but I pushed those memories aside. This was Amina's time.

We laid the wreath on the slab, and stood for a moment with our heads bowed. I'm not sure I managed to pray, but I did remember her: the wide-apart eyes, the straight shoulders, that absolute refusal to bend.

Then we went outside to join the other women, and a few minutes later, Alcimus appeared and led us down to the ships.